THE SECRET
HOURS

Also by Mick Herron

The Oxford Series
Down Cemetery Road
The Last Voice You Hear
Why We Die
Smoke & Whispers

The Slough House Novels
Slow Horses
Dead Lions
Real Tigers
Spook Street
London Rules
Joe Country
Slough House
Bad Actors

The Slough House Novellas
The List
The Marylebone Drop
The Catch
Standing by the Wall: The Collected Slough House Novellas

Other Works
Reconstruction
Nobody Walks
This Is What Happened
Dolphin Junction: Stories

THE SECRET HOURS MICK HERRON

SOHO
CRIME

Published by Soho Press, Inc.
227 W 17th Street
New York, NY 10011

Library of Congress Cataloging-in-Publication Data

Names: Herron, Mick, author.
Title: The secret hours / Mick Herron.
Description: New York : Soho Crime, [2023]

Subjects: LCGFT: Spy fiction. | Thrillers (Fiction) | Novels.
Classification: LCC PR6108.E77 S43 2023 | DDC 823'.92—dc23/
eng/20230303
LC record available at https://lccn.loc.gov/2023010236

ISBN 978-1-64129-600-7
eISBN 978-1-64129-522-2

Interior design by Janine Agro, Soho Press, Inc.

Printed in the United States of America

10 9 8 7 6 5 4 3 2 1

For Jo

THE SECRET HOURS

PART ONE:

DEVON, SOON

The worst smell in the world is dead badger. He'd encountered it on his morning walk down a green lane; had caught the odour without seeing the corpse, but had guessed what it was before returning later with a shovel. Whether they all smelled that bad or whether this one had expired of noxious causes he didn't know. As it turned out, he couldn't do anything about it either—the creature had crawled into a tangled nest of roots to die, and it would require heavy machinery and a strong stomach to recover it. Lacking the former, and not wanting to put the latter to the test, Max opted for a third way: he'd walk a different route for a while, and see if one of the local farmers shifted it in the meantime. Which was why he wasn't sure the badger would still be there a couple of nights later, when he was running for his life.

The first of the intruders entered through the kitchen window. Max hadn't been asleep, though anyone watching the cottage would have been forgiven for thinking otherwise: the lights were out, the curtains drawn. He'd been lying in bed, not so much struggling with insomnia as letting it do its worst, when he'd heard the window latch being finessed open: a piece of wire sliding through the draughty gap he'd been meaning to repair, lifting the metal hook from its eye. Quieter than taking out the glass, but a long way short of silent. He'd pulled on jogging pants and a sweatshirt, slipped into a pair of trainers, then froze in place, caught between two lives, trying to remember where he'd stashed his flight kit . . . You could worry you were losing your mind. That they were coming too late, and you'd long ago turned into whoever you were pretending to be.

(Max Janáček. Retired (early) academic; still footling around with a history book, but mostly just passing the days—taking long walks, cooking slow meals, losing himself in Dickens.)

The stairs were an out-of-tune orchestra of squeaks and whistles, every tread announcing that Peter or the wolf were on their way, unless you'd practised descending, and knew where to put your feet. So almost noiselessly he reached the sitting room, whose doorway was catty-corner to the kitchen, and plucked the poker from its stand by the wood-burning stove. Not a great weapon, for all its iconic status in fiction. You needed high ceilings to accommodate your swing. Max Janáček understood a good swing: he was the man you saw walking the lanes, beheading dandelions with a stick. Who lived in a five-hundred-year-old cottage in North Devon, and could be counted on to do the neighbourly thing: keep an eye out for the old folk, whose company he was on the threshold of joining; litter-pick after the bank holiday rush; sign the petition resisting the makeshift industrial estate down the lane—numbering seventeen cabins now. This and more he'd been for more than twenty years, and whether the locals took him at face value or gave less than a tuppenny damn had become irrelevant, or had done until someone slipped the latch on his kitchen window and climbed inside more or less gracefully, breaking no crockery, dislodging no pans, and moving across the flagged floor in careful silence, intent— it would seem—on unlocking the back door and allowing his comrades ingress. Or her comrades, as it turned out. Whether

Max would have jabbed her so hard at the base of the skull with the poker, then slammed her head on the floor when she fell had he known it was a woman beneath the break-in gear was something he could ponder at leisure, if he survived the night. Meanwhile, he checked her for weapons. She was carrying a Taser, which put her outside the range of opportunist burglars, but no ID, and nothing to indicate what she was up to. But he had to work on the assumption that she wasn't alone, an assumption confirmed when he picked up the landline to hear the deep silence of a well on a windless night. Inside the cottage—anywhere down this lane—his mobile made for a useful paperweight. So sitting tight and calling the cavalry wasn't an option, and wouldn't necessarily have been a sensible move anyway. Sometimes, it was the cavalry you had to watch out for.

The cottage sat midway down a sloping lane, and was half of a twinned pair. In the other lived Old Dolly, who had probably forgotten a time when she'd simply been Dolly. Certainly she'd earned the Old by the time Max moved in, and still regarded him as three quarters a stranger, though he'd long reached the point where he was doing most of her shopping, all of her firewood gathering and a strong seven-eighths of listening to her bang on about immigration, which left him less uneasy than her habit of leaving a gas ring lit, to save striking a match for every cigarette. The next cottage along, a hundred yards distant, had been empty since Jonas Tripplehorn had gone to live with his daughter in Exeter; the cottage opposite—"cottage" by local tradition; it had four bedrooms—was a second home, and invariably unoccupied during the week. And farther down the lane were other dwellings, some housing young families, some retired labourers, and some home-based industries—IT and retro clothing; bespoke greetings cards and editorial services—and beyond them, on the other side of the railway bridge across which the London-Plymouth service rattled, the field now playing host to the makeshift estate which had roused such local ire. Corrugated iron structures had been erected, one at a time, and makeshift barns built, now storing the kind of heavy machinery you could dismember a dead badger with. Since this shanty town's foundation, traffic had multiplied tenfold, most of the vehicles heavily laden vans, with scaffolding poles tethered to flatbeds as the drivers headed to renovation jobs in the surrounding area; work which hadn't extended as far as repairing the potholes their vehicles left behind. Even now, as Max slipped out of a side window, he could hear an engine coughing in that direction, as if it were having one last drag before lying down for the night.

When he hit the ground he dropped into a crouch, and waited to see what happened next.

Which was nothing, for a while. A pair of small owls hooted in the distance, a familiar duet of hunt and swoop, while on the main road, a quarter mile away, a lorry banjaxed the quiet, hauling freight westward. There was cloud cover. Max knew the skies well enough to guess what stars he'd be looking at, this particular time and date, but had to be content to see them with his mind's eye only. More practically, from where he crouched he had a cross-section view of the lane and a full-frontal of the cottage opposite, which enjoyed enough shadowy places—the baggy hedge in front; the nook behind its outjutting porch—to conceal a ninja army. But if there were an actual professional threat lurking there, would they have sent a lone warrior into his kitchen? One he'd made pretty short work of, come to that? But it was pointless trying to second-guess an enemy whose purpose he didn't know. The owls hooted again. You could set your watch by them. If you were a mouse, it was probably wise to.

He wasn't sure how long the woman in the kitchen would be out, but no more than a few minutes would be his guess. It wasn't like calculated violence had been a habit even when he'd moved in circles where, if not the norm, it was at least an accepted accomplishment. No: the force with which he'd banged her head on the floor had more to do with outraged householder sensibilities than long dormant expertise. It would be sensible, though, to at least attempt to don the thought processes of the professional. Whoever they were, they suspected already and would soon know that their first incursion had failed. What they did next depended on their operational priorities. They wanted to be quiet, but they also wanted Max, and they might abandon thoughts of the former if the latter was within their reach. What, after all, would be the outcome of pandemonium? Lights going on in cottages, and a phone call to the police? Which might bring a rescue party, but not within the next thirty minutes, given the village's isolation. So it was a risk they'd doubtless take. In which case, he'd better formulate a response to an all-out assault on the cottage.

Legging it through the dark was the best he came up with.

And this wasn't the worst idea ever. They'd presumably arrived in a vehicle, maybe more than one, but they hadn't driven down the lane, or he'd have heard. So they had likely parked at the junction, where another lane headed to the main road, and a choice of exit routes. That would be their objective, and whether he'd be lying back here with a hole in him or trussed up in the boot of their vehicle while they achieved it, he couldn't know. The Taser, rather than—say—a knife or a gun or a cruise missile suggested that killing him wasn't Plan A, but all plans have contingencies, and if they couldn't take him alive, they might prefer to leave him dead. Neither outcome held appeal for Max, who, if he could make it twenty yards up the road, could slip through the hedge and into the field where their vehicles couldn't follow. He knew the terrain; they presumably didn't. He'd walked that field at night times without number; he'd lain on his back and admired the stars there, which was not a habit he boasted about to the neighbours. He wouldn't claim to know every bump and hollow, but familiarity should give him an edge. Still, he was a long way from being persuaded that this was the way to go when the decision was made for him: a familiar clunk and sigh told him the front door was swinging open. The woman he'd laid low was back on her feet, and her reappearance had galvanised the waiting troops: a shape, two shapes, materialised out of the darkness and ran to join her. There could be others. If he was going to move, it had to be now.

People entered his cottage, and over his head an eerie light broke through the window. They were using torches, and his sill clutter—plant pots, vases, candles on saucers—came briefly alive, casting ghostly shapes onto the night air. Slipping out of the lee of the wall, he crept round the Volvo, whose keys were on a hook by the front door, and onto the lane. This was thickly hedged on both sides, its surface rockier than it used to be, thanks to the recent heavy traffic. It curved as well as sloped and the gap in the hedge allowing access to the field was at the point where the junction ahead became visible. He was walking by memory, trusting his feet. His jogging pants were deep maroon but the top he'd pulled on had a silvery sheen, and if there were moonlight he'd show up as a ghost; a disturbance in the dark, the shape of half a man. But there was no moonlight; there was cloud cover, and the black vault of a February night, and a bitter chill he was increasingly aware of, and then—no warning—the twin head-lights of a parked vehicle at the top of the lane, pointing in his direction. He was pinned like a butterfly against a velvet cloth. Noises erupted behind him; not a circus, but a battery of urgent whispers. Torch beams picked him out as he reached the gap in the hedge, and slipped into the field.

It was like stepping through a curtain and finding himself

backstage. The light vanished, and the only way of telling up from down was by using his feet. With arms outstretched, so when he tripped he'd break his fall, he tried to run. The field was a set-aside; no crops, just the rocky rubble of soil, grass and weeds. If Max chose one direction, he'd come out onto a lane; another, and he'd reach another field. His eyes were adjusting; the car's headlights were creating a spooky glow behind him and then there were torches again as his pursuers reached the gap in the hedge, and spilled through it.

Almost immediately he heard a cry of pain, as one of his pursuers took a tumble and broke—Max hoped—an important bone.

He didn't pause, concentrating instead on running without falling flat on his face, but thought he could discern two separate beams of light playing across the ground. How far behind him? No way of knowing. How far to the road? Another few hundred yards, and the ground easier now he was getting used to it. But that went both ways: his pursuers would be picking up speed too, and they'd be younger than him, like most everybody else these days, and fitter too. An engine growled into life, and everything shifted up a gear. The bastards were no longer intent on silence, whoever the bastards were. But they couldn't, at least, follow him across a dark field in a car; an assurance that was of some comfort for two seconds, until the motorbike broke through the hole in the hedge, filling the field like an angry bull.

Time grows elastic at moments of stress. Apparently science supported this proposition, though for Max it was lived experience: the ever-slowing thud of his feet hitting the ground, the speeding up of the racket behind him. He gathered there were people who could identify motorbikes by sound alone, but he relied on counting their wheels, which was to say they were all the same to him, though this one worse than most. Somewhere up ahead was a padlocked five-barred gate, on the other side of which lay a lane. A little way down that lane was a turn-off: a steep hill leading past two cottages to a three-way junction. If he could reach there uncaptured, and far enough ahead, his pursuers would have to split up. But all of that was in the future, which was arriving too slowly, unless you were riding a motorbike across a rough-toned field, spitting stony soil behind you. The light grew brighter, and Max tried to run faster, as if it were a near-death experience he was hoping to avoid. Sixty-three years old. It was true it was the oldest he'd ever been; at the same time, it wasn't like seventy. Eighty. But time would take care of that, if it ever got back to behaving itself, and the bright headlight was swallowing everything now, clutching Max in its beam: he could see his own shadow rising up before him like a giant. In a fairy tale, it would turn and smite his pursuers; pound them into the soil. The motorbike was all but upon him; he could feel its breath on his arse. Then the gate materialised out of nowhere: he gripped its top and hurled himself over, hitting the ground like a beanbag. He'd be feeling that tomorrow, if tomorrow ever came. Behind him the motorbike screamed in anger, and scattered stony pellets: Max could feel them settle in his hair. He scrambled to his feet, and half stumbled, half ran down the road. The motorbike revved once, then twice, perhaps bearing Steve McQueen in mind as it considered jumping the gate, then roared back the way it had come, pausing halfway to confer—Max guessed—with the foot soldiers, still slogging across the field.

It was biting cold but he was covered in sweat, and had no idea what was going on. Somewhere in the darkness, probably at the junction at the top of his own lane, a car came to life, and more headlights split the night. His motion became smoother as his legs found their rhythm. They wanted a chase? Here's a chase. Before the headlights could pick him out he'd reached the turn-off and was sprinting up the hill, along a lane no more

than seven feet wide: one of Devon's narrow passages, allowing
only one vehicle at a time. The memory of a recent walk was
stirring. His breath grew painful as he passed the first cottage,
which, like its companion, was elevated above the lane itself: its
short driveway, on which a battered Land Rover sat, was damn
near vertical, and its garden wall, as tall as Max himself, was an
ancient thing of overgrown rocks, held together by crumbling
mortar and ambitious moss. He could hear the car slowing, its
occupants trying to work out where he'd gone: whether he was
still on the lane below, or had turned up this narrow passage and
disappeared into its shadows. The second cottage was a little
farther on. This was what he remembered: here, the cottage's
garden wall was bulging dangerously at the level of a passer-by's
head, so played upon by time and weather that it looked ready
to collapse, to spew rocks and soil and earth across the lane.
Perhaps that hint of impermanence was why the building was
for sale; a sign announcing the fact had been planted in the
patch of lawn behind the wall. Max turned up its driveway and
grabbed the sign with both hands: FOR SALE, and an estate
agent's details, atop a five-foot wooden pole . . . It came free
from the ground surprisingly easily, as if he were Arthur releasing a sword, and he was king of the moment for as long as it
took him to bury it again, push it down into the crumbly soil
near the bulging wall as far as it would go. And then a little
farther. The lane lit up: the car had made its decision, and was
coming to collect him. Easier to conquer that steep hill on four
wheels: his own legs were trembling now, partly with the cold,
mostly with all this effort. Not so long ago, his worst problem
had been insomnia. With the pole deep in the ground he
adjusted his efforts; no longer pushing down he leaned on it,
turning it into a lever. The lane was awash with headlights; the
bushes on the other side glittering with life. He felt the earth

give. The car was moving slowly, as if it suspected something. He leaned harder, putting all his weight into it. It was there, almost, just slightly out of reach, that release he was straining for, and the car growled louder, and something splintered in his grip, as if the pole had broken off in the ground, and if so that would be it, game over, except it wasn't, because everything gave in the same moment; there was a dull tumble as the first of the wall's rocks slipped free and thudded onto the lane below, and then the earth was moving beneath his feet, and with a roar Max felt rather than heard half of the garden spilled onto the road: the rocks that had held it in place tumbling first, followed by the soil that had long been their burden: great wet chunks of it, with a looser gravelly content unfolding in its wake. He gave one last encouraging push on the pole and stepped back sharply, and the crunch he heard next was the car grinding into one of the larger rocks and coming to a graceless halt. He hurled the pole in that direction, and in a better life would have seen it pierce the windscreen rather than bounce off, but you couldn't have everything. He jumped back onto the lane, on the right side of the barrier he'd just created—scooping up a hand-sized rock as he did so—and ran off into the dark. Lights came on in the other cottage as a householder peered into the night, in search of the cause of the earthquake, while from the car two figures emerged. One scrambled over the rocks in pursuit, while the other hung on to the door for a moment, trying to gauge the damage, and possibly contemplating insurance issues.

Another headlight appeared at the foot of the lane. The motorbike was back.

Max wasn't looking at any of this; he'd reached the three-way junction and had taken the middle option. A hundred yards on, he knew, lay the opening to one of the green lanes he frequented on his morning walks: narrow tracks with stony footing—riverbeds in waiting—hemmed either side by trees and bushes, and if you didn't know they were there, you'd miss their entrances. A network of them mapped North Devon, and once you'd entered their geography you could lose yourself beyond hope of capture. Provided you made that transition unseen.

The rock in his hand was a comforting keepsake. Behind him, someone was making heavy weather of pursuit, the noise of their feet slapping the ground suggesting swift motion was a novelty. But the motorbike was there too, growling in the distance, and he didn't expect it would take it more than thirty seconds to negotiate the obstacle he'd caused, after which it would come roaring after him again, eating the distance with a lot less labour than the overweight goon between them. But thirty seconds in the dark could make up a small lifetime. That much he remembered from the long-ago, a memory awake now in his bones.

Sooner or later, he would need a plan. And before he'd got that far, even, he'd need to recover his flight kit, provided these hooligans hadn't found it already.

The entrance to the green lane was just yards away. He was running as quietly as he could, hoping he was invisible; that the thug on his heels was too busy flirting with a heart attack to be paying close attention. Though also, as a contingency, he was tightening his grip on the rock in his hand.

. . . Flight kit. It sounded like a piece of tourist equipment. And so, in a way, it was, though most tourists have a destination in mind, and this particular bag was for those focused on departure. His passport—the word "his" designating ownership rather than identity, but it was a passport he'd paid for, and definitely bore his photograph—plus a grand in cash and two prepaid credit cards worth 5,000 US dollars and 5,000 euros respectively. One change of clothing, a basic toiletries kit which included hair-dye and tinted contact lenses, and a pair of insoles that would alter his gait enough to fool a computer. Or that was the notion, though computers were more sophisticated than they used to be. He'd spent years in the country, becoming a bumpkin. Surveillance technology, meanwhile, had been hanging out in city centres, picking up tricks. But you did what you could.

The bag was beneath a floorboard under Max's firewood basket, next to the burner in his sitting room, a hiding place he was reasonably confident would have eluded this bunch of amateurs, but there was no accounting for luck. And even if it remained secure, he had to get back there undetected. But one thing at a time.

Here was the entrance to the green lane. He risked a look back, just making out the grumpy shape of a driver finding his land legs, and took a chance, hurling the rock with all the force he could manage. It missed its target, but not by much, and his pursuer flinched as it whistled past his head, and dropped to a crouch at the exact moment the motorbike reappeared, becoming a lump in the middle of the road the bike skewed to avoid, its cone of lamplight washing the hedgerow yellow. Someone—the cowering man; the bike rider—shouted in fear or anger, and Max slipped off the road and onto the green lane, where he ducked behind the first tree, no taller than he was, and held his breath as the hedgerow healed behind him, and the long grass drew its curtain. He could feel damp seeping through his trainers, and cold sweat on his back and arms. His chest ached and the taste of old coins filled his mouth. Meanwhile, rearrangements were being made; the motorbike's headlight levelled and found a straight line heading west. A moment later the machine itself roared by, leaving a deeper blackness in its wake, and Max heard but didn't see the luckless car driver lumber past. His breathing scored the night like tearing paper. Max waited until it faded before drawing air himself, feeling it enter his lungs like a baptism. Getting to his feet again made everything creak. Things like this should happen to a younger man, if they had to happen at all. Presumably someone had a good reason for setting all this in motion. Max would enjoy holding their head down a toilet, should the opportunity arise.

He made his way down the green lane as swiftly as compatible with balance. If it had been dark on the lane, here in this shaded alley things were pitch: the going slippery, except where tree roots and jagged stones offered trip hazards instead. The low branches were heavy and damp, and he was whipped in the face every other step. Noise magnified in the dark, and he felt as stealthy as a hippo. But for now, at least, he'd evaded his pursuers, whoever they were. Soon, he hoped, he'd have time to put his mind to that. At the moment, he was kept busy making sure he wasn't eaten by the country.

It became a counting game—every ten steps he'd pause and stretch his hearing. Scratches and rustlings were all he heard, as the green lane's inhabitants warned each other of his approach. Once he stumbled, and in the act of falling had a whole string of painful premonitions: a broken ankle, a painful night, a quiet day. The green lane would reach around him, and by the time his body came to light it would be wrapped in roots: a rustic mummy. But an outstretched hand saved him from worse than a jarred skeleton: he felt the impact in his teeth, but no real harm done. As he clambered up again his fingers curled round a stick, as if the world were offering an apology. Nothing like a stick for helping maintain balance. God, he was going to be good at being old, if circumstances allowed. He reached a junction with another green lane, and without pausing turned left—sometimes the best decisions were the ones you hardly made, the ones that made themselves for you. Though it was best not to make too severe an accounting. It could start to look like the life you'd lived had been a series of accidents; of unintentional explosions, and unwilled alterations. Another ten steps and he paused to listen. The motorbike was back within earshot, though it couldn't possibly be heading down the green lane. But it was.

Panic can be time-consuming, and there were better ways of getting through the next little while. Max had two obvious choices: keep going or bundle himself into a clump of hedge and hope the bike would pass by without seeing him. Now that he'd branched off from his initial route his chances of avoiding detection had improved by some precise mathematical element he couldn't currently determine, but maths was a tricky bunch of bastards, and he'd sooner trust his stick. The motorcycle's noise remained at a set distance, or seemed to: noise magnified in the dark, but also played games of its own. It could lurk round corners, or jump over hedges. Max continued on his way, trying not to hurry: less haste more speed, and other English word games. The world was dark and strange and familiar all at once. In his nighttime ramblings, he never entered the green lanes. This was why: they could swallow you whole without even bothering to spit you out. Idiots sometimes drove them in vehicles they didn't care about any more than they did nature, but darkness contained risks even idiots steered clear of. Rocks shifted, stones rolled, and roots reached out and grabbed you. Cars that could bully their way through daylight found themselves wrecked by night's tricksters. Pedestrians like Max moved slowly, exploring the barely visible terrain with a stick, and keeping one foot on the ground at all times.

Somewhere behind him, the motorbike roared and revved. He hoped its rider was unprepared, and wearing non-protective gear.

When the stench hit him it was with the force of an avalanche, as if gravity were rolling boulders down a slope.

It was the dead badger. He'd not been aware he was approaching its ambit, and even now couldn't tell how close he was—it had gathered power since he'd first encountered it, its atmosphere expanding like an untended chemistry experiment—and his eyes began to stream, his head to fill. The worst smell in the world. He'd undersold it, calling it that. It was the smell of an afterlife gone bad; all the disappointments of eternity balled up into a single sensation, and delivered with the subtlety of a shovel in the face. The motorbike ceased its slow progress and growled from a crouching position. When Max turned, a static glow lit the bushes a hundred yards back, where the green lanes met. His watering eyes made the scene a kaleidoscope, fragments of light scattering and reforming, under which the motor hummed with indecision. It would follow him or not. There was nothing he could do about it. He turned again and made his way forward, half blind, his rustling inaudible as long as the motorbike grumbled, and the air he was walking into grew solider with every step. The badger's death was crawling with life, its corpse a feasting table for insects, its putrid flesh, its rotting fur, a palace for famished worms. The stink was unbelievable. The darkness made it worse. There was something in his ears too, as if the animal's death had scored a symphony in the night: it was all drums and screaming strings and a conductor who'd lost the plot. The motorbike was on the move. Max didn't look back. He stumbled forward, stick in hand, and a wave of nausea splashed over him, splashed all around. He pulled the neckline of his sweatshirt over his mouth and nose, but it made small difference. Light was picking him out, an elongated stickman thrashing his way down a quivering corridor, which grew narrower ahead, and rockier underfoot. He must be passing the badger corpse now, off to his left, entangled in its rooty tomb, and Christ the smell couldn't get worse but it did: like walking into a wardrobe and having the door close behind you. The motorbike was throwing shapes as it heaved and rattled over the stony ground, its headlight's beam a wandering yellow scoop. Max's vision began to clear. Leaves were dancing ahead of him, and he couldn't tell if this were a breeze or the motion of the motorbike sending turbulence ahead to rummage down the lane, but either way he felt an approaching storm. The sweatshirt slipped free of his nose and the stench redoubled but he was past the epicentre now, and the motorbike hadn't reached it yet; still about eighty yards behind him, its progress cautious, its driver anxious not to spill on the rough terrain. Behind its headlight's glare there was only a grotesque lump, as if driver and machine had fused into a single being. This was how monsters were made.

Max had no idea why this maelstrom had been unleashed tonight. He was well pissed off about it, though.

There are advantages to being the one on foot in a motorbike/pedestrian smackdown, but none came to mind. What arrived instead was a shift of focus. Using people, changing the game, taking what came to hand—things didn't have to be broken to need a fixer. This wasn't so much Max remembering who he used to be as the person he used to be realising he was now Max. One or maybe both of them was gagging at the toxic shock, but at the same time that shock was slotting into place in the world he found himself in. Here on the green lane was a sphere, a snow globe, a goldfish bowl. It was a perfect circle everywhere you looked, and inside it was the worst smell in the world, and outside was everything else. And you were either in that sphere or not, and right that moment Max's advantage was that he knew this was so and the man on the motorbike didn't. Soon he would, and while he was adjusting to that new reality would be a good moment to interrogate his professionalism. Lots of people could do two things at once. Many had difficulty doing three.

The air was starting to clear, and the motorbike was twenty yards behind, truffling its way along the gnarly passage, its human—Max could now see—being tossed around like a rodeo rider by the roots and rocks its wheels were crunching over. Any moment now. He took two more steps, prodding the ground with his stick as he moved, then looked back. Any moment. Another step, and again he looked back. The headlight's glare was sprawling between them, and he focused on the ground it illuminated, trying to map it—it would be good to know where the worst rocks were, the biggest roots. Any moment. The motorbike rocked and roared, an impossible beast, and Max had the sudden notion of himself as a horseless knight facing down a dragon. Which bucked and steamed and wasn't expecting what happened next: that Max should fling himself towards it, holding his stick like a lance. He was ready for the stench this time, re-entering its sphere as the motorbike joined it from the other direction, and knew without being able to see that the rider was already confused because this wasn't right, the quarry didn't become the hunter. All the rider could do was wrench the bike sideways to block Max's escape. Though escape wasn't what Max had in mind; what he wanted was the rider to experience the impact of the badger's last gasp, which was happening now, he guessed—the bike, slanted sideways across the narrow green lane, was an effective barrier, but the rider had thrown his head back in disbelief or horror or shock, or whatever word best described being assaulted by airborne filth. His stick grasped lengthways, Max leaped, catching the rider chest-high, and the two of them piled onto the ground, the bike tumbling with them, trapping its rider's right leg and sending its headlight's beam directly into the sky, a yellow column in which insects swarmed. It might have been all over then, if Max could have got one headbutt in, but the driver wore a helmet: its visor raised, but his temples and forehead protected. His lungs weren't doing so well though. He'd gasped on impact, taking in a bucketful of busy air, and his face was screwed up in disgust. One of his arms was pinioned by Max's stick; the other he raised feebly in an attempt to batter Max's head, but the tide was against him. Some moments ago he'd been upright and mobile, astride a motorbike; now the bike was astride him, and he was breathing poisonous fog. Max shifted position, so his stick was across the man's throat, and pushed hard, and as he did so he brought his face close to his enemy's and bit his nose. Jesus, he hadn't known he'd had that in him. His victim squirmed and screamed, his hot breath spraying Max's face with germs, but there was a time for worrying about hygiene and another for just getting on with the job. Between his teeth was gristle and grit. Between the two men the motorbike trembled. Between one moment and the next the fight was done: his victim wasn't struggling any more, he was crying. Max relaxed his jaws, released his grip on the stick, took careful aim, and punched the man in the face just once, partly for reasons of caution, but mostly because he could still remember when his biggest problem was insomnia, and now he was cold, wet, muddy and scared. He got to his feet, trembling. The motorbike growled, like a wolf he'd fought to its knees, but it wasn't going anywhere. Keeping his breathing shallow, Max turned and stumbled away down the green lane, where, within a minute or two, the foul air faded. It took longer than that before the motorbike's noise was just a background whimper, mingled with its rider's sobs. When Max spat, it wasn't just saliva he cleared from his mouth. He noticed he was muttering to himself, and not in English either. But it was a little late to worry about maintaining his cover.

Back at Max's cottage, the woman whose head he'd banged against his kitchen floor had taken a couple of surreptitious ibuprofen halfway through her assigned tasks—"Find out where he'd go. Find his phone, his laptop, his diary"—but her head throbbed, and she'd have a face like an aubergine come morning.

The only phone was a Nokia brick on his bedside table. She'd dropped it into a freezer bag. There was a laptop too, old and battered and heavy, but nothing resembling a diary. Her stomach was churning, and she wasn't sure whether that was the assault, the medication swallowed dry on an empty stomach, or the whole burglary enterprise. Which hadn't gone swimmingly well, she'd be the first to admit, and also the first to be blamed. But there was always the chance she could redeem herself, and the best way of doing that would be climbing back into the car heavy-handed. Sometimes, guilty souls packed for a swift getaway. It was possible the bastard had an escape kit—go home with that, she'd be next best thing to forgiven.

It could be anywhere, of course, but easy reach was the thing. So she was checking his sitting room, which had walls of unequal length and a curved windowspace, both suggesting hollow cavities, and keeping an eye on her watch at the same time when her phone trembled in her pocket. It had been sixty minutes since the flag dropped, which was way outside the ideal envelope. When things went bad, they went bad the way soap operas did: they got worse all the time, and didn't stop. She leaned against the wood-burning stove, one hand resting on its companion firewood basket, and took her boss's call in a whisper.

"Anything?"

"Phone and laptop."

"Letters, postcards, Post-its stuck to the fridge?"

There hadn't been.

"Money? Anywhere?"

"A few quid."

The boss paused. Then: "Put a tracker on his car."

Which answered an unspoken question. "He got away, then."

"No, we've got him here. It's a promotional thing, we're giving away free trackers this week."

"... Sorry."

"Jesus."

He disconnected.

There were trackers in her kit bag, fastened to her belt. She looked the consummate professional, all the tools hanging at her waist. Probably the reason the target had heard her climbing through his window.

Rubbing the side of her head again, she straightened up and left the room. Then re-entered, walked back to the stove, opened it and peered inside. Nothing. Worth a look though, and worth another thirty seconds to root through the firewood basket. Again, nothing. She kicked the basket in frustration, shifting it half a yard, and left the room once more, unzipping the pouch containing the tracker as she did so. At the front door, she scooped the target's car keys from their hook: forget the wheel arches, forget the exhaust pipe, forget all the places guilty people checked. She'd stick the bastard thing under the passenger seat. If he waited until they'd gone and doubled back, hoping for a motorised getaway, she'd be the one laughing come morning. Aubergine-faced or not.

The last watcher departed at 6:34, as the first builder's van trundled down the lane towards the industrial encampment. The sky had lightened enough that trees had shapes instead of character, though the rolling clouds suggested that the morning would be smeary and grey, with a better than even chance of turning dismal. Once the watcher's car reached the top of the lane and made the right turn that would take it to the main road, Max emerged from the hedge in which he'd been crouching and creaked his way down to his cottage. The birdsong, normally a pleasure, was unusually irritating this morning. He needed a shower, proper clothes and breakfast, and was aware that a clock had started ticking. He had to find out what had just happened before it happened again. Which meant he needed to be in the car and away as soon as possible.

He was in and out of the cottage inside twenty minutes, locking up behind him and poking his head round Old Dolly's door thirty seconds later, a half-eaten fried egg sandwich in his hand, a rucksack on his back. His neighbour was up by five most mornings, in case—he surmised—they made smoking and being curmudgeonly illegal overnight. Every moment asleep was a moment wasted.

"I'll be away a while, Doll. A few weeks maybe. Possibly longer."

"And you're telling me this because?"

"So you'll remember, when you start starving to death, why you're running out of food."

"I managed all right before you turned up."

"We were twenty years younger then. The Queen Mother was managing all right." The last of his sandwich in his mouth, he opened her fridge. Most of the veg he'd bought last time was still there, in varying states of decay. The only green thing inroads had been made on was the bottle of Gordon's. "I take it back. You're going to live forever." He shut the fridge. "Unless you're already dead. That would explain a lot, come to think of it."

"What was all the activity last night?"

"You have very vivid dreams."

"Don't gaslight me, you shiftless refugee."

"Speaking of which." He turned off her gas ring. "There are cheaper ways of lighting up, you know. And a box of matches wouldn't hurt the planet."

"Tell that to the tree they're made from." Suggestibility at work: she reached for the cigarettes she kept in her housecoat's pouch, an action that, for Max, always brought a kangaroo to mind. "And you're changing the subject."

"It turns out I have unpaid bills. Someone came round to collect."

She nodded, as if this confirmed a long-held suspicion. "Being a deadbeat's caught up with you, has it? Always pay your debts, that's my motto."

"Unless it's to your neighbour, right?"

"Did I ever ask you to do my shopping? Or did you just poke your nose in?"

Mention of noses wasn't welcome. Max made a face he hoped Old Dolly wouldn't notice. "I didn't like the idea of you starving to death, and someone moving in who kept the TV low. I've been listening to the rubbish you watch for free all these years."

"Then don't pretend I owe you anything."

Max made the *doof doof doof* noise of *EastEnders'* drums, and came forward to light her cigarette with the plastic lighter she kept for igniting the gas ring. As he bent to apply the flame, he kissed the top of her head gently.

"Piss off, paedo!"

"Don't open the door to strangers. Jonas's number's on that postcard next to the phone. He'll sort you out if you need anything."

"What would I need, my age?"

"It's too early for the big questions, Doll."

Another van rumbled down the road, and she scowled. "Bloody pikeys. Someone should have a word with them."

"Always full of good ideas." Adjusting the rucksack which hung from one shoulder, Max gave her a three-fingered salute which she returned half-heartedly with two of her own. He imagined her still scowling as he drew the door closed and set off down the lane. In his mind Old Dolly was always scowling. It was difficult to picture someone acting entirely out of character.

Four minutes later—a bell was tolling seven—he was at the

encampment at the far side of the village. A mini industrial estate established by stealth, and hoping to convince the local Council that it had acquired established-use status, this was run by an exile from Plymouth, known for complicated reasons as Neezer. It was Neezer who bore the brunt of the villagers' ire for having brought this makeshift builders' yard to their border, though as Neezer pointed out, when he could be bothered, the field he'd purchased with what he consistently referred to as "legal cash" was separated by the railway line from the village proper, "and is therefore outside your jurisdiction, squire," a form of address he used gender-neutrally. This technical nicety not-withstanding, no self-respecting local set eyes on Neezer or any of his cohort without resort to that brand of freezing contempt perfected by teenagers, French waiters and the English middle class. Which, Max surmised, Neezer was all broken up about on the inside, because it never showed anywhere else.

This morning, as at every other hour of the day, Neezer wore a pork-pie hat and a plaid waistcoat over a white shirt and black jeans, an unlit roll-up in the corner of his mouth completing the outfit. When he heard Max approaching over the redundant cattle grid, he was making coffee in a microwave hooked up to a generator that had the kind of dry cough that would call for a lateral flow test if a human had it, and benignly watching a man who looked about eighty trying to load a dishwasher into the back of a van. "You want to be careful, squire," he said as Max came into earshot, and if it seemed he were addressing the elderly labourer, his follow-up put that right. "Get seen hobnobbing with the likes of me, your posho neighbours'll have you tarred and barrelled."

Max would have grinned at the idea of Old Dolly being "posho" if he weren't feeling the effects of a sleepless night. "I think you mean feathered," he said, slipping the rucksack off his shoulder and leaning against the wooden upright holding Neezer's corrugated iron rooftop in place. The sheltered area contained a rocking chair, a small kitchen table on which the microwave sat, a standard lamp, a cardboard box holding three bottles of wine and a carton of milk, a small lockable cupboard of the kind found next to hospital beds, and which was indeed stamped "Property of Exeter Hospital," and—because the world was full of people, and every last one of them unique—a three-shelved bookcase, about a foot wide, stuffed with teach-yourself guitar manuals. Nowhere in Max's field of vision was a guitar.

"Yeah, I'd not put weight on that, I were you." The microwave pinged, and Neezer removed his coffee. "It's a bit non-load-bearing, if you catch my drift."

Max stood straight, keeping a grip on the bag with one hand, and dipping into it with the other. "That must give you a nice secure feeling."

"Temporary structure. Need permission otherwise." He wrinkled his nose as Max came nearer. "What's that odour?"

Despite the thirty-second shower and change of clothes it was in his hair, and clinging to his skin. "I'm using a new moisturiser."

"You should sort it out, squire. Smells like dead fucking badger."

"It's on my list." He counted a hundred in tens from the wedge of cash he'd taken from the bag. "Here's my parking fee. Car ready?"

As well as signing a petition against the encampment Max had stowed a car there, a fourteen-year-old Saab he'd bought in Exeter from a man in a pub. This had been eighteen months ago, after it became clear that the camp wasn't going anywhere soon, and replaced Max's previous parking scheme, whereby he'd left his secret wheels in a lock-up in Newton Abbot. This had been okay as a fallback, but its drawbacks included Newton Abbot being a fair hike away. If Neezer had been amused at providing Max with a hideaway garage in the camp at the same time as Max was adding his voice to the chorus of outrage at the camp's existence, he didn't mention it. It was possible that such examples of man's Janusian nature no longer surprised him. That, or the hundred quid a month stifled his own outrage adequately.

He made a vague wave towards a nearby structure, similar to the one under which he was sitting but larger, beneath whose tin roof were various shrouded shapes almost certainly cars. "As you left it, squire. If it went then it should go now, provided time's whirlywhatsit hasn't wrought its rusty changes." He sipped his coffee and made a face, whether of approval or disgust wasn't easy to determine. "Maintenance and valeting, that was never part of the arrangement."

It had been, was how Max recalled it, but there was little point arguing. He handed the notes to Neezer, who stuffed them into his waistcoat pocket without counting, and couldn't resist asking: "Do you own a guitar, Neezer?"

"No. Why?"

"Just, you seem anxious to learn how to play."

"Oh, yeah, right. No, I am learning. Still doing the theory though, squire." Coffee cup in his left hand, he mimed holding the instrument, twiddling the fingers of his right. "Day I actually pick one up, I'll already be an expert. Know what I mean?"

Max sort of did. Fetching the car keys up from the belly of his bag, he gave the same three-fingered salute to Neezer that he'd bestowed on Old Dolly, and headed off to rescue his car from its canvas shroud.

Watching him leave, Neezer tapped the roll of cash in his waistcoat pocket, and called encouragement to the octogenarian struggling with the dishwasher. "You wanna bend your knees, squire. Don't wanna do your back in, not at your age."

Then he poured the rest of his coffee away, pulled a book from his shelf, and started to read.

PART TWO:

MONOCHROME, THEN & NOW

As everyone in the know knew, and many on the fringes guessed, the establishment of the Monochrome inquiry—announced with less fanfare than the then PM's mini-break at Peppa Pig World—was intended to leave the Service rattled. There was history there. Prior to his ascension the prime minister had enjoyed a sabbatical as Foreign Secretary, a period of what one observer described as "bubblewrap diplomacy," with the emphasis on bursting bubbles rather than offering protection; its lowlights included an extended sentence in a foreign prison for a British subject innocent of wrongdoing, and a number of indiscreet liaisons on a number of continents, the only context in which the word "continent" might be applied to the minister's activities. While such behaviour was regarded by those around him as priced in, warranting no more than shrugs or backslaps, several of his new-found friendships raised concern at Regent's Park. That the minister's predilection for being wined and dined overcame scruples about the company he kept was hardly headline news, but the roll-call of those he was carousing with was starting to resemble a casting call for a Bond villain. After an incident in Gdańsk in which the Foreign Secretary had allowed a new chum to install a dating app on his official phone—one which, he was assured, was two hundred per cent discreet—it was felt that enough was enough, and his then boss was informed that her minister of state had come dangerously close to giving a foreign intelligence service access to the restricted Downing Street network. With an alacrity which suggested that she'd been waiting for the opportunity she sacked him, whereupon he, in turn, parlayed his new-found victim status into a leadership bid. The rest was history, in the long-term sense of being both tragic and farcical. But whatever tactical advantage the incoming PM had gained from the Park's interference, he nevertheless regarded it as an act of pre-emptive treason. Which ultimately led to the Monochrome inquiry, and the notification of its schedule that reached Regent's Park after circulating Westminster.

The inquiry will be panelled by an all-party body, it ran, *with two independent appointees to ensure objectivity.* Its remit: "to investigate historical over-reaching by the intelligence services." Its duration, open-ended. *Any and all matters regarding potential misconduct by officers of the Service in pursuit of official instruction are to be regarded as material to the inquiry. All officially held informational resources save those pertaining to live operations are to be made available to sitting members.*

Or, in other words, unlock your doors, open your cupboards.

This can't be serious, was the verdict from below decks.

"The guv'nor will have him on toast," was an opinion generally held. "He's just emptied his kettle on a basket of rattlesnakes."

Because among junior officers at the Park—as the headquarters of the intelligence services, located at Regent's Park, was familiarly known—it was so firmly believed as to have become more nearly a law of physics than mere article of faith that in any contest between its top banana, more formally called First Desk, and the PM, it was the latter who'd be queueing at the dentist's afterwards, carrying his teeth in a sodden handkerchief.

But in First Desk's office, with its frostable glass wall overlooking the boys and girls on the hub, the reaction was curiously muted.

"It's his idea, obviously. But I suspect his head gnome has had more than a little input."

This being Anthony Sparrow, the PM's special adviser and, in the eyes of many, glove puppeteer.

"He probably imagines he's just stolen the keys to the sweetie cabinet," she continued. "He'll be needing fresh underwear as we speak."

But even so she did not, in the view of the young woman who was her administrative assistant that season, seem unduly worried by the prospect.

"It seems more than a little victory," this woman offered, somewhat uncertainly.

First Desk didn't answer, and the assistant—whose name was Erin Grey—wondered if she'd spoken out of turn. Her appointment was still a daily source of wonder to her, even if its actual duties bordered on the mundane. She collected mail, she managed a diary, she fetched and ferried, and above all she carried out a kind of temporal origami to ensure that all First Desk's commitments were met in the allotted time frame. But she didn't generally have conversations, above and beyond "Good morning" and "Yes, ma'am." She was starting to recalibrate her expectations, beginning with wondering what job she'd have come lunchtime, when First Desk spoke.

"It's a preliminary inquiry, not a select committee," she said. "Its function will be to amass a coherent body of evidence. And I wish them luck with that."

"But if they're given access to our records, won't they find it? I mean"—a hurried addition—"anything can be made to look like misconduct if it's examined from the right angle."

"Oh, doubtless. And just between you, me, and anyone who's ever read a newspaper or watched TV, the Service's hands haven't always been entirely clean when it comes to operational practices.

It'll shock you, I know, but some of my predecessors might even have been a little less than, well, we can't say 'lily-white' any more. But you get my drift."

Even leaving aside the one who was a fully paid-up asset of the Russian Secret Service, she didn't add. There were some details that even the Park's archive chose to draw a veil across.

"But it's not finding the material, it's knowing what to do with it. Start tugging at a loose thread from a tapestry like ours, and you'll be years in the unravelling. No, we keep records for our own devices, not to provide a ready-made history for anyone who comes looking. Between the worknames and the coded locations, this Monochrome outfit'll be lucky to piece together who did the coffee run yesterday, let alone who shagged who in a safe house in 1987." A deliberate downplayment: they'd be looking for criminal activity. "So let's not lose sleep over a minor irritation."

"It's all just politics, then."

"It's all just politics, and we know how long politics takes. Any finding the PM hopes to make stand up will take years of investigation. Say four, to err on the cautious side. And I give him eighteen months tops. He's a walking non-disclosure agreement, and if his domestic entanglements don't undo him, his disregard for the truth will. No, fucking things up is a legacy project with this one. Forget about him now, and save time later. Now, what did I just say about a coffee run?"

When Erin had left, First Desk turned to other business, or at least, appeared to. In reality, her mind continued to churn over the Monochrome memo. Grey seemed competent, and might even last a few months, but whatever her other attributes, she had a significant inability to keep interesting information to herself, which was a more common failing in Regent's Park than might be hoped for, given that it housed the secret service. So First Desk's trashing of the memo would be all over the Park by close of play: nothing to see here, nothing to worry about. The boys and girls would kick the topic around a while longer, but something else would soon grab their attention—this, hopefully, being along the lines of an in-house romance rather than, say, a terrorist atrocity—and the level of concern would drop back to negligible. Which was mostly, she thought now, where it should be. Because it was as she had said: while the PM was capable of following through with a course of action provided the gratification was immediate and overwhelming, anything involving patience was less likely to reach fruition. True, the fact that he'd instigated the inquiry indicated that he had support on the Limitations Committee, which was a less important way of saying that she herself had enemies there, but this was hardly news: no First Desk ever had the complete backing of the committee, and her tendency to go off message when circumstances required had long tarnished her image in the eyes of some of its dustier members. No, this was an empty threat: a bit of dick-waving to signal the PM's fury at earlier slights. But as well-known as he was for carrying grudges he was also currently carrying a wagonload of debt, and it wouldn't be long before solving his liquidity problems took precedence over anything else on his to-do list. So the boys and girls of the Park would be better employed getting on with their actual jobs than wasting time fretting about an inquiry that would go nowhere, slowly. End, as used to be said, of.

By the time Erin returned with coffee First Desk was operating in regular mode, which is to say that she accepted the offering without looking up from her screen. But if she appeared to have put Monochrome out of her mind, several issues continued to gnaw. One was the question of how the PM would go about solving those liquidity problems, and how big a headache that might cause for those in his orbit. The other was a more general irritation, and should really be dismissed forthwith; the nagging awareness that, times without number, what started out an inconsequential piece of mischief could gather quiet momentum, the way a drip-drip-drip in an otherwise silent house heralded the ceiling collapsing under the weight of water.

Yes, this should really be dismissed, but still. It would be as well to prepare a contingency plan.

She was First Desk, after all. Contingency plans were what she did.

So she returned to the memo that had Westminster in a tizzy and studied it once more, paying careful attention to its phrasing.

It was two years after that morning that a dark-skinned woman in her fifties, wearing a knee-length beige raincoat and carrying a blue umbrella, stepped on a loose paving stone while crossing Bishopsgate and drenched her left trouser leg in dirty water. If she were the type to swear she might have let rip, and wouldn't have been alone—the city was full of angry pedestrians, hooted at by angry drivers and sworn at by angry cyclists, while angry buses trundled past full of angry passengers, and the angry sky rained angry rain, and the angry morning would never end. But she kept any fury to herself. Her mind now throbbing with extra tasks—when to get to the dry cleaners, and what to wear on the alternate days of the week she'd earmarked these trousers for— Griselda Fleet managed to cross the road at last without being sideswiped by vicious road-users, and half limped the rest of the way to her destination, the wet fabric of her trouser clinging nastily to her leg, like a wound dressing.

Monochrome was her destination; monochrome her journey too, the greys and blacks and whites of London in the rain on full display, all its grime and filthy litter, its pavements reflecting the clouds. Takeaway wrappers and discarded face masks bundled in the gutter, causing puddles to swamp the side streets.

She had to make diversions to avoid getting her feet wetter as she toiled past cycle racks and e-scooter bays, past the lobbies of tall buildings that encroached on pavement space. Before reaching the grim black bridge across which trains rumbled, Griselda turned right. This was a far narrower street, though it broadened after a hundred yards, featureless walls giving way to a parade of genteel townhouses—she was ashamed to admit she couldn't identify their era, but Georgian seemed to fit—and then a string of low-rise blocks, most tenanted by media companies and "creative agencies," whatever—her daily observation —these might be. But there were vacancies, too, plenty of vacancies, available for long- or short-term lets: "attractive office space in the heartland of London's start-up district." Estate agents threw words at the wall, and hoped some of them stuck. But it wasn't the attractive space or the creative location that had led to this street being her daily destination, it was economics. A few short years ago, hustling young firms would have wrestled naked for the opportunity to house their workers here. Post-Covid, many of those workers would even now be setting up Zoom calls in their kitchens, the Monday-morning commute a memory from a fever dream. Griselda was reaching for her lanyard as she approached the door, was stringing it round her neck one-handed, the other still hoisting her umbrella, as she mounted the steps, then shaking that umbrella free of rainwater while Clive the doorman buzzed her into the lobby.

"Good morning, Mrs. Fleet."

She'd long ago given up trying to impress *Ms.* upon him.

"I've known better, Clive. And it's barely eight A.M."

The trouser leg clinging to her own was making her feel clammy all over.

A tabloid lay on the reception desk. STRIKES TO CONTINUE screamed the headline, which, as a summation of the national weather, was either woefully vague or admirably concise.

She took the lift, once Clive had activated it, a security measure that was a hangover from the building's previous tenants. She wasn't sure which of those firms were still active, if any; they had all had interesting-sounding names—Hodge-Podge, Trackless, Indigo Mean—which was never a sign of robust longevity. The new working-from-home norm, embraced as a lifestyle enhancement by the young and thrusting, had gone hand in hand with the shedding of employee benefits, the imposition of zero-hours contracts and a rise in mental health issues among workers. Official statistics offered rosier pictures—average salaries had risen across the board, according to a recent government release—but painting by numbers was an illusory business. When you axed lower paid jobs, the average rose without anyone becoming richer. And when people tightened their belts, companies whose focus-grouped names obscured their actual functions tended to go to the wall. Which was how Monochrome had come to be housed here, a year's lease having been taken up at a fire-sale rate, and negotiated downwards when an extension proved necessary.

Past two semi-busy floors, past two totally vacant. Fifth and top. Not enough of a view to crow about; more than enough stairs to make fire drills a pain in the calves. Using her lanyard to beep open the door, she propped her umbrella in the waste-paper basket and hung her coat on the stand in the reception area. As ever, the imprints on the carpet tiles had her mentally furnishing this otherwise empty space: a desk, a receptionist's chair, a table on which, no doubt, fashionable magazines had been strewn, two visitors' chairs arrayed around that table, and a cabinet of some sort behind the reception desk, where Griselda liked to picture coffee equipment: *Can I get you something while you're waiting? Latte, cappuccino?* Or the vegan equivalent. But she really should stop bitching about the imagined conditions previous occupants had luxuriated in. Or if that was too difficult, at least find new things to bitch about.

Reception area aside, Monochrome's kingdom consisted of, to the left, a conference room, and to the right, two offices—the largest of these had been claimed by Sir Winston; the other was used by Griselda herself, by Malcolm Kyle, and by the other panel members when work or emails or online shopping demanded their attention—plus a small break-out area, a name enjoying blackly humorous connotations post-virus, and a bathroom with three cubicles. Whatever entertainment the break-out area had once boasted—a dodgems arena, or maybe a mini-golf course— had been reduced to three plastic chairs, a small fridge and a kettle. On one wall hung a whiteboard, on which a long-erased message could still be made out: *You can all fuck off home now.* It was possible the previous occupants' existence hadn't been as idyllic as she liked to imagine.

Entering the office, she put her briefcase on the table which was its sole feature, aside from the stack of plastic dividers against one wall. These, once used to shield the members from each other when they were in session, looked smeared and greasy even when newly wiped, and sitting between them had made Griselda feel like a supplicant in a welfare office. Their removal had been a relief, though she had insisted they be retained in case a new variant bounced into being, like a nasty little spacehopper. Meanwhile, their absence promoted, according to Sir Winston, a more relaxed atmosphere—a more collegiate nexus of relationships— and this was possibly true, though it was difficult to imagine how a more fractious vibe might have been achieved. Even now, the panel resembled a workshopped demonstration of a passive/ aggressive recovery group.

Setting her phone to charge, Griselda rootled in her handbag for a brush, then half limped—that damn puddle—along to the bathroom to repair the damage. But the bathroom was occupied. It could only be Malcolm. Nobody else would arrive forty minutes before the day's session was due to start, let alone take sole possession of a bathroom with three cubicles in it. Smothering her frustration, Griselda stalked back to the office to prepare for the day ahead.

When the door rattled, Malcolm Kyle was fixing his tie in the mirror. At an early point in his not overlong life—he was thirty-two—he'd received a parental lecture on the importance of first impressions, and as a result now found himself reknotting ties and retying laces before entering a meeting. Paranoically early for appointments, even those involving people he'd long since lost the opportunity to impress, Malcolm found his list of necessary adjustments kept growing: in addition to a comb and a cloth for buffing his shoes he now carried tweezers, in case nasal hairs sprouted without warning. One day, he thought, in a rare bout of self-awareness, he'd find himself hefting so much equipment he'd be unable to leave his flat; would ever be anchored there, tweezering and combing and incessantly adjusting his appearance, all the while nagged at by a glimmering suspicion that nobody cared how neat he was, or wasn't. Nobody thought about him at all.

It could only be Griselda at the door. Who else would be here this early? And Griselda, anyway: what kind of name was that? Her parents might as well have had her christened wearing a witch's hat. *Griselda.* His boss, sort of. He should probably vacate the bathroom.

He sniffed the air anxiously, then squirted two brief blasts of minty breath freshener over his head before leaving. Can't be too careful.

Avoiding the office, where Griselda would be lurking, Malcolm made for the conference room, which was comfortingly empty. He'd already stacked the day's papers on his table there, for distribution to panel members, who this morning, on day 371 of proceedings, would hear evidence from witness #136. Three hundred and seventy-one days, spread over two years, that he'd never get back. This was where careers were lost, in the gaps between the pages of the calendar.

When he'd been informed by his actual boss, the DM, that he was being seconded to this panel—"Monochrome, it's called"—his first thought was that it would be a useful entry on his CV: an inquiry whose findings would be pored over by anyone who wielded power down Westminster way. Which meant that his name would be on all those powerful lips: Malcolm Kyle, collator, selector, ratifier. Second chair, true, but on panels like these, once you discounted the actual members—who were at best an interchangeable array of backbench lightweights, quasi-famous names and a stiff trolleyed in from the Lords to add a dash of ermine—and focused on the admin staff, who were there to make sure that whatever was supposed to happen happened and nothing that wasn't did, the second chair was the sturdiest on which to sit. First chairs were chosen not so much as a safe pair of hands as a handy pair of Marigold rubber gloves—disposable once soiled. Second chair was the back-up plan; the one called on to provide the true picture in the event that the findings didn't match preliminary expectations. Being selected for this role was a promise of promotion, a promise that remained implied, obviously. When you moved in these circles, almost everything went unsaid.

So in the weeks before Monochrome kicked off Malcolm did his research and found that one Griselda Fleet was to be first chair, and she, surprisingly, was nobody. This too was a good thing: if nobody was running the inquiry, second chair was an even more exalted role. But her appointment was a puzzle. From her point of view it would feel like preferment, which meant she must have done something to earn it. The obvious solution was that she'd slept with someone, though that seemed unlikely once he'd met her; so perhaps she had done someone a favour, though what kind of favour she'd been in a position to do was another head-scratcher. The kind of nobody she was was Home Office–stamped: she ran interference in the personnel department, which effectively meant overseeing the dozens, hundreds, sometimes thousands of appointments the Home Office made in the course of a year, whether to a departmental role, to an affiliated research post, or simply as an approved supplier of equipment or commodities, which was less about making the decisions approving those appointments and more to do with ensuring that each individual's paperwork went to the right address. It was possible she'd helped someone fill out a form correctly, but you could get apps that did that, and apps didn't secure seats on boards of inquiry, though facilitated a lot of decision-making by those who did. But none of that mattered, or not in the short term. Whoever Griselda Fleet was, and however she'd come by her supposed patronage, Malcolm Kyle—currently carrying bags for the deputy manager of the Cabinet Secretary's Office, and by his own reckoning the second-highest achiever of his year's intake (there was a straw-haired PPEist from Magdalen who could do no wrong)—was going places. Either Monochrome would provide a launchpad for a full-blown investigation into wrongdoing by the intelligence services, in which case he'd be a golden boy, or he'd be called upon to explain how Fleet had driven her bus into a wall, which, given the Civil Service ethos, would earn even greater kudos. Win/win. Or that was how things seemed, back before Day One. Since then, that launchpad had more closely come to resemble an accident site: all it needed was a bunch of flowers tied to the nearest railing. That, though, would have required people to be paying attention. Instead, all he heard when he fixed his tie in the mirror, when he buffed his shoes, when he plodded round the conference room table distributing the day's papers, was an empty echo of his crumpled-up ambitions, blowing like litter across a vacant lot. That, and the faint faint sound of a straw-haired PPEist, laughing.

Day One had been spent in a waiting room; an almost beautiful joke, in retrospect. There are waiting rooms, and there are waiting rooms, and if some are intended to make the waiter comfortable, others fall short of that ambition; their chairs a little too nasty, their adornments a little too cheap. Others still are never intended to promote relaxation at all. The room Malcolm and Griselda had found themselves in, two years ago, had been of this variety. For Malcolm, it was a taste of what it might be like on the wrong side of a power gap. He had thought about mentioning this to Griselda, whom he had met for the first time the previous day, but something held him back.

The room in question was two floors down in Regent's Park. Gaining access to the headquarters of the intelligence service had been a surprisingly swift business. Beforehand, Malcolm had assumed that a rigorous security procedure would be imposed, something like boarding an aeroplane to meet the Princess Royal. Accordingly, he had taken care to divest himself of anything that might be construed as a weapon, including—painful as this was— his comb, and had even considered wearing laceless shoes, though that would have involved buying a pair. But in the event they were ushered through the gates with something approaching welcome: if there were few smiles in evidence, the words "First Desk is expecting you" were clearly uttered. He'd heard stories about First Desk's office down on the hub, as the centre of operations was called; it had a glass wall which could frost to opacity at the flick of a switch. All very James Bond. He imagined a swivel chair, black leather, and a white cat, though was aware he was crossing the line from rumoured foible into fictional villainy. But still. In a short while from now, he'd be face to face with the real thing.

Which was more or less the case, though not in the anticipated way. Because as it turned out, his imagination was given free rein for the next three hours, which was how long he and Griselda sat in a bare, windowless room—no table; just two bucket seats, one of which had the rubber knob from one of its feet missing, giving it a terminal case of the wobbles. The floor was tiled and scuffed. On a wall hung instructions about what to do in case of a fire. In place of the usual floor plan was a diagram of the room they were in: a square outline, with the single door marked. "Use this door," the instructions read.

"Do you think they're trying to make us nervous?" he'd asked Griselda, adjusting his spectacles.

"'Trying'?"

Malcolm would have laughed that off, but a nervous frog had him by the throat, and was squeezing gently.

He had gone to the door after a while, mostly to make sure it wasn't locked. That's what he'd been expecting by now; to turn the handle to no effect, to rattle the door, and then to break down into rage or terror, whichever burst through his defences first. Rage was unlikely, to be honest. But the door hadn't been locked, and he'd opened it on the same corridor down which they'd walked earlier, now with a table at the far end, behind which sat a man who was royally uninterested in Malcolm, and barely appeared to hear what he was saying. Which was, anyway, a jumble of words that might have defeated even a well-intentioned listener. Waiting, hours, First Desk, thirsty, appointment, busy people. The hard stare drove him back to the room, where Griselda appeared to have entered a state of Zen calm.

"It's a game," she told him, her eyes closed. "Don't even think about trying to fight it."

"I'm going to make a complaint about this."

"You do that."

"An *official* complaint."

"The best kind."

"You're not offering much support."

"Malcolm, trust me. The best I can do for you is encourage you to sit down and suck it up. Because nothing you do will improve the situation, and you're only making yourself stressed."

"How come you know so much about it?"

He could hardly believe he'd said those words aloud.

"Every Black woman does."

He could hardly believe she'd said that either.

As the minutes ticked into aeons, he found himself thinking of his boss, in the Cabinet Secretary's office: the DM, the deputy manager, and with what little reluctance she'd agreed to his secondment. "You take care, Malcolm. Seize the day!" He felt like the day had seized him; grabbed him by the ankles and dangled him upside down. His liver and lights were all a-tumble. Had she known this might happen? He'd been her faithful second, her loyal lieutenant; had she really sent him to walk the plank without a word of warning? And was a certain straw-haired PPEist in on the joke? Checking his watch: "He'll be in Regent's Park dungeon now, ma'am." Chuckles all round. "Nice cup of tea?"

When the wait ended, it did so without warning or apology. Despite absolute silence in the corridor, on whose floor Malcolm's shoes had tip-tapped like a billy goat's on a bridge, the door opened and a woman entered, her expression that of someone fulfilling an unpleasant duty. She didn't introduce herself. She didn't need to.

"We've been waiting for three hours," Malcolm told her, the tremble in his voice attributable to—he hoped—barely suppressed rage, though he was acutely conscious that one wrong move and he'd succumb to tears instead. "Three. Hours."

"Yes," said First Desk. She was an exceedingly handsome woman—late fifties? He was no great judge—with immaculately tended light brown hair, which hung at her shoulders, and wore a grey skirt and jacket over a white blouse. It was by now afternoon, but she appeared as fresh as if just risen from an unbroken eight hours' sleep. She carried nothing. He'd have expected a folder or file; a ledger heavy with his and Griselda's sins.

"Now. You're Monochrome."

"We're its admin staff," Griselda said. It was the first time she'd spoken in a while, and Malcolm was impressed, despite himself, at the steadiness of her tone.

"We all know how these things work. The admin staff is the inquiry. The rest is stage dressing. You have premises near Liverpool Street, I gather."

"Yes."

"And a panel's been drummed up or summoned up, or whatever it is you do with panels. Beat them, come to think of it. Now there's an idea."

"Are you trying to frighten us?"

"Good God, no." She looked genuinely aggrieved. "If I was trying to frighten you, trust me, you'd be left in no doubt about it. Now, Monochrome. You'll be calling witnesses, I'm told."

"Whomsoever we choose," Griselda said.

By this stage, Malcolm was so disoriented—almost convinced he'd nodded off while reading Orwell—that he didn't even find the use of "whomsoever" amusing.

"I'm sure you'll exercise that power wisely."

"We could call you."

"You could." First Desk's attention was solely on Griselda now. "You could summon me before your panel and subject me to all kinds of questioning. You could keep me tied up for days on end. Weeks, even. It would be a kind of revenge for you, wouldn't it? Payback for having been kept waiting in this rather functional little room for however long it is you've been here. Three hours?"

"Three hours," Griselda confirmed.

"And if you did that, do you know how I'd respond? Can you imagine what my reaction might be?"

Griselda was silent.

"No, that's right. You can't. Best keep it that way, don't you think?"

There were all sorts of things he could have said. All sorts of gritty, sardonic responses that would have crushed First Desk like a cartoon piano; she'd have waddled around shapelessly for a while, then popped back into being with a befuddled squawk. While he, Malcolm, gazed on, unimpressed and nerveless.

This almost cheered him up for almost a second.

First Desk said, "Now. Your remit is quite clear, as are your rights of access. You can summon up any file from the archive that you wish to see. Any at all. That's far beyond the leeway any inquiry has been allowed in the past. It's almost as if someone has it in for the Service, don't you think? As if they were hoping to inflict humiliation and reputational damage. My goodness, it's the kind of license that would put whoever initiated this inquiry in an extremely strong position were their intention to augment their own powers at the expense of Regent's Park, don't you agree?"

She let that question remain unanswered for a full seven seconds.

"I said, don't you agree?"

Griselda said, "It's certainly one way of looking at it."

"That's right. It is. Anything to add?"

And now she turned her gimlet gaze on Malcolm, who had

been feeling a spectator. Promoted to a speaking part, his mouth dried. He swallowed nothing, and croaked, "We're simply carrying out instructions."

"Of course you are. The battle cry of the jobsworth since time immemorial. Now, a few details. You won't need to take notes. You're unlikely to forget any of this."

First Desk stood straighter, or seemed to. Malcolm wasn't really sure this was possible.

"Now. The sad truth is, whoever wrote up your remit was a little lax when it came to the small print. Your right of access refers to 'informational resources' only, and makes no mention of entering secure premises. And as they stand, your security clearances wouldn't get you into the recycling room. So take a good look around and soak up the atmosphere, because this is the first, last and only time you'll be allowed into the Park. Any future attempt at ingress will be treated as a hostile act. As for the archive, well, that's here in the Park, so you can forget about browsing its contents, and running your grubby little fingers along its lovely shelves. With me so far?"

There was nowhere else for them to be.

"You have the right to examine any case file you want, that's been established. To activate this right, submit a request to my desk in writing, specifying the reference number of the file in question, and I'll make sure a copy is despatched to your offices. That, I take it, is the manner in which such proceedings are conducted."

It wasn't a question, but Malcolm found himself nodding anyway. It was a relief to be on familiar ground, if only for a moment. He had studied the regulations concerning the conduct of such inquiries, and was certain that First Desk had accurately relayed one of the methods by which classified documents could be transmitted to a panel. It was good to know that, however hostile she might be, she did not intend to actively impede their progress. The goodness of this knowledge lasted not quite as long as a sneeze.

"But those reference numbers will need to be correctly transcribed. As civil servants, you'll hardly need reminding that any inaccuracy will be met with refusal, and indeed, I'll regard such sloppiness as a waste of my extremely valuable time. Such irritation on my part will result in a strongly worded letter of dissatisfaction being sent to your current heads of department. Again, are you with me?"

Again, through lack of choice, they were.

"Good. Then we're on the same page. Oh, and our cataloguing system, by the way, is a tribute to Daedalus. Nice Oxbridge boy like you"—and here she addressed Malcolm—"won't need reminding that he created the Cretan labyrinth. So if you do happen to stumble upon an accurate reference number, well. My congratulations in advance. You'll have earned whatever emoluments are coming your way."

She opened the door and paused on the threshold, not looking back. "Someone will be down to show you out. Do not attempt to leave on your own. We won't be meeting again. Goodbye."

The door swung shut behind her.

They sat in silence for five minutes, Malcolm feeling as if he'd just been hammered into the ground like a tent peg. Griselda might have been feeling the same way: he couldn't tell. The man who came to lead them back into the world—impossible not to see it in such terms; they'd wandered into a grim fairy tale, and wanted only release—didn't speak as he showed them to the lift. The table at the end of the corridor had disappeared. So had the best of the day: back on London's streets, the light had dwindled to a dull grey film, and rain was starting to fall.

"We'll get the wording amended," he said, as they stood on a corner, waiting for a break in the traffic.

She didn't reply.

"We'll have Monochrome's terms and conditions adjusted. Simple as that. This time tomorrow, we'll be back there, listening to her grovel. And then we'll be down in the archives with a wheelbarrow, and we will bury. That. Place. Under. Ten. Tons. Of shit."

"Malcolm," she said softly.

"What?" He was trembling again, but knew it for rage now; knew it for undiluted anger. "*What?*"

"They won't adjust the wording. Sparrow would never allow it." She shook her head softly, as if breaking the news of a pet's death. "It would be an admission of defeat, an admission of weakness. And we both know that Sparrow, the PM, none of them, will ever admit anything of the sort." Cars hummed past, their wheels beginning to spray rainwater behind them. "They will do what they always do, and pretend this never happened. And we will do as we always do."

"What's that?"

"Our jobs. We'll keep doing them until we're told to stop. Come on."

A car had slowed and flashed its lights for them, and she led him across the road in safety.

For reasons he could never articulate, because they were unfair and he knew it, part of Malcolm blamed Griselda for what happened that day. She was First Chair on Monochrome; it should have been up to her to prevent its being defanged and neutered even before it had set up shop. There had been a principle at stake, and also his career. That day should never have happened. It shouldn't have been allowed to happen. Or if it had to happen, it shouldn't have happened to him.

Now it was two years later, and he still hadn't decided whether the wording of the original remit had been drafted by an idiot or by someone very clever; nor had an explanation been forthcoming as to why the wording couldn't be redrafted. Griselda's theory remained all they had to go on, and the more time went by, the more plausible it seemed. This was Westminster, and London Rules were in play, which—right below *Never apologise, never explain*—stated *Never admit you made a mistake*. Besides, when the situation was reduced to first principles, it became pointless to agonise over the details: the purpose of Monochrome was to fuck with Regent's Park, and the one thing First Desk had made clear was, You do not fuck with Regent's Park. Maybe whoever worded the remit had been honeytrapped into leaving this loophole there, or maybe the Limitations Committee had suckered Number 10's hatchetmen into walking up a garden path, only to lock the door behind them, leaving the stupid idiots shivering on the lawn. But in the end, like everything else, it didn't matter how. It didn't even much matter why. All that really mattered was that, in the Grand National of his career, Malcolm Kyle was riding a donkey, and as it laboured round the course for the 371st time, the only glimmer of hope he could remember had been quashed months previously, when the PM who'd set Monochrome running had suffered the inevitable conclusion of his bin-fire of the vanities and been sacked by his own party. Malcolm had got drunk that night, not so much in celebration of that event—or not only—as in anticipation of his own release. Monochrome had been the offspring of a personal vendetta, and while it was true that, in Westminster circles, things happening swiftly were against the natural order, the first thing an incoming prime minister looks for is allies, and no newbie would want Regent's Park on their back before they'd had a chance to re-paper the flat. So within a week or two, or so Malcolm toasted himself, he'd be back where he belonged: in the office of the deputy manager to the Cabinet Secretary, a campaign medal affixed to his chest, and the respect of his peers for a job not bollixed, or not through any fault of his own.

A week or two that had expanded and bloated and here he still was, his bright glittering future a catastrophe, as unfixable as a trodden-on bauble from last year's Christmas tree.

He'd been fiddling with the knot of his tie again, while these memories carouseled around his head. Its previous symmetry would have been destroyed, though he had no mirror to check. But what the hell, the only one who might notice was Sir Winston, and even Malcolm no longer cared what he thought. Picking up the stack of papers relevant to witness #136, he began to allocate each set to a seat round the table.

The career might be a car crash, but the job still had to be done.

If Malcolm's morning had been shot through with painful memories, Griselda's had been little better. Then again, several decades older than Malcolm, she'd grown used to that. And if, unlike her younger colleague, she'd never had much time for London Rules—that unwritten guide to self-interest that powered the careers and choices of so many Westminster denizens—she had at least collected a number of observations that went some distance to explaining how this environment worked. She'd long been aware, for example, that those who've garnered more power than wiser minds would have allotted them tend to think themselves above the reach of law. What added shame to that awareness was remembering how easy she'd found it to be sucked into that way of thinking. In her case, the price of her soul had been a party invitation.

Not just any old bash, though: Griselda had attended one of the infamous Downing Street garden parties thrown during the first lockdown. In weaker moments, she told herself she'd gone along in a state of disbelief—how could this be happening on the day that a government minister had warned of the dire consequences of flouting Covid restrictions?—but in fact, she'd had no such compunction. Instead, she'd fallen prey to the obvious if furtive pleasure of being among the chosen, her attendance underlining her position in the charmed upper circle, or so it felt at the time. In retrospect, it simply rendered her complicit in a vulgar display of misplaced confidence. She had imagined herself among the then PM's favourites, but the PM, as events had so frequently demonstrated, didn't have favourites, he had human shields. She'd eventually received a fixed penalty notice, and hadn't ever pretended it was a badge of honour, or equated it with a speeding ticket. The fact that few people around her seemed to find the statutory punishment worthy of comment made her feel no better.

But shame aside, what made the occasion hard to forget was that it had been the first on which she'd met Anthony Sparrow, then the PM's special adviser. Sparrow had been as clear an illustration as anyone might require of the dangers of believing oneself immune to public opinion. He'd been riding high, and would continue to do so for some while, and if the immediate impression he left on others was one of Rumpelstiltskin-meets-the-Penguin, his self-image, if his interminable blogging was any clue, placed him somewhere between Montaigne and Nostradamus. On that afternoon he'd interrupted a conversation Griselda had been audience to: two of the younger members of her department had been celebrating their importance by mansplaining to their immediate colleagues how crucial their roles were. Sparrow's effect on this performance would have astonished anyone who hadn't known who he was, the appearance of his unkempt, graceless figure causing the self-congratulatory pair to dwindle into repetitive babble. Embarrassing as their display had been, it caused Griselda equal discomfort to see Sparrow's pleasure at their squirming, especially when, once they'd stumbled into silence, he'd asked their names, making a point of repeating them. It had been like watching a lion adding a pair of Christians to its to-do list, which might have been why Griselda offered her own name too, to reduce the moment to one of general introduction. The more empathetic of her colleagues picked up the baton, and if the episode were not entirely detoxed, it was at least rendered less vicious. Sparrow, though, had stared at Griselda while the circle completed its roll-call, an unsmiling assessment that had gone on far longer than she was happy with. Her name aside, they didn't exchange words. But within a fortnight she had been summoned to his presence, at an hour just outside the working day.

If that initial encounter had triggered this summons, he made no reference to it. Instead, he kept her standing in front of his desk while he made careless amendments to a memo before, without looking up, saying:

"I'm told you're capable of keeping accurate records."

"That's part of my job, yes."

"And of conducting interviews."

For the previous month, during her line manager's Covid absence, Griselda had been interviewing hopefuls for research posts in her own department and two others which fell under the same Home Office umbrella. Most candidates she spoke to, being public school- and Oxbridge-educated, had proved more ebullient than herself, and she'd emerged from at least one encounter with a vague sense of having failed the interview. But she didn't suppose Sparrow wanted to hear about that. "I have some experience, yes."

He grunted, as if she'd interrupted a chain of thought.

Sparrow's office, within the warren that was Number 10, was

large and functional, though attempts had been made to stamp eccentricity upon it. In place of more traditional artwork, framed progressive-rock album sleeves adorned the walls—Marillion, Gentle Giant, Yes—while an array of baseball caps hung from hooks evidently intended for more sober outerwear. On a chair against one wall, next to a door she hadn't entered through, sat Sparrow's famous satchel. The door, Griselda supposed, accessed the PM's room. She had a sudden image of Sparrow summoning the prime minister to his presence while not looking up from whatever memo claimed his attention.

"State education, it says here. And University of East Anglia."

"That's right."

"Not the traditional route to the Home Office."

She didn't reply. Though his own educational background, in common with about ninety per cent of the local population, had followed a path well-trodden by family footsteps, Sparrow liked to present himself, in common with about sixty per cent of the local population, as a self-steering maverick, who had broached the Establishment citadel by dint of guile, cunning and panache.

"But I suppose ticking the obvious boxes helped."

He was referring to her skin colour, she supposed, along with her gender.

"Not that those advantages have propelled you to particularly giddy heights, it has to be said."

He really said that, she thought. He really just said "advantages."

"I'd have risen higher if not for the bullies and the bigots," she told him, or would have told him, or even should have told him, as she chided herself later. But the truth was, the bullies and the bigots were among the more minor obstacles she'd faced, and in many ways the easiest to deal with. Because if the casual racism she encountered on a daily basis was at least overt, the institutional variety, embedded in the structures within which she worked, tended towards the impalpable, veiled and obfuscated by Civil Service procedures that had been hallowed by time, and bore "no relation to the personal circumstances of any officer" as one ancient email had put it. This had been in response to Griselda's suggestion that the department's Classic Film Club choice of *Zulu* did not, perhaps, project an image in keeping with its purported values.

Her subsequent reputation as a "troublemaker" hadn't stopped her, though, or not in the early days, and she had a tribunal ruling in her favour to prove it. But she'd also had long periods of stasis; years spent behind the exact same desk while the colleagues around her changed. After a while, the message had seeped through. *Don't rock the boat.* Besides, she was tired, those same years having peeled away some of life's wallpaper, revealing the stained plasterwork beneath—a bad marriage, a difficult daughter. No, not difficult, impossible—how could such a perfect, brilliant and beautiful young woman have come into existence? It challenged all logic. But the fact remained that wrangling Melody into adulthood had drained Griselda of energies she'd once enjoyed, and her moments of principled resistance had become fewer and farther between. Her last spirited episode had been at the garden party, when she'd tried to deflect Sparrow's contempt from its frankly appropriate target, and look where that had got her—sitting here, while the embodiment of privileged white manhood dismissed her career with scorn. Her Kenyan mother would have rolled her eyes and carried on. Her Essex-born father would have invited Sparrow outside. Griselda preferred fighting her own battles—or that was the phrase she'd have reached for—but experience had taught her that the happiest battlefield encounter was one you walked away from unscathed. And there was no fight she could have with Sparrow which would leave her the victor.

Strangely, she had the feeling he was about to offer her something, but whatever it was she already knew she didn't want it. *Give me no challenges, set me no targets.* That bumping noise she used to worry about, the sound of her own head hitting the ceiling: she was used to it now. Having a ceiling prevented you drifting away. But these thoughts were getting in the way of her being here, and listening to what Sparrow was saying.

"There's to be an inquiry. Internal, though the results will doubtless be available for public consumption."

"An inquiry? Have we—the department, I mean—has something happened? I wasn't aware of any problem."

"I'm sure your department could be found to have committed more than enough errors to warrant investigation. But no, this is a different matter, one the PM is keen on pursuing. I see no harm in it. It might even prove a handy stratagem in the long run, which is the only kind we're interested in." He seemed about to head off down a whole new corridor, as if embarking on one of his directionless blogs, but reined himself in. "No, we're planning on taking a look at the intelligence services."

He might as well have specified extraterrestrial life for all the relevance it had to Griselda. "The intelligence services?"

"So called. There's frequently a lack of common sense, let alone actual intelligence. And there's long been concern that the current administration is beating its own pathway, rather than following the government's lead. But what you'll be focusing on is the frequent lapses in discipline over the years, and the damaging consequences these have had. We'd like these to be above the fold, as they say. The bullet points."

"I'm sorry. *I'll* be focusing on?"

"Well what did you think you're doing here? Do I usually run policy decisions past you?"

"I—"

"What it is is, it's essentially a fact-finding exercise. Your findings will point the way towards a fuller investigation into how Regent's Park is straying beyond its remit into areas of ethical dubiousness or actual illegality. Once we're at that stage, we'll have some serious bodies to sit on the panel. For the time being, we'll find the usual bunch of scarecrows. Your job, the current objective, you're simply exploring the mine shaft. Think of yourself as head canary."

It didn't seem worth pointing out what the head canary's inevitable fate was. He almost certainly knew, and definitely didn't care.

"Mr. Sparrow. This is a signal honour, and I'm grateful you thought to consider me for the role. But it's outside my skill set, and not something I'm competent to handle."

"That would be entirely up to you, of course. I'm not in a position to make anyone do anything they'd rather not." The mere thought of doing any such thing was enough to bring a curl to his lip. "But refusal would leave you in a vulnerable position. I'm sure you're aware we're looking at cutbacks across Whitehall. Removing a few snouts from the public trough, that sort of thing. It's popular with the voters, though can make life uncomfortable for those in the firing line."

He waited two moments for this to sink in, though did not seem to require a response.

"Shall I continue with the details? It's not a new appointment, as such. You'll be on secondment. Pay and conditions to remain as is. But there'll be various bursaries to draw upon, and some limited expenses. You'll probably get a few lunches out of it." He glanced at her figure, seemed about to add something, and decided against it. "A list of probable panel members will be with you by the end of the week. I'll let you know when it's been whittled down."

"How long is this expected to last?"

"We won't be setting a term. First couple of months should give you an idea of the probable scope. But you can expect this to keep you busy the next couple of years. Well into the next parliament, more than likely."

"So this is independent of the current government?"

"No, it's the PM's baby. But I'm not expecting to lose an election in the near future." He gave the first smile she'd seen him give, possibly the first he'd ever attempted. He might have been reading instructions from the back of a box. "Unless someone fucks something up, of course. That's the real art of politics, Ms. Fleet. Knowing when the next fuck-up's due. And arranging for a human sandbag to be standing in the way."

Afterwards, she recognised this as the key moment in their conversation, the point at which he revealed his outlook. *Always decide who's to blame before anything goes wrong. It makes the subsequent investigation much simpler.*

Back to business. "You'll hear from someone about premises and so on. There'll be a budget, you'll need to handle expenses and fees for members. But if you've any sense, you'll pass that on to whoever ends up your sub. I'll have someone bring you up to speed. It's well below my pay grade." He looked down at the papers on his desk again, and she wondered if that were that; that having finished talking, he expected her to fade away. What, for God's sake, was his home life like? Or did he just sit behind his desk all night, plugged in to recharge?

"Griselda," he said suddenly.

"Yes?"

"No, I meant the name. Your parents watch a lot of Disney cartoons?"

"I never thought to ask."

He nodded, as if that were the answer he'd expected, then

indicated the door with a nod of his head. "Someone will be in touch."

It sounded more like a threat than a promise.

That was how she came to run Monochrome.

Other, minor details—the word pettifogging was used more than once—were handled by lesser beings from Sparrow's office. "Hours of work can vary depending on witness availability, so you'll be expected to maintain timekeeping records. If you fall under your weekly obligation, make the hours up at a future date." The notion of a future happening was a comfort. It had occurred to her that if she were kept from her desk for longer than a year, it might be handed to someone else, or removed entirely. And then, too, there was the nagging suspicion that her unexpected elevation—if it could be so described—was a tactical move by a disinterested player. London Rules again. *We're all in it together* might have been the public mantra, but everyone knew that you never took a ride in a hot-air balloon without knowing who you'd throw overboard first.

"As for panel members' expenses, stationery requirements and so on, your sub can handle all that."

Her submarine, her sandwich. Ridiculous what the mind threw at you. Sub meaning subordinate, because if Griselda Fleet were so insignificant as not to have a junior answering to her, then why were Sparrow's seconds wasting their time briefing her?

"Has that appointment been made?"

She'd been handed a Manila folder, and this was her introduction to her sub, her junior, her ongoing thorn in the flesh.

"Malcolm Kyle."

Memory gave way to the present, and Malcolm himself came into the office, mumbling a greeting, his tie unexpectedly askew.

Day #371 was under way.

Monochrome—Day #84
Witness No.68: Mr. L█ G████
(Redaction level Two: FOI exempt)

Distribution key: A—F

Panel:
Sir Winston Day (President)
The Right Honourable Shirin Mansoor, MP
Mr. Guy Fielding
Ms. Deborah Ford-Lodge
Mr. John Moore
Mr. Carl Singer

Secretary (first chair): *Ms. Griselda Fleet*
Assistant (second chair): *Mr. Malcolm Kyle*

Excerpt from interview:

Sir Winston Day: Now, you've come to us because you have serious concerns about the administration processes at Regent's Park, which is—
Mr. L█ G████: Yes.
WD:—which is the centre of operations of the intelligence services here in the UK.
LG: Yes.

WD: And you're a former agent of those services, is that correct?

LG: For nearly two years.

Ms. Shirin Mansoor: Mr. G, before we begin, can I just make sure that you understand the gravity of what you're about to do? Any testimony you, ah, deliver that pertains to classified material—

LG: I understand that.

SM:—**must** remain within the confines of this room. If any of it is repeated outside, you could well find yourself liable to prosecution under the Official Secrets Act.

LG: I understand.

WD: Well, on behalf of the committee, I offer you our appreciation.

LG: You're welcome.

WD: Now, your written approach to the committee suggests that a bullying culture pertains at Regent's Park. You're aware that this isn't precisely the remit of the current inquiry?

LG: I have literally nowhere else to turn.

WD: I see.

LG: Literally.

WD: Then perhaps we should begin.

Ms. Griselda Fleet: Before we do so, Sir Winston?

WD: . . . Go ahead.

GF: Mr. G, before we begin, there are one or two matters it's necessary to address. You say you were employed by the intelligence services for nearly two years—

LG: That's correct.

GF:—but records indicate that your actual period of employment was thirteen months and eight days.

LG: I was rounding up.

GF: I see. And it also says that the reason for the termination of your employment—

LG: I don't see that that's relevant.

GF: The reason for the termination of your employment was that on three occasions you used Service equipment, on Service premises—

LG: This is not relevant.

GF:—to access pornographic material of a particularly abusive nature. And the officer who reported this activity, resulting in a disciplinary hearing and the subsequent termination of your employment—

LG: She's a lying bitch.

GF:—is in fact the woman named in your testimony as the officer you claim to be the chief instigator of this "bullying culture."

SM: "Particularly abusive" pornography?

LG: It's an addiction. Who's really the victim here?

SM: [Inaudible.]

(The deposition of L⬛⬛ G⬛⬛⬛ was terminated at this point. The above testimony was not included in the draft report that existed at the time of the closure of the Monochrome inquiry, and would not have been included in any final report, had such a document been prepared.)

To deal with the humdrum details: of the panel members convened to sit on Monochrome, some names will be familiar, others less so. Of the former, Deborah Ford-Lodge was the glamour appointee, an espionage novelist whose recent decalogy about a mole hunt in the upper echelons of what she referred to as the Fairground had her pegged by some as the heir to Le Carré—one of an admittedly long list of legatees—and if some observers questioned the appropriateness of her appointment to a panel adjudicating on the activities of the real-world intelligence services rather than its fictional counterpart, most accepted that this was how things worked these days. A Twitter following in the hundreds of thousands was a more certain indicator of expertise than, say, a career spent studying the topic at hand. Of the rest, Shirin Mansoor, a northern constituency Labour MP who had weathered thirty-two years in the Commons, was regarded by all who had never worked with her as a reliable operator, while Guy Fielding and John Moore, backbenchers both, were experienced committee-sitters, happy to make up the numbers whenever warm buttocks were required on padded seats, provided the padding also applied to the expense accounts. That neither had ever troubled the official Hansard reports much was presumably a tribute to how carefully they weighed each thought before putting it into utterance. Carl Singer, meanwhile, was the face of modern British entrepreneurship, lacking only an endearing foible or two, like a taste for helium-assisted flight, blatant megalomania or a much taller wife, to have him elevated to the status of a household name. Singer's company—actually, a string of affiliated companies, whose interdependent financial relationships would have resembled, on any accurate diagram, instructions for a three-legged ceilidh to be performed by thirteen drunken quadrupeds—had most recently bothered the public at the height of the Covid crisis, when it was awarded a multimillion pound contract to furnish the NHS with PPE, and in a development that was startlingly unexpected actually managed to fulfil the contract. So, anyway, its PR department announced with great fanfare, and if the quoted delivery figures were subsequently disputed by NHS administrators, alongside a damning critique of the reliability of the equipment that actually turned up, the headlines had been written by then, and the news spotlight moved on. Attempts to refocus it met with weary contempt. "There is nothing more despicable," thundered the then Health Secretary, "than seeking to undermine the achievements of those making very real sacrifices in the battle against this evil virus." The Health Secretary left his post shortly afterwards to spend more time with his mistress, but soon enough secured employment as a spokesperson for Singer Industries. For his own part, Singer made occasional noises about going into politics, but so far had restricted himself to issuing regular pats on the back to the current administration. His appointment to the panel was largely due to his interest in the security services: Singer Industries' portfolio included several firms whose operations covered areas more traditionally patrolled by organs of the state, and was known to be interested in expanding farther into this area.

Finally, and adding much-needed gravitas, was Sir Winston Day, whose features seemed moulded to adorn a bust, or possibly a stamp, and whose forehead was so evidently bulging with grey matter that it would have been impertinent to inquire too closely into the actual achievements his half century of public service had produced. His recently published memoirs possibly cast light on this enigma, but given that such details were not provided until after the thirty-page mark, they might as well have remained state secrets. Sir Winston was happy in the role he'd been allotted, inasmuch as it allowed him to bark questions at strangers, an occupation he pursued with such alacrity that it bordered on the vocational, and he might have made a name for himself as an interrogator had he paid much attention to the answers. But he was doing his duty, and that was the main thing. Or so Sir Winston believed, and as nobody contradicted him, it was almost certainly true.

On the morning of day 371 all the empanelled members arrived within an eight-minute time span, though none in such close proximity to another that anyone had to share a lift. It was the first time they had gathered since the week before last, and such gaps were fast becoming the norm—the spaces between convened days growing ever-larger, in pace with the diminishing number of witnesses with testimony deemed worth hearing. That last condition had become more stringent since day 279, which would have been the inquiry's nadir had the word not implied subsequent improvement.

Today, Griselda and Malcolm aside, Carl Singer was first to arrive. Singer was a middle-aged man in whom youth could still be seen, mostly through his choice of footwear. Griselda had never warmed to him, largely because he seemed keen that she should, though in a way that suggested he was intent on expanding his demographic rather than his friendship circle. He was on his mobile as he entered, his tone curt and businesslike, and his greeting to Griselda was engineered via eyebrows alone. She caught a whiff of his cologne as he hung his raincoat on a hook. Something woody: Why was that not a surprise? She frowned slightly, miming fierce focus on her iPad as, one by one, the others peeled in, bringing a little of the weather with them. The damp air, the coats beaded by rain, the presence of traffic. Last was Deborah Ford-Lodge, who had taken time to gussy up before making an entrance, or at the very least, run a comb through her jet-black hair. Easily the youngest and most attractive of the company, she neither took this for granted nor let her standards slip. Today she was dressed—beneath her raincoat—as if it were spring. John Moore and Guy Fielding, in contrast, had arrived decked out for monsoon season, and more than ever looked like two halves of one dismal whole. Then again, on their best days they had the appearance of men who had spent their middle decades slipping round the back for a smoke, a rare example of appearances failing to deceive.

And she, Griselda Fleet—she found herself thinking—how did her appearance strike them? Fact was, it probably didn't, much. She was there, that was all; a fixture of the inquiry. They'd pay more attention to a Nespresso machine.

Malcolm had disappeared, busy with the day's admin—there were expense claims to be made, as the end of the month grew near—though she suspected this was more to do with avoiding company than ensuring said company's needs were met. That was okay. Something had gone out of Malcolm a while ago; if he'd never possessed much of a spark, he had at least resembled someone who got out of bed in the morning intending to achieve something before crawling back into it. These days, it appeared that crawling back into bed was as much of an ambition as he could muster: everything else was just killing time. She ought to do something about this. Talk to him? If Malcolm had a full-blown breakdown there would be an accompanying HR headache, which she didn't need any more than she needed the actual one drilling into her head: small, but as sharp and insistent as a dentist's tool.

"Our venerable President the last to arrive again, I see."

Speaking of dentists' tools, Shirin Mansoor's frequent observations regarding Sir Winston were sharp and pointed. Griselda suspected that she believed the President's role should have been hers, though it remained mysterious why she would have wanted it. But perhaps once your ambition stretched beyond the hope that you could make it safely through the day, it knew no limit.

Carl Singer said: "Seeing as he's the one we can't start without, and he prefers us all to be here when we do start, that's the most efficient way of beginning proceedings promptly, wouldn't you agree?"

"I'd need to see a Venn diagram first," said Moore.

"Anyone read the Chancellor's piece in the *Telegraph*?" Fielding asked. "About the need for alternative funding of the emergency services?"

"I thought Deliveroo was already self-funding."

"He made a fair case," said Singer.

"Do you think so? Because it sounded like a death knell to me."

The last thing Griselda wanted was a political debate, and the next-to-last would be any other kind. "I think I hear the lift," she said.

"Oh, good," said Moore. "I was worried today's session would be cancelled at the last moment."

"Yes, wouldn't that be awful?" said Mansoor. "You'd have to claim your attendance fee without actually earning it."

As with many committees, in the absence of a testifying witness, the panel members settled for tearing one another to pieces instead.

Monochrome—Day #187
Witness No.86: Ms. J█ D█
(Redaction level Two: FOI exempt)

Distribution key: A—F

Panel:
Sir Winston Day (President)
The Right Honourable Shirin Mansoor, MP
Ms. Deborah Ford-Lodge
Mr. John Moore
Mr. Carl Singer

Absent: *Mr. Guy Fielding*
Secretary (first chair): *Ms. Griselda Fleet*

Assistant (second chair): *Mr. Malcolm Kyle*

Excerpt from interview:

Sir Winston Day: And that was the year you had your second child.

Ms. J█ D█: Yes.

WD: Again, by Mr. Stephen Buckley.

JD: That's correct.

WD: And were you still involved in the, I'm sorry I can't quite recall the—

JD: It was called Millennials Against Oppression?

Mr. John Moore: Mao!

JD: . . . What?

Ms. Griselda Fleet: Your preferred . . . form of address was Em Ay Oh, is that right?

JD: MAO, yes.

WD: And your belief at this time was that Mr. Buckley, far from being the activist he claimed to be—

JD: Yes.

WD:—was in fact working for the intelligence services.

JD: Yes. As an undercover agent?

WD: And his task, so you believed, was to undermine . . . MAO with the ultimate intention of having its members— including yourself—prosecuted for subversive activities. For activities designed to undermine the state.

JD: That's right.

Mr. Carl Singer: Can I just ask—

WD: Of course. Of course.

CS: What form did these activities take? The subversive activities?

JD: Oh, well. Well. It was more of a planning stage?

CS: A planning stage.

JD: Yes. That's to say, we hadn't actually actioned any of our plans yet. Which, can I just say, I'm actually glad about now?

CS: I see.

JD: I appreciate that we might have been a little misguided.

WD: Indeed. And to get back to the topic at hand, Mr. Buckley was at that time also a member of MAO, is that correct?

JD: He seemed to be, yes.

WD: And what exactly was your purpose in forming a relationship with Mr. Buckley?

JD: Well, it was to keep him occupied? To lull him into a false sense of security?

WD: With a view to . . . ?

JD: Ensuring that his mission failed.

Ms. Deborah Ford-Lodge: And this . . . *lulling* of Mr. Buckley, this involved bearing two children by him, yes?

JD: It was a long-term situation?

Ms. Shirin Mansoor: Ms. D█████, Stephen Buckley was not, in fact, an intelligence operative, was he?

JD: . . . No.

SM: You were quite mistaken in this belief.

JD: Well, only in the end.

SM: I'm sorry?

JD: Well, all the time I believed he was an undercover agent, he might as well have been, don't you see? Because all the time I thought he was, that's how I acted. As if he was spying on me, and I was pretending not to know that's what he was doing?

Ms. Griselda Fleet: Ms. D█████, none of the . . . testimony you've delivered in front of this committee actually concerns actions undertaken by the intelligence services, does it?

JD: . . .

GF: It relates, rather, to actions undertaken by someone you mistakenly believed to be a member of the intelligence services, and whom, throughout your five-year relationship, you thought was deceiving you and your fellow MAO members. Though he was, in fact, a member of MAO himself.

JD: . . . Yes.

WD: I see.

JD: He was just an ordinary man.

DF-L: Are you still together, Ms. D▮▮?

JD: God, no.

(The testimony of J▮ D▮ was not included in the draft report that existed at the time of the closure of the Monochrome inquiry, and would not have been included in any final report, had such a document been prepared.)

It had indeed been the lift, which did indeed contain Sir Winston, which meant that they could have one of their "where-do-we-stand-now?" conversations, most of which could be replaced in their entirety with the phrase "same place as last week." Griselda sometimes wondered how many similar groups were convening around the capital on any given morning, deeply embroiled in meetings whose only resolution, "going forward," was that another meeting take place in the near future. Which might be the bare minimum requirement for any group's survival, but lacked a certain firmness of purpose.

Before he could initiate such discussion, however, Sir Winston had to divest himself of his rain gear, which included galoshes, a source of fascination to Griselda, for whom they had only ever been a rumour in children's books. Straps and buckles . . . Not for the first time, she wondered about the fetishism of the upper classes; about their clinging onto the ways of childhood—the nannies and

the school-dinner menus; the club ties—and about the wisdom of
putting those mired in their own pasts in charge of all our futures.
But these thoughts were not conducive to a day's work, so she
shunted them aside as Sir Winston adopted a well-met air, and
demonstrated his ability to communicate across any number of
divides by addressing the assembled company as one, just as Malcolm re-entered the room:

"Everyone have a good weekend?"

Since the only answer to this in polite company, despite the
weekends in question having run the gamut from interminable
arguments with offspring (Mansoor and Fleet), through the
usual whirl of constituency pubs (Moore and Fielding), a brief
Parisian jaunt complete with ballet and Michelin-starred grub
to woo some interested money (Singer), an ear-splitting row
with spouse followed by an eleven-thousand-word writing jag
(Ford-Lodge) to an unbroken thirty-three hours in bed with
two pizzas, a bottle of vodka and Apple TV+ (Kyle) was "yes,"
this was duly uttered by various voices, and if the ensuing
moments of silence indicated that the company was reliving
any particular aspect of its separate weekends, that silence
wasn't any more fraught than it was companionable. To fill it,
those who'd brought indoor shoes changed into them while
checking their mobiles, while those who hadn't simply checked
their mobiles. Satisfied that his genial inquiry had established
him as a figure on whom the rank and file could rely for a spot
of paternal interest, Sir Winston—whose own weekend had
involved a rather pleasant time in the country as a guest of the
party chairman—moved his tobacco pouch from one pocket to
another and his pipe from that pocket to the one the tobacco
pouch had occupied. It was good to be organised and important to set a standard. That—let's be frank—squirt Kyle looked
like he'd let a squirrel do his tie this morning, and there was no

excuse for that. But it wasn't like anyone was looking to young Kyle as an example of anything.

Sir Winston cleared his throat, and those around him tensed in anticipation.

"So," he said. "Where do we stand now?"

If cost was the main reason that these offices had been chosen for Monochrome, the conference room went some way towards justifying the decision on practical grounds, being uncomfortable enough to dispel any notion that the proceedings it hosted were frivolous, and not quite austere enough to pretend to any grand purpose. That said, it was designed for full accessibility, should circumstances require. In the centre of the room long tables were set as a three-sided square, with panel members sitting on either flank, Sir Winston at the head and Griselda next to him, her chair at a slightly oblique angle to the table, to signify her lesser status. To her left were Moore, Singer and Ford-Lodge; to Sir Winston's right, Fielding and Mansoor. Malcolm, meanwhile, sat at a school-desk arrangement in a corner of the room, a position which seemed to say more about him every day. At the open end of the arrangement was the witness's chair, next to a low table on which sat a jug of water, a glass and a box of tissues. Windows, with a view of the back of an office building in the next street along, were adorned with six rows of venetian blinds, at least one of which was always slightly out of synch. Malcolm sometimes wondered if Clive from downstairs came into the offices out of hours and subtly fucked with the furnishings. He was aware that this was improbable, and in fact approved of Clive inasmuch as Clive addressed him as "sir," but it wasn't always possible to dismiss outlandish fancies once they'd landed. Paranoia was parasitical; it dug its talons in and fed off what it found. Malcolm had reached for his comb without meaning to, and smuggled it back into his breast pocket, hoping no one had noticed.

The daily procedure underwent few variations. If a witness were being heard, this happened in the morning, only occasionally extending past the lunch hour. If the panel were meeting to discuss what Sir Winston described as "matters arising," and the others as "expenses specials," this happened in the afternoon. When no witness was to be called, and no discussion deemed necessary, only Griselda and Malcolm attended the office, their non-panel sessions revolving around the examination of witness testimonies; the transcription of depositions, which—owing to their potentially classified nature, and the limited budgetary resources for administrative assistance—fell to Malcolm, despite his near sedentary typing speed; and the trawling of public records to identify "material of interest." There was little of this, most news stories suggesting possible wrongdoing by the spook services dissolving into graspless matter when reached for. In a folder marked "Miscellanies"—because you couldn't be too careful— were kept clippings and printouts of the grimmer hints encountered over the past two years; a suicide of someone known to have worked in the shadow world; a fatal accident involving a person of interest. But these were whispers, nothing more, follow-up investigations yielding an open verdict in one case, a finding of misadventure in the other. If Monochrome had had access to Regent's Park's archive, there'd have been a whole dark world to explore: Malcolm, for one, grew more convinced of this with every passing day. But the doors to that treasure trove remained firmly shut. And boy, did the days pass.

Hints had been made at the outset that running the inquiry might be less than full-time, but the reality scotched that notion. For the panellists there were the expenses, and the opportunity to put the entire thing out of mind for days at a stretch; it was drudgery, but reasonably well-paid, and didn't last more than a few hours a week. But for Malcolm and Griselda it was daily servitude. A rational bureaucracy would have applied the brakes, but the wheels of Westminster were like the wheels on the bus: they went round and round, and round and round, all day long.

Some of those days, of course, were worse than others.

Monochrome—Day #279
Witness No.116: Mrs. E█ F█████
(Redaction level Two: FOI exempt)

Distribution key: A—F

Panel:
Sir Winston Day (President)
The Right Honourable Shirin Mansoor, MP
Mr. Guy Fielding
Ms. Deborah Ford-Lodge
Mr. John Moore
Mr. Carl Singer

Secretary (first chair): *Ms. Griselda Fleet*
Assistant (second chair): *Mr. Malcolm Kyle*

Excerpt from interview:

Sir Winston Day: If you'd just like to tell us in your own words, Mrs. F█████, the reason for your appearance before this panel?
E█ F█████: I saw it in a magazine. That you were investigating wrongdoing in the intelligence services.
WD: We were in a magazine?

Ms. Griselda Fleet: There's been a certain amount of media coverage, Sir Winston.

WD: Hmph. And could I ask what the magazine was?

EF: The one that little man runs. Who does that thing on the telly.

WD: I'm not sure I—

Mr. John Moore: Would this be *Have I Got News for You*?

WD: Have you got . . . ?

EF: That's right.

JM (*sotto voce*): Yessss!

Mr. Carl Singer: You mean *Private Eye*, then. The magazine.

EF: That's right. *Private Eye*.

JM: Which wasn't especially complimentary about our procedures.

Mr. Guy Fielding: It's not especially complimentary about anything. That's rather the—

WD: If we could just . . . Thank you. So, Mrs. F██████. You saw an article in *Private Eye*, and decided you had information that might be relevant to our, um, our mission.

EF: That's right. On account of I work at GCHQ, that's the place at Cheltenham, you know?

[Pause]

JM: We're familiar with GCHQ. Thank you.

EF: Yes, well, only the magazine, which I don't read myself, only there was a page pinned up on the notice board, it said you were looking at malpractices and the like? In the security services?

WD: . . . Ah, yes, that's correct.

EF: Because there's stuff going on at GCHQ you should definitely know about. Definitely.

[Pause]

WD: Would it be possible for you to provide us with some details as to the nature of this . . . stuff?

EF: Well, all sorts. I mean, take the canteen. Everyone knows it's run at a loss, but it's packed to the gills every lunchtime. I mean, how can that be? You answer me that.

CS: . . . And this is the information you've come to share with us?

EF: Well that's what it said in that article. Malpractices. And I'm not pointing the finger, but has whoever runs the canteen been asked to explain where all the money's going? That's all I'm saying.

WD: The money?

GF: If I could interrupt, Mr. Chairman?

WD: If you really need to.

GF: Just a point of consistency. Mrs. F█████, in her original offer of testimony, stated that she worked for GCHQ. Now she's saying that she works *at* GCHQ. It's a small point—

WD: It's a *very* small point.

GF:—but it might be best to be sure we're not going up a blind alley.

Ms. Deborah Ford-Lodge: I agree. Language is too important to be used in a careless manner. Especially in—

WD: Yes yes.

DF-L:—*especially* in proceedings such as this.

CS: These.

WD: Yes, all right. If it'll save all this palaver. Mrs. F█████, if you wouldn't mind. I'm going to ask you to clarify your position at GCHQ.

EF: I work there.

WD: Yes, we've got that far. But could I ask you to be more . . . specific?

EF: Mondays and Thursdays.

WD: Just those two days?

EF: Well, not when the Monday's a bank holiday.

WD: I'm not sure I . . .

GF: Could you tell us which department you work in, Mrs. F███?

EF: I'm on the cleaning staff.

WD: You're on the cleaning staff.

EF: What I just said.

WD: But you don't actually—you're not employed by GCHQ itself?

EF: We do have security clearance, you know. Which is just as well. The state of the toilets some days—

WD: Thank you, Mrs. F███.

EF: All I'm saying, you're in charge of the nation's security, you could be a bit more careful with your toilet doings.

(The testimony of E███ F███ was not included in the draft report that existed at the time of the closure of the Monochrome inquiry, and would not have been included in any final report, had such a document been prepared.)

(The above is notable for being the last reliable set of minutes submitted by Malcolm Kyle. Subsequent transcriptions, though signed off by the Chair, were rarely accurate in detail, and never a complete record of testimony provided.)

Everyone needs a code name, so they'd settled on Ratty and Toad—he was Ratty, Toad was his mole, and in the increasingly unlikely event that Monochrome bore fruit, he'd be first to know. Of course, the fruit wasn't the kind Monochrome had been intended to pick, but any harvest counts.

Tonight, a February evening, the scheduled contact would be by phone. There was a certain nostalgia in this. Once upon a time, in another place, phone calls required rigorous protocols: phones were chosen with care, usually in busy locations—the railway station, the post office—and the conversation's subject matter bore no relation to its meaning. Nowadays, in a world whose surveillance techniques had become so sophisticated you'd hesitate to have a chat within earshot of your fridge, precautions still mattered, but at least you no longer had to put a coat on. In Ratty's case, you simply retired to a windowless room, flipped the switch that activated white-noise interference and answered a mobile, the prepaid unregistered one that took calls from only one number.

Then you answered it not saying anything, waiting for Toad to break the silence.

"It's me," said Toad.

"And what do you have?"

There was more silence, the kind mobiles supply if their user is in a corridor, all of whose doors are closed. "Just the usual."

"Don't sound so disappointed. You have no idea what matters to me. Only that I pay well for hearing it."

So Toad began the recitation: the month's witnesses, the discussions that ensued, their increasingly fractious nature, and the lack of anything amounting to hard-core evidence of wrongdoing by Regent's Park. Five minutes later it was done, without anything having been said that rang bells, pulled strings, or caused Ratty's brow to furrow.

He waited a count of five, to allow Toad time to wonder whether information of significance had been unknowingly delivered, then said, "The money's in your bank."

"This can't carry on much longer."

There was an interesting open-endedness to this; Toad could be referring to Monochrome itself, or the betrayal of its workings, or Toad's own reluctance to continue in the role of traitor. Which was not, as Ratty could have explained, an accurate epithet. To be a traitor, you first had to have faith. Otherwise, it was all just gossip.

"It'll carry on for as long as it does," he said. "As will our conversations."

It was possible that Toad had a different opinion about this, but since Ratty terminated the call at that point, this didn't matter. Unheard objections were like unacknowledged offspring: If no one knows about them, could they really be said to exist?

He didn't go in for philosophical rumination. On the other hand, he was prepared to see the funny side of most things, provided the joke wasn't at his expense.

Fishcakes were five pounds for a packet of two, or three packets for twelve pounds. The saving was obvious; the underlying issues were, did Malcolm want to commit himself to three fishcake meals in the short- to mid-term future, and how much room was there in the freezer compartment of his not over-large fridge? He tried to visualise the space in question, but all he came up with was an Arctic image, a vast emptiness into which he might wander and not return for some time. The fishcakes were cod, with a mushy pea mixture involved in the coating. Which sounded acceptable, but not, perhaps, a way of life. So he loaded only the single packet into his trolley, focusing on the seven-pound outlay he'd save, and moved down the aisle, recalling a TV commercial featuring a middle-aged gay couple shopping in a supermarket: the healthy choices being made, the mock-squabbling over the chocolate biscuits, the shared joy at the savings on offer. The hand contact as they left the store. Supermarket shopping as relationship adventure: it was every bit as close to reality as those adverts showing happy young things squealing their pleasure at a casino site, instead of, say, a fat man in a tracksuit smoking outside Ladbrokes. That it was a gay couple made it better, or ought to. But it didn't.

He paused at the fridge, wondering about cheese. Cheese was on his list—he never went anywhere without a list—but he hadn't thought about what kind, and didn't seem able to work that out now. Gruyère? He liked a piece of Gruyère. He liked Brie, too. But his budget demanded that it be one or the other . . . Not for the first time, he resolved to be more sensible about shopping; to start patronising one of the cheaper chains, even if it required a longer trip. Anything to diminish that sense of dread when the credit card bill dropped into his inbox.

When Malcolm had arrived in London, fresh from Cambridge, it was to take up a room in a shared house with one university friend and three strangers, and for a short while it had worked nicely. The new people were friendly and welcoming, and he'd had high hopes of the original friendship—which had once or twice (twice) edged into something a little more physical at college—developing further. But this didn't happen, or at least it didn't happen with Malcolm (it did with two of the other housemates), and things stopped working nicely, and there was a big meltdown one weekend, by the Monday of which it had been agreed by all parties, save Malcolm himself—who turned out not to have a vote—that the atmosphere would be vastly improved by his absence. Since then he'd been living in a one-bedder in Walthamstow, whose rent accounted for sixty-four per cent of his monthly pay cheque. It didn't feel like he was living the life he'd planned. It certainly didn't feel like he ought to be spending five pounds on two fishcakes.

He looked down at his trolley. Apples, oranges, a lot of vegetables, so he was doing something right. Then he turned at the end of the aisle and bumped into someone coming the other way.

Could have been a meet-cute, in other circumstances. In these, though, it was a woman whose trolley he'd sideswiped, and a none-too-stable trolley either: their collision—and she'd been moving fast; really quite fast indeed—caused it to veer sideways, banging into the freezer compartment, upon which the damn thing toppled onto its side, sending shopping flying: a slew of packets of pasta and string bags of fruit, of ready meals and cartons of juice, of pints of milk and jars of olives or capers or whatever—all of it. Everywhere. Nightmare.

"God, I'm sorry!"

"Damn damn damn!"

"I'm sorry! So sorry!"

"Could you just—please!"

Malcolm abandoned his own trolley and scrambled to set the fallen one upright, a task which sounded easier than it proved to be. A bottle of wine almost joined the buffet on the tiles, and wouldn't that have made an unholy mess? As it was there was chaos, not entirely dissipated by the outbreak of fellow feeling among other shoppers, the nearest of whom began gathering up the tumbled shopping and stacking it back in the trolley while a store assistant went for a mop and a hazard triangle. A broken bottle of passata sat in a red puddle. A man wearing a bow tie gave Malcolm a hand with the trolley.

"Easy does it."

The woman whose shopping this had been had gathered herself somewhat; was studying the produce being reloaded into her wagon. She looked like she was having second thoughts. Had she really been planning on buying all this? All bashed about, it was significantly less appealing. She was young to be doing such a big shop—so Malcolm thought, but what on earth did he mean by that?—and had red hair mostly trapped in place by a green beret. Freckles. The sleeves of an oversized jumper poked out from the sleeves of a long overcoat. "I might have been going a little fast," she said.

"Dangerous, these floors can be," someone assured her.

Conversation, in these situations, was a free-for-all.

"I'm very sorry," said Malcolm, though he too thought she'd been going too fast. A mop was on its way, hoisted by an overalled woman also wielding a bucket. "Do you have everything?"

She leaned in, conspiratorially. "I think I'm going to abandon this."

Broken pasta, dented tins. He'd have done the same, if he could be sure of not being recognised next time he came here. *The man who walked away from his shopping.*

They were asked to step aside, somewhat curtly, by the bucket-and-mop, and Malcolm found himself momentarily askew: What had he been thinking, doing, pushing, two moments ago? His trolley . . . There it was. He turned to make another apology, because the three or four he'd issued so far didn't seem enough, but the young woman was gone. Her reloaded trolley stood against the freezer, no longer the centre of attention, and now resembling, in the ill-stacked, haphazard way its contents were organised, the food-bank collection by the exit. The man with the bow tie had evaporated, and the woman clearing up the tomato paste was muttering under her breath. Malcolm shook his head. He wanted to be out of here; he didn't care what remained on his list. He made his way to the self-service checkout, where there was no queue for once, and began loading his purchases onto the machine, fruit and vegetables first.

Under the bag of oranges, he found the envelope.

Winter trees scratched the skyline, and through their outstretched talons First Desk traced the wing lights of a west-bound airliner. There had been a time she could barely notice an evening aeroplane without wishing she was on it, but the years had a way of laying such aimless desires to rest. Among other things, they did that. Tonight—just gone six—she let it fly, returning her attention to the coloured lights and concrete of the south bank across the river. A typical London vista: the hustle and bustle of the city that can't relax. Two different beats from two different sound sources collided mid-river, and on the banks the traffic and the people danced to whichever they pleased.

Behind her, a car slowed and a door slammed. The car pulled away. Footsteps approached. She turned to meet them.

"Chancellor. Good evening."

"First Desk." Then: "That's ridiculously formal, isn't it?"

Maybe so, but the office was more important than its holder. Rather than point this out, she said, "Oh, best to keep things on a professional footing. That's why we're here, after all."

"Well, you have the advantage. I have no idea why we're here."

There was a slight nervousness to this admission, which was as it should be. When the head of the intelligence service suggests a quiet chat, only a fool would fail to feel queasy.

That same head said, "I was interested in hearing your views on the current situation."

Outside the Westminster bubble, the term "current situation" covered enough ground to build a city on: Russia, spiralling inflation, the virus, climate change, the energy crisis, the NHS, knife crime, the royal family, cancel culture, petrol prices, *I'm a Celebrity* and sex trafficking. Some of these overlapped. Inside the bubble, it only meant one thing: party leadership.

"Oh, my loyalties lie entirely with the PM—"

"And yada yada yada." First Desk's hand conducted an invisible orchestra for a moment, then cut it off. "You'll be loyal unto death, obviously, but supposing you wanted him to fall under a bus? Because if it helps, I've a set of bus timetables you can borrow."

"Oh, please. Why would I even want to think that? He's only been in office six months. I think the country's in agreement we're in turnaround—"

"The country's in agreement we're in a handcart, heading for the traditional destination."

"I hear enough doom warnings from the left-wing media. And if you're simply going to vent, I've a dinner engagement I'm late for. I'll leave you with your thoughts."

"Your dinner's not for twenty-seven minutes. Let's walk."

They did so, First Desk allowing the silence to widen enough for the Chancellor to fall into. "I'm not interested in hearing declinist nonsense. We have a new leader, new standards to meet. Honesty, integrity, transparency, accountability—they're all back on the table. We accept that mistakes were made, but we've moved on. That's what good governance is about."

"We might disagree that good governance is about burying your mistakes, but that's by the by. Let's face facts, a reckoning is coming. Partygate, the care home death toll, the twenty billion in Covid-response funds that . . . went missing, we can agree that everyone's forgotten about all of that. But spiralling mortgage rates? No, your party broke the pound last year, which is why it's now polling lower than a sunk punt. You'd be better off calling an ambulance than a general election, but that can't be avoided forever, and when it does, and the few survivors are marooned on the opposition benches, the top job will be up for grabs again. As I'm sure you've worked out for yourself."

The Chancellor gave her a sideways look. "Are we actually having this conversation?"

"No."

"You're not recording?"

"There's such a thing as deep fakery, remember? If I need a tape of you whispering treasonous nothings, I'll have a couple of my desk jockeys fix one up." She let two paces intervene before adding: "Joke."

"You're not famous for your sense of humour, are you?"

"I quite literally have trained assassins in my employ. If I say something's funny, it's best to go along, don't you think?" Without waiting for an answer, First Desk reached inside the black leather tote bag on her shoulder, and produced an A4-sized envelope. "Don't open this just yet. Tuck it out of sight, there's an idea."

The Chancellor had automatically taken hold of the envelope when it was offered, but looked to be already regretting this move. "What's inside?"

"Let's call it a bus timetable. You're familiar with Fabian de Vries?"

"Of course. The payday loan man."

"Among other career highlights." These had included online gambling, a national chain of escape rooms, and virtual reality porn. Currently, he was the favourite to bag the vetting services tender that had arisen under the Green Shoots initiative—doing background checks on applicants for sensitive government positions—and there was a view that he could get half the job done by ruling out anyone on his customer lists. "Were you aware what a close friend of your boss's predecessor he is?"

There fell a pause.

"No, not *that* close," First Desk clarified.

"It painted an interesting picture, though," the Chancellor said, and the pair shared a moment. But back to business: "I'd heard De Vries can be generous to his friends. I mean, the PM was always scrupulous about declaring gifts and holidays—"

"Famously so."

"—but he was understandably . . . *hazy* about details. I mean, he had a country to run. Who can keep on top of every last box that needs ticking?"

"Someone with staff? But you're right, De Vries has been a very generous man. And continues to be so, as these . . . timetables will show."

The Chancellor stopped walking. "Can we leave the fun and games to one side? What exactly are we talking about?"

"Potential outcomes. Your new boss might have an expiry date tattooed on his forehead, but your old one's not yet accepted that the work event's over. Sorry, I meant party. Once the dust settles after the next election, he'll come creeping out of his treehouse."

"You think he'll be back."

"Like Covid, I'm sure he'll be with us forever. Which is an argument for booster shots if ever there was. But yes, I'd say the biggest threat to any future ambitions you might harbour isn't a current colleague, it's the prospect of the man with the mandate re-emerging as your party's saviour. And your party being too shell-shocked by election loss to remember the lies, the corruption and the toxic narcissism he brings with him. So if you want to assume the leadership mantle, you'll need to be sure you're equipped to deal with the king of the zombies first."

"And he's who you really plan to drop a bus on, isn't he?"

"And maybe another bus on top of that one. Just to be sure." First Desk nodded at the envelope in the Chancellor's hand. "As we were saying, De Vries is a generous man. In fact, I think you'll be surprised quite how generous. A veritable fairy godfather, which in his case is a particularly apt description."

"Is this another gay slur?"

"No." First Desk's voice had altered: she wasn't playing games now. "It's more of a Disney reference. The fairy godfather, standing over an infant's crib and granting wishes, you know? Only in this case, it's daddy's wishes he's making come true."

The Chancellor had come to a halt, and was looking across the river. The sole security officer visible stood fifty yards off, hands at his sides, watchful and alert. Nevertheless, First Desk came quite close to say what she said next.

"You'll see from those documents that an avalanche of costs has come the former PM's way in recent years. Legal costs. Associated with a superinjunction, which as you know—"

"Means we shouldn't even be discussing the fact that it's in place."

"Quite. But here we are. And the issue of this particular superinjunction is, well, an issue. His eighth or ninth. Is anyone still keeping count?"

A couple approached, arm in arm, and the security man made himself three inches taller, but the pair paid no attention to anyone but each other as they passed. For a moment their conversation lingered, and then it was gone.

First Desk continued, "And even if anyone were, they're prevented from doing so by the aforementioned superinjunction, the acquisition of which has been cripplingly expensive. But luckily for the PM, those costs have been met by his good friend Mr. De Vries."

The Chancellor said, "Ancient territory. Whatever the former PM's domestic shortcomings, they didn't then and won't now impede his public ambitions. Besides, if there's a superinjunction in place, what use is your evidence?"

"Oh, you just have to show it to the right person."

The Chancellor considered this for a moment. "De Vries."

"Yes. This isn't so much a case of following the money as running after it, shaking a stick. Let De Vries know this is the reason his tender for the vetting service is being rejected, and he'll get the message. Leaving your old boss high, dry and low on funds. And your own path that much clearer."

"You want me to ensure that his bid fails? That's not my decision."

"Yours is the loudest voice in Cabinet. If you can't swing a simple veto, do you deserve to sit in the big chair?"

This wasn't worth a direct response. "You seem very certain you know what the future holds."

"Because some things never change. There'll always be sock puppets thinking they're messiahs, and there'll always be moneymen behind them. And the moneymen don't like being in the limelight. It leaves them open to awkward questions. Such as, where did the money come from?"

"Is that the real reason for all this? To keep De Vries from muscling in on your territory?"

"It's a good fifty per cent," First Desk admitted. "Let's face it, any problems the Service has with funding and resources aren't going to be solved by outsourcing. They're going to be solved by funding and resources. And he's a dark horse, our Mr. De Vries. He has obscure origins. You might even wonder if he wants to own the vetting office to avoid the process himself."

"Russian?"

"I think even your old boss would have noticed that's not a great look. No, he has a Dutch passport. Which could mean he's Dutch, I'll grant you. But another way of looking at it is, he's a porn-peddling loan-shark who's made millions exploiting the poor, the vulnerable and the weak. Just this once, could that not be enough?"

"My God. An idealist."

"How very dare you." But First Desk smiled, even if it were thinly pasted on. "Maybe an environmentalist. One stone, two birds. How's that for husbanding resources?"

The Chancellor said, obscurely, "No wonder he was always frightened of you." The lights on the south bank tilted and wheeled in the background. "And in return for this . . ."

"Helping hand."

"Careers guidance. In return for this, I suppose you'll want that, what's it called, Monochrome? I suppose you'll want the Monochrome inquiry terminated."

"To be frank, I don't understand why it's still ongoing. It should have been put out with the rubbish when Number Ten had the cleaners in. Or were there too many empty bottles for it to fit in a recycling sack?"

"I'm aware you think it's part of a vendetta. But you should understand that it's long been felt Regent's Park is too . . . independent. That's not an ideological standpoint. More of a cross-party consensus."

The noise First Desk made might have been agreement. Might not have been.

"And one it's hard not to agree with. Dirty tricks like this . . . it's why no one likes you."

"We're the secret service. We're not here to be liked."

"And you fly that flag proudly." The Chancellor gave these next words some thought: "Before he was PM, he was a minister of the Crown. You cost him that job. Did you think that endeared you to the rest of us?"

"There was no entrapment, no black-bagging. Just routine surveillance and an impartial report." Largely impartial. "No minister who does their job without endangering national security has anything to fear from the Park."

"So you say. But you can't blame us for wanting to see you kept in check." They walked in silence for a dozen yards, and then the Chancellor said, "All right. I'll see about spiking De Vries's guns. Not that I entirely trust you, or buy your Nostradamus act. But we've had enough of dirty money swallowing British assets. I'd rather not see it edging in on British security concerns."

"Thank you," First Desk said. The fact that putting British assets in the hands of dirty money had been a governmental priority for the past three administrations didn't seem worth raising. "And trust me or not, I never forget a favour received."

"Noted." The Chancellor signalled the security man, who waved towards the road. The car's purring became a quiet growl. "Can I offer you a lift?"

"Thank you, no. The walk will do me good."

The Chancellor nodded, and a moment later, First Desk was on her own.

She waited a while and then, content that she was unobserved, lit a cigarette and stared into the water. If the city never relaxed, the river seemed to, sometimes . . . Studying it gave a moment's peace. And speaking of peace, it would be a relief, a small one, to have the Monochrome panel silenced. It might be a joke but it had gone on long enough, and as with an infinite brigade of monkeys, there was always the possibility it would stumble on something significant. Well: it wouldn't now.

Checking her watch, she decided to be on the move. She had another two appointments this evening; another two senior cabinet members to meet, another two envelopes to deliver. The same conversation to have.

She was a great believer in spread-betting, when it came to democratic outcomes.

Mozart/Q1–94/OTIS/Berlin (BM).

This was handwritten on the top right corner of the grey cardboard folder that the envelope—large, brown, its flap sealed with tape—contained.

The man with the bow tie? The woman with the beret? Somewhere in the middle of that maelstrom, one or the other, or someone else, had placed the envelope in Malcolm's trolley, secreting it under his shopping. And now here he was, back in his flat—fishcakes uncooked—a large glass of Shiraz in his hand—trying to will it out of existence, while a one-word situation report wrote itself:

Fuck.

On the way home he had nearly walked into a streetlight, so intent had he been on looking over his shoulder. He had stared at the windows of houses, expecting to see shadowy figures twitching curtains. And what about his mobile—had it been hacked, was he transmitting his location to the intelligence services? And what difference did that make, seeing as he was heading home? The envelope on the table, openly in his possession, was a crime in progress. Any moment now his door would be reduced to splinters, his flat crawling with uniforms. In possession of state secrets—it didn't matter that he had no clue what they were, that the file remained unread. Of course he had opened the envelope, he would say, repeatedly, in a small basement room in Paddington Green. He imagined it was advertising matter, some gimmick the supermarket had adopted—money-off vouchers. Or, who knew, some sick individual had planted pornography among his apples and oranges, or some tired heart a love letter.

But you already knew it was neither of those things. Didn't you, sir?

Of course I did.

The large glass of Shiraz had become a half-full glass of Shiraz. But it was still large.

He had drawn the curtains, and now he was the one peeping out. Two floors below, the street looked normal for a February evening: dark, with a hazy halo around the lamps. On the pavement opposite, a dog walker ignored his charge as it took a dump on the kerb. Someone slouched past, smoking. A car, and then another car. Way up high in the sky above, an airliner's red lights winked behind cloud cover, the sound of the engine they were attached to following at a lazy distance. No drone strike imminent.

Monochrome, the creaky, thwarted inquiry with all the forward impetus of a slapped moth, had just gone live. Or so, at any rate, he was supposed to believe. But the file could contain anything. If it was a hoax, then he was sweating over nothing: rather than being in illegal receipt of classified documents, he was the punchline to a Regent's Park prank. How likely was that? He made himself sit and take the question seriously: it was possible. Regent's Park wasn't cooperating with Monochrome—was pretending it didn't exist—but there might easily be enough rancour there for someone to attempt sabotage, and steer the inquiry onto the rocks. True, Regent's Park was going into managed decline regardless of any finding Monochrome might make, with privatised companies taking up its slack: vetting procedures, some aspects of data management, other ancillary functions, these were being hived off. This was little more than the redrawing of administrative boundaries, but probably felt like the end of civilisation if you were riding a Regent's Park desk. Which would be reason enough to run a spoiling operation. So that was scenario one.

His heartbeat was returning to normal. This was what he did, he reminded himself; he ordered facts into reasonable columns. In this manner, the world could be made to seem sensical.

Scenario two: it was real. Some disaffected agent of the state had just handed him a pilfered file whose contents would blow a hole through tomorrow's headlines.

That was a far more frightening possibility, since it put Malcolm back in the crosshairs. Special police were on the staircase, their black van round the corner. The file on the table glowed like radioactive waste.

A third scenario: it was both things at once—real and not real; a hoax and the truth. He finished his Shiraz while his mind folded around this, grasping for the light beneath the bushel. Perhaps the file was real, containing actual historical dynamite, but the impending explosion was intended as a distraction, nothing more. Something to occupy the headlines, which currently shouted nothing but woe: the spiralling cost of living, the rumble of distant wars, the creaking infrastructure of a nation giving up. Imagine, instead of that, weeks in which the media fell over itself reporting some old spook scandal, recent enough to have contemporary traction, but long enough ago to leave the current administration untarred. The nineties, say. *Q1–94.* The sins of a different era, dragged into the light, and served up with enough spook glamour to keep everyone happy.

Which meant Malcolm was safe. He was the current plaything of some shady government department, but he was safe. Because the whole point of that scenario would be to have the file delivered to Monochrome, where its contents could be discussed, and duly leaked to the press. (His money would be on Singer, or possibly Ford-Lodge.) No one was going to arrest him; he was having his strings pulled, that was all.

Well, he thought, at least that would result in movement.

Because he'd long since stopped being an effective second chair—here and now, getting up to refill his glass, he could admit that, if only to himself. He'd long stopped doing his job, and was just waiting for it to be over, so he could get back to the heart of Whitehall, where he belonged. His role on Monochrome was to miss nothing and make sense of it afterwards, but his mind was out of the window half the time, and his shorthand thirty per cent accurate at best. Everything was recorded, obviously, but his transcriptions in recent months had been poor to non-existent, and once he and Griselda sat down to write up the final report, she'd know that too. So wherever else Monochrome ended up pointing its finger, Malcolm was front and centre. Dereliction of duty was the worst a civil servant could do. Even if no one cared about the overreaching of the Service any more, Malcolm really should find it in himself to care about that.

All of which got him where?

Nowhere, was the honest answer. Nowhere except a little drunker and a little more scared.

Three scenarios, and there might be a fourth, a fifth, a sixth that hadn't occurred to him. But however many there turned out to be, he'd read enough books, seen enough films, to know what happened to the patsy, and that role currently had his name all over it. He tucked the file back in the envelope, already trying to forget the catalogue coding on its cover, *Mozart/Q1–94/OTIS/ Berlin (BM)*, but knowing it would buzz through his mind like an earworm all night. Mozart: Didn't that indicate the level of clearance required? Don't even think about it, he thought, but couldn't help himself. He re-sealed the envelope, coaxing its stickiness back into life. Yes, Mozart was the clearance level; Q1–94, that indicated the date. OTIS: who knew? Berlin, obvious, and BM . . . He shouldn't be thinking about any of this. But the BM abbreviation snagged on his mind, because he'd initially read it as DM. A Freudian twinge of a misread, but it suggested a plan of action, or at any rate, a port of call. He raised his glass to his lips again, and drank. This had better be his last. He wasn't going to get any sleep tonight, but he'd need to be fresh as he could manage in the morning. DM. It was as if he were being sent a message . . . Leaving his wine unfinished, Malcolm took one last look out of the window, then went to brush his teeth before lying down in the dark.

The alarm didn't wake Griselda because she'd been awake for some while, a familiar carousel of worry spinning her round the same old circuit until she felt like uncollected baggage. In an attempt to reclaim herself she rose early and tried to shower bleak thoughts away, then dressed, and prepared the table for Melody's breakfast, even though she wouldn't emerge until after Griselda had left. *Lectures don't start till ten, mum!* Juice glass, muesli bowl, yoghurt spoon, she couldn't help it: her little girl was a young woman now, able to lay her own table, but if there were some things you couldn't do for your child there were others you could. Then she opened her laptop and investigated her finances, a ten-minute ritual practised several times a week, which always left her feeling worse, but which had to be done.

Life in the red. It was starting to feel as much an address as a condition.

And if it were an address, it was one wished upon her, as if she'd been placed in witness protection: she'd awoken one morning to find the conditions of life had changed, though most of its externals remained familiar. The house was the same house, her child still lived in it, the wardrobe remained full of her clothes, the drawers of her cutlery. Except it now seemed her husband had a gambling habit, and that was a newsflash. She'd known he enjoyed the occasional flutter on national occasions (the National itself, the boat race, the FA cup) but hadn't been aware that it had metastasized into a daily obsession, apt to fix its attention on less obvious competitions, such as which of two cartoon boxers on an online website might knock the other down. It was a way of rendering the irrelevant crucial, she supposed, and had wondered since if that had been the point? Perhaps life with Griselda had been so lacking in consequence that Ray had reached for the nearest means of adding a frisson of risk. But at the time it hadn't occurred to her to interrogate the subtext of this new situation; she had been all wrapped up in discovering its dimensions, and the different ways in which the family's outlook had changed. Their savings were gone. His pension was gone. There were unpaid bills and mounting debts. It was startling how swiftly an apparently secure foundation could crumble like a tapped meringue: this was how people living through earthquakes must feel.

For a while after Ray had confessed his addiction, Griselda had assumed that it was something they'd work through together; that, with the right help, Ray would recover. The crucial part of that was, finding the right help. *When the fun stops, stop,* the adverts recommended, which was not dissimilar from suggesting that, if you found you had a serious heart condition, do yourself a transplant. You needed others to lend a hand. So he did, or so he said; he reached out to a group of people with a similar condition— gamblers anonymous, he described them—and this much was true: they were all gamblers, and he didn't tell her any of their names. But before his association with them was through, they owned everything he'd ever signed his name to, including the house which had been, at the time, their actual address. Not long afterwards, he'd made his final withdrawal from their joint account, this being himself. So now she lived here, with Melody, in the red: a rented two-bedroomed flat in Bethnal

Green, in which she'd never, that she could recall, had a good night's sleep.

At work, she had let it be known that she and Ray had separated, but that was as much as she cared to reveal. In the corridors on which Griselda worked, there were weaknesses you didn't want to show. Bad luck was held to be contagious, and failure a condition requiring self-isolation. Divorce or separation didn't fall into that category, or half of Whitehall would be quarantined, but it was unwise to open the doors to speculation. It helped that she'd always remained at a distance from her colleagues, her trouble-maker reputation having lingered long after she had actively contributed to it, and for a while the usual order of things was flipped: her workplace became a sanctuary, while her new home was where the trouble lay.

"Why didn't you stop him?"

Her daughter's inevitable complaint.

"I didn't know about it."

"Why didn't you know about it? You're *married.*"

And marriages hold secrets, Griselda thought; marriages are made up of secret hours and hidden moments. But there were things you couldn't explain to your daughter, no matter how brave and intelligent she was; things too wrapped in shame and failure to reveal. It was difficult to explain their decline except in the broadest terms: that life was not fair, that things were not equal. Necessary as such lessons might be, there were gentler ways of delivering them, and Griselda would have preferred to defer them indefinitely. Until Melody was, say, a hundred.

She closed her laptop, having confirmed that a payment had been made, if instantly swallowed by debt. It was like trying to seal a dam with Elastoplast. But if the source of the money brought no pleasure, it produced little guilt. Life was not equal, life was not fair, and it sometimes put you in a corner. If what you did to get out of it didn't always redound to your credit, that was hardly front-page news. Or not any more, it wasn't. Before leaving the flat she quietly opened Melody's bedroom door and checked that her daughter was safe and soundly sleeping. Then she made sure she had all she needed for the day, and set off into it.

He knew, because office legend wrote it large—though there were few things office legend wrote small; you were basically a conquering hero if you had the same Tesco meal-deal five days a week—that the DM took breakfast in the garden behind the Savoy every morning, rain or shine. What that breakfast consisted of, Malcolm didn't know. A banana and a bottle of orange juice? A muesli pot? But you didn't need small detail to fashion a big picture. You could paint someone's existence based on their choice of footwear and an Instagram post.

So he was there first thing, pausing at the flower stall by the garden's gates to buy something small, bright and colourful on a glum and overcast day: London being rolled over by a great grey carpet. They were freesias that he bought, and overpriced, a spur-of-the-moment offering he was already regretting as he scanned the path ahead, trying to identify Janet Beckett's presence among the scattered walkers—those with phones in hand, and destinations in mind; those with hands in pockets and no place to go—and the occasional bench-occupier, sipping coffee, eating a sandwich, puzzling out Wordle or staring at the sky. Ms. Beckett was a small woman, but that didn't make her difficult to spot. On the contrary, people left space around Ms. Beckett. A career civil servant. One who never need rise higher than she had done, because the job she had might have been established with her in mind—there might have been a plinth waiting. *Deputy Manager.* Some people were born for the role of deputy. Promote them and they'd freeze in place, ossified by the prospect of policy-making, but stand them behind a chair, a little to the right, and they'd be in their element, implementing every suggestion dropped from on high.

She would never, then, be everyone's boss, but she was his boss for the time being—or had been before his secondment—and therefore the appropriate lap into which to drop his problem. He could see them poring over it together. *It seems to me, Malcolm, you've got yourself into a pickle.* But the whole point of her being his superior was having direct access to her own superior. *I think we'll take this one upstairs, don't you?* A small twinkle. *Leave it with me.*

And there she was, on a bench up ahead. Not much bigger than a child, but dressed in a manner no child of the twenty-first century would tolerate. Her shoes had buckles, as if she featured in a nursery rhyme. And why did she choose to eat her breakfast here, of all places? (Malcolm did not question the notion that, having decided to eat her breakfast here once, she might go on doing so every working day of her life. It was only the initial impulse that escaped him.) Out on the road, the morning ploughed on; here in the gardens, the day waited. A brave blackbird crossed in front of him, running out from shrubbery, running into more. He'd reached Ms. Beckett before deciding how to attract her attention, which turned out to be irrelevant. She saw him before he was ready.

"Malcolm!"

"Ms. Beckett," he replied, in that very short moment realising that he had done the wrong thing, come to the wrong place, was living the wrong life. It wasn't surprise that added that exclamatory lilt to Janet Beckett's greeting. It was shock.

"What are you doing here?"

He noticed he was holding the bunch of freesias out, as if offering a cross dog a biscuit.

"Those aren't for *me*."

This wasn't a question.

"No, of course not. No. I was just—no."

Ms. Beckett was drinking coffee from a reusable cup, or, as such items had once been known, a cup. A folded square of greaseproof paper lay on the bench's armrest, adorned with a few faint crumbs. Office legend had long since passed this story down, from graduate tongue to graduate ears, but to actually turn up and witness it—to see Ms. Beckett at her morning ritual—was akin, he now realised, to storming into her bathroom while she dressed. He had committed one of those sins which, when they happened in actual legends, required the sinner to absent himself for decades, slaying beasts and purging himself, hoping this would do the trick.

"I was just passing, and thought—"

"We both know that's not true."

Even if it had been, Malcolm would likely have admitted that it wasn't. Ms. Beckett's affronted stare was doing the work of rack and poker.

"What are you carrying?"

"The flowers? Oh, they're for—"

"Not the flowers."

". . . My briefcase."

"Precisely. You're on your way to work. Over by Liverpool Street, if I'm not mistaken." Which I'm not, she didn't need add. "And yet here you are. So don't tell me you were just passing."

"I needed to talk to you."

"And you chose to do so here, on my private time? Really, Malcolm. I would have thought even *you* would know better than that."

Which was unfair. Had there been any question as to protocol, the correct manner of going about things in the church in which they both served, Malcolm would have been first to supply the answer, with the possible exception of one straw-haired PPEist. There was no "even *you*" about it. And even as he was allowing that mutinous thought to form, he could see the same knowledge taking root behind Ms. Beckett's eyes, because however much a martinet she might be, she was not unjust. He might be to blame, turning up like this in her private moment, her secret hour, but she was the one who had levelled an unfair imputation. She raised her cup to her lips, but he didn't think there was anything left in it. She was giving herself room to move, that was all.

"It's not proper, Malcolm. Bearding me like this."

"No. I'm sorry. I wouldn't be here, but it's important."

A wind ruffled the grass, giving the impression of a page being turned.

There'd been false hints of spring lately, one day in three, and reminders that winter had barely started in the other two. Malcolm wore an overcoat of plain grey and black silk gloves, which sounded an affectation, but weren't: he'd bought them at a camping shop, assured they were the choice of mountaineers. Ms. Beckett's coat was equally plain, equally grey, though Malcolm suspected that an examination of the lining would reveal a famous name. Her gloves, though, were furry mittens, resting on the bench next to her, being unsuitable for the task of addressing a panini.

She noticed him making the deduction, perhaps. At any rate, she reached for the breakfast wrapper, shook away all traces of its use, and tucked it in a pocket, out of sight.

"If it's important enough to disturb me, you'd better get it off your chest."

This wasn't quite an invitation to join her on the bench, but Malcolm chose to treat it as such. He put the freesias to one side as he sat. His briefcase, he laid across his knees. He might have been a doctor, delivering bad news.

"I'm on Monochrome, as you know."

She raised a hand. "I'm not permitted to hear any complaints or listen to any observations about Monochrome and its proceedings. As you well know. There's a chain of report."

Chain of being, she might as well have said. There's a great chain of being.

"I know. This isn't a complaint. It's about something that's happened. It was outside working hours."

She looked at him. The freesias weren't the only mistake, he now knew. In his time outside the department, his memories of the DM had evolved or degraded or done something. He had recalled her as the voice of authority, the one to whom all issues were taken, to have them broken down into their component factors—categorised, alphabetised, mentally shelved—until they ceased to exist in any meaningful form, and as such no longer constituted a problem. More times than he could recall he had left her deskside feeling lighter, the intractable conundrum he had been carrying rendered a series of unimportant details to be left in other people's pigeonholes. That was the skill he'd been hoping she'd bring to bear on his problem now. What he hadn't taken into account was how much of her magic depended on her desk, its solidity emphasising the official nature of her outlook. Here and now, she was simply a woman in a garden. But he had come this far, and he might be wrong. So he soldiered on; told her, as briefly as he could, of the appearance of the envelope in his shopping trolley the previous evening, suppressing the details that came back as he spoke, and which alone seemed to make the experience real: the broken jar of passata, the bow tie, the sullen mood of the cleaner sent to mop the debris up. Nor did he mention that he had barely slept.

Before he had finished, she was shaking her head. It was clear that he had done the wrong thing, or failed to do the right thing, which—in the corridors they both haunted—were one and the same.

"You shouldn't have allowed this to happen."

"I didn't have a choice. It was just there when I was unpacking my trolley."

"Official secrets? A classified folder? Taking possession of it is embroiling yourself in espionage."

She used the term *embroiling* as if it denoted a particularly labour-intensive manner of food preparation.

"I didn't take possession of it. I don't want anything to do with it!"

"You've brought it with you?"

He took that as another invitation. Nothing he'd have liked more right then than to unload the file onto the DM as if she were a convenient pigeonhole; to waltz away among the black-birds and phone-warblers, weightless again. He had unclasped his briefcase, was holding the envelope out to her, before she'd finished speaking.

There was distaste in the way she declined to take it from him. "Have you examined it?"

"Of course not."

"Then why is the seal broken?"

"I took it out of the envelope, of course I did. But I haven't read it. Haven't even looked at it, really."

"It has a classification on the cover?"

"Yes. It's—"

"I don't want to know. Do you recognise the classification as being part of the Regent's Park taxonomy?"

"No."

She looked puzzled.

Malcolm started to explain that, despite the inquiry's remit, he hadn't had access to Park files, but this too came under the rather large heading, it was turning out, of things that Ms. Beckett did not want to hear about.

"Enough. There's a possibility, then, that this is not what you think it is? That it might simply be a prank?"

Late in the night, at an hour when crocodiles still roamed the streets, he had come to the realisation that his life contained nobody prepared to put time and effort into making him feel uncomfortable.

"It looks genuine."

"I fail to see how you can make that statement, given your assertion that you've never laid eyes on an actual genuine file."

Malcolm too would have been hard-pressed to explain why he felt this way. But it was there in his bones, in his gut. For all his desperate hypothesising, it had been there since the moment he laid eyes on the damn thing. Which was why everyone in sight, Ms. Beckett not entirely excepted, looked to him now like an agent of the state.

"I'm disappointed in you, Malcolm. There is an . . . *ethos*, a way of conducting oneself, that I would have thought you had embraced. No, that's not fair of me. I know you've embraced it, I've witnessed it at work. But why have you let yourself down now?"

"I didn't know what to do."

"And you thought this was an answer? To turn up here and dump it in my lap?"

It still seemed good enough, as far as Malcolm was concerned.

Ms. Beckett sighed. "I can't help you with this. You must return it to its rightful place. The fewer people who take possession of it the better, you must realise that. Social distancing, if you like."

He said, "I'm not sure how to do that. Do I just turn up at Regent's Park? . . ."

"You put it into a bigger envelope and send it back." She

sounded impatient, and he could understand why. Put like that, it was fairly obvious.

"I wasn't sure the post could be trusted," he lied.

"It doesn't have to be trusted. It just has to provide a postbox. Then it's out of your hands."

"Monochrome is nonsense," he found himself saying. "It's as if I'm being punished for something. Literally, nothing is happening there. It's empty complaints about things that don't matter. The final report is going to sound like, like, like an end of term write-up for an absolute no-hoper. *We're afraid young Johnny hasn't fulfilled his potential. In fact, we're rather concerned he has no potential to fulfil.*" He realised, too late, that the voice he had adopted was an approximation of Ms. Beckett's own. "I'm sorry. But it is."

"And I've told you, none of that falls under my jurisdiction. I don't want to hear it, and it's *remiss* of you to put me in such a position."

He couldn't help it, the whine that crept into his voice. This was the real reason he was here, of course. The envelope was merely the excuse. He wanted to make an appeal, to state his case. He wanted to come home.

"I just want to get back to my actual job. Back on the ladder."

"You know that's not possible."

"But will be. Soon. Monochrome can't last forever. Not unless . . ."

Not unless something brought it to life. Something like the appearance of unexpected evidence, which might light a fire under the piles of damp kindling that had accrued. Causing an actual blaze, instead of a damp, patchy smoulder.

But the way Ms. Beckett was shaking her head—ever so minutely—made it clear that he'd gone too far.

And there was something else, besides.

"I'm not sure that was ever the plan, Malcolm."

". . . I'm sorry?"

"To have you return to the exact same position." She fixed her gaze emphatically upon him as she spoke. When she did this, nobody ever noticed how small she was. It would have been like noticing how little a virus weighed. "It's been two years. Things move on."

"What does that mean exactly?"

"That the department isn't the same as when you left. Adjustments have been made. And when something's running smoothly, well. It doesn't make sense to make further changes. It's not policy, actually."

"But that's . . . that's not what I was told. When I was asked to help on Monochrome. I was told it was a secondment, that I'd be reinstalled in my old job once it was done."

"In *a* job, yes. Nobody's suggesting otherwise. But more than likely, not in the same department. And this is a good thing, Malcolm. We all have to move on at some time. Spread our wings, and see what we're capable of."

"But—"

"And if you were prepared to vouchsafe that a change of scenery wouldn't be unwelcome—Birmingham, say, or Newcastle—that would be very . . . helpful. And the road to seniority is less steep out in the . . . Well. They're hardly the boondocks any more, are they? A lot of exciting challenges for a young man prepared to put the effort in."

Malcolm could see his future taking a handbrake turn, right there in front of him, could see it slewing across the path, taking out that passing pedestrian, that litter bin. He had come looking for assistance, and perhaps some nod of recognition that he was involved in bigger things, that he was not inconsequential. *Trust you, Malcolm, to catch the eye of Regent's Park!* And instead he was being told he'd be sent into exile. He could well imagine seniority being easier to acquire in the hill towns and provinces of the nation. He'd have a parking space and a nameplate on his door. And he saw himself on the phone, trying to call London, and being constantly put on hold.

He thought: this is the real reason for Monochrome. It was just an excuse to get rid of me.

Ms. Beckett was preparing to stand. The expression *I'm so glad we had this little chat* hovered unspoken in the air. "I'm sure you'll get on splendidly," she said, as if his future were already settled, and remained only to be lived. "Every challenge is an opportunity, isn't that what they say?"

That depends who they are, he wanted to reply. Conditioning, though, was a sturdy leash.

She pulled her mittens on and looked around, as if seeing the gardens for the first time. A small smile worked its way onto her lips. "My father used to bring me here," she said. "He worked in the Savoy."

Malcolm thought: that's one of the small details you don't need when you're looking at the big picture. But what he said was, "That's nice."

He looked back once, after walking off in the opposite direction, but she'd already disappeared into the February morning. The freesias, though, still lay on the bench, as if marking the place where someone, who had been of importance to someone else, had died.

If there are moments during that morning when the sun breaks through the grey pudding bowl over London, allowing brief scatterings of beauty to brighten its heights and lighten its lows—painting rainbow smudges onto oily roads, and causing pigeons' wings to glitter as they burst into flight—such moments don't reach the lower floors of Regent's Park, one of which houses the archive, its repository of secrets and lies. The light in the archive is blue, except when movement is detected along its aisles, in which case it softly ascends to a warmer, more reader-friendly yellow, though in truth there is rarely much movement in this long room, in which the odd cubbyhole nestles between accordion-style racks of shelving, pushed closed when their contents aren't required. In an ideal world—or a world, anyway, that the archive's chatelaine would find ideal—this room, this whole floor, would be temperature controlled, the better to prolong the life of its files and folders, many of which are succumbing to the vicissitudes of age: they peel and crumble at the edges; the clips and bands that hold them rust and crack; the sticky labels pasted to their covers dry and drift to the floor. But the memories they hold remain intact, available to be recalled and reinterpreted; even—on occasion—revised. Rarely, though, do they blossom or bloom. The archive has long ceased to grow, or at any rate, grows by minute increments only, when a lost detail emerges requiring adjustment, this generally comprising nothing more than a kiss with a rubber stamp: DECOMMISSIONED, DECLASSIFIED, DECEASED. When the past meets the present the present always wins, but the victories are fleeting, mere technical knock-outs. The present wins every battle, but the past always wins the war.

Elsewhere in the Park history accumulates at a brisker rate, the digital cloud where newer secrets are stored holding more pixels than actual clouds hold raindrops, and while this is turning out to present security problems of a kind previously unencountered, things haven't yet reached the pass where wise minds decide that the old ways are best. So for the moment the future is allowed to unravel at precisely the speed of time, while the past continues to brood in its chambers, yielding up secrets only when forced to do so by those brave enough to confront the archive's warder.

Who moves through her queendom this morning, causing the overhead lighting to slip from blue to yellow, as if her arrival had caused the dawn. And like the dawn's, her progress is slow but smooth; she glides, in fact, her vehicle of choice an electric wheelchair—but this places overmuch weight on the word *choice*. Left to her own devices she would travel these aisles without assistance, but then, if that were still possible, it is likely she wouldn't be here at all; that if it weren't for the occasion that robbed her of her lower limbs, her path through life would have taken a different course. This, though, is speculation—an attempted reading of a present unaffected by the past—and, as she has been known to put it herself, all manner of bullshit gets thrown about by those wielding crystal balls. The past lies on shelves all around her, and her rubber stamps can do nothing to change it. Whatever the nature of the adjustment she makes—RECLASSIFIED, REDACTED, RESOLVED—this isn't altering facts but turning them to catch another light, the way one might change a landscape by looking at it from a different place.

The wheelchair arrives at a particular set of shelves, their sides facing outwards to present what appears to be a blank wooden

wall with vertical fractures at regular intervals, and its occupant
reaches down to a metal wheel and turns it counterclockwise,
whereupon the rows of shelves separate at the points of fracture,
allowing access to their stacked contents. The hydraulics involved
aren't complex, and the system is regularly oiled, but still: there's
effort involved, as there always is when shifting history. This
shows on her face, partly obscured by the heavy make-up she
wears; make-up that might have been applied by a child, so thickly
is it plastered on. It is a mask designed to make people turn away,
as if its wearer has long decided she wants no part of their attention; that she would rather slip between gaps in the shelving than
suffer unearned pity. The gap that she is creating now is soon
large enough to allow that escape, and once it reaches the desired
width she executes a neat swivel, her chair—cherry-red with thick
velvet armrests—turning with a grace born of long practice before
easing down the newly created corridor, lined either side with
case histories and situation reports. Halfway along she stops, and
runs a hand along a row of files and folders; some contained in
boxes; others slimmer, requiring cardboard envelopes only. As on
every other shelf in the archive, the contents have been tightly
arranged, leaving no space to add further files. There is little need
to; the period of history to which this area relates is unlikely to
generate further content. That said, as her fingers run along the
spines they encounter a gap just wide enough to insert one more
folder, provided it had only the barest bones to offer on the topic
it covered. The woman in the wheelchair attempts to slip her
little finger into this fissure, but cannot do so. She nods thoughtfully, and then carefully shuffles the folders either side of the gap
until it no longer exists. What would almost certainly have never
been noticed by anyone but her has now been obliterated, taking
with it a small slice of history, the record of which has either
escaped or dropped into a well of its own making. Time will tell,

unless it doesn't. Time can be the best keeper of secrets of all, and hoards them inside its hours and days; places no one ever looks.

Task completed, the wheelchair reverses along the passage into the aisle, where it pauses while its user turns the metal wheel clockwise, putting everything back the way it was. The shelves slide closed, and the wall is re-formed. The fractures remain, though, and while they are barely paper-thick, there's always the possibility that something will leak out, its motion so subtle, so undetectable, that even the light won't notice, as if nothing were happening beneath it at all.

All that's happening now is the wheelchair's withdrawal, as its user retreats to a cubbyhole, and busies herself with the doings of the day. Around the rest of the archive the yellow light dims, as if dawn has had second thoughts, and peace descends. Whether this is the natural state of affairs here, or a temporary victory over the forces of chaos held captive in its folders, is hard to say. But what is certain is that everything becomes very quiet, and soon the only sounds are those of one woman breathing and the past doing nothing at all.

You just put it into a bigger envelope and send it back. Well of course you bloody do, thought Malcolm, and bought just such a bigger envelope before descending once more underground and making his way to Liverpool Street. But something had altered. Envelope in one hand, briefcase in the other, he entered the building to the usual greeting:

"Just you today is it, Mr. Kyle?"

It was. There was no witness hearing scheduled, and Griselda was spending the day at the Home Office, where she was expected to keep track of her old job while the inquiry was in progress. There was no need to rehearse any of this for Clive.

"I'll do the lift for you, then."

He had never worked out how to interact with the Clives of the world, men who were older and in demonstrably inferior jobs that involved the tiny practicalities of life. Plumbers, you could defer to. Mechanics, dishwasher repairmen; anything involving expertise. But those whose job involved opening a door: What were you supposed to say to them? Sorry?

"Thanks, Clive."

"All in a day's work."

He heaved a sigh of relief as the lift door closed.

As it trundled up the building, he reflected sourly on Griselda's position. Spending the day playing catch-up with her old job meant her old job was being kept warm for her; this while Malcolm was cast into outer darkness: Nottingham, was it? Somewhere his mind had failed to grasp hold of, the way prisoners in the dock might refuse to take in the sentence handed down. Sunderland? He imagined, a year hence, sending a postcard to Griselda, which she would glance at from her Whitehall desk, puzzled contempt on her lips, before tossing it into the shredder. All right for her. Being a woman probably helped. Being Black certainly did. A wave of self-disgust accompanied this. But hell—no, *shit*—it wasn't fair. It wasn't fucking fair. He kicked the lift door, then started guiltily. He had no idea if the lift was monitored. Clive might be watching him, his eyes narrowing. Shit.

On the fourth floor, he let himself into Sir Winston's room, one of the minor acts of rebellion he indulged in when reasonably certain of not being caught. He left his briefcase there and visited the bathroom, where he underwent the usual rigmarole of tie-straightening and cuff-checking once he'd washed his hands. There's no one here to notice, he told himself. But he'd reached that heightened state where he considered his every move to be under observation. Sometimes this was a benign surveillance, allowing him to feel he was passing a test; at others it was a glimpse into life under a totalitarian authority. Act innocent. No, *be* innocent. Especially when not.

This time, after entering Sir Winston's room, he locked the door behind him.

The office, larger than the other, contained nothing of interest. A table, two chairs, and a window with a view of the building opposite. Its reservation for Sir Winston's use was a polite fiction, involving the pretence that Sir W might have important, confidential phone calls to make; a fantasy on a par with his appointment to the inquiry being due to a particular strain of acuity, rather than just a willingness to turn up and claim the attendance fee. But such observations were easy to make in the safety of one's own head. What Malcolm needed—what he craved—was a moment of release. *Stuff your pension*. The Sir Winstons of the world wanted a good talking to, and he, Malcolm Kyle, was the lad to deliver it. Or at least, he was when in an empty office.

Putting the innocent envelope on the table, he placed his briefcase on the floor and removed his coat and scarf and hung them on the hook on the door. After checking his phone, which held no messages, he put it in his coat pocket. Everything about these actions suggested a man in charge of his destiny. He sat and, from his briefcase, withdrew the original envelope and removed the file. When he placed this in front of him, he must have looked for all the world exactly what he was: a civil servant, about to review paperwork.

Mozart/Q1–94/OTIS/Berlin (BM).

All he'd wanted was a small guarantee. An assurance that he'd be back in his own department before long; that his life, his career, would continue on the trajectory he'd grown accustomed to before Monochrome. He remembered his thoughts about Janet Beckett, that she was a born deputy, and assigned himself a similar role: stand him behind a chair, a little to the right, and he'd be in his element, implementing every suggestion dropped from on high. Perhaps dreams should be made of brighter things, but ambitions should be realistic. Otherwise most of us are doomed to failure.

The file was a cardboard folder, held together with both crocodile clip and rubber band. The clip had grown rusty in a way familiar to Malcolm, who had sieved the contents of many a filing cabinet, but the rubber band was new, or at any rate didn't snap like a desiccated worm when he removed it. Playing detective, he examined the edges of the folder for a moment. It felt to him as if there were a second ligature mark; as if this rubber band had replaced another, which had dried and broken apart when last this file was opened. He unclasped the clip. It was opened again, now.

This wasn't a crime. He was in full possession of the necessary clearance. First Desk's own words: he had access to *all officially held informational resources save those pertaining to live operations*. No way was this live.

Of course, appended to that permission was a protocol intended to be strictly adhered to, as all such protocols were.

You have the right to examine any case file you want. To activate this right, submit a request to my desk in writing, specifying the reference number of the file in question.

There was no available fantasy in which First Desk smiled after saying these words, and added, *Though obviously, I won't hold you to that.*

Malcolm opened the folder.

The first thing he saw was a photograph, sliding out from among the other papers as if eager for attention. Black and white, it showed three people standing by a wall, two men and a woman. One of the men was in the middle, which seemed off-key to Malcolm; he was large and beaming, and wore a wide-brimmed hat pushed back on his head, though enough hair crept out to reveal it as fair, perhaps even blond. Longish, certainly. He had one arm round the waist of the woman to his left, who wore—in addition to a mid-thigh dress, with big buttons—a shy smile, as if she weren't sure this assignation should be made public. Unless the photograph was playing tricks, she was as tall as the first man and a little taller than the second; had mousy-looking hair which fell to her shoulders, and was pretty in what Malcolm interpreted as an insecure way, as if her prettiness were a late-blooming gift, still something of a surprise to its recipient. All this from how she was standing, and the way her left hand tugged at the hand around her waist; not in an additional gesture of fondness, but more to ward him off. So Malcolm thought, anyway. As for the remaining figure, he was strangely expressionless; caught between two moods was how Malcolm read the moment. About to turn one thing or the other: nice or nasty. His hands were jammed inside his pockets. Like his male companion, he wore a baggy suit and a hugely-lapelled raincoat; unlike him, he gave the impression that these were the clothes nearest to hand when he'd been called upon to rise that day and head into the world. No, this second man was less comfortable than the first, whose confidence was underlined by the jaunty tongue of handkerchief poking out of his breast pocket.

Berlin, 1994. The file's classification number gave him this much.

He stared at the photo a few moments longer, not because it had more to tell him, but because it postponed the next step. He had opened the file, yes, but anyone might do that, simply to ascertain that it was what it appeared to be: a Regent's Park document. Pointless to post something to the Park that didn't belong there. It might contain anything: a collection of newspaper clippings, a set of recipes, someone's notes on a lecture series. So far, there was nothing illegal in his activity; on the contrary, this was due diligence. He was a civil servant with a file in front of him. He could claim a Pavlovian defence.

But first things first. Review the contents.

It wasn't an epic—believe me, Malcolm thought; I've seen some whoppers—containing only seventeen sheets of paper, each stamped ZERO CIRCULATION. The first three comprised what looked like the standard archiving form for the period, information added by typewriter on dotted lines: date, department, required clearance level—this was *Mozart*; before Malcolm's time, but security clearances were once graded according to a supposed hierarchy of musical genius. Mozart was presumably high. The remaining fourteen sheets were a typed report, which Malcolm scanned without reading. The typing made it seem older than it was, because anything created on a typewriter, even an electric one, looked like incunabula now. A neatly handwritten *DC* initialled each page, though there was no clue as to who this might be. But so far so good. He'd opened the folder; ransacked the tomb. And the door had yet to be kicked in by angry—

The door handle rattled.

His heart lurched.

"Malcolm? Is that you?"

Griselda Fleet.

He shovelled the paperwork into an untidy pile and crammed it into its folder.

"Malcolm?"

"I—yes. Yes. It's me."

He attempted to jam the folder back into the envelope, but it caught on the flap.

More rattling. "Malcolm? Would you open the door?"

"Just a minute."

"Why are you locked in? Malcolm . . ."

Unwanted teenage memories ignited in his mind: his mother rattling a similar doorknob; Malcolm attempting to make dissimilar paperwork disappear.

"Just coming!"

Giving up on the envelope, he grabbed his briefcase and mashed everything inside it. He fumbled with the clasp but his fingers were thumbs, and when he tucked it underneath his chair it drooped open, desperate to reveal secrets. But it was a bunch of papers, that was all, and Griselda was hovering: he could feel her presence, her growing impatience. The same thumby fingers made a meal out of unlocking the door, and once he'd done so he pulled it open so brusquely it almost caught him in the face. *Don't act strangely*, he warned himself, but the first words out of his mouth were: "What are you doing here?"

"What am *I* doing here? What are *you* doing? This is Sir Winston's room."

Stepping past him she entered the office, looking round suspiciously.

"He's not in today."

"That doesn't give you the right to occupy it. And why lock the door?"

"Privacy."

"What do you need privacy for? There's nobody here." She glanced at his laptop, open on the table. "Malcolm . . ."

"What?"

"I hope there's nothing going on here."

"What does that mean? 'Going on'? Are you accusing me of something?"

"No, I'm simply wondering why you're acting strangely."

"If I'm acting . . . strangely, it's because I didn't expect you here. I thought you were at the Home Office today."

"It got shifted. I'm going in next week instead."

"Why?"

"Why? What do you mean, why? I wasn't told why and it's got nothing to do with you anyway. Why are you acting like this? Has something happened?"

"Of course it hasn't. Nothing ever happens."

Because she was staring at it, he leaned across and closed his laptop.

"I hope you weren't . . ."

"Weren't what?"

Griselda bit her lip, shook her head, looked away. Then looked back at Malcolm. "I know you're not happy in this job. That's fair enough. But I do expect you to behave like a professional, and not some stroppy teenager. And if you're in any way accessing inappropriate material—"

"That's an outrageous—"

"—then you'll be subject to the usual—"

"—thing to say!"

"—sanctions, which as you well know are very serious. Do you understand what I'm saying?"

"I understand that you're falsely accusing me of something vile. I should warn you that I'm in close contact with the DM, the deputy manager of the Cabinet Secretary's office. We had breakfast just an hour ago. So I'd be careful about hurling slanderous accusations around if I were you. *Very* careful."

He was trembling and his heart was pounding and his hair, probably, was all over the place; he had to fight the urge to reach for his comb. Griselda, meanwhile, had pursed her lips. She was focused, though, on his entirely innocent laptop rather than his guilty briefcase. Setting his own mouth in what he hoped was an expression of grim determination, he folded his arms, then decided this was too defensive a gesture, so unfolded them and placed his right hand on the back of the chair he'd been sitting on. But he leaned too heavily and the chair almost overbalanced: grabbing it before it could fall, he kicked the briefcase underneath, disgorging its contents onto the floor. A cardboard folder, seventeen sheets of paper and a photograph.

"What's that?"

"Nothing."

But the speed with which he attempted to shuffle the spillage away gave the lie to this. He might as well have had a blue light flashing on his head.

"Malcolm?"

"It's nothing. Look, could you give me some space, please? I'm sorry about using Sir W's room, but I didn't think I was doing any harm. It's not like he keeps anything in here." A few old copies of the *Daily Mail*, plus a pair of wellington boots for some unfathomable reason. "And the view's better."

Even before that was out of his mouth, he'd known it for a mistake. The view was exactly the same.

She was staring at the collection of papers he was clutching to his chest. If he'd actually intended to produce the worst possible outcome, it's unlikely he'd have managed anything quite so ludicrous.

"That looks like a file."

"It's just personal papers."

There was an almost kind expression on Griselda's face as she reached across and plucked from his grip the cardboard folder, then read aloud its classification. "Mozart/Q1–94/OTIS/Berlin (BM). A little elaborate for a personal filing system, wouldn't you say?"

He didn't respond.

"Mozart. That's a high-level security clearance, or used to be. Is this what I think it is?"

Malcolm found himself admiring Sir Winston's view, which

was, when you got down to it, slightly different to the one next
door. The same neighbouring building, yes, but from a fresh
perspective. The moment had probably passed for pointing this
out, though.

"It's a Park file, yes? From Regent's Park."

He found himself nodding, dumbly.

For a moment she said nothing but stood staring at him, the
folder clutched in her left hand, her right hand stroking it lightly,
as if it were her new favourite thing. Again, he had the urge to
comb his hair. He needed to get a grip: if only there was something to hold on to. He flexed and unflexed his fingers.

"Where did you get it from, Malcolm?"

Malcolm reached for the nearest available lie, but there
wasn't one.

"Well?"

"I don't know," he said.

They sat at the table, a careful chair's distance between them. The
papers were stacked in numbered order, pages 1–17, with the
photograph on top. Griselda had studied this for a while, without
saying anything, while Malcolm explained what had happened
in the supermarket: the trolley crash, the young woman with
red hair, the man with the bow tie. There were spooks everywhere. They haunt unlikely places.

"But you're not certain it was one of them?"

She wasn't really sure why she was asking. It was clear that
Malcolm wasn't certain about anything.

Eventually he said, "I'm not sure who else it could have been."

If it was Park product, which seemed likely, then the Park was
its obvious source, but that was the final obvious thing about it.
Neither had forgotten their audience, on Monochrome's first day,
with First Desk. Since then, having been deprived of any useful tool

with which to accomplish it, they'd been allowed to proceed with their task without further interference, and this, possibly, wasn't interference but actual support. So why would First Desk have had a change of heart, and why this roundabout way of expressing it? It was certainly true that she never did anything straight that she could do sideways, and she had any amount of talent to call upon, red-headed or bow-tied. But if she were behind this strange game, there was no telling what the rules were. And if she weren't the instigator she was likely the target, which meant Monochrome had just been loaded and pointed in her direction. Somehow, that didn't seem a safe thing to be part of.

The other possibility was Anthony Sparrow, but Sparrow was a busted flush. Griselda's essential opinion of him—that he was a man who wouldn't need to be hungry to grind your dog into sausages—hadn't faltered, but Sparrow had disappeared some while ago, with a speed and thoroughness suggesting that a deity was answering prayers or a fairy granting wishes. True, his deeds lingered behind him like an unflushed toilet, but the man himself was out of the picture, and if he were to re-emerge from the shadows, she doubted he'd do so in an understated way. This was a man who tossed imaginary hand grenades over his shoulder on leaving a room. Subtlety had never been his medium.

Malcolm had said, "The DM says we should just post it back to the Park."

The DM had a point.

"I bought an envelope."

"But you decided to read it first."

Malcolm was quiet for a while. He reached for the photograph, held it aloft as if studying it anew. Nothing about it changed, or ever would. "She told me there was no way back," he said at last. "To my old job."

"They can't sack you."

This was a fundamental truth. They couldn't sack you. It was called the Civil Service for a reason, and sacking you would be the height of ill manners.

Malcolm muttered something which sounded like "Sunderland."

Griselda looked at the pile of papers. Whatever story they had to tell, it was in her possession now. Or Monochrome's, rather. The toothless committee, which had wasted all these months chewing empty mouthfuls.

"Where did you put the envelope? For posting it back?"

It had slipped to the floor. Malcolm bent to retrieve it.

"What stopped you doing that?"

"Nothing. I mean, I haven't stopped doing it. I just haven't done it yet."

"Because you were going to read it."

Just sitting here with him, the file in front of them, made her as guilty as he was. And the longer it went on, the worse it got.

She remembered Sparrow telling her, *you're simply exploring the mine shaft. Think of yourself as head canary.* The self-satisfied smirk that he wasn't actually wearing, but hovered behind every word he said. *Not that those advantages have propelled you to particularly giddy heights.*

Malcolm said, "There's nothing to stop us looking at it. It's there in our terms and conditions. The whole purpose of Monochrome is to examine old case files for evidence of wrongdoing."

"If that's what this is, if it's evidence of wrongdoing, why would the Park put a copy in our hands?"

He didn't answer.

"Besides, we're supposed to request files via First Desk."

"Except we're not able to do that, are we? Up until now, we've not had the faintest clue how to go about identifying them."

"The job parameters were laid down quite clearly. Breaking them now won't do anyone any good."

"It would do *Monochrome* good! We might actually get somewhere!"

"Malcolm—"

"And what's First Desk going to do anyway, bang us up in her basement? We've already been there."

"This isn't a joke. It's a serious matter."

He slapped his hand down on the OTIS folder with a suddenness that made her jump. "*This* is serious. Or it might be. But the last two years have been a joke, and we both know it. Even Sir Winston probably suspects it."

"Just because you're not enjoying the job—"

"It's not a job!"

This time, he seemed to surprise even himself. His words—not quite a shout, but almost—bounced off the walls and windows like invisible rubber balls. For a moment, both waited for them to subside. Then, more quietly, he said, "The PM wanted a war with the Park, and First Desk spiked his guns from the off. Monochrome should have been scrapped then and there, and we both know it. Instead we've had our careers ruined, or I have, just because two narcissists treat Westminster like it was their private wrestling ring. And we're supposed to do as we're told and make no waves. It's never been a job, it's been a political game. Until now." He slapped the OTIS file again. "Now it's a job. We should put it before the committee."

Those things which had always made him faintly ridiculous to Griselda—his neatness, his formality—somehow made him formidable now.

"I thought you were frightened."

He straightened his glasses. "I am. A bit. But I'm also . . . cross."

Griselda looked towards the window, not that there was anything in the view to help her. She tapped the file, as if asserting an equal ownership. "What if it's a fake? What if we're being set up?"

"Oh, like we're being tricked into looking at evidence that's really a pile of crap? I wonder what that'll feel like."

Griselda couldn't help it. A small snort of laughter escaped her.

Encouraged, Malcolm said, "Besides, look at it. It's old."

"It's not that old." But she knew what he meant. The paper, the typeface, the photograph: faking this would have required experts.

Then again, Regent's Park had experts. As did other intelligence services.

She took a breath. It would be safer not to know the answer to her next question, but something compelled her to ask. "What does it contain?"

"I haven't read it yet."

"Seriously?"

"Seventeen pages. A case file. A Berlin operation in 1994. That's all I know."

She shook her head, though wasn't sure why. This was what you did: you made gestures, responses, as a way of filling space while wondering how to respond. "We could end up in serious trouble. Prison-time trouble."

"Yes, but would we? Really? If it was just me, yes, but both of us? The whole panel?"

"The panel haven't seen it."

"Not yet. But we could distribute it. And then what, you think the whole of Monochrome—Sir Winston, Shirin—would find themselves in the dock?" It was Malcolm's turn to shake his head, but this time with purpose. "When it was just me, it could be a criminal act. When it's all of us, it's a clerical error. Someone goofed up and put the file in our hands. What were we supposed to do with it?"

"In a supermarket trolley? That's nobody's idea of correct procedure."

"This is the Park we're talking about. Who knows how they operate?"

"But what if it's not the Park? What if it's another service entirely? Moscow? Or anyone, really."

These days, these years, there was no shortage of foreign services that might enjoy leading the Park down a garden path, or even drowning it in a garden pond.

But Malcolm was shaking his head. "We're already a joke. And if it does turn out to be a hoax, well, we'll find out soon enough, won't we? When we call witnesses."

". . . Witnesses?"

"It's an operation file that's thirty years old. What are the chances everyone named in it is dead already?"

"Yes, but . . . Distributing it, calling witnesses? You're playing with fire."

"You mean we are. Or you are, rather."

"Me?"

"I'm second chair. You're the one who makes the decisions."

And here was the nub of it, the sharp end. Yes, she was first chair, which meant first in the line of fire. Malcolm might have discovered he had balls after all, but that didn't mean he was putting them on the block.

She looked at the other envelope on the table; the one he'd bought to send the file home in. Safest all round, in the long run. There might come sound and fury from First Desk, but any official action would involve admitting a file had been leaked, which would be an embarrassment. So yes: they could make use of Malcolm's brand new envelope and wash their hands of this before things went too far. And then settle back into their established torpor; Malcolm inwardly seething about the derailment of his career; Griselda suffering in silence, they way she'd learned to do the hard way. *Don't make waves.*

All of which meant, she realised, that she'd accepted that the file was real; that it was Monochrome business, and not a red herring. Which meant, in turn, that reviewing the file was part of her job. And whatever else she was, or had been, Griselda Fleet was a career civil servant. Doing her job was what kept her lights on.

That was a good reason. She could find another, if necessary.

She reached out and took the thin bundle between finger and thumb, as if trying to gauge its importance by touch alone, but this was only delaying the moment. Malcolm had removed his glasses and was polishing them on the thick end of his tie, but his gaze remained upon her. Somewhere inside that petulant, uptight young man was an arrogant arsehole trying to get out. She hoped she wouldn't regret extending it a helping hand.

She sighed. "You win."

He raised an eyebrow.

"Let's do our job," she said.

Hours later—dark had fallen again; rain come and gone—after Malcolm had made the eight-minute dash to the office supplies shop; after he'd asked for change for the photocopier to be told, with a roll of the eyes, that it took cards, like; after he'd fed classified documents through a public machine to see seven copies emerge, collated and stapled; after he'd inevitably caught a glimpse of the contents, because he was a reader, and this was what readers did, they looked at a page of text and absorbed a quantity of it without meaning to; after he'd made the eleven-minute dash back to the office, a little more out of breath, and inevitably weaving webs on his way around the slivers of information he'd absorbed, about *Alison North*, about *Brinsley Miles*; after he'd packed the copies into the envelopes he'd bought and booked the usual courier for an early pick-up and delivery (a one-man band, chosen for his cheapness, he didn't operate after six); after they'd sat down again and leafed through separate copies of the file together; after it had become clear that here at last—at last—was evidence of serious wrongdoing by officers of the Service; after he'd collected himself a little, and sat quietly and drunk a cup of tea, reflecting that for all his bravado it was Griselda who'd made this happen, which triggered a squirt of extra shame at his earlier thoughts about her; after he'd decided that she might possibly have her own reasons for acting but that this hardly mattered, because everyone had an agenda; after he'd packed up at last and headed home, giving Clive a cheery good-bye, because they were all in this together; after he'd at last closed his eyes and—to what would have been his great surprise, had he been awake to notice it—fallen asleep with barely a murmur; after all this—after all this—wheels were set in motion by text and phone call and burn-after-reading email, and before the day was done the OTIS file had begun its work, the way a fuse ignites and consumes itself before creating wider damage.

That was the night before the night the team came for Max Janáček, invading his Devon fastness.

The worst smell in the world is dead badger.

PART THREE:

LONDON, NOW

She knew who was calling before she reached for her mobile, an intuition confirmed when her screen proved blank—no "Private number," no "Unknown caller;" just the gif of a ringing phone. Nobody on the line.

Except, of course, there was somebody on the line.

"Shelley."

"Ma'am."

First Desk didn't insist on "ma'am," but it was accepted office code: if you were pissed off, or a lickspittle, that was what you called her.

Shelley wasn't a lickspittle.

"How's the leg?"

"Same as."

"No improvement, then?"

It sounded to Shelley like she was reading off a script. "I have my weekly PT session tomorrow. I'm sure you'll have the report before I've done my laces up."

"Much more of the attitude and I'll have it before you've untied them. If I make myself clear."

Yeah, she did. First Desk didn't need to put a spin on Shelley's medical assessment. She could decide in advance what that assessment would say.

"How can I help you this morning?"

"That's better. I've been hearing strange stories, which are my least favourite kind. Concerning Max Janáček. One of yours, if I'm not mistaken."

"Formerly one of mine. He was reassigned to John Bachelor."

"Being reassigned to John Bachelor ought to be some kind of euphemism," said First Desk. "Like being sent to Coventry. You know, having no one pay attention to you, or call you up. Or do their job."

"I can't be held responsible for what happens while I'm on medical leave."

"Yes, that sounds like it would be fair, doesn't it?"

". . . What happened?"

"An attempted abduction, by the look of things."

"Attempted?"

"Best guess is he, ah, thwarted the bad actors. But he's no longer on the scene."

"Well he wouldn't be, would he? In the circumstances."

In the event of enemy action, evade and drop from sight. That was actually written down somewhere, presumably to offset the chance that it wouldn't occur to anyone to do precisely that.

"And then contact your friendly," said First Desk. "Isn't that how the leg-it rule concludes?"

"I'm no longer his friendly," Shelley said. "As we've established. I went on medical leave, and Bachelor took over."

"And a quick glance at the contact logs indicates that Bachelor has had about as much hands-on time with Janáček as I've had with Vladimir Putin. So if Janáček goes looking for a friendly face, who's he most likely to pick? You or Bachelor?"

"We were never that close," said Shelley. She allowed her face to go misty, as if she were dissolving into a flashback. It was best to adopt the expression your listener might expect to see. "It was all checklist stuff, the usual questions. Any odd encounters, any strange phone calls? Won any competitions you didn't enter?"

"And nothing flagged up?"

"If it had done, you'd have known about it at the time. I haven't seen Max since the accident. Since when, I've been—"

"On medical leave, yes. I remember."

"Once a month I did the duty run, and that was a long slog, let me tell you. North Devon might not be the North Pole. But it's not Clapham, either."

"You have the Service's gratitude for doing the job you were paid to do. Up until you stopped doing it. And he never mentioned anything to frighten the horses?"

"Not even to worry them. What sort of evidence was left behind?"

"Well, that would be need-to-know, Shelley. And you're not so much need-to-know as can't-be-arsed."

Shelley reached for the cigarettes on the floor by her chair before remembering they weren't there, and hadn't been for twenty-two days and eleven hours. "Thank you. I'll add that to the contact diary I'm keeping. You know, for the tribunal hearing."

"If you don't have it on tape, it wasn't said. Isn't that a proverb or something?"

"Is there anything else I can help you with?"

"Yes. You can give me an assurance that if Max Janáček makes contact with you, in any way, shape or form—and I'm including having a dream about him—you'll let the Park know before it's finished happening."

"Duly noted."

"I won't spell out the consequences of your failing to do so."

"That's big of you, ma'am."

"Yes, that's the reason I'm so popular."

Reluctant as Shelley was to allow her boss the last word, it's always satisfying to disconnect first, so that's what she did.

Putting away her phone, she said, "Well, didn't take her long, did it?"

Max nodded thoughtfully.

I'm looking forward to signing her leaving card, thought First Desk. In front of her, along with the day's ongoing clutter—coffee cups and scribbled notes; a tube of hand lotion; minutes awaiting signature—lay a folder thicker than it had any business being. Normally she'd access personnel records digitally, but there were medical documents attached to this one which it would breach data regulations to do so, she'd been told. Just one of the many irritations that cropped up whenever this individual required attention.

Shelley McVie, attached to Housekeeping in the section unofficially known as the milkmen, whose role it was to offer care and support to clapped-out spooks.

And please please somebody complain about that, she thought. Milk*men*. Somebody please make an official complaint. I could do with a stressbusting encounter, and I will squeeze you like an orange.

There was a photo on the inside cover of McVie's file, of course, alongside the usual statistics—height, weight, hair/eye colour, de-dah de-dah—to rehearse which would doubtless come under the heading of Objectification. Besides, what mattered was the medical leave McVie had been on for the past eight months; medical leave First Desk had long suspected was fraudulent. What was "ghost pain," for pity's sake, beyond being irreducible to blunt diagnosis? Didn't show up on an X-ray, didn't respond to treatment. Like those phantom ailments children invent for their imaginary friends, to score a day off school. Any other line of work she'd have been put out to pasture, and good bloody riddance. But she'd been canny enough to cotton on to some small type in the employee regs, so here we were, eight months later, with McVie still on full salary, still absent from duty, and a hell of a bigger pain in First Desk's arse than anything currently afflicting her own limbs. She snapped the folder shut.

Paperclipped to the cover was a page from a memo pad: "Ask about her bloody leg."

"Shall I return that to—"

"Yes! No." She allowed herself a weary moment, during which her laptop pinged a notification: Limitations meeting. One hour. "You'll only have to fetch it up again next time she's given a pass by her physio. Which will be tomorrow."

Hari tucked the file under his arm, and made no movement towards the door. He'd grown to recognise those moments when First Desk needed to vent, and every time he was present when it happened, it bolstered his position. Everybody in power needs someone to confide in. Be on the right side of the door when that happened, you became indispensable.

"A work-related injury, I could get behind that," First Desk said. She was staring through her glass wall at the boys and girls on the hub, whose own injuries rarely amounted to more than a stubbed thumb, but who monitored the doings of agents in the field, who daily faced the possibility of life-altering damage, and pain, and death. "But her work consisted of making cups of tea for pensioned-off joes and listening to their war stories while eating biscuits. If she was claiming to have contracted diabetes, she might have a point."

"So it wasn't line of duty?"

"We're supposed to agree it was. But what happened was she fell and broke her leg leaving a client's premises, and instead of being treated to a slow handclap by those of us who can walk down a staircase without injury, she now has a union rep threatening civil action if we dare suggest she's not in line for a Victoria Cross, or contact her about anything other than her salary and benefits without a damn good reason. And I have to remember to ask about her fucking leg every time we speak."

". . . She has a union rep?"

"Don't even think about it." First Desk closed her eyes briefly, trying to dispel an unpleasant memory. "Three years ago, some bright bulb in HR decided to re-employ most of Housekeeping, including all milkmen, under fixed-hour contracts with a direct line of report to Cornwell House."

Cornwell House was the mothership for auxiliary staff, whose security clearance was second level at best.

"Which means, it has since turned out, that there's wiggle room in their Terms & Conditions. So yes, Shelley McVie has access to a union rep. You, on the other hand, work inside this building, which means if you break your leg, I can have you shot."

Besides which, as Hari almost certainly knew—though it remained officially an off-the-corridors topic—Cornwell House, along with the rest of Housekeeping, completed its transfer under the so-called Green Shoots initiative in six weeks. Though still under government control it would have "independent fiscal identity," meaning, among other things, that any outstanding claims against it had to be settled before then. One way or another, Shelley McVie's grievance didn't have long to run.

Bright enough not to raise a topic guaranteed to boil blood, Hari said, instead, "If she's faking injury, why not have someone spy on her?"

"Assign her a full-time surveillance crew? You think we're made of money? And now you've had your fun, could you get on with some work? I want last quarter's inter-agency co-operation stats updated and distributed to all Second Desks by sixteen hundred."

"Yes, ma'am."

"And any word that comes in on Janáček reaches me the moment afterwards."

"Yes, ma'am. Do you want police forces briefed?"

"No. He might just be counting the dozens." It was an

old-school phrase. "Making sure his tail's clear," she clarified. "Sometimes a bad actor will flush a joe just to find out who his handler is. Because nine times out of ten, that's who the joe runs to."

"And the bad guys follow him."

"So he counts the dozens, which means waiting twelve hours, or twenty-four, before reaching out to his friendly. His handler. To make sure he's alone."

"You think that's what he's doing?"

"It's possible. Whatever happened happened the night before last, so he's had time to count down the clock. And Janáček doesn't have a handler, but old habits die hard." It was an irritation was what it was. Some ancient neighbour had made a phone call to the local cops about night-time disturbances, which had triggered an alarm on the hub. All over the country there were clapped-out spooks haunting little houses, and on top of everything else on her plate, First Desk had to ensure that any time a bell rang, it didn't mean that one or other had had the past reach out to claim them. Which was barely credible in this case. Janáček was of zero significance: Why would anyone target him? He'd had some friends round, it had got rowdy, they were now touring the local cathouses. "On the other hand, we don't know for sure he's been targeted. He might just owe money to a neighbouring hard case, so let's keep an open mind, shall we?"

"It's an education, ma'am."

"Don't push your luck."

"One more thing, your new PS starts tonight. She's called—"

"Can she shoot straight?"

"I believe so."

"Then I don't need to know her name. Thank you. That'll be all."

So Hari disappeared in a flurry of efficiency, leaving First Desk to gaze at the closing door. She liked Hari, but if much more venting went on in his presence, she'd have to get rid of him. The last thing a First Desk needed was someone who'd witnessed her frustrated moments. She remembered—what was her name?—Erin Grey; another promising Personal Friday, who'd seen and heard too much for comfort, so ended up in the archive. That seemed appropriate. The archive was where you put things you wanted to forget.

There were days, she reflected, where you'd put everything there if you could.

"You taking anything for that?"

Max indicated Shelley's leg.

"Just over the counter stuff."

"I'd have thought you'd want something stronger."

She shrugged.

Jesus. You could drop hints, or you could start chopping trees down. "Because I would. If I'd recently been wrestling motorbikes."

"Do you want some aspirin, Max? Or a drink?"

"That's kind. Both, thanks. Yes."

It had been the night before last, but the memory lingered, mostly in his joints. After recovering his back-up car from Neezer he'd driven to Birmingham, taking it slowly, which attracted attention on the motorway but enabled him to gauge who was simply pissed off with his caution, and who—if anyone—wanted to know where he was going. But any eyes on him showed only the blunt contempt of the road-user for the speed bump. Once in the city he'd gone to ground in the traditional way. There were hotels where they gave you a robe, hotels where they didn't give you a robe, and hotels where, if they did give you a robe, you wouldn't want to wear it, and Max found one of these a few streets away from the Bullring, checking in as Ernest Bowman.

He'd come this close to writing *Blofeld*. The rest of the day he'd spent holed up, thinking through possibilities. All of them began in the past, and none gave a clue to the future. He had a passport and a flight fund; he could cab to the airport and lose himself abroad. But he was getting too old and too sore to do that. He was a man who walked country lanes, beheading dandelions with a stick. Or at least, that's who he'd been for so long, he didn't much fancy pretending to be anyone else.

Whoever had come for him, it hadn't been the Park. If the Park wanted him it could issue an invitation, and once he'd arrived, drop him down a well. There'd be no need for nocturnal shenanigans.

On the other hand, given that they'd known where to find him, it was likely his night-time visitors had a source in the Service. Which ruled the Park out as a place of comfort, at least for the time being.

Shelley limped back with whisky and two glasses. Her cane—which had a crooked handle in the shape of a wolf's head, and was evidently from an outdoor goods shop rather than a medical facility—leaned against her chair. He didn't know her well, and they'd only slept together once. That had been, what, three years ago? He remembered it was their second meeting, and she'd made some grousy comment about the distance she'd had to travel; about how Devon got farther away the more you drove towards it. Afterwards, in bed, he'd said something about hoping it had been worth the journey, but she just grunted.

"So," she said now, sitting back in her chair. "It's not the Park looking for you."

"Unless that was a double bluff."

"Nah. She's capable of subtlety, I'll give her that, but if it's her who's gunning for you, and she thought I was involved, she'd send the heavies round on principle." She poured whisky into both glasses and passed him one. Or outstretched an arm; Max had to lever himself up from the sofa to collect it. He felt bruised all over. Nobody told you what a drag it was, getting older. Or at least, people did tell you, but you ignored them, because they were old. "Even so," she continued. "It wasn't a bright idea, coming here. It's the first place a professional would look."

"They weren't professional."

"You said they came kitted out. Tasers. Doesn't sound like your average gangbanger."

"Professional in the sense they were paid," Max admitted. "But they didn't have a clue." He took a sip of whisky: it tasted really really cheap. "I shouldn't have got out. They should have had me hogtied on the garden path." He leaned back again. "No, they weren't Service. Not ours, not anyone's."

Because he'd been thinking about this; in that cheap hotel room in Birmingham; on the drive into Oxford, where he'd shed the car, this time for good; on the train into London, where he'd played catch-me-first on the underground for half an afternoon. Professionals don't burst into tears when you punch them in the face, not even after you've bitten the tip of their nose off. Professionals don't flinch in the dark when you lob a rock their way. They let it bounce off them while tracking its trajectory in reverse.

He'd put the flight kit to use by then: his eyes were now a noticeable blue, and his hair and trimmed beard leaning towards brown. He still looked like Max, but was now trying to look like he didn't. On the other hand, given that he wasn't actually Max to begin with, it was possible the disguise was a roaring success. Anyway, whoever he was, there'd been nobody following him on the tube; no one collecting his movements on CCTV, feeding his image into software. No: in place of that, there was someone who'd hired goons to—what? That remained obscure. Kill him or snatch him, he couldn't say. But at this stage, the Who was more important.

Cheap or not, the whisky was doing its work. A couple of aspirin didn't hurt either.

She might have read his mind. "So now we've established that whatever's going on it's not the Park, maybe you should plan your next move?"

"Anyone would think you wanted rid of me."

"I'm not your handler, Max. I was your milkman, and I'm not even that any more. Medical leave, remember? Your file was handed over to—"

"John Bachelor."

"John Bachelor, who may not be the most reliable card in the deck—"

"But is possibly the drunkest."

"—but he does have this advantage, he is now on your case. And I'm not."

Max said, "I met him once. After that, we had an arrangement. I'd sign off on his feedback forms, he'd send me twenty per cent of his fee."

"Very sackable. Very."

"The risk was all his, and I guess he drank enough to put it out of mind. Besides, no one ever found out."

"Until now."

"The point is, I barely know him and I don't trust him. Inasmuch as all I do know about him is, he can't be trusted."

"And you trust me? That's sweet."

"I barely know you either. Though we did have a moment, I recall."

She said, "Max, that's history. Shouldn't have happened, and I think we agreed to pretend it never did."

"I've got no intention of making your life difficult." He kept his gaze steady, resting his glass on the arm of his chair. "Not when you have so much to deal with already."

"Well, just being here—"

"And I'll be long gone before he gets home. What's his name, by the way?"

She paused. "Graham."

"Graham. And is Graham in the business?"

"God, no. He works for Network Rail."

"Really? That's interesting. Maybe I'll stay and have a chat after all." He leaned forward, confidentially. "Did I ever tell you, my cottage is near the steepest rail incline in the country?"

"You're not chatting with him. Not about anything."

"Don't worry. Train talk only. It's unlikely our long-ago dalliance will come up." Max sat back. "Could I have another shot of this filthy whisky? I might be developing a taste."

She waited him out, her face a hard mask.

He said, "All I want to know is who might have accessed my records recently."

"I am not on good terms with the Park. As you might have noticed."

"But you're not based at the Park any more. You're at, where is it? Cornwell House? Just check my records. That's all I'm asking."

"You make it sound simple. It's not as easy as all that."

"Let's do it on the honour system, then. I'm always told how good you Brits are at that. Do your best, that's all I'll ask. Do your best, and I'll be long gone before Graham gets back. And all memories of our indiscretion will remain forever sealed."

"I'm telling you, they won't even let me in the building."

"Won't know until you try."

"And even if they do—"

"Shelley. Give it a go, yes? And then I'm out of your hair."

He counted to thirteen in his head before she made her response.

Big number. But it was the answer he wanted, which was the main thing.

There had been a time when they were an excuse to leave the building, but more frequently now, gatherings of the Limitations Committee —the Park's fiscal watchdog—happened in Regent's Park itself, in one of the rooms with a view of the outside world: today, bare-limbed trees and leaf-strewn paths; dog walkers, traffic wardens, grown men on electric scooters. First Desk sat with her back to this, partly because she liked to know who spent more time on the view than the agenda, and partly because this was where the best chair was. One or two had dodgy height-adjustment controls, and she didn't relish the indignity of attempting to raise or lower the seat in front of witnesses.

Oliver Nash was leading the meeting. He had either lost a little weight or found a better tailor, and either way wasn't enjoying it as much as he ought to, never a good sign in a man who steered a budgetary oversight committee. His discomfort wasn't difficult to parse. That Nash was a Park supporter had never been in doubt—it was he who had decided that this was a more fitting venue than a Whitehall conference room, largely because it allowed him to visit the hub afterwards, and enjoy a moment on Spook Street—but he was, for all that, embedded in the bureaucratic machinery of government, and never likely to bring it grinding to a halt. On the contrary, he was here to implement official whims, and being clubbable, approachable and generally less apt to bite your hand off by way of friendly greeting, had more support on the committee than First Desk. Besides, the committee as a whole wasn't exactly composed of free thinkers. One or two were capable of independent thought, but when the whip came down, none would throw themselves in front of a foregone conclusion. All over Whitehall, the matchstick remains of once-promising careers warned of the consequences of doing that.

When the room was full and the door closed, there was the usual four-minute mêlée while the weather and the headlines were given a going-over before the meeting settled onto familiar tracks: previous minutes approved; the first quarter's overspend projections delivered; the current hiring freeze of admin and support staff renewed. Through all this, First Desk sat on her hands. *I sought this job to serve the Service*, she thought. *Not to oversee its slow dismantlement.* The occasional glance came her way, devoid of sympathy. No one in the room was glad about these embarrassments, but all had more sense than to make First Desk an object of pity.

The third item on the agenda was what she was saving her powder for. Green Shoots: an update.

Oliver's voice, on cruise control until now, changed register slightly. She guessed, had the opportunity arisen, he'd have gone a stage further and put body armour on. "Item three, people. Following the successful ongoing transition of Housekeeping to a more, ah, market-driven system, Cabinet has agreed that vetting procedures and background checking, that is to say, the work generally falling under Landscaping's remit, should be the next area looked at in terms of streamlining and associated costs-savings, part of what we're calling the Green Shoots initiative. The prime interest here is coming once again from Fabian de Vries, who you might remember showed interest in Housekeeping, but ultimately decided to stay his hand given Cabinet's decision not to allow any individual to have a majority share in more than one decentralised department. Most likely under his aegis, then, but always allowing for another contender to materialise, we're considering, as with the previous procedure, an eighteen-month hand-over period, during which initial difficulties can be resolved, and long-term issues identified. Everyone on board with that? Good. On to item four, then."

Instead of laughter, this was followed by an expectant hush, broken only by the squeaking of chair legs against the floor, as one less than tactful member pushed himself away from the table to get a better view of upcoming entertainment.

Which took the form of a query from First Desk. "'Successful'?"

"... I'm sorry?"

"I'm sure you are, Oliver, but that's by the by. No, you described the transition of Housekeeping duties as having been 'successful.' I'm wondering what criteria you're adopting to arrive at that conclusion. If they involve the late or non-existent provision of goods and services, then yes, I'd be the first to agree, the new dispensation is proving something of a smash hit. If, on the other hand, you bend towards the notion that success requires, at a bare minimum, the fulfilment of promises made and undertakings given, then your use of the word stems from either a woeful ignorance of the situation or a wilful distortion of the true state of affairs. Which is it?"

"I'm aware, as we all are, of teething problems, but—"

"*Teething* problems? We're talking major dental work here. The delivery of services we once took for granted has become non-existent or farcically inadequate, and this isn't simply a matter of inconvenience. Without the necessary support structures in place, the smooth running of the Park, and by implication the security of the nation itself, becomes problematic. Put at its simplest, Oliver, and to pluck three examples at random, the Park requires fully functioning laser printers, it needs vending machines, it *crucially*—and when I say crucially, I'm speaking as someone who attends COBRA meetings and has War Room access, so I know what I'm talking about—it is *crucially* in need of secure waste disposal, because when classified material's being disposed of, we'd all sleep better if we knew it wasn't being recycled. Which is what happened last month, Oliver. Shredded material was taken from the Park and delivered, not to a destruction facility as laid down in the legally binding transition protocols, but to a recycling plant. Do you want to dismiss that as a minor inconvenience?"

"I'm sure it was an oversight with no serious consequences."

"Are you, Oliver? Are you *very* sure? And—forgive me for banging on about this, but it strikes me as important, for some reason—how sure would you say is sure enough? Bearing in mind that if there do turn out to be serious consequences, those consequences could quite literally be devastating? In the sense of 'causing devastation'?"

"I think you're overstating the case."

"And I think you're underestimating the damage already done with this ludicrous and ill-thought-out privatisation scheme."

"We're not calling it—"

"I know we're not calling it privatisation, but that doesn't alter the case. Now, as it happens, De Vries's interest in taking on Landscaping is on the wane, but be that as it may, the fact remains, we're looking at divesting the Service of what could be, in the wrong hands, a saleable commodity—information about many hundreds of our own citizens. And where's it going to end, Oliver? Shall we scrap what's left of our front line operatives and start hiring whoever's cheapest? Maybe WeWork will diversify from office space to office drones, and we could sack the boys and girls on the hub, replace them with school-leavers. Because that would save us money in the short term, whatever it costs in the end. Which will be our national security. Feel free to pass that back to Cabinet. If anyone there's listening to advice, that is, and not just skimming the situations vacant columns."

Nash, who had already raised one eyebrow, raised the other. "I'm not sure where your information regarding De Vries's change of heart comes from, and maybe we'll discuss that later. In the meantime, we all appreciate your strong feelings on the matter, but there's no need to descend into abuse."

"We'll have to agree to differ on that."

"No, that's not how this works. This is a difficult time, but we have to work together. Believe it or not, I have the Park's best interests at heart. We weather this storm together, salvaging what we can, and in calmer times we can set about rebuilding our vessel. But meantime we have to tread delicately. Let's not forget that there's still an inquiry under way, one whose eventual report—"

"Monochrome is a waste of time."

"I know that that's the general feeling, but it's also the case that the very fact that it's sitting, the very fact that the government chose to initiate such an inquiry, is indicative that the Park is not in good odour. And I'm not giving away secrets when I say that it hasn't been since the Westacres bombing."

"Before my time as First Desk."

"But very much during your time as an active and senior figure with the Service." He looked disappointed. "And I didn't think that weasel words were quite your style."

First Desk, in fact, looked shamefaced; a new experience for everyone in the room. "No. That was wrong of me."

"Graciously said. And besides all that, I took a call from Sir Winston this morning, as it happens." He added an explanatory footnote: "Sir Winston is chairing Monochrome." Everyone already knew this, though it was possible some had forgotten. "It seems there's been a, ah, let's call it an *upgrading* of the material falling into Monochrome's purview."

Experienced First Desk watchers noticed her go into alert mode, though this was outwardly signalled by nothing more than an impatient twitch of the nose. "Meaning what, exactly?" Her tone suggested that whatever the answer was, it would be an irritation on a level with a broken fingernail or lost comb.

"Meaning that a Regent's Park file has come into their possession, though he wasn't clear how this came to be. He was seeking clarification as to the legality of subjecting it to examination."

"I see. And your advice was?"

"I didn't provide any. I'm not that foolish."

"I'm glad to hear it." Every pair of eyes in the room was on First Desk. She said, "The independence of a government-sanctioned inquiry is, of course, sacrosanct. However, we will need to be clear as to the provenance of the file you're talking about. There'd be little point in Monochrome bringing its mighty wisdom to bear on fake news."

"As you say. But in the meantime, fake or not, it's in Monochrome's hands, and Sir Winston has informed me that tomorrow's session has been brought forward to this afternoon. I can only assume that at least some panel members intend to treat the file as legitimate evidence. But this isn't really on our agenda. Shall we move on?"

There was a pause, as if all those around the table had momentarily failed to realise that this, coming from the chair, was a rhetorical question.

"Of course," said First Desk. "Back to item three, then."

"Well, perhaps a refreshment break first," said Nash.

Cornwell House, in an ideal world, would have gateposts and pillars, and ornamental pineapples set in niches either side of its front doors, which would be reached by ascending stone steps. Instead, it's a modern four-storey brick building squeezed between two more venerable institutions down a narrow lane behind Mansion House. The lane is cobbled, the pavements uneven, and the facing wall of a severe and dirty stone, studded on top with broken glass. Shelley had no idea what lay behind this: magical garden or private zoo—in London anything was possible, and grew more so the nearer the river you got.

She was still inwardly cursing Max Janáček when she arrived, and buzzed herself through the single-width glass front door with her employee card. Her place of employment was nowhere she wanted to be, even more so now she was on sick leave than when she'd been working. And what was she supposed to achieve, anyway? Her instructions were clear enough—"And use a little discretion, yes?" Max had said—but had he ever met her colleagues? They were presumably capable of discretion when discussing their STDs with their doctors, or hiring hitmen, but in most other circumstances experience suggested otherwise. By the time she was hobbling back up the lane, her surprise appearance would be the sole topic of conversation on the premises, and every word she'd uttered would have been parsed within a syllable of its life.

On the other hand, her marriage. Maybe not perfect—and Max hadn't been her first peccadillo—but she'd been making an effort lately, above and beyond the confinement her injury had imposed. Graham was a sweet man, and they'd been together twelve years, a record worth persevering with. She was done with adventures, and wanted him to remain part of her life; nor did she want to spend great chunks of that life apologising for past misdeeds. And even sweet men hired lawyers. No, she didn't want Max spilling beans to her husband, and while part of her thought Max might be bluffing, she wasn't confident enough of that to take risks. So here she was in

Cornwell House for the first time in months, tucking her card into her pocket and reacquainting herself with her environment.

Which on this level consisted of a foyer the size of a market barrow, hosting only a lift decorated with an Out of Order sign, and a staircase that wrapped around the lift shaft and was steeper than at first appeared. For a moment Shelley stared at the sign, which had an air of permanence, then at the security camera above the door, giving a fish-eye view of her mood to someone, somewhere. "Fuck that," she mouthed, adding a two-fingered salute in case whoever's lip-reading skills weren't up to speed. Holding her cane like a ski pole she began her assault on the stairs, pausing on a tiny landing to find a brush in her bag and do her hair. First rule when breaching enemy territory: look like you mean business.

Upstairs, through architectural sleight of hand, the floor space achieved more depth: a narrow open-plan office accommodated eight workstations, none of which had ever housed Shelley. Milkmen were peripatetic workers, or so designated: "No need for you to put down roots, dear," as her line manager had expressed it. "You can hot-desk as and when." Instead of actual real estate, she'd had a locker big enough to stow roughly half of what she carried about on a daily basis, and a hook in the kitchen on which to hang a mug. This had not always been the way—back in the Park she'd had a one-third share of an office, a filing cabinet and a kettle—but the hiving off of the department, though it had promised to be an upgrade—its own premises; more independence; an accelerated promotion structure—had turned out, surprise surprise, to be the prelude to a fundamental restructuring, the full details of which were just coming to light.

As was her line manager, by unhappy chance. Steaming across the floor, threading between the workstations at which Shelley's co-workers—the landlocked brigade, who had responsibility for

procurement, facilities management and various other administrative burdens, but no hands-on client contact—beavered away,
or that was the impression they liked to give. Some among them,
Shelley figured, had more in common with weasels. As for her
line manager, she was more of a badger, if her relentlessly harry-
ing nature was anything to go by. She had Shelley well and truly
in her sights. Her name was Bobbie Lawlor.

"Shelley. I didn't know you were coming in today."

"No . . . I was passing. Osteo appointment nearby. Thought I'd
stick my head round the door."

"I thought it had been agreed that you'd stay away from office
premises until all this . . . has been sorted out."

The word *unpleasantness* was elided, as if the very syllables
were redolent of the situation they applied to.

"Saying hello to colleagues?"

"With whom you've always got on so well."

A snappy comeback was usually desirable in any encounter
with Madame Bobbie. Well, that or knuckledusters. "Being away
for so long, being off sick, you start to miss people, you know?"
Think fast. "I was going to bring some doughnuts in, but they'd
run out."

She was spotting faces in the background: Pete, Martin,
Lizzie, Glen, Zadie—Zadie! Zadie wasn't so bad. She could
talk to Zadie. And then, in the background to the background,
something else: the view from the rear of the building offered
a partial glimpse of Tower Bridge, but that sliver of postcard
London was obscured today by a piece of hardwood fastened
over a section of window. A man in blue overalls, the global
uniform of the practical class, was measuring the frame and
keying the results on his phone.

"Doughnut World ran out of doughnuts? The situation's more
serious than I'd realised."

Shelley would have made a lousy spy, Shelley decided. She had nothing to offer that except a change of subject: "Someone attempted to escape, I see."

"Ah, gallows humour. The prerogative of the subordinate."

"What happened?"

"A break-in. Nothing to worry about."

"Nothing to worry about?"

"There've been a number of incidents locally. The police are already aware."

"Well, that's a relief. Does being aware of something count as active investigation?"

"Shelley, somebody scaled a wall, broke a window and opened a few drawers. Martin had his squash racket taken and a purse went missing. I'm always telling everyone not to leave valuables in their desks, and I can't be held responsible when instructions are ignored. The window's being fixed, and we can forget all about it. Now, do you want to step back here?" *Here* was where the inoperational lift stood; it was hardly a confessional, but was a mite less public. The same, or a similar, Out of Order notice had been taped to the lift door. Shelley wondered whether Blue Overalls would turn his attention to this next, but it was unlikely he'd get round to it before she had to make the downward journey. "It's as well you put in an appearance," Bobbie continued. "Some things are easier tackled in person."

"Not really here for—"

Riding roughshod was the phrase. "Look, just between us, I hear rumours you're to be offered a pay-off. Little lump sum, easily more than your, er, *injury*'s worth. Just to clear the table before our new overlords move in."

"I'm sure my solicitor—"

"Yes, here's a thing, best not to overburden your solicitor with too many details." Bobbie Lawlor had a look about her, one that suggested she'd faced down big bluffers over smoky card tables. "What I've heard is, the first offer you get will be the last. Hold out for a bigger payoff, and you're likely to find yourself on the wrong side of a professional hardball match. They might just sack you and see how you do on the rebound. Now, if—*if*—a tribunal's satisfied your injury's real, and not the fantasy of a burnout employee who can see her lottery numbers coming up, you could do well out of that. But that's a big if, Shelley. A very big if indeed."

"Is that a threat, Bobbie? Because it certainly sounds like one."

"Not remotely. In fact," and here she touched Shelley lightly on the elbow, "I'm saying this as a colleague and not your line manager. Piece of friendly advice." But it was offered without a smile.

"You're embarrassing me now. I should have made more of an effort to source doughnuts."

"Oh, we're too busy to sit around snacking. In fact, it's probably best if you don't bother your colleagues now. Will you be all right on the stairs with your stick?"

"I can manage."

"Not too much of a disability, then."

"I have a high pain threshold. Makes conversation more bearable. When did it happen, by the way?"

"When did what happen?"

"The break-in."

"Does it matter? A few nights ago. Three."

"Kids, do they reckon?"

"Well it wasn't a pro job. They left glass all over the floor. And a squash racket? Seriously?"

"They didn't take any of the laptops?"

"All securely docked. You'd need a crowbar to release one, and you couldn't do it without breaking the machine. So no, everything's—"

"And nobody's worried that someone might have lifted the *contents* of a laptop?"

Bobbie pursed her lips. "Forgive me. Are you here to bother colleagues, or as a representative of Neighbourhood Watch?"

"It's a legitimate concern, wouldn't you say? Given our client base."

"There's nothing classified on the office laptops, Shelley. The databases contain nothing that would reveal client identities, as you know. If security had been compromised by a childish act of hooliganism, I'd have been the first to raise the alert. But after consideration, I came to the conclusion that there was no sense raising an outcry over a bit of smashed glass. Now. Was there anything else? Because the business of the department continues, with or without your participation."

"Good to know."

Which earned her an impatient *tchah!* that she could still feel protruding from her neck when she reached the bottom of the stairs.

That aside, it was true, she thought, as she limped back up the lane through the drizzle; it was true that the database wouldn't allow a third party to pinpoint the whereabouts of, say, Max Janáček.

On the other hand, it would indicate that said Max Janáček's current milkman was John Bachelor.

And pinpointing Bachelor's location was mostly a matter of finding the nearest pub.

Another rainy afternoon, painting London dismal colours. Tracking along a Shoreditch lane, having treated herself to an overengineered salad from a pop-up booth, Griselda felt her phone buzz.

"I understand you've come into possession of a file."

It was one of the prerogatives of being First Desk that you didn't introduce yourself. "That's correct."

"I'd be interested to know how that happened."

"I wish I could illuminate you. It was . . . wished upon us."

"A fairy godmother?"

"An anonymous donor."

"There's a saying about gifts from mysterious sources. Perhaps the educated Mr. Kyle could quote it for you."

"I'll be sure to ask."

"In the meantime, I'd like that file returned."

"Already done."

She had the pleasure of feeling she'd wrongfooted First Desk. It was doubtful that happened often.

As she reached Bishopsgate a bus blared past, in the way buses did. When you were aboard one, you were mostly aware of halting progress; a series of mini-shuffles between traffic lights. But the ones you observed sailing by when you were on a pavement achieved impressive speeds.

First Desk said, "Right. Yes. I can only assume it's on its way from the mailroom. I take it there's been no distribution of its contents? Yourself, presumably, excepted?"

"Myself and the educated Mr. Kyle."

"I suppose that was unavoidable."

"And Monochrome too, of course."

Which earned her a moment's silence.

Deciding that, since she'd made it she could break it, she said, "Yes, I'm afraid there was an administrative cock-up this end. Before the nature of the file was fully appreciated, our temp had it copied and distributed. So all the panel members are in possession of the contents."

"I wasn't aware you had temps."

"Strictly speaking, we don't. But there was a backlog building, so we borrowed someone from the Home Office. And, well, you know how it is. Sometimes people can be *too* efficient."

The answering silence made her wonder if she'd gone too far, but when the reply came at last, it was wryly delivered. "I can't say I've found that a recurring difficulty. What do you plan to do next?"

"We have an afternoon session, ma'am." No harm in throwing in a little honorific. "Full panel. A witness has been called."

"Yes. Well. Always nice to be kept up to speed." There was another pause while options were audibly weighed. Depending on how close her finger was to the button, First Desk could have a team of Dogs descend on the Monochrome offices before Griselda crossed Bishopsgate. Which would be one way, of course, of revealing how much of a threat OTIS was . . . Besides, threat or not, the simple fact of its being in Monochrome's possession—its having ended up in Malcolm's shopping trolley—must, for a control freak like First Desk, be like having someone go through her shoe collection, mismatching pairs.

Nevertheless, she reached the other side of Bishopsgate unabducted.

First Desk said, "Very well. I'll expect to see the minutes within an hour of the session closing."

"I'm not sure—"

"As for the long-term viability of Monochrome, I suggest you don't get too comfortable. It's not only good things come to an end."

"I'll have Mr. Kyle check the terms and protocols. If it's within our remit, I'll have those minutes dispatched once they're ready."

Her heart was pounding when she ended the call. Sometimes you know you've made an enemy: the anger and bluster leaves you in no doubt. First Desk's calm was a different story. Griselda would have preferred a screaming match.

She was back, and Clive was on his feet to prepare the lift. "Good afternoon, Clive. Everything well?"

"All tickety-boo, Mrs. Fleet. Sir Winston's here first."

"Really?"

"What I said to him. I said, you bucking for a promotion, Sir Winston?" Clive was reaching into the lift, activating the button. "Because you're certainly the eager beaver today."

"And what did he say to that?"

"He said, 'Fifth floor, please.'"

Which was where Griselda found him, in his office, door open. He was holding a stapled stack of papers, seventeen pages thick—not that Griselda could count them, but there was no doubt what the document was. "Can I ask where this file came from?"

"From the Park, Sir Winston. I thought that was clear from the note I circulated."

"But my impression was—the facts definitely were—that we weren't receiving material from the Park. That there was a distinct lack of cooperation from that direction."

Griselda said, "There's evidently been a change of heart. But whatever the reason, we have this new material before us, and access to a new field of inquiry. It would be remiss not to pursue it."

Sir Winston folded his arms, and something about the action

reminded Griselda of the pipe in his pocket—it was the arms themselves, she realised; those and his legs. He was a pipe-cleaner of a man, spindly and archaic. These qualities informed his speech. "It would be equally remiss—nay, it would be illegal, an act of gross folly—to submit a file before the panel which lies outwith our remit. Which is classified material, and subject to the usual restrictions and reservations."

"Classified material falls within our remit. It's there in black and white, Sir Winston. Always has been."

"And yet custom and practice have made it clear that in reality, no such material is ever laid before us."

"Until now. I can only assume that government priorities have changed. Or, indeed, Regent's Park's."

"Perhaps it would be best to await clarification on the matter before going into session."

"I've just spoken to First Desk, as it happens. She's well aware of our intentions."

"And approves of them?"

"If she didn't," Griselda said, "you can be quite sure she would have made that plain. Besides, we have a witness arriving soon. Everything's under way."

"A witness?"

"Witness number one thirty-seven. With the possibility of another to come."

Sir Winston grunted and rustled the papers in his hand. "If this goes pear-shaped for any reason, there'll be no doubt in my mind who's responsible. And I won't be shy about making my feelings clear."

"That's understood, Sir Winston."

"And this witness will be here this afternoon?"

"Yes," said Griselda. "Funny, isn't it? How it all goes painfully slowly, until it doesn't."

An advantage of having the Limitations Committee meet in the Park was the very short space of time it took to return to her office afterwards. Or on this occasion, during. Having had her say on Green Shoots, First Desk invented an emergency, not caring how transparent this was, and had called Griselda Fleet before reaching the lift, called the post room before the lift arrived, and called the wrath of God down upon the hapless intern who answered. But yes, a package had arrived that morning, and yes, it should have been on her desk two minutes later. However, he'd been placed under strict instruction not to leave the post room unattended for any—

An explanation, or even an excuse, had no doubt been appended to that fragment, but the lift had arrived and First Desk was in it.

The package was on her desk by the time she reached her office, and ten minutes later she was leaning back in her chair, staring at the wall she'd frosted to obscure her view of the hub. Which didn't mean she didn't know who was knocking before she called "Enter."

In the way of young women, Erin Grey had changed since First Desk last laid eyes on her. Her hair she now wore in an intricate plait, currently draped over her left shoulder. She wore glasses, too, which was also new, though might be an affectation. Shifting identities—changing cover—wasn't solely a Spook Street preoccupation, and the young could do so without inviting suspicion. Were First Desk to follow suit, a crisis would be diagnosed, whether personal or geopolitical.

"Nice to see you, Erin. How have you been?"

"I—good. Yes, thank you, ma'am, I've been fine. How about you?"

"I've been First Desk. Maybe you remember the symptoms. Constant stream of headaches, constant pains in the arse. Case in point." She tapped the OTIS file on the desk in front of her. "Look familiar? Close the door."

Erin Grey did so, and stepped farther into the room, glancing at the visitors' chair, in which she was not asked to sit. She looked thoughtful.

"That wasn't an invitation to ponder the great mysteries," First Desk said. "It was a question. You've been working the archive. Does this look familiar?"

"It's a file. I can't tell one from another."

"No, but luckily it has a catalogue number stamped on it. Does that help?"

Erin said, "I can tell you it's high clearance, and not far pre-digital. In fact, if the compression programme starts up again, it could well be in the first batch—"

"I'd hate to get the idea you're prevaricating. That might make me think you've something to hide. Let's start with first principles. How in the name of John le fucking Carré can Service product go walkabout?"

"It can't."

"And yet here we are."

Erin said, "I meant, it couldn't be taken other than with permission of the archivist."

"And how often is that granted?"

"All the time. There are always studies going on, historical reappraisals, material required for training purposes. A whole shelfload of material was sent to Oxford just last week."

Oxford, shorthand for the Spooks' College.

"Could this have been part of that consignment?"

"Yes."

"But you're not sure."

"I wasn't involved. You'd need to ask the archivist."

"Oh, believe me," said First Desk. "I'll be doing that."

Erin turned to go, but before she reached the door, First Desk said, "Erin? That folder you prepared. On Green Shoots."

"Yes, ma'am?"

"It proved useful."

Erin nodded.

Once she'd left, First Desk laid her hand flat on the OTIS file, for all the world as if trying to secure its contents. It wasn't often she had the feeling of being on the outside looking in, and she didn't enjoy it. Then again, whoever had put this game in motion wouldn't enjoy it much longer either—she'd just had a text from the Chancellor fulfilling a promise: Monochrome would be history by the end of the day. Which didn't mean First Desk wouldn't find whoever was responsible for the leak and mush them into a paste. That thought left her smiling as she reached for the button that unfrosted her glass wall and allowed light from the hub to spill into her office, moving nothing, but subtly rearranging it all.

"Might I ask that we lower the blinds?"

No one responded to this at first, perhaps because no one was sure to whom the request was addressed. This silence didn't faze the witness, who sat pleasantly, awaiting a herd decision. She seemed aware that, having fallen into the embrace of a committee, no conclusions could be swiftly reached.

At last Griselda said, "Is the . . . light bothering you?"

There was no light, or only little. A grey luminescence smudging the window was more a reminder that darkness would fall than that daylight had settled. At times like this, Monochrome seemed aptly named.

"I just feel it would be more appropriate, somehow."

Sir Winston cleared his throat. Singer and Moore exchanged a glance.

Griselda said, "Malcolm, would you . . . ?"

He scraped his chair leg across the floor in rising, making his acquiescence appear sullen. "Sorry. That wasn't . . ." He moved down the row of windows, lowering then slightly angling the slats, so that a hint of the day painted the room in horizontal stripes. He then made to adjust the overhead lighting in compensation, but the witness demurred.

"Could we leave that as it is? Thank you."

Malcolm hesitated for a moment, awaiting confirmation from Griselda which did not come, and dialled the dimmer switch back to where it had been.

With the lighting adjusted the witness relaxed a little, though was aware that few present would have registered change in her demeanour. There were benefits, there were advantages, to her appearance. And while no introductions had been made—protocol, apparently—she'd done her research, and identified those she was facing. The young man who had adjusted the blinds, "Malcolm": he was Malcolm Kyle. The Black woman was Griselda Fleet, the Brown woman Shirin Mansoor, so the white woman was Deborah Ford-Lodge. These last two, in fact, were familiar faces, frequently appearing on different pages of the same newspapers. Of the balding self-important men it was easy enough to pick out Sir Winston Day, which meant that one of the others was John Moore and the other Guy Fielding. It probably didn't matter that she couldn't tell them apart; she suspected that long acquaintanceship wouldn't necessarily make that task easier. Carl Singer, though, was also a face weathered by newsprint and pixel, and one that had possibly had a little work done. This observation the witness made with no sense of judgement. That we create our own masks was a truth she'd long accepted.

But it was time to get down to it. Ms. Fleet was initiating proceedings, such initiation involving the usual boilerplate attending classified proceedings. Important nonetheless. Listen. "Just

to ensure that the members attending are familiar with the protocol governing today's session, which we've not had occasion
to invoke before, we should start by stating for the record that,
in accordance with Standing Regulation 14.10.04, we will be
addressing you throughout by the workname you were assigned
during the operation under discussion. Similarly, any agents or
operatives mentioned before this panel who are alive and still
in the employ of the intelligence services will also be referred
to by the worknames they were assigned during the operation
under discussion. Are you comfortable with that?"

She said, "And if I weren't, would my discomfort override
Standing Regulation 14.10.04?"

"I'm afraid that question requires a yes/no answer."

"Which leaves me sorely tempted to reply yes/no. All right,
all right. Yes. I'm comfortable with that."

She hadn't even earned a hard stare. Fleet's eyes remained
focused on the notepad in front of her; the pen in her hand, which
had remained poised over the paper while the above exchange
endured, now made its mark.

Malcolm Kyle shifted in his chair. "For the benefit of the
panel," he murmured, in an undertone honed to perfection in a
series of wood-panelled offices. His shoes, she imagined, would
be buffed to mirrordom.

"Yes, quite. For the benefit of the panel, could we ask you to
state that name clearly, please?"

"You're asking me to cast my mind back quite some way."

Fleet looked up. Again, you couldn't call it a hard stare. Nevertheless, her gaze met the witness's with unflinching directness.
"Perhaps we could establish, before we go any farther," she said, "that
the matters under discussion are very serious. In view of your . . .
situation, no one present should be more aware of that than you."

"Thank you for pointing that out."

"So it would be appropriate if these sessions could be conducted in a formal manner."

"'Sessions'?"

"Oh, I doubt very much we'll cover everything this afternoon. You will be required to attend on any further occasions that we stipulate."

So keep the smartarsery under control. Or expect to spend your foreseeable future at our beck and call.

"Of course," she said. And then, rather amused that among her first submissions to Monochrome would be, not only an outright lie, but one that all present recognised as such, said, "My name is Alison North."

"Thank you."

Preliminaries over, it was Sir Winston's turn. "Now, Ms. North. Is there anything you need before we begin? A glass of water, perhaps?"

Or a whole new identity, she thought. A different set of memories. A heightened awareness of when to tell the truth, when to fudge it.

"Oh," she said. "I think I have everything I need."

"Then perhaps we can begin," said Sir Winston Day.

"Please, yes," she said. "Ask away."

"**World's highest** mountain, base to summit? Everest, K2, Mont Blanc or . . . Can't even say it. These proper words or what? Mourner Key?"

"Mauna Kea."

"What I said. Never heard of it. Anyway, s'obvious. Everest."

"I don't think so."

"Nah, you wouldn't, John, because you're an idiot, innit? Any. Fool. Knows"—words punctuated by the slapping of a palm on the keyboard of a pub quiz machine—"the answer's *Everest*."

Lights spun and bloopers blooped, or whatever you might call the electronic flatulence of such a machine when it's declaring an error. It couldn't have been less subtle, thought John Bachelor, if it had blown a dwindling trombone honk, or issued divorce proceedings.

". . . Fuck."

"Like I said—"

"Yeah well *don't* fucking say it again, John. Because nobody likes a fucking . . . speaker."

"Base to summit."

"I don't even know what that fucking means, John. All I know is, this machine's swallowed my fucking money again. Which is why it deserves some of this."

This being a kicking hard enough to have alerted the barman were the kicker in question not someone most barmen would have gone a distance to avoid noticing. He wasn't a big man but didn't need to be, what with the dead eyes, and the way sparks kept popping from his ears, unless they were an optical illusion caused by poorly filtered aggression. In fact, were it not for his accent—pure South London—or the fact that he had several times in John's hearing vouchsafed that he had been born here, lived here all his life, and would go to his fucking *grave* here, know what he meant, John?, John would have had him down as Scottish. He was aware that this might have been viewed as racist in some quarters, but was also aware that those quarters did not include The Fox and Bucket.

"I think it's seen the . . . error of its ways now."

"It's a fucking machine, John. It can't see nothing."

A final kick, and he was done. Scooping up his pint glass, he shambled to a booth in the corner, John tagging along behind.

Tagging along because it was hard to see how he could do otherwise. This is how relationships sometimes worked: you noticed you were in one. Worst case scenario, you were wearing a ring. Other times, like this, you were too many drinks the wrong side of nightfall to do the full diligence, so found yourself brand new friends with unlikely candidates. This afternoon, it was the quiz machine had done the damage. John Bachelor wasn't the sort to feed cash into those things, because by their very nature they were always hard by somewhere he'd rather spend his money, but he was generally prepared to offer advice to those who were. It wasn't that he was a fount of general knowledge. But he had spent a lot of time hanging around quiz machines.

"Come on, John. Get that down you. My shout."

It said a lot about Bachelor's feeling that the day was going sideways that even this, for the moment it took him to finish his beer and push the glass across the table, didn't feel like the clinching argument it so obviously was.

But, he decided, as he watched his new mate stumble to the bar, you couldn't always trust your sense of doom. If you did, you'd never get out of bed, always supposing you were lucky enough to be in one. Besides, sometimes the clues you picked up on, owing to your well-honed ability to read a situation—what with having been fully trained by Regent's Park experts, half a millennium or so ago—turned out to be bent pennies. For example, how his new friend had known he was called John had rung an alarm, given that Bachelor had some while ago ceased giving his actual name to people he met in pubs. But when Sparky—which was what Bachelor was calling him in his head, not having been offered an alternative—also went on to address the barman, two other drinkers, the quiz machine and his own cigarette packet as John, he allowed himself to calm down on that score. Still going to be a long afternoon, though.

"Cheers," he said, when Sparky returned with two pints, only a small amount of each slopping onto the table.

" 'S'all right, innit?" his new friend said obscurely, raising his glass to his mouth.

The Fox and Bucket was mostly empty, which wasn't a huge surprise. As pubs went, it was somewhere between dire and dismal, meaning it entertained locals, but enjoyed visiting custom on a one-time-only basis. John had been among the former for a few weeks now, having put a root down—the situation too precarious for a plural—after acquiring a flatsitting job just that long ago. The owner, acquaintance-of-acquaintance more than friend-of-friend, was working in the States, and wanted someone *in situ* to water plants and feed the cat. John was fine with watering plants, or was when he remembered, but he'd found the cat dead in the bathroom three mornings back. I mean, Jesus, could he ever get a break? Since then he'd been responding to all inquiries about feline health with shameless lies, and planning for an abrupt departure. Not having known what to do with the corpse, and vaguely assuming its owner might want a ceremony of some sort in due course, he'd double-bagged and stashed it in the cloak-cupboard in the hall. That's how nice a flat it was—it had a cloak-cupboard in the hall. But there was no point getting attached: it was unlikely he'd be offered the same gig again. Apart from anything else, there'd be no cat-sitting required.

But for the time being he was a Fox and Bucket local, which was as damning an indictment of his life and career as a long-service medal to a shitshoveller's assistant. Where had it all gone wrong? Where to start? . . . Divorce, the cost of living, the inability to put together a deposit on a rental let alone a mortgage, some seriously bad financial advice capped by worse financial decisions—all in the past, of course, but whoever said there was no point crying over spilt milk hadn't noticed how much milk cost lately. Fact was, it had doubled in price in recent memory, which, if you valued yourself in terms of how much milk you could afford, meant you were worth half as much as previously. So spilling it was heart-breaking, to be honest, and if you couldn't cry when your heart was broken, there was something wrong with you. Any wonder he'd stayed in his seat when a beer was offered? Say what you like about beer, at least you could drink it. Try doing that with spilt milk.

Beer in hand, the world was slightly better. Which wasn't to say there weren't plenty of ways it could still spin out of orbit.

"Hello, John," said Max Janáček, looming out of nowhere. "How've you been?"

"**The events** we're here to discuss took place in the spring of 1994. Obviously we're not expecting you to have total recall of this period, but we would ask you to take care not to embellish your memories. We'd rather have an honest inability to provide accurate minutiae than have you invent detail in an effort to please or impress us."

"I'll make sure I don't go out of my way to do either."

"During the time in question, you'd been working for the Service for less than a year, is that correct?"

"It is."

"And yet you were assigned to Berlin. Was that usual for an agent of such recent standing?"

"No," said Alison. "But then, I wasn't an agent."

This caused a fluttering of brows among the company; a shuffling of paper.

"It would be simpler," she said, "if those listening were *au fait* with the terms in use at the time. Agent was not a word that would be applied, for example, to anyone with a desk job. We were simply officers. Officers of the Service. Agents were those who worked on hostile territory. In Service terms, this meant anywhere outside the Park."

". . . I see. I beg your pardon. Was it usual, then, for an *officer* of your limited experience to be assigned to the Berlin desk, given the importance of that, ah, station?"

"It wasn't unprecedented. I was clerical staff, and every station needs clerks. When permanent staff are on home leave, it's not unusual to have junior-level assistance rotated out to relieve them. But my secondment to Berlin Station wasn't for routine reasons. There were . . . circumstances."

"And they were?"

"Spook flu."

". . . I'm sorry?"

"That was what we called it at the time. A flu bug, a nasty one, came in from Hong Kong or somewhere in that region and laid waste to the Park during March and April of '94. They'd call it SARS if it happened now. It put strong men on their backs. Which meant there were limited numbers of hale, healthy personnel to assign to foreign duties. I wouldn't normally have been in the frame for such an assignment."

"But that aside, such secondments were a familiar method of supplying staff to undertake routine administrative tasks. Tasks that you, if not fully qualified, were at least perfectly competent to undertake."

Alison smiled faintly. "Perfectly competent. Yes."

Singer made a noise that turned into a cough and said, "Excuse me."

"And a routine administrative task is how the secondment was presented at the time."

"Initially, yes."

"Though that was not in fact the case."

"No," said Alison, after a pause. "It wasn't the case."

Finding Bachelor hadn't been the most demanding task. Once Shelley had returned with news of the Cornwell House break-in, he'd persuaded her to do "one last" favour.

"This Zadie . . ."

"What about her?"

"A mate?"

"She's not openly hostile."

Hard to tell whether that was cynical outlook or bald statement of fact, but you played with what you had. "So she'd do you a turn if you asked nicely?"

"Christ, I don't know. She might call in air support. We did lunch a couple of times, that's all. But since *this*"—and she grimaced, pointing at her leg—"I've been made out to be the Wicked Witch of Whatever. No reason to think Zadie feels any different."

But worth, Max thought, finding out.

As things stood, he was as much in the dark as he'd been two nights previously, scrambling down the green lane, but at least it now seemed likely that John Bachelor had been the cause of that particular rollercoaster ride. Bachelor, after all, had known where Max was, which put him in a small group. And while Max didn't know much about Bachelor, he did know this: he'd sell his job for the price of a round.

"Tell her you need a current address for your replacement. That you need to pass on crucial information that's just come to light."

"Like what?"

"Well, I don't know. My birthday?"

She stared.

"Just a thought."

"If I can point you in the right direction, you'll fuck off, yes?"

"Nicely put."

"No hard feelings," she said, fishing out her phone. "But I'm starting to feel like this is a lot to pay for one stray shag."

He let her make the phone call in peace, closeting himself in the bathroom and quietly running inventory, telling himself it was professional interest. On the shower shelf sat bottled product: Jo Malone, Aesop, Aveda. Graham wet-shaved, or anyway had one of those little kits in a leather bag. In the cabinet he found a frugal array of over-the-counter remedies: antihistamines, aspirin, an ancient-looking bottle of cough medicine which was sticky to the touch. He rinsed his hand, listening: in the living room, Shelley had made contact with Zadie. Friendly, by the sound of it. It went on for another five minutes, and five minutes after that, Max had the lowdown on John Bachelor.

Who, it turned out, was a legend at Cornwell House, known for changing his address twice a month and claiming relocation expenses, despite repeatedly being informed that no such emolument existed. You had to admire his persistence. Or if you didn't, you had to heave a sigh of relief that this particular car crash was someone else's. Max Googled his latest living quarters, trying not to dwell on how easy it proved to worm information out of the supposed guardians of former spooks while Shelley watched, at last asking, "Didn't you have one of those Nokia bricks?"

Yes, but it was one thing to play the Luddite while beheading dandelions with a stick, another to deny yourself an advantage when on the run, so among the items in his flight kit had been a smart phone. There was a downside—they were trackable—but anyone looking for you had to know about it first, which in this case would mean having access to his bank records, and noticing the monthly charge. If his unknown enemies were that good, he'd not have got this far.

Besides, there were always loose threads. You could build an identity out of whole cloth, but as soon as you put it on you noticed how the sleeves rode up, how it was already wearing away at the elbows.

Bachelor's current burrow was south of the river.

"So you're what, you'll check out every pub in the area?"

Max waggled his eyebrows in response.

"And then what?"

"I'll ask him who he sold me to."

"We already know the answer to that, Max. He sold you to someone who has money."

"Your point being?"

"That people with money in London are the nastiest on the planet. That's why they come here. It's their playground."

Whereas he was a hick. When they'd come hunting him on a green lane he'd jammed their wheels, but he was on their territory now, whoever they were, and stick his neck out too far, they'd behead him like a dandelion.

"Have you asked yourself who you've upset?"

"No one lately," he said. He thought of Old Dolly. "Or no one rich."

"Let's face it, Max, you've done nothing lately. Whatever this is about, it's ancient history."

The time he'd spent in the bathroom, it had been impossible to avoid his reflection. Ancient history sounded about right.

"So be careful, okay?"

That was a farewell. "Thanks, Shelley. And, you know. Sorry."

She didn't rise to see him out, pointing to her leg as an excuse.

He took the Tube, enjoying the arterial views of the city it allowed. People with money, he thought, never got to see this: the ordinary, the workable. Theirs were the bloodless vantage points of hedge-fund high-rise and laundered helipads. Of course, they didn't come to unscheduled halts underground, either. *We apologise for the delay to your journey.* When Max emerged he was on the other side of the river, but under the same grey sky. He used his phone to locate Bachelor's current flat—in a surprisingly upscale block—and again to pinpoint the nearest pubs. It was mid-afternoon: would his quarry have gone to ground so soon? And then recalled who he was dealing with, and thought, Yes.

In the end, he was seven pubs into his odyssey when he tracked him down.

The Fox and Bucket was on a corner, with tables outside for smokers, and dusty windows through which passers-by could see what they were missing, which included a row of booths against the far wall, each with a big wooden table, a curved banquette and a sconce with a bulb shaped like a burning candle. In one of these sat John Bachelor, holding a pint glass in a way that suggested it was all that was keeping him upright. Max had met him only once, but had no difficulty recognising him: his appearance, even through a dusty window, was of a man nearing the end of his rope, and not an especially reliable rope at that. You wouldn't want to try hanging yourself with it. Their one conversation, of the kind during which you learned far more about the other person than an in-depth discussion of their habits and hobbies would get you, had focused on how little Bachelor received for in-person catch-up sessions, and how that little was inclusive of expenses. Just turning up at Max's door cost him more than twenty per cent of what he was earning . . . Witnessing Bachelor's verbal contortions had been like watching a five-year-old explaining gravity. In the end, Max had acquiesced to his scheme more to avoid having this conversation again than because he'd felt there'd been injustice. Besides, there was never a chance that his relationship with this milkman would follow the same path as that with his predecessor.

Which didn't mean it couldn't offer surprises.

"Hello, John. How've you been?"

"I, Christ, what? Max? *Max*?"

Max slid onto the banquette, forcing John to budge along. He reached anxiously for his drink as he did so.

The aggressive force field around his companion fizzed and sparked. "You looking for trouble, pal?"

"Not remotely. Just after a quiet word or two with John here."

"John doesn't look happy about that."

"I'm fine. Really. No. He's an old friend is Max, an old *old* friend."

In the context of The Fox and Bucket, an old *old* friend might mean anything from childhood sweetheart to last Tuesday's imaginary confidante.

Max said, "And once we're done I'll buy a round and get out of your hair. Deal?"

It didn't require a lot of thought. "Sweet."

Sparky inched out of the booth, leaving the pair alone.

"So, John, how've you been? Making friends, I see."

"No, yeah, well, fine. Just fine. How are you, Max? What, er, what brings you all this way? And how'd you find me, anyway? Or is this just . . ."

His voice trailed away, as if his brain were catching up with his tongue, and recognising the futility of completing that sentence.

There were only three other people in this half of the pub, Bachelor's recent companion included, and all were a reasonable distance away. Nevertheless, Max lowered his voice to say, "No, John. No coincidence. I came looking, and you were easy to find, but then, you're not living in deep cover like I was. But guess what? Turns out I was easy to find too. Wonder how that came about. Do you wonder that too, John?"

"Jesus, Max, I don't know. Leaks at Cornwell House, do you think? The woman who had you before I came along, her name's McVitie or something? She had a bit of a rep, Max. Bit of a rep."

"Yeah, the thing is, John, that won't fly. No, there's only one way they could have found me, and that's if you pointed them in the right direction. Now, I'll give you the benefit of the doubt and say maybe—*maybe*—this happened without you being aware of it. But it did happen, John. And I need to know how, because that might tell me who."

Bachelor looked down into his pint, and for a moment Max had the idea he was preparing to jump into it and drown. That was okay. Max would pull him out and try again. But when Bachelor looked back up, there was something other than self-loathing in his expression. "I know you don't think much of me, and there's no reason why you should. But I only cut corners with you because you didn't need me. If I'd had danger signals, or I thought for a moment there was a breath of worry, I'd have been there for you, I swear it. I'd have called in the artillery. Because I may be a joke at Cornwell House but I take my clients seriously. More than anything. I mean it."

He looked like he thought he did, thought Max.

"No one approached me. No one. And if they had, I'd have sent up a flare."

Max said, "Okay, then. Let's take it a step at a time. No outright overtures, but any strange chance encounters lately? I'm talking in the past couple of days. Any new friends appearing out of nowhere?"

He glanced at Bachelor's erstwhile companion, who had drifted towards the quiz machine again, an unlit cigarette dangling from his lower lip.

"Him? Nah . . . He doesn't even know my name."

"Pretty sure he called you John."

"He calls everyone John."

"Okay . . . Where do you keep your records? I assume you do keep records?"

"Same place everyone does." He tapped his breast pocket. "On my phone."

"Never out of your sight?"

"I do sleep occasionally."

"Good to hear. Tell me about your sleeping arrangements."

Bachelor stared at him for a moment. "I lie down. I close my eyes."

"Nice to know some things come easy. But I'm asking about nocturnal security, not your bedtime routine. Where do you leave your phone overnight?"

"I keep it with me."

"Next to the bed?"

". . . Yes."

"Always?"

"Jesus, I'm not a robot. Usually. *Usually.*"

"But sometimes, maybe, getting to bed, the details get hazy."

Bachelor took a pull on his pint, as if illustrating Max's point. "Well. Okay. You know how it is."

"So think. Think about things that might have happened while you were otherwise engaged."

There were so many possible answers to this, so many philosophies as yet unlogged, it took Bachelor some while to gather some together.

"Anything at all. Out of the ordinary run."

"Well, the cat died," Bachelor said after a while.

"Died? How did it die?"

"I'm not a vet. I got up in the morning, it was dead. There on the bathroom floor."

"So it just dropped down dead?"

"Must've done. I dunno, heart attack? Do cats have heart attacks?"

"Take me through this slowly. You have a cat. How old was it? Was it healthy?"

"It wasn't mine. It belongs—belonged—to the guy who owns

the flat I'm sitting. And who I haven't told about it yet. He'll not be pleased."

The look that flitted across his face was an indicator of just how not pleased, and with what consequences. Max remembered Bachelor having confessed he'd slept in his car more than once. But we've all got problems.

Some more pressing than others. "Look, I really need to pay a visit, you know? The gents. Can I just do that? I'll come straight back."

"You will. You know how I know? Because you wouldn't want to go sneaking off without your phone and your wallet."

Bachelor handed them over with such eagerness, it was as if he wanted to make it clear that sneaking off never entered his mind.

With Bachelor gone Max looked at the phone. If these things could talk, he thought. But he already had a working picture of Bachelor getting home some nights in a blackout, and if he was lucky waking up in bed. Where he left his phone was a matter of chance—in his trouser pocket, in the dishwasher, behind a radiator. The one thing anyone looking for it wouldn't have to worry about was him waking up and shelling out grief. A quick in and out—unless they disturbed the cat, and Max knew enough about cats to know they could make inconvenient noise when they wanted.

Bachelor wasn't a vet: he'd said it himself. And Max wouldn't trust him in a hungover state to identify a broken neck.

Faint music drifted across from the pub's other room. For no sane reason, memory threw up a different dive in a different country, and a ragamuffin jazz trio playing something haunting. It came and went, just as both doors opened at once; the one leading into the other bar, and the one onto the street, through which a woman stepped.

There was no reason he should have recognised her, because he'd barely seen her the first time, when mostly he'd been banging her head on the floor. But there was a clue in that her face was the colour of aubergines. Besides, the way she was looking at him gave most of the game away, and the part that it didn't was covered by the man coming in from the other bar. Max hadn't been out of the game so long he didn't recognise a professional. He stopped and had a quiet word with the couple at the far table, who picked up their glasses without a word and trooped out through the door he'd just come in by.

Leaving only Max himself and John's recent drinking buddy, Sparky, who was leaning against the quiz machine, a sly smile buttering his face. The newcomer stopped by him too, and slipped him some notes he folded carefully before sliding into a pocket.

"Really good to meet you," Max called. "Shall I pass on your best to John?"

"Fuck off."

The woman arrived at his booth, and laid her palms flat on the table.

"Just so we're clear," Max told her, "I'm a lover not a fighter."

She raised a palm long enough to point at her own face.

"It makes you more interesting," he said. "Nobody's going to say, 'She looks dull.'"

"You're coming with us now."

"And if I don't want to?"

"Then we hurt you enough to render your objections inaudible. And you come with us anyway. Don't get me wrong, I'd rather you resisted."

"How's your friend? The one with the motorbike?"

"You bit his damn nose off. How do you think he is?"

"Just the tip," said Max. "He cried like a baby. Did he mention that?"

"On your feet."

Her companion had stationed himself one side of the booth, blocking a swift exit, which anyway wasn't on the cards: extricating oneself from a banquette wasn't the easiest of tasks even with the full cooperation of everyone present. Max grimaced, sucked his belly in and eased himself upright. The woman took a step back. She wasn't visibly armed, but given their recent history it was safest to act like she was.

"There's a car outside," she said.

"Back seat or boot?"

"Don't give me ideas."

She led the way, Max behind her, and her companion bringing up the rear; a procession that got them halfway to the door before John Bachelor appeared from the gents, hurling a plastic swing-bin which hit the man full on the head. He staggered into Max, who stuck a foot between his legs and shoulder-shoved him. While he was hitting the floor, the woman was reaching inside her loose-fitting jacket. *Taser*, Max remembered. He was having one of those slow-time moments whose only use is as a conversation-starter afterwards. *She's going for a Taser*. He grabbed for her arm but she danced backwards, easily evading him. *Once upon a time*, his stupid brain informed him, *you could have scooped up a nice heavy ashtray from a table and crowned her with it*. Best on offer now was a single-stem vase from which a plastic flower poked.

Her hand appeared from her pocket holding, instead of a Taser, a baton that untelescoped with a flick of her wrist: a three-foot-long switch.

"You're kidding," he told her.

"Come on."

"What is this, a bad movie?"

Behind him, Bachelor said, "Careful, Max."

Yes, thanks. He knew to be careful. He knew what sticks could do.

She whipped it onto the table next to him, sending that little vase flying.

"I'm good with this," she said. "I'll open both your cheeks and ruin your face. Like you did to me."

"You broke into my house, what did you expect?"

Her companion was getting to his feet, shaking dancing stars out of his head.

"Take the other door, John. I'll be fine."

"I didn't know they'd read my phone, Max."

"I know."

"Didn't know Sparky was their lookout."

Max didn't bother answering; was too busy focused on the baton. She flicked its tip in his direction, and he felt a stinging sensation on his cheek. Resisted the temptation to raise a hand to its source, but felt his heart racing, and had an impulse to laugh even as the door behind the woman opened, allowing him to grin at the newcomer. "Nice timing." She wasn't fooled and didn't look round, which suited Max because he wasn't bluffing. Shelley McVie's cane came down heavily on the woman's head, splitting in two on contact. The light in the woman's eyes went out, came back on again, and then sort of popped, and she sat down heavily. When Max looked round, Bachelor had picked up a chair, and was either hiding behind it or working out how to use it in a fight, while the man who'd just got to his feet was prepping himself for action. To speed things up, Max smacked his elbow into the man's temple, and when he hit the floor again, Bachelor hit him with the chair, unless he just dropped it. But give him the benefit.

Max said to Shelley, "You followed me?"

"I worried you'd get into trouble." She was breathing heavily, and had her eyes fixed on the woman on the floor.

"Ye of little faith," said Max. He fetched the baton, and as he straightened up realised the bartender was watching from behind his counter. "Sorry about this."

"I've called the police."

"Yeah, we can't stay. Sorry." Then, to Shelley, "We only need one of them."

"She looks lighter."

"My thoughts exactly."

They scooped her up and bundled her out.

Meanwhile, back in the Monochrome offices, witness #137 was getting into her stride.

PART FOUR

BERLIN, THEN

All witness #137 knew, as she explained to herself afterwards, was the instruction she'd been given: IR3, –2, 10.15 A.M. Which, decoded, meant Interview Room Three, second floor down. The time was self-explanatory. And the agenda would be lifecraft, she assumed, because a foreign assignment involved new banking procedures, living arrangements, any amount of detail designed to consolidate a daily existence while she got on with the task in hand, which, in line with her lowly status as a first-year trainee, Housekeeping division, was purely admin. "Assess daily procedures and work-related outcomes." Precisely what a work-related outcome was remained obscure: perhaps this was an initiative test. But however it was looked at, the posting, while superficially glamorous—Berlin Station was a headline operation; the city was still the Spooks' Zoo, even though the Wall was rubble— would swiftly embed itself into daily drudgery: an eye run over these figures, a finger run down this column. So, anyway, she had told herself the previous evening, after news of the imminent posting had arrived in her pigeonhole. A way of tamping down the excitement, because this, her secret self told her, was as good as it got: a junior spook, not field material, heading abroad, and so soon. Those around her—better qualified, many of them— would be spitting feathers when the news broke. If half of her contemporaries weren't flat on their backs mainlining hot lemon and feeling sorry for themselves, she'd not have been in with the faintest shout.

But first there were hoops to be jumped through, because life in the Park for a fledgling was an unceasing bewilderness of obstacle and hurdle—the schedule included compulsory gym sessions, during which trainees were treated like those police dogs made to leap through flaming windows, scuffle under fences and run through lengths of tunnel, actual instances of which, she imagined, rarely presented themselves in the dogs' working lives. Similarly, no junior spook in Housekeeping might legitimately expect to have to scale a drainpipe or repurpose a hairdryer as a deadly weapon, or at least, not unless their domestic lives significantly deteriorated. But more frequently, situations arose aimed at inducing mental and emotional stress; mind games in which there was no winning line to cross, simply a process to undergo. Results were graded on a spectrum, and at which end lay the pot of gold depended on the division you were applying for. There were rumours of applicants for research divisions unwittingly revealing themselves to be field-proficient, and undergoing a swift change of trajectory. *Psychopathic tendencies*, it was muttered. It rarely happened the other way around, though perhaps that was because those who fancied themselves as James Bond couldn't face a desk career, however classified in nature. Though if that did ever happen it might be entertaining, in a desultory sort of way. And then there were the endless complications of joining an organisation whose watchword was secrecy, even if its prevailing ethos was obfuscation. So there were hours spent traipsing down corridors, requisition forms in each hand—for a Service card, without which movement within the building was sorely trammelled; for a Service phone, without which communication was severely limited; for a list of written assignments, failure to complete which would bring training to an abrupt halt—hunting for an office with no identifying nameplate, and whose occupant, if it was ever tracked down, would happily inform you that newly computerised systems meant that such needs could only be met when the applicant had completed the mandatory forms digitally, having first acquired a valid username and password, available on receipt of the appropriate paperwork. Yes, in time such paperwork would be replaced by online transmissions. No, that time had not yet arrived. Glad to have been of help.

It was possible that such small nightmares were themselves ways of stress-testing a fledgling's mental resilience, but equally likely that they were the consequence of an organisation out-growing its resources. Not everything was an initiative test. Unless it was.

All that being so, she should have been prepared for anything when she knocked on the door of IR3, –2 at 10.15 a.m. on a cold day early in 1994 and was invited to enter. But of the faces she might have expected to encounter on doing so, none belonged to the man behind the desk in the centre of the room.

"Please," he said. "Sit down."

"I—yes. Thank you. Sir."

The slightest twitch of what might have been irritation shaded into benignity so smoothly, it was possible to believe it had always been intended as such. "Oh, we can dispense with all that. David will do."

Because this was David Cartwright, who had once been pointed out to her in the lobby at the Park. *There's the man who drives the whole shebang.*

But he's not—

First Desk? No. She couldn't now remember who had told her this; one of the previous year's intake, Susan? Fiona? *But he's the one who makes the big decisions. Or that's the rumour.*

Like any large organisation, Regent's Park ran on rumour, except when it was flying on legend.

That one time apart, she'd never laid eyes on him, though he often featured when conversation among the fledglings turned to the higher powers. His precise role was difficult to determine, since his actual job title was obscure, or at least, proved impossible to pin down despite the insider knowledge some of those debating the point claimed. Chief of Internal Resources, perhaps, or Head of Domestic Strategy.

"Makes him sound like a bursar," someone objected, and those with Oxbridge memories, almost everybody, nodded in agreement.

What was certain was that there was no desk involved: not First Desk, obviously, but not Second either, though that particular job title was going through a boom period. Second Desk (Ops), Second Desk (Comms), Second Desk (Strategy)—time was, Second Desk had meant just that, opined one young Methuselah, the burden of fourteen months' service heavy on his shoulders. You had an actual role, an actual . . . *domain*. But David Cartwright was the exception to the rule book, the one that demanded an appendix to itself. A mixture of Rasputin and Robespierre, it was said, though in person he looked kindlier than either description suggested. High forehead, with light brown hair starting to whiten, and alert blue eyes behind spectacles, one of two pairs he wore on a chain round his neck, the easier to switch to reading mode when required. Lips rather full, not something she found attractive in a man, but it suited David Cartwright, she decided. Underneath his tweed jacket he wore what might be a woollen waistcoat, and below that a dark blue shirt, whose top button was undone. His fingers were long, their nails neatly clipped. A man, clearly, who ensured that he was all in one piece before leaving the house.

More importantly, a man who was immensely busy, what with being a legend. So what on earth was he doing here, gracing her send-off with his presence?

An open file lay in front of him, and while she was as practised as any would-be Mata Hari at reading upside down, its topmost sheet was blank, aside from a paragraph of neat, ruler-straight handwriting so small she might have needed a magnifier were it the right way up.

"And I," he said, "will call you Alison."

Which was when she understood that the whole thing was an embarrassing mistake. He thought she was someone else, and she would now have to explain this to him while somehow maintaining the fiction that it was her fault, not his; that she had inveigled her way into this interview, though without evil intent, and that he, vastly senior in rank and indisputably male, had made no error of any kind. And then all that went away, to be replaced by a single thought. *Workname.*

He was watching her, expectantly.

"I'm already used to it."

"Good. Good."

And Alison North, as she now was, and would remain for some while, smiled her agreement.

"Now, Berlin. Been there before?"

She shook her head.

"That's fine. No experience necessary, as they say. Read the dossier?"

There were dossiers on every placement location, supposedly updated bi-monthly, though Alison wasn't sure the Berlin entry had been tackled in years. Most of it read as though the Wall still stood, and Berlin remained subdivided: checkpoints and conning towers, spotlights and barbed wire. But then, there had always been stories about those posted there; about how those who spent time on the Berlin Desk never really came home, but remained mired in a different reality. Perhaps the unaltered dossier was intended to allow a glimpse into that separate domain, the one in which Berlin's spooks still moved, even if to outward appearances its fittings and furnishings had been replaced. Then again, perhaps it was about underresourcing once more.

"I've looked at it," she said. "It's . . . helpful."

"If you're of a nostalgic bent, yes." He laid his pen down and removed his glasses, folding the arms neatly before allowing them to drop into their chain's caress. "You were expecting lifecraft, of course."

She nodded.

"All that will be taken care of." There was a knock at the door, and a young woman came in. Ignoring Alison, she bent and whispered something in Cartwright's ear. "Thank you, Diana. I'll deal with it later." Diana, since that was her name, left. Cartwright went on: "But there's something else that requires attention. In Berlin, I mean. That's why we're here."

There was something cold in those blue eyes, something his spectacles had concealed. Alison thought, Rasputin, Robespierre—yes, okay. She could see that now. *Assess daily procedures and work-related outcomes.* That was how the memo had run. And this was what her task would be, except that wasn't the story at all, was it? No, that was the cover.

What he was about to tell her was the story.

So tell me, she thought, and in that moment became a spy.

The Station House was on a mid-city street, which must once have been prosperous, and was still lined with trees, some caged behind railings to prevent the depredations of dogs. One side was given over to retail premises—grocery stores and bakers, a small supermarket—and the other to what were once professional premises, with proud front doors at the tops of flights of stone stairs that dentists and doctors and lawyers once descended, with watch chains and waistcoats and wallets. But the houses were shabby now, their stone facades having taken a pasting over the years, and their steps were chipped and broken, accidents waiting to happen. A group had gathered on one flight, their appearance suggesting that a certain kind of professionalism still held sway, and a number of eyes watched her progress as if awarding points for comportment. "Looking for the spooks, baby?" someone called, in English. "Three houses down. With the fancy door."

Laughter accompanied this.

Alison was too British to respond.

The next house along was dead, its windows boarded up and tagged with names so ornately sprayed, so intricately imagined, that they were illegible to the amateur eye: false identities writ large and indecipherable. She didn't want to look back, but felt the stares on her shoulders as she walked past it, the next house too, and then heard another spillage of laughter as she found herself looking up a flight of steps in no better repair than the others, leading to a front door on which had been painted a cartoonish ghost, a white omega-shape with round black eyes. Seriously? When she wondered later about this gross breach of security, Young Alan, who was for a while her main source of local information, explained that anyone who might want to know where they were already knew. The Spooks' Zoo, Berlin was called. And a thing about zoos was, the animals were on display.

There was an intercom, and when she pressed the buzzer she was asked in German who she was and what was her business? On the first day wearing her new cover, it took her a moment longer to answer the first question than the second. The door clicked open and she stepped through it into an unshabby hall-way to be greeted by someone she expected was the building's security man—at the Park, they'd started referring to these as the Dogs—but who didn't especially look the part, inasmuch as he was needle thin and about seventy. He did, though, have a

gun under his jacket—she saw it quite clearly when he reached
to take her Service card, which still felt shiny and stiff. Everything about her screamed newbie, including that slight start she
gave at the gun.

Another figure appeared from a doorway to the left. "Alison
North." It not only wasn't a question, it sounded like an instruction. "You're here from London."

The speaker was from London herself, to Alison's ear, but she
made the city sound as if it were a failed project on a distant
continent. "I'm Theresa. House mother." She did have a mother-
ish air about her, but the kind of mother who'd eat her young at
the first sign of a harsh winter, and her sharp-looking suit made
Alison worry she'd gone the wrong way with her calf-length
denim skirt and red sweater. "Thank you, Ansel. I'll take it from
here."

"Welcome, Miss," said Ansel. His voice was as thin as his arms.

Theresa said: "We'll do introductions later. He's said you're to
go straight up." That this didn't altogether meet with her approval
could be gauged by the tautness of her lips as they shaped the
words. "He likes to catch them early. He says."

"Mr. Bruce?" said Alison.

"Robin? God, no. Miles. You're to go straight up to Miles's
office. Top floor. You can't miss it."

"By myself?"

"It's a staircase, not a labyrinth. Do you want to leave your
coat?"

Again she felt herself watched as she began her ascent. These
two, she supposed, were the more expert scrutineers, given their
employment by the British intelligence service, but the going-
over she'd had from the ladies on the corner—not all of whom
had been ladies—had felt more rigorous, somehow. They'd seen
right through her first glance. This pair still thought she was

who they'd been told she was: Alison North, from London. Who was to go straight up to Miles's office, where she could assume her role of spy.

Top floor was six storeys up, which felt like a lot of floors. Espionage, she thought, ought to be a more crabbed business; shouldn't take up this much space. There were offices on every floor, most with their doors closed, and there were notice boards on several of the landings, which also struck her as unnecessary. Back in the Park the walls were clear, legislatively ordained notices regarding health and safety practices aside. Three floors up, she took a peek at what was on offer. Someone was selling a scooter; someone else was looking for a new apartment, one "without a naturist landlord." "Without" was underlined three times. There was a plea that a missing scarf be returned. It was decorated with Disney characters, and had great sentimental value.

None of it classified information. In fact, she reflected, you might even think it made for good cover, allowing for the fact that anyone standing here would know it was nothing of the sort. But perhaps this was the biggest secret of all: that spies were just like everyone else, especially when you locked them in an office.

She continued up to the top floor, where Miles's room was one of three; the only one with its door not wide open, displaying an uninhabited space.

There's a chap there at the moment, David Cartwright had said. *You've probably heard of him.* He gave a name. Alison had, vaguely; he had something of a reputation, of the mixed variety. He was either as clever as a barrel full of monkeys or so twisted he could see himself coming back. Not for the first time, she reflected that much of the Service's slang belonged to the Second World War, which probably had something to do with the age of those in its driving seats. She wondered, too, whether its moral outlook dated back to the same era, and whether this was a good thing or a bad thing. Far too much there to reach a conclusion about in the time it had taken her to nod a response to Cartwright's comment. "I've heard of him."

"Yes, well. There are those who say he'll either be running this place in a decade's time, or buried in one of its cellars."

"And which are you?" she dared ask. But he merely smiled briefly, as if admiring her move.

"You'll be reporting to him." He glanced down at his sheet of paper, though she was certain this was for show; that any details he might rely on for the purposes of this conversation were already fixed in that brain, behind those owlish glasses. "Brinsley Miles. That's his Berlin workname, so that's what you'll call him."

"Brinsley?"

"These things are assigned randomly. There's some kind of . . ." He waved a vague hand. "Algorithm, they call it. Goodness only knows. I assume 'Brinsley' has, what do they say, the right kind of *vibe*. Though I imagine he goes by Miles."

Which he evidently did.

She knocked, feeling her breath come faster. There was a noise from within, which she took as invitation, and she entered the room. Brinsley Miles was standing behind his desk, his body angled towards the window, which he'd evidently been gazing through, but his head turned towards her. First impression: here was a man who was going to be larger in the future, and was only just managing to contain himself now. He was average height, though might be taller if he didn't slouch, but his shoulders were broad enough that he came across as bullish, and not someone you'd force into a corner. His hair, the colour of dirty straw, looked like shampoo was a twice-weekly luxury, and several days' stubble graced his cheeks and chin. His hands, one of which rested on the window frame while the other hung by his side, its thumb hooked into a trouser pocket, were bears' paws modified for human use, and his fingers were thick and blunt. But his eyes were what drew Alison's attention: they were grey and calm and watchful, and possessed of a certain grace. Watchful, she repeated, underlining the ridiculousness of that observation: wasn't that what eyes were for? But she had the sense that once he saw things, they went unforgotten. He was recording as much as seeing, and she felt herself memorised as she stood in the doorway; her image stored in his mind, in case she should prove useful later. Other details: his suit was well cut but shiny at the cuffs; his shoes were scuffed. An ashtray on his desk contained a single stub. On the wall hung a smeary-glassed print of a bridge, spanning a European river.

She had the feeling that everything about the man, perhaps everything in the room, had been constructed; could, if necessary, be dispensed with at a moment's notice, only to have a different man leave the room and walk into a different identity that would itself be complete and singular. But she didn't know why she thought that. On face value, he was just another man, still south of forty. Brinsley Miles. Not his real name, but the one she would know him by.

"You're out of breath," he said, and if it wasn't quite a growl, a little more smoking would see it there.

"There's a lot of stairs."

"It's worth it for the view."

It was difficult to gauge the sincerity of this remark. The view, much of which he was blocking, was concrete and autobahn, a grey-bound spectrum across which, at this time of evening, dashed red and yellow lights, going and coming. But perhaps he was reading within it the possibilities of travel.

"A point, if I may?"

Without appreciating the interruption, the witness assents.

"What time of day is this, exactly?"

". . . Does that matter?"

Sir Winston looks around, as if mustering his troops. "It's a question of detail. If we're to rely on your testimony as being an accurate summary of events, we need to be sure that you have sufficient grasp on them."

There are one or two nods from around the table, including from heads which do not look up from the papers in front of them.

"It was late afternoon. Early evening."

"But there was still activity in the, ah, Station House?"

"It didn't keep normal hours."

"I see."

"There was mostly someone around. But people worked as and when they chose. It wasn't unusual for Miles to go back to the office after a night out."

"It doesn't sound very orthodox."

"It was how things were done." She shifts in her chair. "Different time. Different place."

"As you say."

"May I continue?"

He waves airily, and she does so.

"I'm Alison North," she said.

"Congratulations."

"I'm supposed to report to you."

"So report."

"I mean, that's what I will be doing . . . I haven't done anything yet."

"No? How long have you been here?"

"I arrived this afternoon."

"And nothing's happened yet? You're not doing Berlin properly, are you?"

So she told him about the taxi ride from the airport, whose driver had appeared to be learning his core skill on the job, and the apartment she'd been loaned: a flat-share in the Kreuzberg district. One of the Embassy's support staff—an events manager—was on compassionate leave, her mother having recently died back in Berkshire; Alison was occupying her bedroom, and sharing the rest of the space with—

"Cruella."

"Carola. Yes. Is she a friend of yours?"

Miles said, "And you're here to keep us on our toes."

"I'm to conduct a compliance study, yes."

He leered. "Cruella's the best place to start, then. Word is, there's not much she won't go along with, you get enough drink inside her."

She pretended not to hear that. "So if you let me know where my office is, I'll start settling in."

"'Office'?" He gave a low whistle, not much more than a rattle between front teeth. "They've spoilt you, back at that shiny new Park. Over here, we take what we can get. Which in your case would be a desk on one of the landings. We don't have a spare chair, mind. Upturned bucket do you?"

"I'll also need a computer, and someone to talk me through your network and assign me a password and all the rest."

"Only a bucket might come in handy. There's two lavs, and one of them's constantly blocked. Someone round here—and I'm pointing no fingers—someone's in dire need of a whole new diet." He was holding a cigarette suddenly. It wasn't clear where it had come from. "I blame the street food, personally. There's a lot of it about. And some people, well, temptation's just another name for opportunity, right?"

"I'd rather you didn't smoke."

He smiled, apologetically. "I heard a guy in a bar the other night, a woman said that exact same thing to him. He told her, 'And I'd rather you didn't menstruate, so that makes us even.'" One of his hands was padding around his desktop, searching for matches. His gaze didn't leave Alison's face. "I thought that was rather rude, myself."

"Is this meant to impress me?"

He glanced around, deliberately misreading her. "Oh, there are worse places to work. And you know what they say. Uncluttered desk, uncluttered mind."

"I'm not sure they do say that. And I meant your manner, not your surroundings."

He found a box of matches, and plugged the cigarette into his mouth. "Well, pardon me all the way to fuck and back. But just to make sure we're on the same page, I'm the one in charge and you're the visitor, right? Or did I get out of bed the wrong person this morning?" When he struck the match the head flew off, a little blazing beacon that landed on the carpet, fizzing to itself.

Alison stepped across and ground it out underfoot. Burnt spots here and there suggested this wasn't an unusual occurrence. When she looked back at him, he was having more success with his second attempt, and the smell of cheap tobacco drifted across the room. Reaching deep inside herself, she brought out the woman who could have been head girl. "Getting out of bed the wrong person would likely be an improvement," she said. "But as it is, if this is to be an endurable experience for either of us, you're going to have to behave like a civilised man. I'm not only here to make sure the Berlin office has been running according to official protocols and procedures, I'm also, invited or not, your guest. Which means I expect to be treated with respect. And if that bar's too high, you can at least refrain from treating me with contempt. Do we understand each other?"

He stared for a long while, his face partially wreathed in the smoke his cigarette was sighing. And then, quietly but unmistakably, he farted.

There'd be moments in the years to come—and this was information she did *not* share with the panel listening; this was a thought she hugged to herself in her secret hours, in her shutaway life—many moments when she'd wish she'd turned then and there and left that office; walked back down those never-ending stairs and lost herself in the thrumming Berlin streets. There are so many pivots on which a life spins. Wheels, and wheels within wheels. But instead of embracing any other possible future, she said, "Is that your final answer?"

He grinned broadly, showing uneven teeth. "We're short on staff right now," he said. "That flu bug going round. So there's desk space in most offices, if you don't mind emptying the odd drawer. The computer guy's called Benny, and he'll see you're cleared for network usage, though I gather the system crashes or burns or does whatever you call it when it's not working properly about four times a week. Any problems with that and you talk to Benny, or whoever's nearest, but you do not, under any circumstances, discuss it with me. Carola's a stuffed animal enthusiast who's been decorated for services to virginity, so you needn't worry about strange faces at the breakfast table. And I smoke in my office whenever I feel like it. There's a petition going round, and you're welcome to sign it, but I should warn you, that's what blocked the lav last time. Welcome to Berlin."

She chose an office on the next floor down, a larger and tidier space than Miles's room, and found herself sharing with a woman named Cecily, who was hardly ever there, and a constant timid presence known as Young Alan, though whether this was with reference to another, older Alan, nobody explained. She soon learned to address him in that manner herself. He didn't seem to mind.

Another interruption:

"This, ah, Brinsley Miles. I gather he's still with us? I mean, not just on the planet and so forth, but the actual Service, yes?"

The question is addressed to Griselda, who has no need to consult her iPad. "He's still alive, yes, and still employed by the Service."

"And will he be gracing us with his testimony?"

Though these questions, like their predecessor, are aimed at Griselda rather than at the witness, they seem to amuse the latter, whose face rearranges itself for the smallest moment into a private smile. But that might be a trick of the light.

"That's the intention, yes."

Nobody else pays much attention to the exchange, it having become clear to all that Sir Winston must make his voice heard at regular intervals, perhaps fearing he will cease to exist if he fails to do so, or perhaps simply concerned to earn the fee his presence commands. For now, he is satisfied that he, too, is still on the planet, and still audible. He nods and, when that proves not enough to start the world turning again, says, "Quite. Quite. Please go on."

So the witness goes on.

The sad truth of a spy's life is, you live the cover. This was what Alison discovered in Berlin. Her assigned task was one that needed doing, if those around her weren't to start wondering what she was actually up to, so she had to absorb and understand the processes that kept the Station House running: the messages, the outcomes, the deliveries. "Messages" was the in-house term for tasks and operations, the details of which fell outside her remit, but focused on the fallout from reunification: an ark full of former eastern bloc agents had joined the exodus when the Wall came down, and some were keen on selling their wares, and others equally keen on hiding theirs under bushels, though whether this was because they were naturally shy or because treasures kept under bushels attracted higher prices was the abiding question. But one way or the other there was a fire sale still burning, and some of the goods on offer were fake, and some of those kept hidden were fake too, which meant hours of intelligence work applied to chasing down rumours and setting traps for ghosts. Around the Station House, the word was that Miles was the man you wanted when ghosts needed trapping. Miles had been a ghost himself, or as good as; had been a fixture behind the Wall, when casting your shadow upon it offered you good odds on being shot. He might look like he'd given up a career as a ticket tout in favour of one selling double glazing, but he was the closest the Station House had to an oracle. Which was a handy position to be in, Alison reflected, if other people's trust was your stock-in-trade.

"Outcomes" were what they sounded like: the bottom line reached when an operation closed. This happened in hours in some cases—as long as it took to get the weasel offering his or her birthright good and drunk—and weeks in others, but sometimes they endured for months, or even years. Trawling the paperwork, Alison caught glimpses of these ops, like catching sight of a whale out at sea; a sudden view of a broad back rolling over before the creature returned to the depths. Measured in spook years, such beings were ancient, and Miles, she knew, was involved in all such operations, though his name rarely appeared in the files. The assets they centred around were from the dark ages; those who'd spied for the west from the other side of the Wall, and who had remained there now it was gone, but still required care and consolation; not least, the cynical might say, because walls could be rebuilt, and dark times fall again ... But these were the exceptions. The vast majority of the work product involved day-to-day encounters with minnows, whose scraps of information were small change; straw, and never gold.

("Too many loose ends. Too many casual asides, instead of nailed-down certainties," David Cartwright had said, leaning over the desk towards her. "They're supposed to be running an outpost of the intelligence service, whose brief, as the name suggests, is to capture intel. Intel likely to indicate threats to Her Majesty's dominions. Not to skulk around strip bars dishing out sterling to anyone with dirty pictures of their sister to sell.")

But the operational work of the Station House was the background to her assigned task, not its focus. She was here as a temporary compliance appointee, her mission to clean the cogs and strip the gears; to verify that paperwork was filed according to Regent's Park's approved taxonomy, itself undergoing significant overhaul since digitisation had taken hold. To check that expenses were accounted for in the approved manner; that Registry was collating and stacking files appropriately, with classification levels strictly observed. The in-house system was graded according to a local joke—the clearance levels ran from Sausage to Schnitzel—but nobody minded a bit of local humour provided the grades mirrored those that would apply when the work product was transferred to the Park; became, in the jargon, "deliveries." It was on this material—analysed and interpreted by the boys and girls on the hub—that future policy would be based. It was, then, of no little importance—Cartwright's phrase—that the deliveries be sound.

"And I want to hear about the outgoings. How much is ending up in the pockets of supposed assets whose product is fool's gold, dib-dabs of gossip they'd as likely found in local scandal-rags as in the corridors of whatever ministry or barracks they pretend to be attached to."

"I thought all the important ministries were in Bonn."

"But the important marketplace is Berlin."

Already, that soon into her meeting with David Cartwright, Alison's world had turned upside down. She had entered the room a newbie, one of the Park's tadpoles; a flair for assessment—gathering up history was her speciality; she had a talent for spotting recurring patterns, and had been tagged by the resident Moscow-gazer as a future star—and never destined for streetwork. But what Cartwright was preparing her for, by the sound of it, was precisely that: she was to be parachuted into Berlin to cast her amateur eye over the workings of a Service substation. Why on earth had this fallen to her?

"And I'm interested in incoming product. Why they're making the choices they're making. Because they're supposed to know the difference between fillet steak and dog food."

"You need me to find this out for you?"

"I need someone on the ground who can take bearings. You're supposed to be good at that. Acquiring quite the reputation."

She tried hard not to blush. Mostly succeeded.

"Besides, if I send someone who knows the ropes, they'll be treated like a tax-collector. Nobody likes having their workings checked. And all substations start behaving like fortresses sooner or later. They know what it's like out there, and we know sod all, that's their outlook. Some truth there, I won't deny. We can't—we shouldn't—be trying to second-guess those doing the groundwork. But . . ."

"But that's what you're doing."

"After a while, it becomes unavoidable. Making the odd misstep, we all do that. We've all chanced our arm on a bargain, only to get it home and find we've been had. The designer sweater whose sleeves come off. The logo that's spelt wrong. We've all placed our faith, temporarily, in snake-oil artists."

Alison, who'd never unknowingly invested in shoddy goods, nodded.

"But turning down high-grade intelligence offered on the cheap, that makes a mockery of everything they're there to do."

"Has that happened?"

For the first time, his gaze turned stony. "Do you think I'd mention it otherwise?"

"No, I just meant . . ."

But she hadn't known what she'd meant, so didn't finish the sentence.

"Miles isn't in charge of the whole shebang, however much he likes to act like he is, but he's the one who knows the streets, and he's done the hard time staring at the Wall from the opposite side. So he should know what's what."

"And you want me to observe him."

"Observe . . . Yes. I want you to observe him."

"You think he's . . . turned?"

Turned was the word you heard, in the movies, on TV. "Turned" was when you stopped being whoever you were and started being someone else, unless it was when you stopped pretending to be someone else, and went back to being who you were. It occurred to her even as she was saying the word that they could have been discussing Miles's sexuality as much as his loyalty. If you were going to be turned, Berlin was very much the place where this might happen. She'd read enough about the city, and heard from friends for whom it was a clubbers' paradise, to know that much.

But Cartwright said, "Let's not get ahead of ourselves."

"No. I understand."

"You're there to observe," he repeated.

And the rest, as she mentally added later. David Cartwright had a number of things he wanted from her, even aside from the housekeeper's tasks she'd officially be assigned to.

The verifying, the checking, the bookkeeping.

"It's a regular posting. We send someone to work through compliance issues once every couple of years. Someone from the fresh intake, who's had time to memorise the protocols and hasn't yet grown blasé enough to take shortcuts. Over at the Station House, they'll know you for who you are."

And who I am will be Alison North, she thought.

"I'd encourage you to try to win Miles's trust, but that's not an especially likely outcome. So I'll just suggest you try not to annoy him too much. I suspect he can make life uncomfortable for those he'd sooner not be working alongside."

This was offered as if it were a late birthday gift; something to be valued and apologised for in the same breath.

"But you'll be fine, don't worry. I'll be in touch."

She made her way out of the room, but he called again as she opened the door.

"And, Ms. North?"

"Yes?"

"Don't catch the flu, will you? I don't want to have to have this conversation twice."

It might have been meant as a joke, but somehow wasn't. Which brought to mind Rasputin and Robespierre once more, a reminder that this twinkly man was hard as nails; a bastard wrapped in benign swaddling.

And now, here, in the Station House, that Miles was not in charge of the whole shebang was something she had to keep reminding herself of. The actual housemaster, as he was usually referred to, was Robin Bruce, and Alison quickly gathered that he was both popular and effective, or had been, until an affair with the wife of a local dignitary had rendered him, first, distracted by an erotic haze and subsequently, following its demise, semi-drunken and tearful, and apt to break into fits of fury with no apparent cause. There were whispers of smashed crockery, launched at the walls with no warning. There were ominous silences, which dragged on all day. And there was no sign of a controlling presence, though he occasionally put himself together long enough to demand that all work product due for despatch to the Park be run past him by the relevant case officers, which, when this inevitably proved too much for him round about the mid-morning mark, led to afternoons fractured by havoc. That his staff conspired to act as if none of this were happening, or at least that it constituted business as usual, was one of those realities of office life which Alison took in her stride: it would have been normal in London, so why not Berlin? No: for Alison, whom nine months in the Park had rendered unshockable as far as tales of marital infidelity went, the detail that struck her was *local dignitary*. It had a pre-war air, as if the affair had been scripted by Somerset Maugham, or, at a pinch, Graham Greene.

As for Bruce himself, he might have fallen out of the pages of one of those authors' novels, not so much for his appearance as for the self-pity he radiated. Alison's first encounter with him, intended to be a swift sit-down over coffee, became a gruelling morning session in which she was cast in the role of interviewer-cum-psychoanalyst, a part which demanded that she simulate interest and compassion. Coffee in the office became a three-course lunch, most of which he drank, and ended in a clumsy pass, punctuated by the glass of wine he poured into his lap. This did not go unnoticed on their return to the Station House, where Theresa—who had thawed a little, but only enough to show Alison that underneath the ice lay permafrost—let her know that it had been nothing personal.

"Tried it on, did he? He's in a state, that's all. That bitch tore his heart out."

"He does seem rather . . . distracted."

"Poor sod. He's had his hand up every passing skirt, lately. Put lipstick on a pig, he'd give it a go." She put a sympathetic hand on Alison's elbow. "He's just wanting to prove he's still in the game."

It seemed to Alison he was back in the pavilion, but she'd received the message loud and clear. The Station House boss was not himself, and any attraction momentarily felt for the new girl was a symptom, nothing more.

And so the wheels went round and round. By her second week in, she found herself quite liking Young Alan, who offered shy advice about eateries and short cuts and the vagaries of the local transport system, and was intrigued by Cecily, whose duties took her out of the office most days, though Alison never worked out why. As for Miles, he too was mostly off the premises, but generally turned up towards the end of the working day, or the beginning—as he put it—of the working evening: he'd be more or less freshly turned out, and she soon noticed that he shaved every third morning. He had a rotation of three suits, two dark, one of which was subtly striped, and the third grey. His two ties were bright and plain, a single-note red, a neon green, and he didn't welcome comment on either. Arriving around six, he'd call for coffee, and Alison would hear him talking to whoever delivered it, a conversation that was never more than a burbling murmur from her desk on the next flight down, but often ended in laughter.

Once during that first week she was more or less alone in the building, the day staff having departed and the night crew still gathered on the ground floor, and she had crept up the stairs to his room, where a lamp still shone, though he had departed on his night's mission an hour before. The door was half-glass, the wavy kind, and the light threw a fuzzy pattern on the corridor wall. Through the glass, she had a distorted view of Miles's domain; the desk whose messiness was apparent even through this prism; the filing cabinets against one wall, their drawers not quite closed; the newspapers strewn about. There was a coatstand in the corner, an overcoat dangling from it like a body hung up to dry. She put a hand to the doorknob, but didn't turn it. It would be locked. Everyone had a key to their own office, and Theresa kept a master set in her room on the ground floor. From which she could hear noises now: hellos, goodbyes, dispersals. Her heart was beating like a tin drum. She wasn't cut out for this. She felt like she'd just run up those stairs twice rather than crept up them once, and her body must be leaving clues of its presence here, there'd be traces of her sweat and breath staining the air, and he'd sniff them out when he reappeared. This could happen in the small hours. He came and went at will, like a cat.

Earlier that day she'd been up here to see him and his floor had been covered in paperwork; not the angry disorganisation of a man failing to make sense of anything, but the deliberate arrangement of entries from separate files, as if Miles were attempting to map a path through a labyrinth only he'd noticed. She'd wondered if she ought offer to help. It was a form of labour she was more suited to, the creation of a route through chaos, than this somewhat hapless attempt at hands-on espionage: staring through wavy glass at a distorted mess of clues. But he had glared at her—nothing personal; it was as if she were an unexpected obstacle encountered during a hike—and her heart had thumped badly on her way back down, much as it did now. Whatever the maze he'd been constructing, it was gone now; hacked back into separate pages and shuffled out of sight.

That same morning, she'd missed a phone call that arrived while she was in the bathroom. Young Alan had taken it.

"Your landlord? Back in London, I mean."

She had a landlady back in London. "Yes?"

"Something about needing access to service the boiler. Could you call him back?"

"Of course."

"Funny," Young Alan had said, returning to his work. "Almost like a coded message, isn't it?"

She called the number her fictitious landlord had left from a box several streets away. There were nearer public phones, but she had an idea that the Station House might keep tabs on them, though how they'd go about this remained an unstructured possibility in her mind.

"How are we getting on?"

Without Cartwright's twinkly presence, it was easier to hear the Rasputin, the Robespierre. His voice was in a hurry, and expected results.

"It's a little chaotic. They've had the flu here too. So it's all hands to deck."

"Yes, I'm sure." A touch of testiness. "But what about Miles?"

"I haven't had the chance to talk to him much."

"*Talk* to him? What good would that do? He's hardly likely to *tell* you anything."

"He keeps his office locked."

"Well of course he keeps his—he's a spook. He's not going to leave his door wide open."

She was keeping a mental list of the things that spooks do and spooks don't. Spooks lock their doors. That seemed natural.

"Do what you can in the office. That's a priority, obviously. But . . ."

She waited, knowing what was coming.

"He has a reputation. They all do."

Here in Berlin, did he mean? Here at the Station House? Or was he talking about spooks, still; those who'd been joes, and learned to live day-to-day, hand-to-mouth? Grabbing what they could along the way?

"For the night life. He likes to get out and about."

She was going to wait for him to say it in words; to use vocabulary and not insinuation.

"Go along with him. Make it an accident, make it whatever. But watch him, listen to him, while he's got his guard down. That's what you need to do."

"Is that why you picked me for this job? Sir?"

"What, because you're a woman, you mean?"

"Yes."

"Well of course it is. What kind of business did you think you were getting into?"

"All sorted out?" Young Alan asked, on her return. Adding: "You could have used the phone here, you know."

"But then you'd have known it was a coded message."

What she hadn't told David Cartwright, what she couldn't have put into words without sounding foolish, was that she was beginning to know what Miles's footprints looked like. She could see them in the files she trawled through, on the pretence of verifying that substation protocols were adhered to. He mostly went unnamed, but there'd be initialled emendations attached to typewritten records—the initials not always his own, or not Brinsley Miles's, but the lettering was similar—which were more often offered as observations than as matters of fact: small bursts of intuition that could turn an operation on its head. This interested Alison, who knew that intuition was a slippery thing. Sometimes it was born of a lifetime's experience in joe country, learning the landscape, reading tracks on the snowy hillsides. Or it could be calculated, treacherous; the way a card sharp can read the hand you're holding, because he was the one dealt it.

But that wasn't the sort of insight that would be welcomed in a report.

This time it's Carl Singer who interrupts.

"I'm sorry—"

Rather embarrassingly, he's raised a tentative hand, as if hoping to attract a teacher's attention.

"Are we to understand that David Cartwright—who, I gather, was something of a mover in the shadows—"

"An *eminence grise*, yes." Sir Winston allows his wisdom to fall on the assembled company like a benediction. "Without ever holding the highest office himself, he was a close adviser to at least three First Desks."

"Thank you, Sir Winston." There's something in Singer's manner which rings not entirely true, from the hand-raising to the over-punctilious way in which he addresses the committee chair. "So, a grandee of the Park, at the very least—and are we to understand that he mistrusted this Brinsley Miles? Thought that he might be a traitor?"

Silence falls.

Breaking it at last, Griselda says, "I think that's a question for the witness?"

"Was it?" Ms. North asks. "Oh. I thought he was addressing a meeting."

Malcolm Kyle stifles what might have been a cough.

Ms. North says, "Cartwright knew that Miles had spent time behind the Wall. That he'd been a joe, which few of those wearing suits at the Park had ever been."

Ms. Deborah Ford-Lodge says, "A joe is an agent in the field."

Alison fixes her with a stare that would level a lesser ego. "That's right. And what Cartwright said was, if Miles had decided to fold his tent the wrong way, he wanted to know about it." She pauses. "There was a tendency at the time, there still is, for those behind desks at the Park to adopt fairly colourful language. I think it makes them feel more . . . active."

In the brief silence that follows, Deborah Ford-Lodge's pen can be heard scratching across her notebook.

"All right if I go on?"

"Please do."

"I was talking about Miles's intuition. It might have been real enough. Because just a day or so after Cartwright instructed me to spend time with Miles outside the office, Miles invited me out for the evening."

But only because she'd waylaid him on the stairs. It was after eight, and the Station House had adopted that echoey air places of work assume once the day shift has departed; she was young enough that this made her feel more adult, as if she'd been left in charge. She'd been working through a stack of expense accounts destined for Regent's Park, ensuring that each submission was accompanied by receipts, and fell under one of the approved headings. Miles's sheet showed everything listed on the right-hand side, under a caption she quickly ascertained he'd added himself. *Miscellaneous.* Well, that covered the waterfront. There were receipts attached, but no indication as to what goods or services they related to, and several were little more than sums scrawled on scraps of paper. Some of these were nicely rounded figures. Others were simply gross. None of this caused her great surprise. And the fact that Robin Bruce had approved the sheet meant that if the Park wanted to query any of it, it was him they could take it up with. The burden of leadership.

Bruce's own accounts were neater, despite the chaos of his current style, his receipts amended by hand to indicate their validity. "Petrol," he'd added, or "Dip lunch." "Dips" were diplomats; lunching them part of his job, though when it occurred to her to check the receipt from their own lunch together, there it was again: "Dip lunch." She was more amused than scandalised. But none of this was indicative of treachery. The only oddity she found among Bruce's accounts was a slip for a cash withdrawal for US$5,000 from House funds, at the top of which was printed, in Bruce's neat capitals, "Basilisk." She was still scanning documents for another such reference when she heard Miles's office door close, and the scratching of his key in the lock, and—clutching the nearest folder to her chest—she scrambled to make sure she appeared on the staircase as he was descending. It was her first sighting of him that day. He wore the suit with the stripe, the green tie, the overcoat, and a scarf decorated with Dumbos.

"I see you got your scarf back."

He gave her a strange look. "What are you on about?"

"Doesn't matter. Could we talk about your expenses claim?"

"No."

"Only it doesn't accord with the official template."

"Is that a fact?"

He'd splashed some aftershave on in the recent past, which almost but didn't quite mask the odours of tobacco and liquor—whisky, she assumed. There'd been a bottle of whisky, a German brand, on top of a filing cabinet in his room that first time she'd been in there; its level had dropped, glass by glass, in the fortnight since. As far as she was aware, he wasn't in the habit of offering it to visitors, which meant he'd got through almost a whole bottle by himself inside two weeks.

"I need you to fill it out again. Properly."

"Do you have it with you?"

It was tucked against the folder she'd brought with her, so she unpeeled it and handed it to him. He glanced at it, nodded, crumpled it up and tossed it down the stairs.

"Very adult."

"I hear you had a little adventure with Robin."

"That's overstating the case."

"Well, Jesus, it's gossip, not courtroom testimony. You want some advice?"

"Very much not."

"If the head of House makes a pass at you, don't pour a glass of wine on him. Either uncross your legs and offer it up for the good of the Service, or use the bottle and slap him round the head."

She said, "He poured it over himself."

Miles laughed, a sudden seal-bark. "Okay. That makes sense. Robin's hand-eye coordination's been shot to bits since Frau Blasen gave him the elbow. And I speak as one who's stood next to him at a urinal. You hungry?"

"Not since hearing that."

He shook his head. "If you're gunna let the odd coarse notion put you off your food round this place, you'll lose more weight than you can afford to."

"Round this place or just around you?"

"I *am* this place. Now get your coat. I could eat a whore."

". . . I beg your pardon?"

"I could eat a horse. What's the matter, your ears need syringing?"

Offer it up for the good of the Service, she thought.

"Give me a minute," she said.

Which was as long as it took him to hail a cab. The house three doors along was relatively quiet this evening, with just a pair of women, dressed for the beach, adorning its front steps. They watched as Miles clambered into the taxi, leaving Alison to walk round the other side. "Got yourself a real smooth operator there,

baby," she heard. Then Miles gave the driver an instruction she
didn't catch, and they were on the move, one of the women wav-
ing them off with the hand not clutching a parasol.

Sometimes life happened like this: one moment you had a
plan, your evening mapped out in increments; the next you were
being taken you didn't know where.

But if she was expecting a tour guide she was disappointed,
because other than a rapid exchange in German with the driver,
Miles said nothing as the car ploughed through streets that grew
lighter and broader—past any number of restaurants that looked
like they'd do the job—and then narrower and darker again, as if
the journey were some kind of parable. Restaurants gave way to
takeaways and corner shops, and boarded-over premises that
might once have been either. From some boarded-over windows
slivers of light extruded, glinting off the rows of motorbikes
parked outside. Garages and tattoo parlours; a shop with a giant
inflatable parrot in the window. Posters peeled from most available surfaces, a mixture of pop and politics. When the cab came
to a halt, it didn't seem to Alison that they'd arrived anywhere.
Miles produced banknotes he didn't glance at, and passed them
to the driver. In return, he received what looked like half a dozen
receipts. Once on the pavement, he stood motionless until the
taxi was out of sight.

You bring me to the nicest places, she thought. *Got yourself a
real smooth operator there.* There was a row of shops ahead, four of
them, each specialising in sexual novelties, or that was how she
interpreted the slogans plastered to their windows. But the novelties on display wouldn't have struck a Victorian as innovative,
the storefront mannequins attired in faux-leather lingerie, which
was almost certainly not as cheap as it looked. A blow-up doll,
its mouth an astonished O, had slumped against one window, and
Alison wouldn't have been surprised to hear it complain of a

headache. The backdrop was a montage of naked women in the throes of ecstasy, no men in sight. On the pavement a group had gathered, smoking joylessly. As Miles led her past she felt their gazes brush against her, without lingering long. I should be made of plastic, she thought. Or imitation leather. Anything but real. Real was a turn-off.

The early evening had shaken off the working day; it was darker and colder than when they'd climbed into the taxi. She resisted the temptation to shrink further inside her coat. It would have looked like she was trying to hide.

Beyond the four sex shops was an amusement arcade, though any amusement it brokered was as genuine as the ecstasy on offer. Its soundtrack was Lou Reed, serenading New York not Berlin, and the tune lingered in the air for twenty yards. As it faded Miles stopped at an open doorway, its inner recesses obscured by a bead curtain that wouldn't have looked out of place in a 1970s kitchen. The man outside was obviously a bouncer—black jeans, black T-shirt, black jacket, black hat—and greeted Miles like an old friend, but without using his name. When Miles pushed through the curtain, its rattling noise triggered a distant memory she couldn't pin down. On the other side a flight of stairs descended: the light was dim, the walls red, and the stairs uncarpeted. Short of a sign suggesting they abandon all hope, it couldn't have been less welcoming.

So she felt little surprise that, behind the heavy wooden door at the foot of the stairs, a strip club waited. Or a club in which stripping was taking place, though nobody seemed interested. A bar took up most of one wall, and a red sticky carpet most of the floor. Miles had stuffed his Dumbo scarf into a pocket and shrugged his coat into the waiting arms of a young woman wearing a flesh-coloured leotard; without glancing behind him, he then followed another, similarly clad, to a table against a far wall. With little obvious choice, she did the same. The room wasn't full, but it was fuller than it had a right to be, given the time of day and the day of the week. Alison—this might have been a puritan streak rising to the surface—had the notion that strip clubs prospered only once the working day had been drowned in drink. Here, the atmosphere seemed almost preprandial. Meanwhile, a skinny girl in her teens worked her way out of some complicated underwear.

"I'll have a whisky," Miles said, slumping into a chair with his back to the wall. A professional habit, Alison guessed; somewhere he could stay alert to the room. Though also, the best view available of the stage. "Large. Whatever's cheapest. No ice."

They were both looking at her expectantly.

She asked him, "Do they do wine?"

"Take a wild guess."

"Red, then." She turned to the woman in the leotard. "A glass of red wine, please."

Miles loosened his tie, and turned his attention to the skinny girl, now all but naked, gyrating to "Tainted Love." To Alison, it seemed not so much erotic as an illustration of a desperate life-choice. Or the absence of choice. "Did we have to come here?"

"Yes."

"Why?"

"Because if we were in Paris, we'd go to a restaurant. And if we were in Amsterdam we'd go to a brothel."

"Or an art gallery," she said.

"It's possible one of us might," he conceded.

Around them, conversation bubbled like eggs in a pan. She was far from the only woman in the room, even apart from those who obviously worked here, some of whom were leaning against the bar, chatting with customers. Even clothed she could tell they were strippers, because the clothes they were wearing would have made her feel naked. She hated feeling this, hated what it said about her. She wasn't uptight, wasn't a prude. But she'd have liked to know that these women felt good about their lives.

Miles lit a cigarette she hadn't noticed him unpacking from a box. There was an ashtray in front of him, but he tossed the used match over his shoulder anyway, as if in deference to local superstition. It hit the wall and dropped to the floor.

She stared.

"Did you want a cigarette?"

"No."

"Then shut up."

"This is where we're having dinner?"

"The food's surprisingly good."

"I'll be surprised if it's actually food."

But at least the drinks, which arrived that moment, were real. Miles picked his up, and she thought he was about to offer a toast. Not sure it would be one she'd go along with, she let her glass sit on the table. But all he was doing, it turned out, was admiring his alcohol by the lights spat out overhead: a glittering disco ball, slowly rotating, rearranging the colours in the air.

He said, "So how's the, what are we calling it? Your visitation. Your examination visitation. How's it going?"

She said, "It's going."

"Please. Your enthusiasm's giving me the bends."

"It's plod-work, that's all. Working my way through your protocols. Messages, outcomes—"

"Deliveries."

"Deliveries."

"Expense claims too. That's going to the heart of the matter."

"You know what it's like at the Park. They keep a tight hold on the purse strings."

"This your first foreign holiday?"

"Well, it's not exactly a—"

"Spook speak. Anything that takes you away from your desk's a holiday."

"Oh. Right. Yes."

"How long are you in the job, anyway? A year? Eighteen months?"

"More like ten."

"Sweet Jesus."

"I came in the top quarter of my intake."

"They should drop the bottom three quarters, just to keep standards up. Which would put you way down there in a dunce's cap."

"Thanks for the support."

He shrugged modestly, and tasted his drink. Alison tried hers too. It was wine. It was very ordinary.

"So what earned you the dream posting?"

"It's a regular thing," she told him. Reminded him? He should know about this; he'd been an agent long enough. "And they always send a newbie. Part of the training."

"Yeah, see, that's what's puzzling me. I've never been in-house while an audit's been done, on account of I've had real jobs to do, which keep me out the way. Risking life and limb for Her Madge, that sort of thing. Fair enough, she's clocking on, can't be expected to do it herself. But from what I've heard, when they're going over the books, they send a heavy team in, not a fledgling. Because if they do find anything dodgy, someone needs leaning on. That something you're good at, Alison North?" There was a hint of mockery in his use of the name. "Leaning on people?"

"We won't know until I've tried it," she said. "Brinsley Miles."

He laughed, and returned his gaze to the dancer. To Alison's eyes, he didn't seem remotely aroused or even much interested in the emerging nudity, or the method by which it was achieved. He might have been watching someone waiting for a bus, without being invested in whether it turned up or not.

She said, "And whatever you've heard, you heard wrong. It's standard to use a newbie. David Cartwright told me that himself."

His eyes remained fixed on the dancer, but something inside him shifted. "The old bastard. Did he really?"

They weren't alone any more. The newcomer had arrived so quietly, so unobtrusively, it startled her. "Hello, Miles," he said. Only he didn't say Miles; he used another name. He was a short thin man, with dark hair trained back across his head so closely, it looked like a plastic mould. His eyes were twitchy, and his hands might have been too, but they were jammed inside his trouser pockets. These trousers had seen better days. So had the jacket. She formed the impression they'd been bought off the peg, by somebody else. He was smiling, and his teeth were small and sharp and grey. None of these details seemed to matter to Miles, who continued staring at the stage, even though it was vacant now, its recent occupant having completed her task and retreated into the shadows behind.

"Not going to introduce me to your new friend?"

His voice was reedy and insecure.

"Dickie Bow," Miles said in a flat voice. "Alison North. Alison, Dickie Bow. Alison's a visiting fireman, aren't you, Alison? She's here to make sure there aren't any cinders about to burst into flames. And Dickie Bow's a resident, what shall we call you, Dickie? I want to say ratcatcher. Except you're not so much a catcher as a rat, when you get down to it."

All this without looking Dickie's way.

"He's having a laugh, miss. Aren't you—Miles? Sorry about that slip. Names are tricky things, when they change on you."

"Everything's tricky to the constantly challenged. And you'll know when I'm having a laugh, Dickie. You'll know because I'll be laughing." His face, saying this, was set like concrete. You could as easily imagine an Easter Island statue having the giggles.

Dickie said to Alison, "You're new in town. I can tell."

"You can tell because I've just told you," said Miles. "That's what 'visiting' means."

"I'd know anyway." Dickie Bow's voice had the artificial merriment of a confirmed bachelor addressing an infant. "People new to Berlin, they have this dazed air to them."

"I wasn't aware I looked dazed."

"Well, no, dazed. That's overstating it. You have this fresh look, that's all. Puts the rest of us to shame."

Miles finished his drink, and looked at Dickie for the first time. "Flattery? How far do you think that's going to get you? Bear in mind, we're in a strip club."

"Just trying to be nice."

"Yeah, well, forget being nice and stick to what you're good at, Dickie, which is making sure nobody notices you." He replaced his empty glass on the table, and raised a hand for the waitress. "That very much includes me."

"I will, I will. I am. Only," and here Dickie retrieved his fingers from his pocket and pushed them though his slicked-back hair, like a rat in a cartoon, "if you could sub me for a couple of nights? I just need to get my ducks in a row, know what I mean? There's something stirring in the undergrowth, Miles. Just the sort of thing you like to hear about."

"I've heard this song before. I definitely remember the refrain. It goes, 'Give me all your money, while I take a dump in your hat.' Because last time you came to me with a golden goose, Dickie, that's what I remember ending up covered in. Not glory, just shit. From the head down."

"Not like last time. Swear to God. My hand on your heart, Miles."

"If you think I'm letting your hand anywhere near my vital organs, you've another think coming, old son. Same again."

This to the waitress, newly arrived at their table.

Alison hadn't finished her wine yet. Had barely started it. "Nothing for me, thanks."

Dickie had settled into the spare seat. "And I'll have—"

"He'll have a long hard look at himself," Miles said, and then, when the waitress frowned, spoke a few sentences in German. She shrugged, collected his empty glass, and returned to the bar. He went on, "And another thing. Last time we got up close and personal, I remember a certain property being mentioned, on sale for a certain price. Only when further inquiries were made, it turned out the price had skyrocketed, on account of the seller having become aware of my interest. Which is what it always comes down to with you, doesn't it, Dickie? Always pulling the old one-two shuffle. And instead of being right in front of me, you're behind me with something large and pointy in your hand. Do feel free to contradict at any point."

"Miles—"

Miles pantomimed someone finding a handle poking out of their back. "Almost as if the favour you were doing was for some-body else entirely."

"It was a misunderstanding, that's all."

Miles stared at him with no visible expression. He might have been examining a light bulb; trying to work out, by appearance only, whether it still worked.

"I'm not carrying water for anyone else."

"Sure you're not."

"I mean, we're friends, right?"

"Dickie Dickie Dickie." Miles reached across and laid his hand on Dickie's forearm, giving him what was probably a mild, fraternal squeeze. The look on his companion's face morphed from beseeching to anxious. "We can enjoy the occasional drink. We can share the occasional story. Money might even change hands, time to time. But we can never be truly friends. You understand why?"

"...Because that's how it goes on Spook Street."

"No. Because I can't stand the sight of you. Now fuck off, Dickie. And, Dickie?"

"What?"

"Stay fucked off."

When Miles released his arm, Dickie Bow rubbed it before standing up. He nodded at Alison. "Very nice to meet you, Ms. North."

Alison wasn't sure of the etiquette, but Dickie seemed familiar enough with it, slipping through the crowd and vanishing before reaching the door. Again, she had that image of a rat in her mind. They could vanish too, the moment you took your eye off them. Which made it difficult to know whether it was preferable to be looking at a rat, or not to be able to see one.

Miles, with an air of unconcern which didn't seem feigned, was scanning the room. His fresh drink sat on the palm of his right hand, as if he were weighing it.

"You weren't very nice to him."

"No? What gave me away? Telling him to fuck off, or saying I couldn't stand the sight of him?"

"You seemed to know each other well enough. You could have told him he was a friend."

"Friends are just strangers you haven't pissed off yet."

"That's not as clever as you think it is."

"I doubt even Dickie Bow's as clever as I think he is. And I think he's a fucking moron."

"You swear too much." She regretted the words as soon as they were out of her mouth; the oral equivalent of sticking her head over the parapet. But he simply grinned, and took a first taste from the glass in his hand.

Alison said, "What did he mean, anyway? That he wasn't carrying water for anyone else?"

"He meant he doesn't sell gossip to anyone but me. But he was lying. Dickie Bow would carry water for whoever asked, provided they had the price of a shot of rum or an Alka-Seltzer. Depending on the time of day."

"He can't be all bad. Or you'd have jettisoned him long ago."

"He's good at following people," Miles said. "I'll give him that. Otherwise, he's a fuck-up." He weighed his glass again. "And fuck-ups are dangerous. If I had my way, they'd have a department all to themselves. Keep 'em off the streets."

"While you make sure the strip clubs are safe."

"Someone's got to do it."

"And what else do you do? Listen to people like Dickie Bow, and give them money for the stories they tell?"

"It's most of what I do, yes. What did you think? That it was all tuxedoes and Aston Martins? They call Berlin the Spooks' Zoo, you know that, right? What happens in a zoo is, the animals get fed. You shouldn't lose sight of that."

"And who feeds you?"

"Is that what Cartwright sent you here to find out?"

"No."

"You're going to have to learn to lie better than that. And something else you're going to have to learn."

"What?"

With a swiftness that almost amounted to conjuring, the glass that had been on his palm was suddenly at his mouth, was suddenly empty. "How to make your expenses claims seem both plausible and necessary." He raised the empty glass, and their waitress appeared as if part of the same magic trick.

Miles made the universal gesture for another round.

"I still haven't finished mine."

"We'll add that to your list of things that need work. Oh, and here." He was stuffing something into her hand. "You'll need these."

A bunch of receipts, crumpled into a single ball.

In the meeting room, the more-or-less silence that prevails when a group of people are listening to an individual speak is starting to strain at the seams. Shirin Mansoor has a persistent dry cough, never shaken off after a bout of Covid—"the Omicron variant," she insists on specifying, as if this were an upmarket brand, more in keeping with her status—while Guy Fielding and John Moore, not the most attentive of the company at the best of times, both seem occupied with other matters: a surreptitious game of sudoku in one case and an ongoing struggle not to fart in the other. The amount of note-taking Deborah Ford-Lodge is engaging in suggests she may be multitasking, listening to Alison North with one part of her brain and achieving her daily word count with the other, and Sir Winston, having laid down a marker with his earlier interruption, thus establishing that he is awake and paying attention, is quite possibly no longer awake, and almost certainly not paying attention. Only Carl Singer seems fully on-message, studying Ms. North as she delves into her memories, the furrowing of his brow indicating that he is sharing her journey, a phrase he would no doubt employ if the need arose. As for Griselda Fleet and Malcolm Kyle, their status as civil servants puts beyond question their devotion to the proceedings, and their concentration is as total as it is unobtrusive. Nevertheless, Ms. Fleet—part of whose occupation it is to attend to the needs of the panel—is not unaware of the general drift taking place, and feels it important not to allow this to go too far, as it risks testimony slipping by without being given due weight. She therefore decides that now would be a good moment to call a twenty-minute recess, to allow bathroom needs to be satisfied, and cups of tea or coffee taken. Mr. Kyle, if his commitment to the Monochrome inquiry might be questionable, is never less than punctilious when it comes to refreshment breaks, and has kettle and biscuits organised before the assembled company has risen and stretched and scraped chairs back under tables. There is the murmur of phatic conversation, it being the convention that discussion of testimony is frowned upon during breaks, especially those at which the deposing witness remains present. Mr. Kyle opens a window and fresh city air breezes into the room while the panellists collect their favoured cups.

But Alison North remains at the table in the centre of the room. Mr. Kyle approaches and asks if she needs anything—she does; a cup of coffee—but she makes no move from her allotted position, leaving to him to fetch her drink and carry it back. As he places it on the table, within her reach, she murmurs a thank-you, but this is clearly an automatic response, and might have been triggered by the new air now circulating. He backs away, a little unnerved by her preoccupation. And her coffee sits untouched while Alison herself remains inside the memories she has awakened, her narrative continuing unheard by the company; a private recollection, long locked away in a corner of her mind.

After that first night, there were others. She didn't recall what they'd eaten, if they even had, but remembered drinking more than she was used to, which was a drop in Miles's ocean. That he'd managed to make the bottle in his office last nearly a fortnight now seemed worthy of comment, though a comment she kept to herself.

As to whether she'd enjoyed herself, or Miles's company, that wasn't relevant. *Try to win Miles's trust.* Cartwright's words, to which Alison's footnote was, And how better than to watch him drink? He seemed to want an audience, at least some of the time, because every other evening or so he'd appear at her office door as she was getting ready to leave. *Buy you a drink* . . . It wasn't a question. Or even a generous offer, given that he expected to be bought drinks at least as much as he bought them. At the end of the evening, he'd present her with the receipts he'd collected, some of which related to rounds she'd paid for . . . It was a game, she thought. He didn't care about the money; he just wanted to be on the right side of any hustle going. And she wondered whether that was part of the drive that had sent him over the Wall as a joe, or something he'd brought back with him when his undercover life cracked apart.

At the same time, she wondered whether that undercover life had ever really been abandoned. Miles was as open and relaxed as an iceberg, though she couldn't be sure whether the submerged majority was frozen solid or fiercely burning. Only once did she think she caught a genuine reaction from him, when the three of them—because they were a trio by then—found themselves in a club with a band in the corner: violin, upright bass and drums. Otis had been telling her about how the young of the east, many of them, saw reunification as occupation, with established operators from the west cruising into sought-after jobs in universities, businesses, even the police force, making themselves unpopular in the process. Which meant there wasn't a lot of cooperation going on with the new boss class, and when you applied that equation to law enforcement, it allowed a certain leeway to the criminal element. Drug dealing was enjoying a heyday, and hadn't exactly been in the doldrums beforehand . . . Otis was capable of remaining in lecture mode indefinitely, but he'd not got much farther than that when they noticed Miles was paying even less attention than usual; was focused, instead, on the band.

After waiting a beat to see if the spell would break itself, Otis said, "Nice tune."

Miles grunted.

"You want me to find out what it is?"

"No, what I want is for you to stop banging on like a social studies broadcast and order some drinks. I've known teetotallers quicker to the bar."

But Otis had had a word with the bassist regardless, and told Alison later that the tune was called "Sleep Safe and Warm."

"I never thought our Miles had a musical soul."

His name wasn't really Otis, of course, but that was the name plastered on the folder that would ultimately capture these events. At the time, they called him Rutger, though that wasn't his name either.

Sometimes, it could be difficult to keep up with all the pretence.

Griselda Fleet has reassembled the weapons of her trade—iPad, notebook, tin of mints, reading glasses, pencil, because she's always preferred pencils to pens, and who cares what this says about her self-confidence?—and is ready to restart the session, just as soon as the chatter has died down. This can take a while, and she is usually reluctant to call the panel to order, being conscious that the majority of the witness testimonies they have been listening to lately have been, well, tedious. Interminable tales of accounting errors; epic narratives of withheld identities. But today is different. Alison North has a story to tell, and though all present—having had access to the folder that person or persons unknown slipped into Malcolm's shopping trolley—know the bare bones of her tale, and cannot fail to be painfully aware of its outcome, the details she is offering put flesh on a skeleton. It is akin, Griselda decides, to viewing the artist's model, rather than the mere sketch. And the artist's model deserves consideration.

A clearing of her throat suffices to alert the panel members that their attention is now required, and all but Sir Winston break off their audible musings. His focus is the weather, and his uncanny ability to gauge its diurnal fluctuations, a more than useful gift when one is planning one's outerwear before leaving home for the station. He pauses for effect, or perhaps a smattering of applause, and Griselda seizes the day.

"And now we should resume. Ms. North, are you ready?"

Ms. North is ready.

"You've described an evening spent with Brinsley Miles. I believe it was on a similar evening that you first encountered the man referred to in the report as Otis, is that correct?"

It is correct.

"And 'Otis,'" Griselda notes, "is another workname, yes?"

No.

It boils down to this: an agent has a workname, and will of course be absolutely aware of what that name is. An asset, however, or a target, or even an innocent, unwittingly involved in a Service operation, will have a *code*name, of which they are entirely ignorant, and which will never be used in their presence.

"But you're going to be calling him 'Otis' throughout?" Again, it is Mr. Singer who requires clarification. "Doesn't that mean that your recollection can't be viewed as being entirely reliable? I mean, that is to say, that it won't be wholly accurate?"

"Oh, it will be accurate," Ms. North submits. "It just won't be entirely true."

"I'm not sure I follow."

"Well, I may have got that the wrong way round." She pauses, and seems for a moment to be about to dissolve back into her break-time reverie, and forget about those attending on her words.

But she hauls herself back from whatever brink she was approaching. "The names are the least important part of it. I mean, I'm not the same woman I was then myself. Whatever name you call me by."

The panel digest this in silence; or at any rate, Griselda does. She cannot speak for the mental workings of her companions.

Ms. North appears to be waiting.

Griselda says, "Tell us about Otis, please."

Tell us about Otis, and for some reason, the day of the aborted picnic is the first occasion that comes to mind, ridiculously enough, given what else occurred in his company. But perhaps it was the car that triggered this reflex: a pearl-white 1969 Chevrolet Camaro convertible with a red interior, which made Alison feel like she was in *Grease*. "You're kidding," had been her reaction when the pair arrived at her apartment building on her fourth Saturday morning in the city, sounding the horn until she appeared at her window. "Where did you steal this from, a rock and roll song?"

Otis pretended offence. "It's a design classic. Not a teenager's plaything."

"Well, you're certainly not teenagers," Alison agreed.

It was Otis's car, it turned out. He had bought it, he explained, from an under-secretary at Clayallee.

"The Yank embassy," Miles interpreted, sprawling across the back seat like a Roman emperor in his chariot.

"Not that I'd encourage you to mix with that crowd," Otis said. "You know why they call diplomats 'dips'?"

"Because it's short for—"

"Because they're all pickpockets. Steal your name, nick your boyfriend, rob you blind. No, you want to watch out for the embassy lot."

"In case they sell you a car, mostly," said Miles.

"Where are we going?" Alison asked.

"The Großer Wannsee," said Otis. "You'll love it."

A lake to the south-west of the city: she'd read about it in the in-flight magazine.

"A picnic?" she said.

"Of course."

She turned to Miles. "You packed a picnic?"

"I've brought a bottle."

"Food? A rug? *Glasses?*"

"There'll probably be a kebab van."

Otis was wearing a pink jacket and cream-coloured trousers, putting Alison in mind of an ice-cream sundae. Miles wore one of his regular suits, recently enhanced by a fresh stain on the lapel, one he'd evidently attempted to wipe away with a damp cloth, spreading whatever it was over a slightly larger area. His green tie was knotted an inch lower than usual, to mark the weekend.

"You're not exactly dressed the part," she told him.

"I had a leather jacket once," he said. "Made me look like Van Morrison."

"Well, that's not so—"

"Now. Like Van Morrison looks like now."

"Oh. I'm sorry."

Otis was the driver she'd have expected; borderline oblivious to other road-users but prone to over-notice pedestrians, to whom he would offer relationship advice or style guidance. That young man there, the girl he was with: it wouldn't last ten minutes. He was her starter-boyfriend, you could tell by the stiff arm round her shoulders; not so much seeking contact as claiming territory. This pair, though, the two women: just the way they were walking down the street should be taught in schools. Otis used both hands to express his admiration; Alison used one of hers to force them back onto the steering wheel. Unabashed, he segued straight from the women's statement lipstick to Alison's own unadorned features. "You don't wear much make-up, do you?"

"Oh, I wear it. Usually when I feel like hiding."

"You don't feel like hiding today?"

"The way you're driving, I feel like entering a nunnery."

Miles said, "We'll probably pass one. We're passing everywhere else."

"Scenic route. Have you seen the Brandenburg Gate yet?"

"I haven't seen anything," she said. "I've been working."

She wasn't to see the Großer Wannsee that day either, because machine-gun fire ripped the day apart before another word was spoken; an onslaught causing Alison to shriek and Otis to swear and Miles to react in no way at all, and the car to swerve wildly across the road while horns blared and brakes squealed. Beneath that was a sound like the sea going out, and then a thump, which was the car hitting the kerb, and Alison's insides leaped inside her. The car made choking noises, while— as she learned afterwards, once her senses had wrapped themselves back into place—a black cloud rose up behind it, keeping its shape far longer than seemed plausible. It brought to mind the cartoon spook painted on the Station House door, though this one was grinning.

A hand was placed on her knee. "Are you okay?"

"I thought—"

"She thought it was gunfire," Miles said.

"I think my heart stopped."

"Just a little engine trouble," Otis said. "It does this."

And you didn't think to warn me?

But Otis was dismissing automotive failure with a breezy hand. "This is not a problem. This is exactly what happens most of the time. Just needs a little TCL."

A snort from Miles. "You need to get your TLAs in the RFO."

"Three Letter Acronyms," Alison explained, when Otis raised an eyebrow. Her heart was beating again, no mistake about it. Was making a break for freedom. She folded an arm across her chest. "And, ah—Right Flipping Order?"

"Where was it you're from again? Regent's Park? Or Pogles' Wood?"

Passing traffic indicated the usual levels of concern directed at those whose cars don't work by those whose do. The Camaro had at least reached the side of the road, or the front of it had. The rear was jutting out, causing something of an obstruction.

"Come for a drive," Miles quoted. "Let's take your little friend for a spin." He lit a cigarette, oblivious to—or in defiance of—the smell of petrol in the air. "I might have known a jaunt with you would have all the dignity of a sidecar funeral."

"Why not entertain the lady," Otis suggested, "while I deal with the practicalities?"

He dropped his jacket onto the seat, and rolled his shirtsleeves up as he went round to the front of the car, ignoring a jeer from a passing Volkswagen.

"There's an idea," Alison said, her voice shaky. "A tap dance? Card tricks?"

"I heard a joke the other day."

"Is it offensive?"

"Only if you're French."

"I don't want to hear it."

"And disabled. Maybe female."

"I definitely don't want to hear it."

"Reported back to Cartwright yet?"

The change of gear so slick, she nearly gave an honest response. Which was presumably the point.

"I—he's not in my line of report. He's, he's, he wouldn't even know who I was."

His eyes were closed again, but she couldn't help feeling that he was studying her closely nevertheless.

"But you've encountered him."

It wasn't a question, but she felt compelled to respond. "Well, yes. Obviously. I mean, he's around the Park a lot."

Which he wasn't, but Miles wasn't to know that. And she needed a reason, in case more information slipped out, why she might be familiar with that sleeveless pullover, or the glasses he wore on a chain round his neck.

"I've heard he's a grandpa now," said Miles. For a moment, he chewed this over, as if contemplating all the futures that might await David Cartwright's grandson. Then: "Pity the poor kid."

"I think that might be it," Otis said, still bent over the motor with the bonnet up. Or hood, rather—an American car: it was probably a hood. "Try the ignition, Alison?"

She shuffled into the driver's seat and turned the key. Nothing happened.

"Not entirely the response I was hoping for," Otis admitted.

"There's a bar over there," Miles said, without indicating any particular direction.

But then, there was always a bar over there, or if not over there, over here—any time she was with Miles outside the Station House, and any time Otis arrived, there'd be a bar sooner or later. Still, she often thought of him as he'd looked that day, standing upright in front of the crocked car in his shirtsleeves, grinning despite the spanner in the morning's works. It wasn't the first time they'd met, of course, but memory has a way of choosing its touchstones. And there was little point in arguing with that now.

A man of substance, the phrase went, and it was to do with materiality, with worldly goods. A man of substance was landed and housed. Alison didn't know then whether Otis was either of those, but he was substantial: first glance told her that much. Not fat, but big, and loaded with the ability to swagger. Even then, she could tell this was a quality which wouldn't abandon him if he were homeless; he'd have the same lordly carriage pushing a trolley down the street, piled with his only possessions. Shaggy-blond and big-jowled, he wore two days of stubble as if it were a fashion statement rather than neglect, and his eyes were the kind of blue you got in books; eyes that were "piercing," or possibly "cold." Though that couldn't be right, because Otis himself came over as warm, a person you'd want to be standing next to in a bus shelter on a snowy night; positively burning with something, call it energy, call it a luminous capacity for friendship. He was the sort of man you expected to find on Spook Street; one who'd spend all night swapping stories and drinking you under the table, and in the morning carry you off to a small café only he knew about, where they poured you a breakfast that set the world to rights. A myth, in other words. Otis wasn't a man, he was a legend.

She had evidently had too much to drink. Her mind was in the wrong gear; speeding along streets without pausing at junctions, reaching a destination she hadn't known she was headed for.

She'd met him a few hours previously. It might have been the fourth occasion she'd spent the evening with Miles, might have been the fifth, but she was pretty certain it was the one she'd asked him why he valued her company. As with some other questions she'd voiced, this puzzled him.

"What makes you think I do that?"

She indicated their surroundings. Another club, this one without strippers at least, or without strippers who were on the clock. No shortage of female forms, though. She'd noticed, if you wanted to be somewhere with a high proportion of women, you had to come to a club like this. On the streets, men outnumbered women five to one. Perhaps it was the way they dressed that put women off. Alison hadn't seen so much paramilitary gear and short-backs-and-sides since watching footage of a skinhead rally. The techno clubs, where the young men flocked, must be like indoor battlefields.

At least the clubs Miles favoured had seating and table service. And the music was a background lilt, not an aural assault.

"You keep bringing me to beautiful places."

"Everyone else has flu."

That was a slap in the face, though was true, or near enough. It was presumably the same strain that had laid waste to London, and even Theresa had succumbed, after some days struggling in like the martyr she wanted you to think she was, instead of the idiot she was being. So Alison was currently sharing her office with nobody, Young Alan being on his second day of absence, and Cecily—well, it was hard to tell with Cecily. But Alison had only a vague recollection of what she looked like.

The flu. This is why I was sent to Berlin, and it's why Miles has taken me under his wing. Don't tell me, if germ warfare's ever declared, that the germs won't win.

Such were her thoughts when Otis strode into shot, her first impression being that here was a man occupying that hazy ground somewhere between an oak tree and the captain of a pirate ship.

When Dickie Bow had sidled up without warning, Miles had reacted by taking potshots at him, his indifference as to whether they struck home or not making the encounter all the more excruciating. But when Otis arrived, bearing a commandeered tray—champagne, so the label claimed, and two glasses, plus a shot of the bar's cheapest Scotch, no ice, thus confirming his credentials as Miles's familiar—Miles went so far as to grunt a welcome, or at least, refrain from grunting a dismissal. By this time, Alison was starting to learn the codebook. She couldn't have put his feelings into words, but was able to eliminate certain possibilities: murderous rage, or overweening joy.

"Sir, madame, the finest bubbled elixir this hostelry has to offer. Plus, some awful piss in a shot glass for the lout with the comedy tie."

His voice was gravelly, and the accent reasonably local, but the vocabulary was a surprise.

Not to Miles. "The sign on the door mentioned a strict entrance policy. No barbarians."

"I slipped the thugs on guard duty your sister's phone number." Placing the tray on the table, he stage-whispered to Alison, "Are you here of your own free will? Say the word, I'll escort you to safety."

"That's useful, thanks."

"I'm Otis, by the way. This monster hasn't the manners of a zoo-bred warthog. Though he does have the looks and the charm, as you've doubtless discovered already."

"Alison. Alison North."

"Very glad to meet you, Alison North. Are you one of his spook crew?"

That gave her pause. "Is there anyone in Berlin who doesn't know what you are?" she asked Miles.

"Well, I thought the couple next table along were still in the dark," he said sourly. "But that cat's out the bag."

"Here's your rotgut," said Otis, sliding the whisky across the table. Miles caught it before it achieved liftoff, and raised it in ironic salute. Otis ignored this, being busy pouring Alison a glass of the fizz, while raising the now empty tray high with his free hand. A waitress materialised. "Would you mind? Thank you so much."

"I'm just passing through," Alison said. "How do you know Miles?"

"About as well as anyone can. He overdoes the man of mystery, don't you find? Even allowing for the needs of the job."

"I'm an open book," said Miles. "You know that."

"But a lot of your pages have fallen out," said Otis. "Anyway, shut up. Alison is going to talk to me. How are you finding Berlin, Alison?"

"It's . . . different."

"I'm sure you're right. If it was the same, we'd have abandoned it years ago." His face crumpled into what she would come to recognise as his habitually self-mocking expression. It was a carrier bag of a face, she'd decided since. Sometimes it was empty, waiting to be filled; at other times it bulged here and there, never in the same place twice. Alcohol probably played a part in this. Drugs too, perhaps. And it didn't detract from his looks, strangely, provided you were okay with the well-travelled, heavy-baggaged type. "Who'd put up with all the shit if it's just ordinary shit?"

"Okay, then. It smells different."

"That'll be the beer and sausages."

She rolled her eyes.

"No, I apologise. You're right." He put a finger in his mouth and held it up as if testing the air. "The wind's blowing in from the east tonight. What you're smelling is coal."

"From factories?"

"Car exhaust. GDR cars, that's what they mostly run on."

"That and beer and sausages," said Miles.

"Forgive him," said Otis. "He thinks it's funny to make inappropriate comments."

"When I need a lesson in the use of appropriate language," Miles said, "I'll not be looking for it from a slack-jawed square-head."

Otis leaned across the table and tapped his glass against

Miles's. Then against Alison's. To her, he said, "Fasten your seat belt. It's going to be a bumpy night."

"Tell me more about Berlin."

"Oh God," said Miles.

"Berlin," said Otis, ignoring him. "You have to understand that, for years, Berlin was a city unlike any other in the world. More than a city, it was like some giant car crash, where everyone stops to look at the damage, and a bottle gets passed around, and before you know it there's a party underway, right here at the accident site, where the flames haven't even died down yet."

"You sound dangerously like a poet."

"Dangerous is what poets ought to be. Dangerous and drunk. Please. You haven't damaged your glass yet."

Which he meant metaphorically, though it could have gone either way. Slightly entranced, and aware that she was slightly entranced, Alison raised her glass to her lips. She wasn't sure it was real champagne. The bubbles were authentic, though, and danced on her tongue, waking it up.

"Above all, Berlin is a liberal city. You can't enjoy yourself in Berlin if you don't have a liberal soul." Miles groaned. Otis ignored him. "And liberalism is always aided by a little compulsion, don't you find? It's best to be tolerant when you're outnumbered. And everywhere interesting in the city, you're outnumbered by punks and hippies and queers."

"Gays," said Alison. "Gay people."

"What?"

"They prefer to be called gay. Queer . . . Queer's a horrible term."

"Well, it's what the ones I know call themselves. But tell you what. I'll introduce you to a few, you can explain to them what they like to be called." Before she had time to take offence, he was topping up her glass. "Here. A peculiarity of the local champagne. Once opened, it must be drunk inside thirty minutes, or it falls flatter than a, than a." He turned to Miles. "Tell me something flat?"

"Your conversation."

Alison said, "If it's local, then it can't actually be—"

He roared, drowning out her objection. Otis occupied a chair, she thought, the way a duvet might, and his attention seemed split three ways, between her, the room and Miles. But mostly Miles. She had the sense that, even when he wasn't watching Miles, he was observing him. As if Miles, left unattended, might turn nasty.

Otis was offering another toast, while simultaneously summoning the waitress, who, when she arrived, bore a tray with another glass of whisky. "Standing order," Otis explained. Then said to Alison, "A short history lesson. *Very* short, because the more time things take, the less drinking gets done. Here in the west, in West Germany, there was conscription. But not in Berlin, because Berlin already had so many soldiers that adding more into the mix, especially native German ones, well." He lowered his glass and clasped his hands together briefly, then made them explode in a hubbub of waggling fingers. "It would have been a recipe for . . . excitement."

Miles grunted. He seemed to be part-enjoying Otis's assumption of the limelight, part-scornful of the theatricality involved. "You have to bear in mind while listening to this man," he warned Alison, "that he's two-thirds bullshit to every one-third bollocks."

"And yet each word is crystal-true," Otis went on. "No conscription in Berlin so it became something of a . . . Canada. Something of a Canada for West German youth of the non-military mindset. You take that meaning?"

"The way American kids headed for the border to evade the draft," said Alison. "But I'm not entirely—"

"Exactly. And of course, along with the anti-military mindset come certain other values."

"Anarchy and dope," said Miles. "Oh, sorry. Did I tread on your punchline?"

Otis ignored him. He was focused on Alison now, as if his lecture were a form of seduction. "Anarchists and deadheads, yes. And artists of every kind, from piss- to post-apocalyptic. And musicians, most of them making very loud noise with very little harmony. And most of them men, of course. This is one of the upsides you're going to find to being here. There are an awful lot of single men in Berlin."

"What makes you think I'm looking for a man?"

"I don't mean to imply you're looking for one. Just that it's difficult not to find one, unless you really try."

Miles snorted.

Alison decided to bypass the topic of the romantic quest in which she was not engaged. "I haven't actually seen that much of the place. I haven't had a lot of free time."

"Well, we shall have to put that right."

She half expected Miles to put up a roadblock here, and point out that Alison's time was his and his alone to allocate.

"And you'll love it. That's axiomatic. Am I using that word correctly?"

"Do I look like I care?" Miles asked.

"He's all sweetness and shite, isn't he? I heard him say that once." Otis clinked his glass against hers once more. "You'll love it," he repeated. "Because the best thing about Berlin is, if you don't love it, just wait twenty-four hours. It'll reinvent itself."

"That must keep the tourist board busy."

"They're mostly occupied spreading the word about the coming recovery." Even in the hubbub she could hear the inverted commas around that word. "Ten years from now, twenty, Berlin will be the financial capital of Germany. Maybe of all Europe."

"But you don't think so."

"No." He paused. "Yes. I don't know. Maybe. But Berlin has the habit of avoiding its obvious destiny. So maybe this is what it will always be, a city of dreamers."

"And dope-smokers," she said. "And anarchists."

"And neo-Nazis." He gave her a sideways look. "Not all dreams are happy ones."

"Did you grow up here?"

"What do you think?"

"I think," she said carefully, "you've been here long enough to pass as a native."

"That would be my wide-eyed idealism showing through."

"No," she said. "I think it's more the dangerous poet."

"Fuck me sideways," Miles put in, his tone more than usually disgruntled. "If I have to listen to you two falling in love, I might just puke all over the table."

Otis laughed, but Alison echoed Miles's disgruntlement with a little of her own. Love at first sight? She wasn't going to fall in love with Otis.

That wasn't what she was in Berlin for at all.

And now Sir Winston stirs uneasily, and barks, or she thinks he does. And then she unscrambles the last few moments, and his noise becomes: "Is all this detail required?"

She pays him the courtesy of considering the question. "No," she says at last. "I don't suppose it is."

"Well, then—"

"But I'm not doing this for your benefit, I'm doing it for mine. So if you want to hear anything, you're going to hear all of it."

"That's not how this inquiry works."

"I won't pretend to be on the inside track when it comes to Whitehall gossip," Alison says. "But even I've heard that this inquiry doesn't work at all. A screw-up start to finish is one of the kinder assessments. So, given I'm the only witness with anything to say that you couldn't find on Twitter, might it not be best to just let me get on with it?"

Too surprised to do anything but raise his tattered eyebrows, Sir Winston allows her to do just that.

So Otis became a fixture, though she afterwards puzzled that he hadn't done so sooner. For it quickly became evident that he and Miles were companions of long standing, who knew each other the way card sharps know the deck: each could read the other by studying the back of his hand. She also realised that the clubs they now frequented were not those Miles had taken her to before she first met Otis. So had Miles deliberately been keeping them apart? If so, why? And why the current change of heart? For it wasn't simply more often than not that Otis was now with them; it was ten times out of ten. And sometimes felt like eleven, given the height and width of his presence. And the fact, too, that they sometimes encountered each other outside of Miles's company.

One lunchtime, a few days after they first met, he was waiting outside the Station House when she left, on her way to a sandwich at a nearby café.

"Should you even be here?" was her greeting.

"Is it top secret?" he responded.

Well, yes. Sort of. But the cartoon ghost on the Station House front door gave the lie to that. Ansel's attempts to scrub it away had only emphasised its presence, muddying its edges so that it appeared more spectral, more spooky.

"Maybe Miles painted it," Otis said.

"That's ridiculous! Why would he?"

"To stop anyone else doing worse?"

Already, she knew him well enough to know a longer explanation was forthcoming. He took her arm, led her along the street. He knew a little place: they could have a quick meal, a quicker glass of wine. No one would even know she was gone. It wasn't that she agreed with any of this, or made a conscious decision to fall in with his design. It was more that it started happening, and continued to do so, before she'd made any objection.

"Berlin is a city of spooks," he told her as they walked. "Always has been. Nobody worries about them. They worry even less when they're made fun of, and that's going to happen, believe me. So you step in first and make fun of yourself. Pretty soon, everyone remembers the punchline, no one recalls the joke."

"Like hiding in plain sight."

"Like just standing around in plain sight. So people forget you're hiding." He offered her a cigarette, and she refused. She was smoking, sometimes, in Berlin. But not yet in broad daylight. "Besides, it's not like he's behind the Wall any more. Miles has a whole different set of games going on."

She must remember that: that Miles was no longer behind the Wall. A lot of the time, it felt like he still was.

"Are you a spook, Otis?"

"I refuse to answer on the grounds that it might incriminate me."

Which was a yes. Unless it was a no.

She said, "I thought you were taking me to a 'little place'?"

"Next time. For now, let's just walk. There's things I can show you."

"I'm supposed to be right back."

"Will they send out the dogs?"

She thought, for a moment, he meant something else. "I don't suppose so."

"Then let's head east."

East was nearer than she had supposed, but then here, more than anywhere else she'd been, east was a matter of crossing a line. At first, that line was imperceptible, Berlin remaining Berlin—the architecture hadn't changed, nor had the sky. But it was grimier, she slowly noticed, the buildings having a patina of neglect not apparent in the west. She was reminded of a split screen detergent commercial, a bedsheet, before and after, and soon other differences appeared. Flags and banners hanging from buildings. A mixture of cultural icons—the Velvet Underground's banana—political statements—the hammer and sickle, the golden crescent—and those which had become a blend of the two: the bearded, bereted Che.

Otis noticed her noticing.

"Squatters. This is how they mark their territory."

"There's a lot of them."

"It's nowhere you'd want to be a landlord, that's for sure." A quick smile went with this, as if he were recalling a private joke. "There are many squats in East Berlin. Squats where people live, squats where people throw parties. Berlin is where you come to when you want to throw a party, or just to recapture the one you were having when the rest of the world grew up."

"You make it sound like one big commune."

"It kind of is. Everyone welcome. So you've got the punks and the dreamers, the junkies and the jokers. The soixante-huitards, hoping to recreate time past, and all the hippie fuck-ups, who haven't come to terms with time present."

"And all they want is a party."

"Perhaps 'party' undersells it. What did they call them in London in the sixties? 'Happenings'?"

"I wasn't invited to any. Being two when the decade ended."

"But maybe you've heard tell of them since."

"They were called happenings, yes. I've never been really sure what they amounted to. Though I think George Harrison attempted to levitate the Albert Hall once."

"Did he succeed?"

"If he had," said Alison, "it probably wouldn't be The Beatles he's remembered for."

They were passing a vacant space between buildings, where a man whose boots didn't match was punishing a stray breezeblock with a hammer, its head wrapped in tape which came halfway down the handle. This muffled the noise to a subdued *doof! doof!*, which might have been the point. More likely, the tape was to keep the head from flying off.

"He's making Wall," said Otis.

"It looks like he's smashing one up."

"Yes, but when he's broken it into bits, he'll sell the chunks to tourists." His voice became comic: roll up, roll up. "Get your genuine bits of Berlin Wall. Pieces of history, buy them here."

But he tossed the man something folded over several times, to give it purchase on the air: a banknote.

"When the Wall was up, the east was like the 1950s. Russian cars, bad teeth, smuggled jeans and no telephones. And the war was everywhere. Not the cold war, the real one. Smashed-up buildings and pockmarked walls. Bullet holes, you know? Never mended." He finished his cigarette, and tossed it into the gutter. It wasn't warm. He wore a thick black coat, though it was only thigh-length, and underneath it, a suit of dark grey. "Well, it's still like that. Reunification happened so fast, we're still catching up. Still chasing the ever-receding spectacle of an economic miracle. There—didn't you say I was a poet? Spectacle, miracle."

"Wall, fall."

"Nice. All this, it looks like a city, but it's really a black hole—you've got a lot of investors lining up, pouring money into it, then going away empty-handed, because all that's happening are the parties and the clubs. Techno. You like techno?"

"I'm not really clued up on it."

"Well, all you need to know is it's got a beat and you can take drugs to it. Which means you need space, which Berlin has in spades. All the empty supermarkets, all the empty stores, all the places the money disappeared. That's what the parties are about. They're celebrating the freedom won when the Wall came down, but because all they're doing is celebrating, the freedom never takes off."

"You sound like a diehard capitalist."

"I'm a concerned citizen, that's all."

"By birth?"

"Alison, Alison. This is Europe, not tight-arsed England. You can be a citizen of anywhere you choose. You think Miles considers England his home?"

She said, "I'm not sure what goes on in Miles's head."

"Probably safer that way." He produced his packet of cigarettes again, stared at it for a moment, then shook his head and put it away. "You're not really a spy, are you?"

Despite his earlier levity on the subject, something serious in his tone took her by surprise. "I can't talk about that."

"I mean, whoever pays your wages, you're not a professional liar. But Miles is. You know that, don't you?"

She laughed, but it was forced. "Are you warning me about him? I should be wary of my virtue, is that what you're saying?"

"I'm saying you should be careful, that's all. I like you, Alison. I like Miles too. But he's not safe company. And he's stayed in Berlin for a reason."

"Which is?"

"He's hunting a tiger."

"He picked a strange place to do that."

"It's a zoo, remember? Of course we have tigers."

"But tigers in zoos are safe."

"It depends which side of the bars you're on."

They'd reached a junction at which a car had stalled. A crowd of youngsters had gathered round, though whether their intention was to get it moving again or strip it clean wasn't obvious. "I should probably be getting back," Alison said, releasing herself from Otis's arm. She hoped to pass somewhere she could buy a sandwich, but in the end went hungry that afternoon.

Strange to recall details like hunger, all these years on, but she can, if required, add weight and colour: say that the smells of other lunches kept reaching her desk—a hot soup warmed up in the Station House kitchen, or a spicy concoction carried in from a nearby stall—and describe how they tormented her all afternoon; explain how famished she was by the time evening rolled around, and she was able to eat. This would not be lying; would be mild fictionalising, at worst. Such embellishments provide context, and encourage hidden details to emerge—the past lies behind a wall, but memories, given encouragement, clamber over. Invention can give birth to truth. Another example of wheels within wheels, and she knows about wheels, Alison North.

But none of this is what the inquiry wants to hear. A few less dangerous poets; a few more operational details. As it is, memories are beginning to flow through her unbidden, now the tap's been turned; it's as if she's reliving, in fast-motion, those weeks that took place in another millennium, and feel like it. It seems to her that the life of Alison North was a fully achieved cycle, complete unto itself, with little or no connection to her subsequent existence, apart from the obvious. Her Berlin days had been like time spent in lockdown, and she feels about them the way she does when a song she remembers dancing to plays on *Desert*

Island Discs. If she shuts her eyes, she can almost pretend she's not pretending when she imagines herself still there. Still dancing.

As for the conversations she has been recalling, they didn't take place on any single occasion; are fragments from different days, different meetings, but running together in her mind. It has, she finds, a certain elegance to look back on those separate episodes as a single continuous happening. Like anyone else, Alison North is prone to seeing her past as if on a screen—when she recalls events she is watching herself participate in them, rather than recreating the sense of having them happen to her. Which makes her current situation an anomalous one; she is both spinning the web and caught in its centre. So when the web breaks—which it does now—it's a dizzying moment, one in which the past comes crashing down onto the ruins of the present.

This moment is heralded by a note struck from a bell in another room. Or that's how it reaches her, though the actual noise is no more than a ping, the tolling of an incoming text. As is usual on such occasions, no one is at first clear whose phone is responsible, and therefore everyone reaches for their own, but out of the assorted fumblings, clarity rises.

"I'm sorry," says Griselda Fleet, and then clears her throat and repeats herself: "I'm sorry."

Phones are laid aside; expectant faces turn her way.

"A message from the Home Office," she says. "It seems Monochrome has been discontinued. With immediate effect."

In the blur of chatter which follows only Griselda, Malcolm Kyle and witness #137 remain seated, while the rest of the company, after a few moments of indecisive shuffling about, reach the communal decision to treat this as an unexpected *exeat*. In this mood they leave the room, their chatter becoming a buzzing behind doors, then a murmur, then a memory. Not all of them have taken all their papers. In the conference room the three figures remain, as if still wrapped in the web so recently spun there, its strands and filaments sticky on their surfaces. A clock chimes. They have no idea where.

At last, Malcolm stands. "So," he says, and begins to stalk around the tables, collecting abandoned pages, unnecessarily arranging them in order. Both women watch, but neither offers comment. When his task is done, he stacks the papers on his own corner desk, clears his throat and says it again. "So." His voice has a curious flatness to it, like that of a man interrupted while deep in fantasy. "That seems to be that, then."

And so it does.

PART FIVE

LONDON, NOW

"Our friend has had a turn. She'll be fine."

Shelley was holding a bottle of water to the woman's mouth, in a vague approximation of someone who knew about turns, and how to handle them.

"Have you called an ambulance?"

"It happens a lot. When her meds kick in, she'll be fine."

"If you're sure . . ."

Max gave a thumbs-up gesture, which surprised even himself. The concerned dog-walker, civic duty done, moved on, and Shelley screwed the cap on the bottle. Their female captive, propped between them, gave a low moan.

He wasn't sure where they were, but it involved a bench, a grassed-over area hemmed by trees, and a children's playground that was currently deserted. Behind the wall at their backs was the main road they'd recently crossed, having cut through several side streets, all named after Dickens characters: a ten-minute walk from the pub, which had taken nearer twenty because of their burden, and if the pub landlord had actually called the police they'd be answering serious questions by now, or wearing serious handcuffs. Aggravated assault and kidnapping: neither of them pursuits that academics should be involved in, even if they had retired early.

Their burden, meanwhile, slumped forward, and would have slid from the bench if Shelley hadn't prevented her.

"She needs medical attention," she said, in the tone of one stating a fact rather than recommending a course of action.

"How do you think I feel?" said Max, touching his cheek where the woman's baton had whipped him. No blood, but a weal had arisen.

"You'll live."

Two nearby dogs quivered in the gloom, taking the measure of each other, while their walkers waited, leashes in hand.

Max said, "Thank you. By the way."

"I'd say you were welcome. But I still wish you hadn't turned up at my door."

"Yet there you were when I needed you."

"What else was I supposed to do? Let you wander into a lions' den by yourself?"

"It was a pub crawl, not a safari."

"Wildlife turned up, didn't it?" she said. "It occurred to me that if you had the idea of going hunting for Bachelor, they might work out the same thing for themselves. And be waiting for you."

"Whoever they are."

"Whoever they are, yes. But whoever they are, banking on them being less smart than you wasn't the clever option."

"In the circumstances," he said, "I can't argue with that."

Other current circumstances included their having shed John Bachelor's company on leaving the pub, a decision reached by mutual consent, or would have been had discussion preceded it. As it was, Bachelor had simply waited to verify the direction they'd chosen, then made off in a separate one. Max had no problem with this. The milkman had done his duty: above and beyond, actually. He'd have put money on Bachelor remaining in the gents once he'd clocked the newcomers' arrival.

He said, "He's not a great advert for Cornwell House, John. On the other hand, he didn't betray me, or not deliberately. And he came out fighting when it mattered."

"So did I."

"So did you. I've spent time with joes. Long time ago. They came with different stripes, but most were brave good people. You'd make a fine joe, Shelley."

"Thanks."

"Even though you're lying through your teeth about your leg."

Her stick lay in two halves back in The Fox and Bucket, but she'd got this far without obvious difficulty.

On the green, the dogs had reached a rapprochement in the traditional canine way, and were conducting nasal examinations of each other's behinds.

Shelley said, "Yeah, I'd rather you kept that to yourself."

"Of course." He had a sudden urge, his first in years, to smoke. "Do you mind if I ask why? Why the play-acting?"

"Because the job's going tits up, that's why. Cornwell House, it's not Park, it's a separate entity, and becoming more separate by the minute. If I go back, which is unlikely, but if I do, I won't be working for the Service, I'll be working for a private company. And the first thing that'll happen is, we'll be cut to the bone."

"Ah."

"Yeah. Welcome to the new austerity." She turned to face him over the slack form of their docile companion. "You're not the reliant type, Max, but then, you're still relatively young. My older clients, they're not going to be getting the help they need, because there'll be a whole new set of criteria operating. Heating bills? We'll supply extra blankets, encourage them to huddle up warm. Food bills? Older people eat less, we all know that." She shook her head. "They've already made sacrifices for the good of the country. Won't kill them to make a few more."

"Except it might."

"Except it might." She inhaled suddenly, and Max wondered if she too were imagining a cigarette. She said, "Bachelor's for the shove, I can tell you that for nothing. And if I stayed, I'd end up with a client list five times as long and half as many resources to support them with. And a new contract, more than likely, with what they're calling de-emphasised terms and conditions."

"Right . . . And this is happening across the board? The Park's being sold off, bit by bit?"

"They're calling it a streamlining. Auxiliary services can be better met by the private sector, unquote. Vetting will be next. That's the big money spinner. Not that many clapped-out spooks, in the grand design of things, but everyone needs vetting. New intake, applicants for senior positions, elected officials, bidders for government contracts. Everybody, when you get down to it. We all get turned inside out in the long run. And it won't stop there. Surveillance? Why spend vast sums on providing the security services with tech when you can get the same stuff from source with in-house operators as part of the deal? Intelligence gathering? The social media giants have got that covered. We just need to reach some friendly arrangements. Timeshare their satellites or something. Jesus."

"So you're getting out."

"They'll pay me off, to get me out of the way while the handover goes through. Troublesome employees are the last thing you want in this line of work."

"I don't know," said Max. "I've met a few. You kind of want them on your side."

The woman between them said, more or less distinctly, "Fuck."

There were fishcakes in the fridge—he hadn't got around to them yet. And maybe a wilted lettuce and a softening tomato, and certainly two inches of vodka in the bottle he'd shamed himself with at the weekend. And their job had just hit the bumpers: they'd been dropped by text, like a rock star's girlfriend. So all in all, home was where he should be heading. One last meal, then he could pull the duvet over his head and practise having nightmares about living in the north.

Instead, he was with Griselda in what had been Sir Winston's office, and was now merely an empty room, Sir W having ferried away his wellingtons, and grandly allowed that they might recycle his abandoned newspapers. The other panel members had likewise packed and departed, Shirin Mansoor—to Griselda's surprise and Malcolm's alarm—having first treated both to an enormous hug. "It has been such a joy working with the pair of you." For the others, it was clearly more of a joy to cease doing so, though all were gracious and friendly except Carl Singer, who put the sweet sweet sorrow of parting behind him in less time than it took to scan his mobile and find something more important to do. He waved a sketchy goodbye from the doorway, and set the lift in motion without waiting to see who else was ready to leave.

As for the witness, she'd been composed, seemingly unsurprised to have her testimony cut short. Then again, Malcolm reflected, interruption wasn't the worst thing she'd suffered. He'd accompanied her downstairs once the lift was free, and found himself on the pavement with her, as if she were a fragile relative he was unlikely to meet again. She used his full name when bidding him farewell, and laughed when he called her Ms. North. "You shouldn't worry, you know," she said. He hadn't been aware that he was worrying, or to be more accurate, hadn't been aware that it showed. "It feels like an ending, but it's only a setback." As he rode back upstairs, he wondered whether she'd been referring to Monochrome or his career. Either way, she was clearly in error.

Now, alone with Griselda, he said, "I'll tell you what puzzles me. The speed with which she—Alison—the speed with which she agreed to appear. We called her, she dropped everything. Almost as if she'd been expecting us. And couldn't wait."

"If she'd waited," Griselda said, "Monochrome would have been over before she'd got here."

"What do you think happened?"

"I think someone at Regent's Park—"

"First Desk."

"—First Desk, I think First Desk didn't like the fact we had OTIS. Didn't want the panel to hear the witness elaborating upon it."

"She certainly added details that aren't in the file."

"And we haven't reached the major parts yet," Griselda said. "The stolen money. The trap they were building."

"Alison wants us to know what was really going on," Malcolm said. "And First Desk doesn't."

"But maybe just on general principles. I mean, it's called the secret service for a reason."

Whatever. He should leave now. It was over. He need never return; could say goodbye to Clive, and never again be disconcerted by how he was supposed to treat him. He could try for straightforward friendliness, he supposed—simply wish him well, and hope for good fortune . . . One day he would be beyond all this; the overcalculation of the everyday. He would just live his life without wondering what mask he should be wearing. But he didn't know how to make that come about.

"What are your plans?" Griselda asked.

"Plans?"

"You know. What will you do next?"

"They're going to send me into the desert."

"You mentioned Sunderland."

He shrugged. "Sunderland. Nottingham. Swansea. Doesn't matter where, it's out of reach of anything important. I'll spend the rest of my career knee-deep in local policies. This is as high as I'll go."

"There are worse fates. Swansea's a nice city. And there's the sea, and the opportunity to build a new life."

"I like my old life."

"Really? Because you don't look like you do. You look like you're being put through a wringer, most days."

For a moment, he was dumbfounded. Couldn't remember the last time anyone had said anything so personal to him, let alone a fellow civil servant. Her response should have been, "Well, quite." Or perhaps, "Of course." The topic thus shut down, they could have gone on to discuss other things, such as the likelihood of rain later. Instead, he was forced into saying, "Yes, well, that's because of bloody Monochrome. I was doing fine until Monochrome."

"Were you really?"

"Second-highest achiever in my intake," he said. "That's not nothing."

"And how do they measure that, exactly?"

Well, who could answer that? There were no actual metrics involved. That would have been insane. "People know," he said. "That's all."

It wasn't logical; it wasn't *maths*. If it were all according to immutable rules, he wouldn't have been assigned to Monochrome anyway. He'd have been too valuable to waste.

She said, "Look on it as a positive. If you stay in Westminster, trying to grope your way up a dirty ladder, you're not going to have time to build yourself a life. Take it from me."

"Why should I? It's not like you got far. I mean, you were in personnel, right? That's hardly lighting up the skies."

"We have different ceilings, Malcolm. Besides. There are challenges I've had to face that you haven't. It really is that simple."

His response surprised them both. "I shouldn't have said that. I'm sorry."

"Oh . . . Well. Thank you."

He felt something give inside him. He should have been on his way home to an overdue fishcake supper—an exhausted salad on the side—but here he was with his colleague of two years, who'd been with him through countless blasted days of pointless witness testimony. If anyone knew how he felt, it was her. "Besides," he said. This was his tongue doing the work now; it was kind of interesting, finding out what it would say next. "You seem pretty sorted."

". . . Right."

"I'm sorry, I just meant—"

"Malcolm, I had a marriage that went sour. Happens to a lot of us. In my case, I lost my house and all my savings. I live with my daughter in a rented two-bed, and I wouldn't reach the end of the month safely if I didn't—oh, never mind. Let's just say, 'sorted' isn't what I think when I think about where I am right now."

He said, "I spend sixty-odd per cent of my salary on rent. I turn the heating on for an hour in the evenings. Two at weekends."

"Look at us. Last of the high achievers."

"I'm going to have a cup of tea. Want one?"

"Thank you."

He took the kettle to the bathroom, filled it, brought it back and switched it on. Then fussed about with the contents of the tea tray. "I might steal these teabags. Unless you want to share them?"

"Knock yourself out."

"What were you going to say just then? You wouldn't reach the end of the month if you didn't do what?"

"It doesn't matter."

"Believe me, if you've got tips about making money stretch, I'm all ears."

She said, "My marriage broke up because my husband had a gambling addiction. Which I didn't find out about until he'd spent every last penny, and then some. A lot of the debt he built up is in my name. So it's a struggle to get to the end of the month. My salary runs out before the days do."

"I'm sorry."

"So I've been taking money from his parents."

"Taking . . . ?"

"I mean, not stealing. Accepting. I've been accepting money they offer, even though they can't afford it. Their life savings. Just a bit at a time, month by month. They want to make up for what he did, even though it wasn't their fault. It was his. And this bit, taking their savings from them, that's mine."

"Not really. I mean . . ."

But it wasn't a thought he could finish, and he had to leave it floating in the air while the kettle picked up steam, and blasted it into nothingness.

He poured water into mugs and let the bags float helplessly. "What about you?" he said.

"What about me?"

"What are your plans? You get to go back to your old job, right?"

"When this one's over."

"Well, that's now, isn't it?" Malcolm used a spoon to flatten a teabag against the side of a mug. "We're past that stage. Monochrome's a dead duck."

"But is it really?" Griselda said.

Only so many descriptions can be made of the Park's nerve centre after hours, and all play on themes of light and shade: First Desk's office, with its frosted wall—behind which a dim bulb gleams, as if a nativity were witnessed from a distance—and the hub's close-kept darkness, interrupted at intervals by the glowing of monitors, their blue screens reflected in their users' spectacles. In the corner a coffee machine waits patiently, one green eye winking, while on the ceiling pulse the faint red LEDs of cameras and smoke alarms and ever-watchful sprinklers, ensuring that activities below can be monitored, screamed about and watered down, a faithful reproduction of the work done on the hub itself. In the absence of calamity, after hours in the Park is a quiet time, most meetings being scheduled by a civilised clock, but even when apparently peaceful the hub is alert for disturbance, whether in the world at large, on the streets of the safeguarded cities, or at the next workstation along, because—as the whispered mantra has it—*You never know*. You never know when treachery might strike, or from what quarter. This is true whatever the time, but especially true after dark, since how we act in the light of day is largely for other people's benefit, but what we do in the secret hours reveals who we really are.

In her office, First Desk was weighing up the day's contents, an exercise which, as ever, promoted mixed feelings. Monochrome was over; a mosquito slapped against a wall. De Vries, too, had been dealt with, or so the email she'd received an hour ago promised: his tender for control of the Service's vetting procedure had been quietly withdrawn. Details had not been given—and wouldn't be, in an email—but she assumed that weight had been brought to bear, his association with the former PM held up as the reason for his disfavour. Both sides would know this for just another round in the eternal game. After all, it was late in the day to claim that foreign nationals had no place in the governance of the nation—you only had to glance around London, its statement buildings erected on laundered money, to know that foreign nationals had been using the city as a playground for decades—but there were lines to be drawn in the sand all the same. You could buy a prime minister, but you couldn't buy the office. De Vries would get that. But he'd also get that his next move was not to make one: to wait, instead, for the wheel to turn again. There'd always be another election, and with it, another set of bills falling due. At which point, there he'd be again, having unobtrusively formed new alliances while the curtains were drawn. This battle won, First Desk knew, she could wake up one morning and discover the war to be lost. But she could only protect the nation one threat at a time.

Restless, she decided to patrol her domain. The boys and girls on the hub were used to this; her silent presence at their shoulders, watching them at work. This evening, most were engaged in surveillance of a trio of young women whose recent purchases at a variety of hardware superstores suggested their involvement in a bomb factory, which meant that their phones were being tracked, their conversations recorded, their movements analysed, and their immediate futures planned. One would, unknown to her, soon be texting the others to let them know she'd be staying with an aunt that weekend, and out of touch for a few days. A room was currently being prepared in a secluded unit on an industrial estate in Hertfordshire.

"Good job," First Desk murmured.

This was passed round the room like a parcel at a party, all present unwrapping a layer, and handing it on.

She continued on her rounds, along the corridors, down a flight of stairs. At the next landing she paused, reconsidered her intention to patrol the Kennel, as the Dogs' floor was inevitably known, and continued down the staircase, each of whose landings was decorated with a single portrait of one or other of her predecessors. She stopped when she reached Charles Partner's likeness. Strange to have his picture still hanging, given his ancient treachery. But like many an ancient sin, Partner's had been buried deep; it might be whispered of in careless corners, but had never been officially recognised. So here he still hung—a hanging too good for him—but at least on a rarely visited wall. For First Desk had reached the archive level, Molly Doran's domain.

The lighting here was dimmer than elsewhere, any instruction First Desk had ever issued to have it strengthened having been countermanded by Molly. That Molly could countermand her orders despite the gulf separating their respective positions remained a mystery to all concerned, except, presumably, Molly. Now, First Desk felt glad of it for no reason she could put a finger on, other than that it was soothing, sometimes, to remain in shadow. When the door swung shut behind her she felt sealed off from the rest of the Park in a way no other door could achieve. Again, a mystery, except probably to Molly.

She walked the length of corridor and paused on the archive's threshold. The silence of libraries was unlike any other kind, and the silence of this one particularly acute. It was as if unintentional noise might release a secret. A thought accompanied, a moment later, by an intentional noise; the clearing of a throat.

Stepping inside, she saw Erin Grey at a desk a little to the left, a lamp angled to pool its light precisely on the book in front of her. Her hair was tied back, and she wore spectacles, as if in conscious homage to a stereotype.

"You're still here," First Desk said.

Erin nodded. "I do my best work at night."

So did I, when I was your age, First Desk thought. But not always at a desk. "We're not currently on an amber alert," she said, "so daylight staff went off shift an hour ago. And as far as I'm aware, there's been no relaxation of the overtime rules."

As far as I'm aware was one of those verbal decorations that soften a concrete absolute. Anything she wasn't aware of didn't happen, so far as the rules went.

"Don't worry, ma'am. I'm not on the clock." Erin showed the cover of the book she was reading: a recent history of the British empire's involvement in the slave trade.

"A little light reading?"

"I'm thinking of doing a master's."

"Very commendable. But if it's promotion you're after, an MA in Sino- or Slavic studies would be a better bet."

"I was thinking more of a sideways move, ma'am. Maybe academia."

"I see." The last thing she wanted—last thing she needed—was a seminar on career opportunities, but the leakage of talent from the Park was an issue that couldn't be ignored. "You're not happy here?"

Meeting her gaze, Erin Grey seemed to be wondering whether to take the question seriously. At length she removed her glasses, folding them neatly and placing them on top of her book. "I have been," she said carefully. "It's important work, and I've been glad to be part of that."

"But no longer."

"We spend more time fending off threats from within than we do defending ourselves from dangers without. With all that's going on in the world, why is playing politics our prevailing narrative?"

"I can see you're practising the jargon you'll need in your future career, but don't let it blind you to facts. I've just come from the hub, where there's work being done that'll prevent tragedy. Real-time tragedy, with severed limbs and crushed lives. *That* is our 'prevailing narrative.'"

"I'm glad to hear it, ma'am."

Which irritated her no end. *Say what you mean, girl*, she thought, but had too much control to say it. "Say what you mean," she said, instead.

"It's fiddling while the city burns, isn't it? Look at Green Shoots . . . I mean, we barely know which way we should be facing. Looking under stones for the next bomb factory, or over our shoulders for whichever Downing Street heavyweight you've—*we've*—pissed off."

First Desk said nothing.

After listening to quite enough of that, Erin said, "Sorry. You asked."

"If this was the military," said First Desk, "that little outburst would see you in front of a court martial."

"Only during wartime."

"Then it's as well we're not at war. You seem to be under the impression that government policy towards the Service is dictated by personal animosity."

"What else is Monochrome about?"

"Monochrome's finished. And Green Shoots—well, see it as a way of funding important services, or just another example of cash cows being herded towards government cronies, but the fact is, we're a country on the edge of bankruptcy, and if it's a choice between taking money that we're not sure where it's been, and seeing no money at all, then it's clear which side to come down on."

"It's not the colour of the money though, is it? It's handing over control of services to people who shouldn't have it."

"You made that clear in your assessment of the initiative, for which I've expressed gratitude. But as for how to deal with the characters involved, you let me worry about that. Now, where's Molly?"

"Home, I expect."

"I didn't think she went home."

"People can surprise you."

"Rather the point of our profession is making sure they don't."

She made to leave, but hesitated and turned back. "You can rely on me for a reference if you need one. Obviously it won't say anything, but I'll put my name to it, and that will open doors. But remember this. You only get to spend your days looking at the past because some of us are guarding the present. And yes, that can mean wasting time and resources on fighting battles that shouldn't need to be fought. But if I don't fight them, the Park loses. And if the Park loses, then it doesn't matter which way we turn to face the enemy, because the enemy's already won."

A speech she thought about afterwards, back in her office, with the wall left unfrosted so she could see her staff, the night crew, at their tasks. It was true, she thought. She had to fight some battles to allow these people to fight theirs. It was simply unfortunate that all her fighting seemed to be done with one hand tied behind her back.

Another email had come in from the Home Office—from, in fact, the Home Secretary. Say what you like about politicos, they didn't go home early. It was, in her own words, just a heads up: the new front-runner for the vetting tender was cleaner money and a UK passport. His name was Carl Singer.

Now, thought First Desk. Where have I heard that name recently?

Griselda opened her bag and produced more paperwork. The world had long been heading towards the paperless office, an environmentally necessary destination, but Malcolm understood the impulse—how could he not? He and Griselda were part of the same pack, and tilted heads to the same whistle. Until an instruction was down on paper, it lacked authority.

She was rifling pages like a card sharp, at length plucking one from her stack and laying it in front of Malcolm. "These are the instructions I received from Sparrow's people two years ago. Because I was—still am—attached to the Home Office, it was decided to make that department Monochrome's controlling body in order to preserve existing chains of command. Sparrow was no fan of the Civil Service, but he recognised its usefulness when it suited him. Now, Sparrow's crew followed his lead, inasmuch as, when it came to establishing how Monochrome should operate, they used existing boilerplate to save themselves starting from scratch. Which means Monochrome's constitution incorporates, among other things, the standard regulation regarding the presidency, that is to say, that in the absence of the president, his appointed second shall fulfil his or her duties and obligations, and in the absence of such second, regulation of the panel shall fall to its secretary."

"You," said Malcolm.

"Me," agreed Griselda.

"Congratulations," he said. "You're in charge. But what's the use of that when Monochrome's been shut down?"

Asking the question because it had to be asked, but already seeing the answer arise from the paperwork.

"Has it? Did you hear Sir Winston close it down?"

"What's the instruction?"

She had it ready. "Blah blah blah, granting the president the power to close Monochrome's proceedings upon being called upon to do so by the Home Secretary or his or her appointed official. Following which, he shall instruct the secretary to prepare and deliver the panel's findings within a period not exceeding six months of the date of termination of proceedings, unless an extension be required blah blah blah."

"And he didn't so instruct," said Malcolm.

"Not in my hearing," agreed Griselda. "As far as I'm aware, Sir Winston left the building without saying or doing anything which might be interpreted as an official termination of proceedings."

Malcolm sipped his tea. It should appal him, the president's failure to conduct proceedings correctly, even—especially—if the failure meant not administering the last rites. But it should equally appal him where Griselda was going with this. And it didn't.

He said, "That being so, what do you intend to do?"

"I intend to do exactly what Sir Winston would have instructed me to do had he grasped what was required of him. I intend, with your help, to prepare and deliver the panel's findings on the subject it was convened to investigate."

". . . Oh." He couldn't help but feel disappointed. Something just out of his reach, something intangible, had been removed before he could appreciate what it might have been.

"Of course," she went on, "we can't complete the report without hearing the rest of the testimony."

And there it was, back within reach.

He said, carefully, "We'd be inquorate."

Griselda shuffled another page loose from her stack. "Closed proceedings. When the president so requires, proceedings may take place in camera, attended by as few or as many members of the panel as the president deems requisite for the occasion." She put the page down. "Well, as acting president, I so require. And I think the pair of us will be more than requisite."

"Is this wise?"

"We're past wise, Malcolm. Somebody got the wind up when we called a witness in about OTIS. Now you're being sent into the wilderness, and trust me, I'll find myself reorganised before I've learned the new code for the photocopier."

"Reorganised." A civil servant, the word made him shudder.

"So why shouldn't we, just this once, wag the dog?"

Warming his hands on his mug of tea, he gave it some thought. Why shouldn't they? Because there'd be consequences. At every stage of his career to date, that would settle the matter—consequences were best avoided, everyone knew that. Results were what you were after; results put an end to a matter and allowed it to be filed. Consequences suggested that things would remain ongoing, which in turn suggested that they were not under control.

"It feels like an ending, but it's only a setback," he said.

". . . What?"

"Something Alison said. I'd thought she meant . . . Well. Never mind."

Griselda sorted the papers into a neat stack. Tapped them into shape. Placed them on the table. She seemed to be addressing them rather than Malcolm when she said, "So what do you think?"

"I think . . . I think we need to call the witness back."

"Right."

"To hear the rest of her testimony."

"You think she'd be prepared to continue?"

"Oh," said Malcolm, "yes. Just my impression. But yes, I think she would."

Max said, "You might have a bit of a concussion. You've almost certainly got a mother of a headache. And you've currently got a choice. Tell me who you're working for, or I'll drown you in the nearest puddle."

"That's not necessary," Shelley chided.

"Whose side are you—"

"No, I meant there's a pond over there."

"I bow to your local geography."

". . . People," said the woman.

"She's telling us there are people about," Shelley said.

"There are," agreed Max. "So I'll be taking a risk." He scanned the gloom. The people in evidence were dog walkers, homegoers, youths with a skateboard. "But not as big a risk as you."

"... Shout."

"You want to shout, go ahead. But you've not the breath to kill a candle. So we'll be all right a while yet."

Shelley said, "Our friend here, he's already mashed your face into his kitchen floor. And I just broke a stick on your head. You're two strikes down, and we're both upright. How much are you getting paid for this? Because it's not enough."

"... Fuck you."

"I think she's feeling better," said Max.

Though it took a while before information started to flow. And when it did, it came slow and sticky.

"Fucking animal," she said.

It was a start.

"Are you talking to me?"

"You're gross. Disgusting."

I'm not the one busting into your house late at night, he thought. Armed with a Taser, and backed by a gang of thugs.

"I don't know who crossed your wires," he said, "but I intend to find out."

"Yeah, what'll you do? Kidnap me? Rape me?"

"We've already kidnapped you," Shelley offered. "Technically."

"Fuck you, scum." She made to stand up, but Max prevented her with an arm made stiffer by the baton secreted up his sleeve.

"Listen, call me all the names you like, but let's hear some background first. Who did they tell you I am? What did I do? Because whatever you were told, you've been lied to. I'm a retired academic. I read books, I write articles, I live in a nice little cottage with a dodgy window latch. Until your gang turned up, my only excitement was signing the occasional petition."

"Let me go or I'll scream my head off."

"Yeah, if you were going to do that you'd have done it already. So why so bashful?"

"She's been told to keep a low profile," Shelley guessed.

"That makes sense," Max said. "No police, no public. You don't want the attention, do you? Not while wandering around with a deadly weapon."

"It's not deadly."

Max tapped his sleeve. "You haven't seen me using it yet."

Shelley said, "There's a whole bunch of you, using strongarm tactics and weapons you bought online. You're either fucked-up vigilantes or private security. Which is it?"

"Screw you, paedos."

Max and Shelley exchanged glances, light dawning.

Shelley said, "That's why you attacked his place? You think he's a paedophile?"

"Who's paying you?" Max asked.

"Screw you," she said again.

"Because there's someone behind this. If it was an online pile-on, a case of mistaken identity, I'd have heard about it."

"Alarms would have rung."

"So this is private enterprise, not a public ruck. So who's pulling your strings?"

The woman didn't reply. But nor did she swear at them.

"If you're legit," said Shelley, "what are you frightened of? Tell us who pays your salary and we'll walk away, no harm done. But keep playing the hero, and Max here will break your leg."

"And I'm not a professional," Max said. "Which means it'll hurt. A lot."

He flexed his arm, and the baton dropped into his palm. It had the heft of a good stout stick, he thought, and he was a man who knew what to do with a stick.

She mumbled something, but neither he nor Shelley caught it. "Say again?"

". . . Four Corners."

"Feeling better yet?"

It was the concerned dog walker, on his second circuit, and if his question was addressed to the woman, his eyes darted between Max and Shelley, scanning for suspicious vibes. His dog, half lurcher if Max was any judge, lowered its hindquarters to the path, its gaze on its human. Max's fist closed round the head of the baton, hiding it from view. "All good now," he said.

"I wasn't asking you."

The woman said, "I'm okay. Are you heading towards the high street?"

"I can do."

She got to her feet. The dog, too, stood on its hind legs briefly, leaning against the pull of its leash, and panting a welcome.

"Take care now," said Shelley. "Don't be a stranger."

The woman was wobbly but upright. She handed Shelley's water bottle back to her. "I spat in that."

"That's fine," Shelley said. "So did I."

The dog walker, unsure of what he'd got himself into, was sticking to his guns. "Come on then." He moved on, and the dog leaped forward too, testing the leash's length. The woman, her bruised face bestowing a last evil-pumpkin glare at the pair of them, went with him, and until they were ten yards off, Max heard urgent muttering from the dog walker.

"That was . . ."

"What?"

"Kind of heroic. People can be quite heroic, really." He stood. "And we want no more of that shit. Come on."

They set off towards a different gate that gave onto the same main road.

"Four Corners?" said Max.

Shelley was already busy on her phone. "Private, ah, personal protection services, it says here. It also says 'urban ranger squad,' which is a bit RoboCop for my liking."

"Where do buses go from here?"

"Thanks for asking, because doing lots of things at once is my specialty. I don't know, Borough Market?"

"And who runs these personal protection services?"

"The thing about this kind of enterprise, actual names of actual people tend to be buried in the background. But I'll find something."

Which she did, ten minutes later. They were north of the river by then, on a bus heading towards Aldgate; Max was mostly looking out of the window, not so much checking that they weren't about to be boarded by a hostile crew as mesmerised, a bit, by the lights and the action. Traffic going all directions, people scuttling in and out of shops. Darkness had fallen, and life was stretching its envelope. It tugged at hidden memories, all this activity. It was a distant shout from his Devon fastness, and dragging a different identity to the surface.

She said, "The name Carl Singer mean anything?"

"Not a thing."

"Because he's head hobnob. Carl Singer, CEO of Singer Industries. Of which Four Corners is a subsidiary, though not one of the headliners. Some way below the fold, in fact." She looked up from her phone. "He's reasonably well-known. I mean, I've heard of him. He gets interviewed on business pages."

"Does he really?" Max said. "Impossible to believe he's mixed up in skulduggery, then."

"Such a cynic." The bus jolted, throwing her against his shoulder. "Sorry. So. What next?"

Max was looking down on the streets again, at all the lonely people. What next? Good question.

He said, "Probably ought to look him up, don't you think? Carl Singer. I mean apart from anything else, I've a window latch needs paying for."

PART SIX:

BERLIN, THEN

And here we are again, she thought, surveying Monochrome's conference room: the blinds covering the windows, the tables forming their open-sided square. An unnecessary number of chairs, because there would be no panel today; there would be Griselda and Malcolm only. Nor, Alison assumed, would there be a report. The request that she attend once more had been presented as an administrative necessity, without which proceedings would remain incomplete, but the pair were either lying or deluded, and she was comfortable she knew which, and did not care. The lighting, per yesterday's request, remained dim, and the rain that had been threatening since the early hours was tapping out messages in Morse on the window pane. Sometimes it felt that the city might never stop raining; was about to wash itself away on a wave of its own making.

She had been ushered in—again, like the previous day—by Clive, and had been pondering the man since. Clive was interesting in exactly the proportion he lacked obvious interest. Of indeterminate age—thirties? forties?—and dressed in a uniform (grey suit, red tie, lanyard on a blue ribbon) that obliterated individuality, he made it easy to imagine him as more than he pretended to be, his *Yes, sir*s and *Good morning, ma'am*s mere tradecraft. She remembered the strippers she'd encountered in Berlin, all spooks in their own way, and how they'd put on identities before removing their clothes, one kind of covering masking a different disrobing. Clive's uniform might mask naked treachery. Maybe he was on the phone to the Park the moment

Monochrome convened each day. Maybe he had the offices bugged, and was compiling his own dossier . . . If Alison knew nothing else, she knew this much: that it was the small betrayers, the watchers, who were the cogs of the secret world. Without them, the machinery of Spook Street would grind to a close.

"We're very grateful you agreed to come in today," Malcolm says.

She finds that she likes Malcolm, despite—or perhaps because of—a strong suspicion that he doesn't much like himself. But he is young enough for this to be a phase, and even those who know her well—a number that, most days, she would peg at no higher than two—might be surprised to learn that she hopes this is the case. But life, she feels, is too fragile to waste in self-loathing, unless such disgust has been adequately earned.

But all she says in reply is, "It's mildly inconvenient. Nothing more."

Griselda coughs, and examines whatever notes she took yesterday. "We can begin," she says, "whenever you're ready."

Alison is ready.

Familiar sequences in black-and-white movies show a breeze catching a calendar and blowing its pages away. The current process was more like trying to catch those pages and stick them back on the wall, pinning the day, the month, the year, to actual memories. The first time things happen, they do so in the correct order. Afterwards, there's more of a scattergun approach. Nevertheless Alison was sure, or reasonably so, that the night she broke into Miles's office was the one that had started in the club below the apocalyptic supermarket—apocalyptic because there were still raggy banners everywhere reading "Everything Must Go." She was indebted to Otis for the translation. Otis's running commentary rarely left things unnoticed.

To reach the basement, you had to descend one of the pair of unmoving escalators, on which it was—Otis again—traditional to slap the red button when you reached the bottom; the one that would have brought it to a halt once, and which you'd be fined for pressing without cause. Downstairs, you were among the mirrored pillars consumers once road-tested lipstick in, onto which were now taped album sleeves displaying Bowie in different guises, alongside a gallimaufry of would-be iconic images, from snarling punk posturing to the prog-rock fantasies of Roger Dean. Some had been painted over, perhaps to indicate evolving tastes, but perhaps just meant people got handy with spray cans sometimes. Alison thought she saw a swastika, but it might have been an accidental conjunction of angles; a collision of unfinished squares. Within moments of their arrival Miles had found a table, which was probably how the club had acquired it: found it, that is, on a skip or a wasteground. It was tin, its surface knobbled and dimpled as the moon's. Other nearby tables were upturned trunks or glass-topped display cases. Lamps were dotted here and about, several plugged into extension leads that snaked out of sight, becoming trip hazards elsewhere. The noise lived down to the décor. The sickly-sweet smell of hash, thick upstairs, was thicker here.

Alison's chair was a milkmaid's stool, generously stickered with smiley faces and anti-nuclear slogans. Sitting, she said, "Is this club famous?"

"Not sure." Miles looked at Otis. "They named a disease after this place yet?"

"The night is young."

But the place was heaving. Another thing to add to her Berlin album: the smell of sweat, hash's undercoat. It wasn't that the people weren't clean; just that, to find them so, you had to catch them the right time of day.

Otis noticed her eyeing the pack. "On a weekday evening, too," he said. "Does it still shock your bourgeois soul, all this partying?"

"It doesn't even shock me that old hippies still say 'bourgeois soul.'"

He grinned: that wide mouth, doing what it did best. "Think of it as delayed reaction. The partying, not my vocabulary."

She surveyed the crowd again. It would be good to be part of it; swaying and swashing and surrendering to the beat. That afternoon she'd had a showdown with Robin Bruce, who now knew she was under false colours; soon, she'd report this encounter to David Cartwright, which would magnify her sense of treachery. And it was impossible that Miles would remain unaware of her true role much longer, if indeed he was unaware, and not playing his own game. Perhaps tonight would be her last time sitting at a table with this pair among crowds of young Germans. Some older ones too. A trio at a nearby table were well past youth, drinking clear liquor from an unlabelled bottle, and eyeing the dancers like butchers assessing a coop.

Otis, who never liked leaving a thought unfinished, said, "Berlin has always known how to enjoy itself, even under severe conditions. Every bridge has its campfire, every campfire its dancers. There's always music."

"I hope this is going in your report," said Miles to Alison. "It's like listening to the fucking BBC."

"I'm not making a report."

"What do they call it now, then? 'Downloading your impressions'?"

Otis said, "And so it goes and so it goes. But where it goes, no one knows." He hoisted his glass: beer, in the establishment's absence of champagne. "Here's to the dancers. May they always keep the beat."

"There are nuns drink faster than you," Miles observed sourly. His own glass was empty.

"We need another round here," Otis called, to nobody in particular, and a waitress was at his side within seconds. "Darling," he said, or something like. "More of all of this for all of us."

On those occasions—which was most of them—when the establishments they were favouring offered table service, Miles allowed Otis to order the drinks, and also to pay for them. The receipts, though, he scrupulously collected.

He turned to Alison now, to practise his small talk. "You're looking peaky."

"Thank you. Nothing a woman would rather hear."

Miles shrugged. "If you're up the stick, I've a number you can call."

It took a moment for this to sink in. "You can be a real prick, you know that?"

"Mr. Otis?"

It was one of the nearby trio; forties, at a guess, with lank dark hair and trim beard, mottled with grey.

Otis lounged back on his stool, a dangerous manoeuvre, but one he accomplished with grace. "I'm not sure I've had the pleasure."

"No, but you're a well-known figure about town."

The newcomer took in the company, nodding at Miles, then Alison. "Sir. Miss."

Miles grunted. Alison said, "*Guten Tag.*"

"Ah, English." He switched languages. "It is a pleasure to meet you."

"We'll be the judges of that," Miles said.

"One of the things I admire about your people. Their grace when abroad."

Miles showed his teeth. This might have been a smile.

"Always happy to make new friends," said Otis, continuing in English, "but what was it you had in mind?"

"I understand you've come into possession of a property."

"Bought it, you mean. Yes, I've bought a property."

"It's an ... unusual thing to do, in today's market. In that area."

Otis said, "I have great faith in the coming economic boom. Soon property prices will rise, and I'll be a rich man." He raised his still unfinished beer. "To capitalism."

"You're aware there are squatters in the building."

"A temporary inconvenience."

"Of course. But, and this is what I crossed the floor to mention, but if it turns out that you wish to rid yourself of this inconvenience, I can perhaps be of assistance."

"Really?"

"Yes. The company I represent has experience in these matters. It is a small occasion, swiftly done. And for a reasonable price."

"I see. Well, that's kind. If I decide to use your services, how would I get in touch? Do you have a card?"

The man gave a pantomime shrug. "Alas, I gave away the last half an hour ago. For the time being, perhaps you could just remember the name? Dieter Schulz."

"Dieter Schulz," Otis repeated.

"Yes. Mention it anywhere." He looked around the club. "You'll be put in touch."

"I like a man with good connections."

Schulz nodded, as if this were hardly worth mentioning. He said, "It has an interesting history, your building."

"Yes. That's the main reason I bought it." Otis stretched his palm across the table, and Miles, not normally one for playing the straight man, placed a cigarette in it. "I'm a collector of curios, you might say."

"That is also interesting," said Schulz. "Because I had

heard you were more of a, what is the word for it? Fixer. Yes, I'd heard you were something of a fixer, Mr. Otis. Is that true?"

"I prefer to think of myself as a people person."

Schulz produced a lighter. "And how about ghosts. Do you believe in ghosts, Mr. Otis?"

"Not so much." He inhaled, then removed the cigarette from his mouth and brushed at his shaggy hair. The lock he displaced immediately fell back to its original position. "But I do believe some places retain . . . impressions. Impressions of what went on there."

"Really?"

"Yes. In fact, you could even say that some events leave records behind."

"I have heard that."

"This particular house," said Otis, "you only have to step through the door. It's uncanny."

"It's hard to say," said Schulz, "whether you're a very lucky man or a very unlucky one."

"Isn't it, though?"

When Schulz left, Alison looked from Otis to Miles and back. Neither said anything, nor even exchanged a glance. Otis finished his beer as the waitress arrived with a fresh round. Alison's—a red wine—joined the almost full glass in front of her: a pair of sentries, alert for anything.

"What," she said at last, "was all that about?"

Otis shrugged. "Exactly what it sounded like."

"You've bought a house?"

"Did you think I was homeless?"

"But not one to live in."

"He wouldn't want to live in it," Miles said. "It's haunted. Weren't you listening?"

"Plus, squatters," said Otis.

"You're both very annoying, you realise that?"

Miles stage-whispered: "She's touchy tonight. Scared she's pregnant."

"Oh do fuck off!"

Her own vehemence surprised her: she should have been used to him by now. But she was getting to her feet before she'd finished swearing, knocking over a glass of wine as she did so: luckily this didn't impede her progress, as it fell in Miles's direction. He made a number of sounds, each more irritated than the last, while Otis leaned back and watched with amusement as the tabletop's dimples filled like a valley floor in a flash flood. *Don't look back*, she told herself, and didn't look back; forced her way through the madding throng like a woman on her way to do damage. It was possible Otis—Miles?—called her name, but equally possible he didn't. And anyway, wasn't this the opportunity she'd been looking for? Miles ensconced for the evening, and the Station House a ten-minute walk. It was as well the mirrored columns were plastered with album sleeves, because she wasn't sure she wanted to see her face. Guilt was like wearing too much make-up: everyone knew you were masking something. When she reached the outside world she took deep breaths, thankful she'd not drunk much. She remembered David Cartwright saying *I'd encourage you to try to win Miles's trust, but that's not an especially likely outcome*. He was naturally suspicious, naturally untrusting, naturally a spy. And here she was, a spy too, in his own backyard. There was every chance it wouldn't end well.

She walked on, hurrying but trying not to appear hurried. Didn't look back, because why would either of them follow?

That afternoon she'd had a showdown with Robin Bruce.

"I need a word, Robin."

"Of course, of course." The affable Housemaster: that term suited him. In another life—or in the same one, played out differently—he'd have occupied a study in a minor public school, a grey cardigan under his scholar's gown. The sadness bowing his shoulders might have had a different cause, but it would have come to the same in the end. He turned his back on her to open the window, letting air into the room that carried with it the now-familiar ribbon of coal and street food and something else she would never identify, but would ever after pain her when she encountered it. "Come in, sit down. Alison, Alison. Are you settled in? What can I do for you?"

Her heart was pounding, but this needed to be done. "I'd like to know what 'Basilisk' is."

"I'm sorry . . . ?"

"Basilisk." She closed the door and took up his invitation to sit, while he watched her with words like *viper* and *bosom* sidling round his mind. "There's a withdrawal been made, a sizeable one, from House funds. In cash. US dollars. You authorised it, and marked it 'Basilisk.'"

"I see." He lowered himself into his chair, reaching for the packet of cigarettes by the telephone. "Well. I wasn't expecting that. Perhaps I should have done. What exactly is your role here?"

Assess daily procedures and work-related outcomes. But what she said was, "To make sure everything's running as smoothly as possible."

"A broad remit."

"But that doesn't mean I need turn the House upside down. All I'm interested in are procedural errors, Robin. Nobody's looking to capsize the ship."

She didn't know where that had come from, the nautical metaphor. But it was enough that she was making some kind of sense, she supposed. Her heart was beating so loudly, it was a wonder the window pane didn't tremble in response. If he called her a silly girl, she'd flee the room weeping.

That, anyway, was what her inner imp suggested, the one whose job it was to make sure she didn't get above herself. She tamped it down, and it guttered like a candle. She had a job to do. She was authorised. She was in charge.

Besides, Robin's own imp was clearly rattling cages. He'd lost colour, and was flexing and unflexing the fingers of his left hand. "Cartwright's got it in for me, hasn't he?" he said. "That's what this is about. That's why you're here."

She shook her head. "I'm so low down the ladder, you wouldn't believe it. I don't take instructions from Mr. Cartwright. He doesn't know I exist."

"One bloody slip-up." She was afraid his eyes were glistening as he plucked a cigarette from the packet and lit it with a flourish. Shaking the match, he placed it carefully in his ashtray, watching it as if it might burst back into flame. Smoke curled from his fist. "They give us these jobs to do, these roles to play, and they forget we're only bloody human. It's not like I walked into a honey trap. I fell in love, Miss North. Not with an agent of a foreign power, or a, a, a, a bloody blackmailer. Just an ordinary, ordinary . . . person."

This was an improvement on the twenty-minute biography of his former lover that he'd embroidered over their first lunch, but to fend off a relapse to that self-pitying mess, she nudged him with a word. "Basilisk."

He stared, as if she'd trodden on his soliloquy. Then shook his head. "Nothing of interest. Truly."

"I'll have to be the judge of that, I'm afraid."

"You mean, whoever's pulling your strings back in London."

"We all have jobs to do."

"You're too young for that defence."

"It's not a defence, Robin. It's a statement of fact."

"Hard as nails. Every last one of you."

Women, she assumed. Or younger women. Or maybe just other human beings, who hadn't suffered the way Robin Bruce had.

He regarded the cigarette between his fingers with bewilderment, as if someone else had put it there, then took a drag. "Basilisk is one of Miles's. All above board, don't worry about that."

"It's an operation?"

"Not exactly."

But it was an operational codename, or that's what it sounded like. "Then what?"

"Basilisk is, is, is, well. You might call it post-operational. It's welfare, when you come down to it. Damn it, is that thing shut?" He stood suddenly, and for a fierce moment Alison thought he was about to assault her. Instead he marched to the door and checked it was firmly closed. When he turned he seemed about to say more, but clamped his mouth round his cigarette instead, as if smoking were a cardiovascular exercise requiring serious effort. "Look, you can't breathe a word of this. It's not that it's classified, it's just . . . a touchy subject." Back behind his desk, he slumped into his chair, which softly groaned. "Miles had an asset, back when the Wall still stood. An officer in the Stasi. Codenamed Bogart. A lot of assets, most of them—look, I shouldn't be telling you this."

And I shouldn't be here, Alison wanted to reply. Her life suddenly seemed very far away. Her friends back in London thought she worked in local government, in a role so dispiritingly dull it had become a brushaway joke: one reference to it allowed in every gathering. But that was a necessary falsehood, for everyone's benefit. Here and now, deceit was more damaging. Robin Bruce had offered her a welcome, even if that welcome were required by Regent's Park; the others, too—Young Adam, the elusive Cecily, Benny, even Ansel and Theresa—all had shuffled aside to make space for her in their own ways. What she was doing here, characterised by David Cartwright as duty, had turned into betrayal. She wished she'd not come. But it was too late for wishes.

So what she said was, "I need to hear all of it. Otherwise I'll take it to the Park."

The look he bestowed upon her was one of regret, as if she were simply the latest in a long line of women who'd sought to disappoint him. "It's a grubby game we play, isn't it?"

"An officer in the Stasi."

"Yes. Can you imagine what bravery that must have taken?"

"Not really."

"Quite. Anyway. Anyway. Most assets, after the Wall fell, came over to us, to receive their just rewards. What we called the passport package. A new life under safer skies. Seems a fair reward for those who'd been risking their lives year in, year out. But Bogart turned the package down."

"Why?"

"Said it was a time for rebuilding, not abandoning. Said working with the west had been about working for freedom, and now that freedom was here, it was time to ensure that it was enjoyed by all. Idealist, you see? Less of that about than you'd imagine. Putting your money where your mouth is, I mean. Though in this case, no money changed hands. Bogart never took a penny."

He allowed a moment's silence to laminate that fact, while smoke from his cigarette curled ceilingward.

"The Wall might have fallen," he said at length, "but people have long memories. Over on their side, they must have known they had a leak, because you always know. That's the conventional wisdom, anyway. You always know. But what they didn't know, and what they somehow found out, don't ask me how, was that Bogart was a woman."

The picture in Alison's mind, tilted sideways until now, righted itself. "When did they find this out?"

"A year ago. Or not quite."

"So this is what, three years after the collapse?"

"Or two since reunification. Or one since the dissolution of the USSR. They're only dates, Alison. History alters the landscape, it doesn't change the people. Bogart was our hero but she was someone else's traitor, and she paid that price. Not only her, either."

"What do you mean?"

"We can only assume that they received incomplete information. That Bogart was a female officer of a certain rank, but nothing more than that. Still, it more than narrowed the field. There were only two other women of that rank during the time frame Bogart was working for us. Only three possible suspects. And plenty of former Stasi officers, KGB too, prepared to avenge themselves on those who betrayed them."

Alison felt her stomach contract.

"Never let anyone tell you this isn't a dirty world."

She wouldn't.

Robin said, "All three were hanged. With piano wire. We received a photograph, it came through the post like a catalogue. Three of them in a row, in a forest. Miles's joe, and two other former Stasi officers. Innocent, obviously, though of course that's a relative term, given what the Stasi got up to . . . There were . . . things tied to their feet. Irons, I believe. To weigh them down. Makes the wire cut that much tighter, I gather."

Alison tried to say something, but there was nothing to say.

Robin mashed his cigarette stub out.

"The photograph showed the three of them, and there was a man with them too. Back to the camera, because he wasn't a fool. Possible he was just a lackey, of course. I mean, it can't be an *easy* job, can it, hanging three women, there must have been a whole crew involved . . . Christ, I'm burbling. Miles still has the photograph. As far as he's concerned, that man's the architect, the one responsible for the . . . slaughter."

"But you don't know who he is."

"No. Though believe me, Miles is keen on finding out."

They sat in silence for a while, the smell of cigarette smoke thinning in the draught from the window. The image of three hanged women was difficult to dispel. The cost of heroism—of betrayal—was high; it was the same cost, seen from opposite sides. And the same cost applied, it seemed, if you were neither hero nor traitor, but simply occupied the same neighbourhood.

At last she said, "Where does Basilisk fit into this?"

"The Basilisk funds, it's simply a name for the money, technically they belong to Bogart. Like I said, she never accepted payment, but the Park doesn't trust idealists. If you're not taking money you're playing a game, that's how the Park sees it. And if you're playing a game, you can change sides. So when Miles set up the Bogart line, he told the Park she needed paying in dollars. That's the language they understand. The product was good—she was an invaluable source—so the money was forthcoming."

"But it wasn't actually going to Bogart."

"No, it was sitting in one of our boxes." She raised an eyebrow, and he said: "Well, we couldn't keep it in an account because sooner or later it would have been noticed, and then the ceiling would have dropped in. It's one thing spending money you're not supposed to. But not spending money you've been authorised to spend, that's a serious business. Careers have . . . foundered."

"So," she said. "For some years, Miles was running an agent who didn't require payment, but the Park was paying her anyway. And that money was piling up in a deposit box."

"It wasn't as outlandish as you're making it sound."

"And now, with the agent dead, and the payments presumably ceased—that's right, isn't it? The Park isn't still paying her?"

"The payments stopped when she died."

"Okay. So now, a year or so on, suddenly you're spending the money. Why?"

"Because Miles made contact with her family. A son. And persuaded me that the money was rightfully his. As it happens, I agreed with him. Still do. The money's not ours, it was paid to a brave woman who died because she'd helped us. Why shouldn't her son have it?"

Alison could see no reason why not.

"How much does it amount to?"

"All told, a shade over forty thousand, I think."

It sounded like Bogart had been a bargain.

Bruce read her thoughts. "If she'd wanted paying, she could have held out for rather more. But she didn't know the money was being disbursed, and I think even Miles forgot about it. So she remained bottom of the scale, despite her value."

"And now you're accessing the funds, why are there receipts? If this is all under the counter?"

"Because we weren't stealing the money, damn it! We weren't then and we aren't now. Every penny's accounted for."

"Have you met this son yourself?"

His face hardened. "If Miles says he's paying her family, he's paying her family."

"You trust him."

"With money? A hundred times over. She was his joe. So yes, he'd have gone out of his way to find her family. Who probably didn't even know what she did, and might not welcome the news. But it's a debt of honour."

That word hung in the air for a while, as if he'd deliberately spun it that way. She felt, perhaps unfairly, that he'd intended it to hurt.

Perhaps that was true. Certainly, as she stood up to go, he said, "I can't say I'm not disappointed."

"We're all here to spy, Robin. It's our job."

"I suppose you're going to ask me to keep this to myself."

"I didn't think I'd have to," she said, leaving the room.

When she reached the Station House it was in darkness. Well, it wasn't like there was a war on. Her main worry was the Comms office annexe with its camp-bed, which, according to Young Alan, Benny from IT was using on a regular basis, fights with his live-in girlfriend having reached a 48-hour cycle. Why don't they just split up, Alison had wondered, to which Young Alan had blushingly suggested that the concurrent 48-hour cycle in which they patched things up was an argument for keeping things as they were.

The streets, elsewhere wilder than London's, were quieter here: there was noise nearby—an ambient roar; the noise the sea makes when there's no one on the beach—but the place was mostly deserted, save for the usual group on the steps at the corner, and a huddle of teenagers over the road, passing round something that glinted like foil in the half-light. At the door, she fumbled for the key while the cartoon spook shimmered and pulsed. *Who you gonna call?* Her heart was the loudest beat in the city. It almost drowned out the harsh squeak the door made when it opened, alerting everyone in Berlin to her whereabouts.

I left some papers behind
Robin asked me to collect a file
I can't find my purse and I wondered if

But her excuses, dangling as they were, weren't called upon. If Benny was on the premises, her arrival hadn't disturbed him.

Closing the door, she stood in the dark hallway waiting for her heart to slow down, which it didn't. This was her new beat; the rhythm of her next little while. It would see her through the treachery she had embarked upon.

The keys for the various offices—the spare sets—were in Theresa's room, its own door kept open during the day, "in case of walk-ins." Even Alison hadn't needed a phrasebook for this: walk-ins were what they sounded like, people coming in from the street, shouldering secrets they hoped to swap for worldly goods. In the weeks following the Wall's collapse, the story went, the Station had considered setting up a numbered-ticket system, like at a deli. Whether that had really been the case she didn't know, and all that mattered was whether Theresa's office remained unlocked outside office hours. Her heartbeat counted out her steps across the tiled floor, passing the cubbyhole where Ansel spent his days, perhaps hoping for a moment during which he could demonstrate his abilities as guardian of the house; perhaps hoping such a moment never came. Her eyes, adjusting to the gloom, made out his mug on a shelf, a folded newspaper on his small table. She reached Theresa's door and tried the handle. The door was locked.

So she went home, her internal narrator supplied, *and went to bed, and the following morning pretended this had never happened.*

Instead she stayed where she was, internalising the problem.

The door's locked. You can't get in.

A group of people walked past the front door, talking loudly. She caught scraps of their dialogue; something about a party happening somewhere.

The longer she remained like this, the less sense it made. None of her threadbare excuses would survive the time spent loitering in the dark.

Which didn't make sense either—being in the dark. Either

she had reason to be here or she didn't. She reached for the light switch, and a moment later the hallway was bathed in a warm yellow glow, though everything remained unfamiliar, as always happened out of hours. That childhood fantasy, that fixtures and fittings come to life when the family's asleep, there was a reason that persisted. The row of coat hooks on the wall had acquired a sinister air. She tried Theresa's handle again, but the door remained locked. Think. This office was the Station House's hub. It was where the post arrived; it was where you went when you ran out of anything. It was where the kettle was kept; the one Ansel boiled to make his tea.

This was the thought she'd been waiting for.

Ansel's doorless cubbyhole didn't contain much, especially when it didn't contain Ansel. His chair; the table for his newspaper. A shelf, on which his mug sat, next to three worn-out paperbacks. The table had a drawer, just big enough to contain a box of matches, a tube of ointment she didn't examine closely, and a key on a length of string. With this, she opened Theresa's door.

Again, she turned the light on. No show of innocence would help if she were caught now, but there was no sense hampering her own efforts. The office keys were kept in a cupboard on the wall; it was locked with a small padlock, the kind that secured a bicycle. Alison checked the nearby surfaces, on which no padlock key lurked; she opened drawers and found nothing. A teacup missing a handle sat on Theresa's desk, and she upended it to discover a mess of paperclips and elastic bands and a device for unclasping staples, but no padlock key. She rattled the lock again, but it hadn't stopped functioning since her first attempt. The hook-and-eye fitting from which it hung was a flimsy affair, and the leverage a wooden ruler afforded would be enough to prise it free. This would render useless any attempt at covering her tracks, but she'd come this far, and if she turned back now might as well head straight to the airport . . . She sorted through the paperclips again, knowing already that doing things twice was the first step towards panic. Better just to tip everything back into the broken cup, put the cup back where it had been. No point going through the drawers again, but she did so anyway; found a pair of compasses—a pair of compasses?—and for a moment imagined herself picking the padlock with them; recreating herself as a lockbreaker because that was what the moment demanded. But there was no sense trying, and meanwhile the minutes were ticking by.

In the end, she took Theresa's wooden ruler and prised the hook-and-eye free.

It dropped to the desktop with a thump, padlock still attached. Splinters poked from the damaged cupboard doors, but at least they opened, revealing the hooks on which keys hung. Alison plucked Miles's set and wrapped her fist round it; pushed the cupboard doors closed again, but did nothing about covering up the wreckage; left Theresa's room, turning the light off behind her. She switched off the hall light too, and climbed the stairs in darkness.

"Notes, memos, jottings."

This was what David Cartwright had said to her yesterday, in one of their furtive telephone conversations. She had listened over the noise of a Trabant kicking up a fuss at a traffic light; blue smoke unfurling from its exhaust like a scarf from a magician's sleeve, a visible pungency ballooning into the sky.

"Why would he keep notes?"

"You'd be surprised. I've known joes keep diaries." She couldn't tell whether he was joking. "I doubt . . . *Miles* would be that foolish. But he'll be foolish in other ways. Look for receipts, you'd be surprised how many old hands hoard receipts. There'll always be an expense account they can hang them on. Evidence of being where he shouldn't be, with people he shouldn't be with."

That's just his daily routine, she wanted to say. That's just the life he lives.

"I'm not expecting photographs or videotape, Alison. I can hang this man with a length of red ribbon. All you need do is find that for me."

A length of red ribbon, she thought, climbing five storeys' worth of stairs. This is what you sent me to Berlin for. To find a length of red ribbon.

On the top floor, she padded across a squeaky landing and stood outside Miles's door. She'd taken a mould of his key in her hand; the impression burnt into her waxy palm. She slipped it into the lock now, turned it one way, then the other. When tumblers fell into place, she turned the handle. The door was locked. She turned the key again. Now it opened. He hadn't locked his door. The splinters in that cabinet; her beating heart. All pointless, because she could have just walked upstairs and let herself in.

She didn't know whether to hate Miles for this, or laugh. Hating was quieter, though. She pushed open the door, and stepped into his office.

The light switch was useless, the bulb having long since blown. And Miles didn't do overhead lighting, though whether that was a habit he'd acquired through being too lazy to replace a bulb, she didn't know. The Anglepoise worked, though, and she clicked its button to release a pool of light that swamped his desk and spilled onto the floor, illuminating scorch marks and dubious stains. The air was limp with the afternoon's smoking. Up here, the city's late-night buzz was muted, as if a partygoer had been bound and gagged and left to roll around on a dancefloor unsupervised.

She started with the drawers. They were a mess; so much so

it was easy to suspect it was deliberate, because who could find anything among this welter of bus tickets and Biros, pencil ends, pen tops, used envelopes, plugs and fuses, scraps of paper, sandwich wrappings, crocodile clips and treasury tags, candlestubs, boxes of matches, packs of chewing gum, cassette tapes and unidentifiable bits of plastic? To work through this meaningfully she'd need to tip each drawer onto the carpet, and still be here in a week's time. She closed each one and turned to the filing cabinet instead, because of course a spy would file evidence of his treachery: probably best to start looking under "T." These drawers were locked. She remembered that a filing cabinet's locking mechanism was operated by a single rod; that if she upended the cabinet she could open every drawer with one vandal act. That wasn't going to happen. Telling herself there was no desperation involved, that she was being methodical, measured, she turned to what lay on the desktop, in open view. No length of red ribbon. An Olympic logo of shot-glass stains, plus the phone was slightly off the hook. When she raised the receiver to her ear, a dead emptiness met her. She put it back the way it was, or tried to, unconvinced she had matched its original careless disposition. Miles kept a paperweight, a lump of rock that might have been actual Wall; might have been a street-seller's knock-off. She wondered which would have more resonance for him, then put that thought aside while retrieving the piece of paper it safeguarded. German words, in a column: a coded list.

"If you're planning on walking out with that, you're looking at twenty years. Minimum."

Her heart had stopped in the time it took him to say this. It started again as he moved into the room closing the door behind him. Coming up the stairs, coming through the door, he'd made no sound at all. He might have been an actual spook, haunting his daylight premises.

"Because this is a Service house, meaning everything here's classified material. And intent to sell, that's not a good look on a fledgling."

When she was sure her voice wouldn't wobble, she said, "This is a shopping list."

"And you think we want that falling into the wrong hands? The Russians discover we're short of bacon and milk, they'll be parking their tanks on Friedrichstrasse in the morning. Uh-uh, lady. Treason's treason whichever way you slice it."

"You're being ridiculous."

"And you're being in my office at one o'clock in the morning. Which of us looks guiltier?"

He'd produced a cigarette, and lit it with a match he then dropped to the carpet and trod on.

"You can start fires like that."

"It's my office. I can start fires any way I choose. The question is, am I going to burn you?"

"I left my purse somewhere. I came looking for it."

"You had it in the club. It was in your bag." Miles exhaled, and for a moment was lost in the clouds. Then his face swam back into view, like a wizard appearing from behind a curtain. "Now you say, how do you know? And I say, because I went through it when you were in the ladies'."

"If you're going to do both sides of the conversation," Alison said, "perhaps I could leave?"

"I'll call you a cab. Did I say cab? I meant police wagon."

"You're not calling the police."

"No, but the crew who turn up will look just like them. Where do you think you are, back in Blighty? This is where the grown-ups play, little Miss North. I can have you back in Regent's Park before the clubs are closed, and your passport'll think you're still tucked up in bed. Am I getting through to you?"

"It's a shopping list," she insisted. "I picked it up. I was curious. That's all."

"You know what curiosity did to the cat?"

"I heard, yes."

"Did you hear what it did to it first?"

"You're trying to frighten me."

"How'm I doing?"

He already knew how he was doing. Could hear it in her voice. She was still standing behind his desk, her back to his filing cabinet. He approached and sat heavily in the visitor's chair, smoke curling around him. An image of yesterday's Trabant flashed across her mind. He leaned and tapped ash towards the metal wastepaper bin, but instead of dropping in a lump the ash feathered and drifted across the carpet.

He said, "Cartwright sent you, didn't he?"

"No."

"Yeah, that's what I thought. You want to reach for that bottle up there?"

The whisky, the German brand, on top of the cabinet.

She handed it to him along with the pair of glasses next to it. Both were streaked with tap water, as if rinsed and left to stand upright.

He uncapped the bottle and filled one glass to the brim. The other, he left empty.

"Aren't you drinking?" she asked.

"You know, the sad thing is, I could probably get to like you if you were here long enough. And I don't really like anybody."

"I thought you liked Otis."

"Otis is my friend. There's a difference."

"I'm glad we don't live in the same world."

"Oh, we do. It's just that you get to go home afterwards. Where were we?"

"I found your shopping list. You were turning it into a conspiracy thriller."

"One dictated by David Cartwright. What did he expect you to find?"

There was no point trying to hide behind a lie. Miles was in flamethrower mood, and lies were kindling. "Evidence of wrongdoing."

"*My* wrongdoing?"

"You turned down an offer of booty." Self-consciously using the spook term: a pirate's treasure. "Sent the seller packing."

He swore under his breath. "Dickie fucking Bow."

"He brought you the booty?"

"He brought me the seller." Miles picked his glass up. He didn't spill a drop, despite its brimfull contents, on its passage to his mouth. "And then sold the fact that I didn't buy it. Money-sucking little bastard."

"Why didn't you buy it?"

"Yes, that's a good idea. Why don't I tell you how this business works? Maybe you could pass the info back to Cartwright. About time he had some idea of how things go, here at the sharp end."

"I don't—"

"Except he fucking knows already, because he's been doing this a lot longer than I have, even if he's been doing it from the safety of a London office and not the streets of a fucking zoo. And he knows as well as I do that sometimes you say no, not because you don't want the information on sale but because you want everyone to think you've already got it."

"And that's what you were doing. Who was the seller, a Russian?"

"Who was the seller, a Russian?" he mimicked. "What are you, ten months into your career? I'm surprised you know what day of the week it is."

"I was just—"

"Yes, he was a Russian. And I knocked him back for the reason I've just given you, so the Russians will think our Service is two steps ahead of them. Except things get a little more complicated now, because this particular Russian was in the pay of the Americans." He threw his head back, poured what was left in his shot glass down his throat, then slammed the glass down on his desk. "Sometimes more than one thing happens at the same time. Or have they not covered that back at the nursery yet?"

She said, "I thought the Americans were our allies."

"And like I said, you're ten months into your career."

"So why would they try to sell us Russian secrets?"

"As an iodine trace. They send information through our system to see how long it takes the Kremlin to render that information worthless, by changing whatever system's been blown. That way, they can work out how efficient the mole in our Service is."

"The *what*?"

Miles bent and stubbed his cigarette out on the rim of the wastepaper bin. It wasn't an altogether effective manoeuvre, scattering more sparks than it extinguished. One or two settled on scraps of paper, where they glowed for a while, wondering whether to burst into flame.

He said, "Lay off the teenage hysterics. No one ever set foot in the Park without wondering what it would be like to ransack it. Or no spook did, anyway."

"You're serious? There's a mole?"

"Probably best not to tell too many people. You don't want to cause unnecessary panic."

An amateur might have thought he was amused. But she'd known him long enough now to see the anger underneath; like a man laughing at tales of adultery, who knows himself a cuckold.

She tugged that thread anyway. "You don't seem too concerned."

"We're spooks. Spooks spy, that's what we do. And when we
run out of enemies to spy on, we spy on each other."

"It sounds like you don't care."

"That's because I don't. Not any more."

"But if there's a mole—"

"Oh, I wouldn't worry about it. We already know who it is."

"... We do?"

"Well, I do. And so does Cartwright. He knows because I told
him. So when Cartwright sends you to find out whether I'm on
the straight and narrow, he's not doing it because he thinks I'm
a traitor. He's doing it for some other reason entirely."

Her head was reeling. There was a mole in the Park? It was as
if she'd come looking for evidence of shoplifting, to find someone
had carried the department store away. She was a ten-month
newbie—well, more than that now—and this stuff was above and
beyond and out of sight. Not only was there a mole, but they'd
already caught him. She felt she'd just picked a book up, and
someone was telling her the ending.

What made less sense than anything, right at that moment,
was what she was doing here in the first place.

"And what reason's that?"

"Yeah," said Miles. "That's the question, isn't it?"

Rain lashes the windows, because this is what rain does. The lighting that witness #137 has chosen—lamp rather than
overheads—seems both inadequate and wholly appropriate, for the
tale she's spinning is one for the secret hours. Everything flickers,
and it's possible that thunder has rolled outside, and lightning
scorched the sky. Or it might just be that every story needs its
punctuation marks, and Alison's has reached one of those moments.

"Wait." Surprisingly, it is Malcolm Kyle who makes the interruption. "Miles told you there was a traitor in the Service?"

She nods.

"But that's not covered in the file." He looks to Griselda for confirmation that the file they've read now twenty times—thirty—contains no word of this accusation; that this knowledge wasn't stored in an appendix that unaccountably slipped his attention. But the look on her face is as wary as that which he knows paints his own. Either the witness has access to information outside the realms of the OTIS file or she has slipped the bonds of reality, meaning that the risks he and Griselda have taken to hear her story have been for nothing. Their careers, their daily lives, might be left smoking by the roadside, and all in the cause of hearing a madwoman weave a fantasy.

Though what she says next is perhaps even worse.

"Of course it isn't. This is not the sort of information that ends up in a file."

Which strikes the two career civil servants like an axe head burying into a trunk.

Malcolm tilts his head to one side, the universally accepted semaphore for failure to understand, while Griselda purses her lips. This much they know: there are files that contain everything that can be known on a topic, and there are other files containing everything that can't be known. But an absence of files entirely—a quantity of information uncaptured by any file whatsoever—that runs counter to their systems. If there were room for religion here, witness #137 has just blasphemed.

But this is a passing fancy, given birth by the strangeness of the moment, and the shadows of the room.

One hand reaches to the knot of his tie and then remembers where it is, and drops to the tabletop. The other rolls a pen between its fingers. Malcolm says, "So you're saying this is true.

That there was a mole in the intelligence service in the early nineties? At Regent's Park?"

"Yes."

"Working for . . . ?"

"The Russian intelligence service. Well." There is a pause, while greater accuracy is reached for. "Initially, the *Soviet* intelligence service. But they were febrile times."

"But how come we don't already know about that? I mean, if Cartwright already knew, if Miles knew—what happened? I don't remember reading about . . ."

He does not remember reading about arrest, trial, or punishment. He knows there were not always trials—that there were uncoverings which took place in secret; that traitors were unmasked and allowed to carry on regardless, as if national security were a slapstick comedy. But always, he had thought, there comes a reckoning in the end. Traitors grow old, they die, and their sins are laid out like a carpet. The establishment hides its living embarrassments in plain sight, but leaves its dead to be scavenged by the media. It's how the ecosystem operates.

Alison North smiles sweetly for him. If subtitles were available, he thinks, hers would now read *Bless*.

Griselda says, "Did Cartwright really think Brinsley Miles was a traitor?"

"No."

"Then what was he after?"

"Anything that would taint Miles."

"Taint him?"

"You don't have to be a traitor to be . . . tainted. Anything will do. And Cartwright knew that there's no such thing as a clean joe. To live that life, to survive while pretending to be someone else, requires so much compromise, so many lies, that no one comes out the other side pure. There'll always be betrayals, always

be damage. And some of that will be to your own side. A successful spy has to love the enemy, that's what it comes down to."

"Despite which, there were some Miles wanted to destroy."

Alison turns her gaze Griselda's way. "Of course. Miles had his
tiger, and he was determined to hunt him down. But not because
of any . . . opposition of ideas. Not because of a conflict of ideologies. But because Miles's tiger ate Miles's joe. That's all there
was to it."

"And that was his taint?"

"You could call it a weakness, I suppose. Excuse me." She
pauses, and reaches for the glass of water by her side. Meanwhile,
London tests the window frames one by one; rattles the glass,
checking for entry points. But London, for the moment, is staying outside. While Alison sips, raindrops pebble the windows, an
invisible benediction because the blinds have been pulled down.
But the sound paints the picture nonetheless: a relentless battery,
as if Monochrome were under siege, and down to its last supplies.

There is a faint click as glass meets tabletop again. Alison says:

"Miles had already uncovered the traitor, and had told Cartwright months previously. Cartwright was sitting on the info
while he worked out what to do. Which I think he'd already
decided, but he couldn't do it himself. He needed Miles to do
it for him. And to make sure Miles agreed, Cartwright wanted
a little edge. Something he could aim and point at Miles. Do
what I ask, or be accused of treason yourself. Of taking funds,
of mismanaging operations, of getting things wrong . . . Whatever it turned out to be. Anything he could use as a weapon. So
if Miles didn't play along, he'd find himself turfed out of the
Service, and that was the last thing Miles could have handled.
It would have been like exiling a sailor from the sea. He'd have
drowned on dry land. It was bad enough the Wall coming down.
Another blow would have killed him."

"What did Cartwright want Miles to do?"

"To kill the traitor. To murder him and make it look like suicide."

Griselda and Malcolm look at each other, the same words scampering through their minds.

Any and all matters regarding potential misconduct by officers of the Service in pursuit of official instruction are to be regarded as material to the inquiry.

"And would that have been an . . . official instruction?"

Alison says, "I suppose it would have depended where you were standing. To a junior officer, any instruction from above is official. To the one giving it, it might be intended as, what shall we say? A strongly persuasive suggestion."

"But it didn't happen, surely."

"You think the intelligence service isn't capable of ordering killings?"

Neither of them think this. Nor does anyone else, out on the other side of those windows, in London and the wider world beyond. Killings happen. It is not a matter of whether this is true or not; it is more a matter of whether it is justifiable.

Malcolm says, "Yes, but isn't that the point? I mean . . . this is the Park. If they wanted someone dead, weren't there any number of . . . agents able to do that? Without going to the lengths Cartwright was going?"

Griselda agrees. "We're not supposed to know it happens. But it happens. So what made this more complicated?"

"Well, for a start, the traitor Miles uncovered was his own former handler, back in the day. His own mentor."

"So?"

"Who went on to become First Desk," Alison says. "The traitor was the head of Regent's Park. That's why Cartwright needed dirt on Miles. It wasn't the sort of job you get just anyone to do. But that happened later. It's not what this story's about. Shall I go on?"

And she does.

At length, Alison said, "Why have you been taking me everywhere?"

"To keep an eye on you."

"Why?"

He shook his head. "Jesus. You know who the Park usually sends on these bean-counting missions? Some gargoyle with bad breath and brogues, who eats fried-onion sandwiches at his desk and spends lunchtime in the porn shops."

"I was told they send someone different each time."

"I didn't say it was the same gargoyle. You, on the other hand, are in the top three in your year, despite what you said. Ninety plus in strategic thinking, and they don't give marks like that for nothing. So I don't care who's got the spook flu, the Park's not sending its brightest and best just to check the petty cash is accounted for. Certainly not here, it's not."

"Avoiding your bad influence?"

"Dream on. They don't send the good ones to Berlin, simple as that. Because they go home broken, if they go home at all."

Alison wanted to sit. Her legs were trembling. If she was a spook, and not just a misplaced deskbody, she'd been caught and pinned on her first operation. If she wasn't a spook, it was even worse. She thought of her bed in the cramped flat a mile away. Carola would be asleep, but a faint smell of hot chocolate would linger in the air, and she could imagine—this bit wasn't true—a nightdress freshly laundered and ironed and waiting on her pillow. She'd be asleep within seconds. Failing that, she still wanted to sit. Even before she'd come creeping around in the night, before she'd been taken to that rathole of a nightclub, she'd done a day's work. She wasn't like Miles, who seemed to function without rest.

He was talking again. "See, the clever ones come out here and they want to stay. Because this is where spooks belong. Not back on the hub, playing games with computers. Not at GCHQ, eavesdropping on the neighbours. The proper trade happens on the streets. Christ, even rubbing shoulders with the likes of Dickie, you'll learn more than a dozen instructors can pound into you."

She said, "I know about Basilisk."

He stopped talking.

"I know you're taking money and I can guess what you're doing with it."

Now he found another cigarette. This much she had come to know about Miles: he always found another cigarette. One of the ways in which spending time with him was like volunteering for an experiment. He slotted it into his mouth and aimed words down it like it was a gun-sight. "Okay, enough career talk. You should probably start being careful now."

"You had a joe, and she got burned. There was a photograph—"

"I said, be careful."

He spoke quietly, but for a moment she suspected she'd seen through several of the layers he wore; that this was the Brinsley Miles who'd spent time behind the Wall, back when it was still blocking half the world's light, and wasn't just a collection of tourist paperweights.

But she'd come this far. The fact that he didn't like it ought to add a little zest.

She said, "You told Robin you were taking the money for your asset's family, but that's not true, is it? Because you're not one for family. You're tribal is what you are. Spooks on one side, everyone else on the other."

The look on his face was unreadable. She had the feeling he was weighing words; that every ounce short she fell, he'd make her pay. *Tread carefully.*

He said, "As long as you're making up stories, where does this one lead? I'm stealing the money to fund my jet-set lifestyle?"

He'd found a match now, and applied it. In its sudden flare, his face was demonic.

Strategic thinking. She never thought of it that way. It was more like jigsaw puzzling: putting broken bits together and fashioning a picture. She had the broken bits in her hands now. She'd been gathering them all along.

"No. You're stealing it so Otis could buy a house."

Miles put his head back and laughed without making a noise. Smoke made shapes in the air instead. One of them had corners.

"Is this the story you're taking back to London? You might want to add a little colour. Try working three little pigs into it, say. Take everyone's mind off the fact that you're Goldilocks. You're Little Red Riding Hood."

"And that conversation you had about ghosts. Places retaining *impressions*. Events leaving records behind. There's something going on with that house."

"Don't look at me. It's your fairy tale."

"Otis said you're hunting a tiger."

And this time she struck home.

"Otis," he said, "has many good qualities. Failing to be a loudmouthed dick is not always one of them."

She'd had this feeling before, once or twice, during training sessions back in the Park. It was the moment a kaleidoscope shifts, and the underlying pattern rises to the surface of its own accord.

"You're laying a trap, aren't you? For your tiger."

"I told you to be careful."

"And I know who he is."

He reached for the bottle again, and this time filled both glasses, one fuller than the other. The smaller measure, he passed to Alison. She took it without hesitation, raised it to her lips, felt the liquor burn into her. It tasted like an oily rag, left overnight in a metal sink. "Otis is right. You should upgrade your taste in whisky."

"Otis might know what he's talking about. You don't."

"But either way, you're not going to pay attention."

He said, "Let's leave aside my taste in whisky and focus on the matter in hand. You have this fantasy I've diverted Service funds to buy property. What are you offering in the way of proof?"

"I don't need proof, Miles. I just need to make a phone call."

"And then what, David Cartwright sends proper trouble to sort me out? I gather they're calling them the Dogs now. And you know what the Dogs'll find? Business as usual. The Park sends money for me to put on the street, because that's how it works at the dirty end. And that's where the money's been going. Nobody'll find any in my own pockets."

"Because you passed it on to Otis, like I said. And I've been through the records, remember? Otis isn't on your official contact list."

"This is Berlin, not some fucking town council. You think I write down names? That's how people get killed."

"Like your asset. Is that what happened? You wrote her name down, and that got her killed?"

"Nobody cares how it happened. It's ancient history."

"Less than a year ago."

"That's how fast history happens round here. Blink twice, it's yesterday. Now, finish your drink and go home. When you speak to Cartwright, tell him Miles told you there's only one rotten apple he needs worry about, and it's right under his own fucking nose. He can leave me to get on with my job."

"People always get that wrong," she told him. "They think one rotten apple, no real harm. But the point is, rot spreads. If you've got one rotten apple, you can lose the whole barrel."

"All the more reason for him to focus." He swallowed what was left in his glass. "Go back to Regent's Park. They'll give you a desk and your very own stapler. A set of coloured pens. You can draw charts and add up columns of figures and do more of that strategic thinking you're good at. But stay away from the sharp end, because out here people get hurt."

"They hanged her from a tree, along with two other women, didn't they? Robin said weights were tied to their feet. I don't know whether that was to make it more painful or make it quicker. What do you think?"

"I think you're treading on dangerous ground."

"He told me there was a photograph, that someone sent you a photo. Because they wanted you to know all about it, didn't they? That they'd found your asset and executed her. That wasn't tradecraft, that was personal. Three women hanging from a tree, and a man looking at them. I'm sorry, Miles. I can't imagine how awful that felt."

He said nothing.

"And that's who your tiger is, isn't it? It's the man in the photo. And you're setting a trap for him, in the house Otis bought. The one you paid for with Service money."

Miles stabbed another cigarette to death, and reached for the bottle.

It becomes quiet when she stops talking. The rain still falls, so the windows are noisy; there is traffic at the far end of the road, but these sounds simply nibble at the edges: the witness's story is the only thing happening. So when she stops talking, the quiet takes over, and settles on all three like ash from a distant bonfire.

Malcolm is thinking: that's a wedge right there. Brinsley

Miles defrauded the Service of operational funds, with the knowledge, if not the actual connivance, of his Station House chief. If Monochrome required a scalp, here it is. But then he reminds himself that Monochrome no longer exists; that, moreover, in the light of what the witness has just revealed— that the Service was run for years by an active agent of a foreign power—the misappropriation of funds doesn't carry the heft it might have done that morning.

He makes a mental calculation and realises that the traitor must have been Charles Partner.

He's barely taken a note, this last twenty minutes. All he wants to know now is how this turns out.

As for Griselda, it's impossible to tell what she is thinking.

The witness continues to speak.

She breakfasted in a small park next morning: a cup of coffee and a hot egg sandwich which she ate sitting on a bench. There were others doing the same thing, one or two having conversations on brick-sized telephones, which looked a lot less convenient than waiting until they'd reached their offices.

What would happen when she got to the Station House, she didn't know.

The fact was, her task was finished—one call to David Cartwright and he'd summon her home, pat her on the head. Brinsley Miles would be brought back too, and made to face music. Nor would Robin Bruce emerge unscathed, because it was one thing to let the job slide in the wake of a splintered heart; another to let a subordinate ransack the till on your watch. As for the others: Who knew? Like any large organisation, the Service was paranoid, and less hampered than some in the way it dealt with failure. The simplest thing to do with a dysfunctional unit was abolish it; bring in a new crew and start again. Alison would be leaving debris in her wake. Not bad for less than a month. It took most people longer than that to destroy everyone they came into contact with.

On the other hand, it was difficult to say how Miles would retaliate, and what manner of comeback he'd have organised by now. Last night she'd seen him move through more obvious emotions than she'd encountered in weeks of his company, from the sardonic contempt she'd grown familiar with, and to which he treated most of those who weren't actively involved in bringing him food and drink, to anger, though he'd covered that up quickly. It had been genuine, though. And she had the sense that Miles, for all his years behind different walls, was a work in progress; that he'd not yet settled on the identity he'd one day fully inhabit.

Meanwhile, if he wanted to whip her legs away from under her, he'd have had time to come up with a plan. This was something she hadn't got used to yet: that she was working among spooks, who thought around corners they'd built themselves.

She walked slowly to work, not caring she was late. By the park gate a young man had spread a blanket to display his goods: stacks of cassette tapes with hand-drawn copies of actual album covers inserted in their cases. The low-rise city allowed for plenty of sky. She was learning to orient herself by Alexanderplatz, the way the Post Office Tower must have worked in London, before everything around it started growing.

It was a rare morning off for the ladies on the corner: their steps were vacant, though an empty bottle had been left standing guard. Miles called the crew here the freaks, and while she couldn't bring herself to do the same, she'd come to recognise it wasn't intended as insult, but a recognition of a status they took pride in.

Ansel was smoking outside the Station House, the cartoon spook floating at his shoulder. He nodded in greeting, rolled his eyes, and tilted his head, to indicate malarkey within. Alison supplied "malarkey." She doubted it was in Ansel's vocabulary.

As ever, her heels tap-tapped on the tiled floor of the lobby. This morning, she felt like she were entering a bank.

If so, it was a bank in a fluster. Theresa stood in her office doorway, face like artificial thunder; angry, but mostly pretending. Enjoying the drama, and about to deliver a speech. Behind her could be seen the ransacked cabinet, splinters protruding where the padlock had been prised free. In daylight, it looked more trivial than it had last night. Still, it was damage done to unlock a cupboard containing office keys. And this was the Station House.

But if need be, she thought, I'll just tell her to get stuffed. I was acting on instructions from the Park.

What Theresa said was, "Don't even talk to me about it."

"There's been a break-in?"

"Of course there hasn't been a break-in. If there'd been a break-in we'd be locked down and answering useless questions."

"Then what—"

"What happened is that *Miles* keeps his own hours, as we all know, only *Miles* isn't as careful as some of us might wish him to be when it comes to looking after his office keys. So when *Miles* turns up after midnight on an urgent mission to examine some file or other that is suddenly crucial for reasons us lesser mortals can only guess at, then *Miles* has to break into my cupboard to liberate his office keys."

"Oh."

"Could you not have picked the lock? I asked him. You'd have thought that a simple task for a trained professional. But no, it turns out *Miles* has never mastered the art of finding his way through a simple padlock. No wonder he's lumped here with the rest of us, instead of out playing James Bond on a speedboat somewhere."

"If it's that simple a padlock," Alison dared ask, "what's the sense of using it?"

"Because otherwise the door swings open. It's an absolute hazard." She rubbed a temple, remembering an instance.

"Where is he now?"

"In his office, amazingly enough."

She climbed the stairs, past her own room, glimpsing Young Alan at his desk, not so immersed in the work before him that he didn't dart a glance her way. She saw in that moment what she hadn't registered until now: that Young Alan was yearning for her. Poor Young Alan. Another time, another place. And even then: no. On and up the stairs: it seemed that all she ever did in Berlin was climb up stairs then climb back down them again. She could smell his current cigarette before she reached the fifth floor. Could smell—though maybe she imagined this—last night's whisky tainting the air.

Miles wore the same clothes, and had neither shaved nor showered. The room was pungent, in a deeply male way. It looked, for reasons she couldn't at first put her finger on, as if at some point he'd swept everything on his desk onto the floor, and at some later juncture piled it all back on again. After a moment, she identified the reason: the desktop looked tidier than usual.

His current cigarette wasn't actually lit, which meant the previous cigarette had been recent. She wondered how much she was to blame for this: an acceleration of his bad habits. The bottle that might have lasted a fortnight, barring her presence, was a dead soldier in the wastepaper bin. The air that might have poured in through an open window remained outside. Even the light from his lamp, necessary given the blind over his window, seemed weaker than usual.

"You're late."

"I wasn't sure whether to come in at all."

"Spoken to Cartwright yet?"

Answering that would undermine her presence here. "He sent me to report back on you. Keeping you informed as to how that's going wasn't one of my instructions."

"Yeah, right, whatever. Have you?"

She stepped inside the room and closed the door. "You mean, have I told him you're on a mission to avenge yourself upon an unknown Stasi officer, and have built him a trap using stolen Park funds? If I had, do you really think you'd not know about it by now?"

"If you imagine Cartwright would have arranged a bunch of heavies to cart me back home already, you have a rosier view of the Park's efficiency than I do."

"But he might have stretched to a phone call."

"Yeah, because telling me what he intends to do would be a good move. Last night you acted like you had half a brain. What happened to the rest of it, you sleep next to a switched-on vacuum cleaner?"

"I barely slept at all." And it was true, she felt like there'd been no interruption between last night's conversation and this. They might have been here all night, padding round the same ground like animals at a watering hole. "Why did you tell Theresa it was you who broke the cabinet?"

"Like I said. Only half a brain." He reached for a hat, hanging on the coatstand. It had been a fixture there these past weeks, but she hadn't seen him wearing it before. Broad-brimmed, it gave him a gangsterish look. "Come on. You can buy me breakfast."

"I've already had breakfast."

"So have I. What's that got to do with it?"

Her feeling that she'd wandered into a morning orchestrated by someone else only increased once they'd walked out into blustery sunshine, and were joined by Otis on the corner.

"Full court press?" she said.

Otis smiled in greeting. He was wearing a hat too.

"I assume he's brought you up to speed," she said. "That I know what it is you're doing."

Otis said, "Quite the Modesty Blaise."

"That's a very male thing, you know? I work out what you're up to, you pretend I'm a cartoon detective. It indicates a certain inadequacy."

He raised his hands in mock surrender. "I'd have said Nora Charles, but I wasn't sure you'd get the reference."

"I'm not in the mood for being charmed."

Miles said to Otis, "Funny, she didn't say that to me."

"And you can shut your damn mouth too."

"Now now. Casual profanity's the sign of a small fucking mind."

"I think we need coffee," said Otis. "A lot of coffee."

Which they took in the same small park, because sometimes days make patterns, laying your footprints ahead of you like tracks in the snow. The boy selling bootleg cassettes was still at his station, but the men with mobile phones had gone. The cardboard cups Otis and Miles carried steamed in the air. Alison had refused one; a self-harming gesture of resistance.

A row of call boxes lined the railings on one side of the park. She could call Cartwright from there and pull the curtain down on this whole mess.

Otis said something to Miles in German, words so fast they might as well have been bullets, and Miles dropped a step or two back, as if he were their minder.

Alison said, "You're not even on the payroll, are you?"

"I have always been . . . independently minded."

"That's desperately interesting of you. How does this manifest? Do you slay dragons, or just chat up waitresses?"

"What Mr. Schulz said last night, when he called me a fixer? He wasn't wrong."

"And what exactly do you fix?"

"Well, once upon a time, I was the sort of person you'd come to if you wanted the kind of things not readily available in the local shops. This was before . . . You know."

Before the Wall came down. Sometimes, the simplest conversations here took on the rhythms of a nursery rhyme.

"So you're a black marketeer. A spiv. We used to bang people like you up during the war. Or shoot them."

"We all have our own way of fighting for freedom."

"Thank you. Very glib."

"Some pay better than others, it's true."

He didn't seem remotely abashed. Probably wasn't. Probably it was she who was at fault: uptight English schoolgirl, still replaying victories at the debating society.

"And now you're helping *him*"—and she couldn't help the emphasis; this was what happened when you spent long in Miles's company; you began to italicise him, as if this were the quickest way of penetrating his layers—"find his . . . tiger."

"Tigers are not good news," Otis said. "One man's tiger is everybody's problem."

"And what did this tiger do to you?"

"He hanged my sister."

". . . Oh."

"Yes, oh. They haven't yet designed a card for the occasion, so words can be hard to find."

"Your sister. She was Miles's asset."

After a pause, Otis said, "Her name was Alicia."

"And she was in the Stasi."

"Imagine," said Otis. "One day she's a little girl, playing with her dolls. The next she's all grown up and working for the state

security service." He thrust an arm her way, offering her a cigarette. "How could you possibly put yourself in her shoes?"

She took the cigarette, her hand shaking. The same park as
earlier; the same big sky, the same squirrels and pigeons doing
their things. But there was a big rip down the centre of everything
now. It wasn't fair, she absurdly thought; wasn't fair that people
should expose the violent terrors history held, and expect you to
know how to respond.

He struck a match for both of them. Miles had fallen behind;
seemed to be absorbed in the scene all around, though Alison
suspected he was reading their body language, supplying subtitles.
This cigarette, her shaking hand. He'd have ticked a mental box.
Now she knows about Otis's sister.

"I'm sorry," she said.

He seemed not to hear, which was perhaps the kindest
response.

She inhaled, felt dizzy, blew it out. The nearest squirrel was
crawling around the foot of a tree, like the victim of a gas attack.
Perhaps it was looking for something. The cigarette was making
her feel sick, but it was something to hold on to. Otis wasn't
speaking; was waiting for her to continue.

She said, her voice harsh, "So you're both hunting the same
tiger. Tell me about the trap. This house you've bought."

Otis fell back into lecturer mode. "When a country undergoes
something as . . . volcanic, as *seismic*, as reunification, there are
always going to be dirty secrets. Those who want to reinvent
themselves in light of the new order, well, they need to bury their
pasts. But the trouble with volcanoes, with earthquakes, is they
bring things to light all the time. Things thought buried out of
sight."

She said, "One thing they never told me, back when I joined
the Service. They never told me how much I'd have to listen to

people talking in metaphors. Is it because you're all frightened of being too easily understood?"

He laughed. "I'm not a spook. I've just been around them too long. And also, speaking your mind, saying what you really think, it was a good habit not to get into. In the old days."

"Pretend they're over."

"I'll try. Last year, a cabinet was found in some rubble under a collapsed house on the former eastern bloc."

"That's better. Whose house was it?"

"It was a Stasi safe house. Not an actual official residence, but a safe house of sorts, or an unsafe house might be a better way of putting it. A house where, if they took you there, you would not expect to walk home afterwards."

An unwanted image assaulted her of a cellar wall, of manacles. Water dripping slowly into a metal bowl.

"What did the cabinet contain?"

"Records of things that had happened there. Interrogations, punishments. Dates and times and the personnel involved."

"For *beatings*?"

"It's a national weakness. We keep records the way you English keep apologising. We don't even notice we're doing it half the time."

"Neither do we. Sorry."

"And it's a hard habit to break. So when they weren't keeping files on everyone else, they were keeping them on each other."

Light was dawning. "Which was a dangerous thing to do."

"To those who wanted to bury their pasts, yes. A career in the Stasi, that's not something to boast about. If you were one of the bottom feeders, who stamped on faces or broke fingers, now you turn your collar up and sit in a corner of the bar and hope nobody notices. But if you're more ambitious, a political animal, or the entrepreneurial type, who hopes to make waves or money in the new world order, well. You can hope no one rustles too deeply into your past, or you can take steps to make sure that that past stays under the rubble."

"Is that what happened with this mysterious cabinet?"

"Yes. It disappeared. But the boys who found it were soon driving a nice new car."

"They sold the records they'd found."

"Which will now be ashes and dust. But what happened once might happen again."

"So you're spreading the word that there's something in that house you bought. Another cabinet. Something that compromises your tiger."

"That's the idea."

And this was Miles, closer behind them than Alison had realised.

"And what will he do to get it back?"

Miles made the universal sign for money, rubbing fingers and thumb together.

"You look like a bookie," she told him. "With that hat."

"Some of my best friends are bookies." He thought for a moment. "And also some of my worst enemies."

"How do you know your tiger had anything to do with the house you've bought?"

"Because our house," Otis said, "was more than just a cellar for beatings and burnings. It was where duplicate records were kept."

"You kept duplicates now?"

He shrugged. "Doesn't seem unlikely."

Miles said, "Schenker was senior enough that his name would appear on any set of records that covered a reasonable amount of ground. So that's the word we've put out. Duplicate records."

"If he was that senior, how come he's stayed anonymous since?"

"He's changed identity."

"But you just called him Schenker. Why?"

"Because that's his name," Otis said. "Karl Schenker. Or that's the name he went by when I met him."

"You met him?"

"Once. It was at a . . . party. A sort of official party. Beards and bigwigs. We were introduced briefly, we exchanged two words. Nothing more."

"Introduced?"

"By my sister."

Light glimmered. "You met him at a Stasi works do?"

"You don't think they met up after work, had a few drinks?"

Of course she didn't. Nobody thought that. But it might have happened.

"Karl Schenker was subsequently identified as having died of a heart attack." Miles. They were double-teaming her. "Back in '91."

"But you don't believe it."

"It's him in the photograph," Otis said, not needing to specify which photograph. "He has his back to the camera. But there's something about his posture, the shape of his body. It's him."

"And the photograph was taken last year," Miles said.

Alison stuck with Otis. "So you were a black marketeer, with a sister working for the state security police? How did that work, anyway?"

"We compartmentalised."

"Family Christmases must have been fun."

"Yes, well, the DDR. Christmas wasn't such a big thing."

She supposed she deserved that.

"The man in the club last night. He was taking your bait?"

"One among . . . well, not many. But some."

"Some," Alison repeated flatly.

"A man with Schenker's history, he'll have his ear to the

ground," said Otis. "A few scraps, here and there. That's all that's needed."

"Chumming the water," Miles said. "It's not an exact science. But it doesn't have to be."

"So now he's a shark, not a tiger."

"Christ on a fucking bicycle. He's got teeth. What else do you need to know?"

Otis laid an arm across Alison's shoulder. She shrugged it off. He didn't mind. "Miles can be abrasive," he explained, as if this were news. "A bit of, what's the best word? A foul-mouthed pig. He was trying this identity on for a joke once, and the wind changed, so he stayed like that."

"And this is your plan? A retread of something that happened last year?" She turned, for Miles's benefit. "What's your biggest danger, do you think? That you'll end up a laughing stock, or that someone'll charge you royalties?"

"Well, not the jokers with the new car," he said. "That was pulled out of the Spree a few weeks later. But at least the seat belts worked."

They'd reached the park gates again, their third or fourth circuit. Alison hadn't been counting. "So this plan failed even when it was new," she said.

"But not for a couple of weeks," Otis said. "That's more than we need. Just long enough for Schenker to show himself."

"And if he doesn't?"

"It's a plan, not a fucking toaster," said Miles. "It doesn't come with a guarantee."

"A plan you funded with money you stole from the Service," Alison reminded him. "Even if it does work, you're hip deep in shit."

"And I'm the one gets called foul-mouthed."

"Children, children." Otis was holding cigarette and coffee cup in the same complicated grip. "Let's not fight." He glanced at his busy hand, perhaps calculating whether a drag would spill his coffee, or a swallow burn his cheek. In the end, he did neither. "Alison. We're not asking you to take part in this. Your hands, they stay clean. We just need you to be quiet for a short while. Let events take their course."

"That's your idea of clean hands? Seriously?"

"On Spook Street?" Miles said. "Grow up. It amounts to a fucking halo."

"You're not helping, my friend," Otis told him.

"You'd prefer it came covered in butter? Look, no offence, but I need a few minutes with my junior colleague. You mind pissing off?"

"Well, given the grace with which you ask." He transferred the cigarette to his free hand and waved with it at the park gates. "If things turn nasty, I'm over there."

Miles rolled his eyes. "I can probably take her without your help."

She wasn't in the mood. She strode on, forcing him to accelerate, but made the mistake of inhaling at the same time, and within yards had come to a halt, dry-retching at the side of the path. Miles watched, sympathy absent, while a man walked past with a poodle, both carefully paying no attention. When Alison was done, she dropped the cigarette and ground it underfoot. "What?" she said, her voice a rasp.

"Help me catch this bastard and you can hang me out to dry afterwards. Cartwright'll thank you for it. Diverting a few grand from the reptiles fund, that's not enough to get me where he wants me. Especially given what I know about the state of the Park, and who's really pulling strings there."

"Where does Cartwright want you? I don't get it. I don't get any of this."

"Oh, you will. If you stick the course. You want to serve your country, right? What did you think that involved, dressing up and playing parts? This job is about betrayal. About persuading people to betray other people. Their countries, their friends, those they work for. And in return, we betray them too in the end."

"It doesn't have to be so bleak."

"Good luck with that. No, if Cartwright sent you to keep tabs on me it's because he wants something, and if you're lucky, you'll never find out what. But take it from me, he's not acting out of idealism or trying to get rid of a bad actor. He's got an agenda, and plans to slot me into it. And whatever it is, it's dirty enough that he needs me dirty too. So you give us a week, ten days, before reporting back, and you'll be golden, because by then I won't just have been dipping my hand in the Service pot. I'll have been running an off-the-book op on foreign soil. More than enough to give him what he wants."

"You're doing that already."

"No, right now I'm just staking a goat. It's only an op when the tiger pounces."

"Some goat. An imaginary filing cabinet."

"The records aren't the bait, Alison. Otis is."

She looked at him, shock finishing the job her cigarette had started, and leaching all the colour from her face.

"What did I just tell you? It's all about betrayal."

"You'd do that? Even when those boys you talked about, the ones last year, ended up in the river?"

"Otis isn't a boy. He knows what's going on."

"He knows this is the plan?"

"He knows how things work."

"You're using him!"

"Help us or not, it's up to you. But the man who hanged my joe in a wood, if he walks away, what do you think he'll do with the rest of his life? Wear sackcloth and ashes? Or raze the ground around him, so he's the only one with a view? Because whoever Karl Schenker is now, we'll be hearing from him sooner or later. Unless we do something about him first."

"Don't pretend you're on a holy mission. You just want revenge."

"Who says it has to be one or the other?"

She walked back the way they'd come, where Otis was waiting at the gate, as promised. He'd shed the coffee cup, shed the cigarette, and opened both arms at her approach. "All friends again?" He looked like a shaved bear, she decided. But not that well shaved. "Good, because I've found someone will take our photo."

Miles, in Alison's wake, said, "Get our picture taken? What the fuck kind of spy are you, anyway?"

"I'm not. I just live here. And you, you look great in that hat. And how many times are you going to look great? Twice in your life? If you're lucky."

A few yards away, out on the pavement, stood a man with a camera right enough, and also wearing a juggler's hat, as if hedging his bets. A cardboard sign, handwritten, outlined his fees. His studio was a stretch of wall on the opposite pavement, and he watched them with a hopeful look, not altogether confident.

Miles said, "Fuck a bunch of monkeys."

It suddenly felt urgent to her that whatever Miles didn't want to do, that was a good reason for doing it. She said, "No, Otis is right. Let's get our picture taken."

"Not as if we have anything to hide," said Otis.

He led the way like a man heading a parade. All he needed was a baton.

Miles scowled. "I should have sent you packing the day you arrived. First you're screwing with my op. Now I'm having my picture taken."

"I'll give you a week," she told him.

"Ten days."

"A week."

He looked her full in the face and suddenly he was smiling, as if she'd offered his heart's content. "Yeah, okay. A week. I can live with that."

"Are you coming or not?" Otis called.

So they followed him from the park, and had their picture taken.

"And that's what you did, is it?"

It's Griselda who's speaking, her voice a little rusty. She reaches for the glass of water in front of her, but continues speaking before sipping from it.

"You gave him a week for his plan to work, before letting David Cartwright know what he was up to?"

Alison might as well be looking through her. "It's what I told him, yes."

"But not what you did?"

"I talked to Cartwright later that day. I let him know Miles had taken money, that he was running an operation against a former high-ranking Stasi officer, seeking revenge for the murder of his one-time asset. And that I thought he was in danger of getting himself or his associate killed in the process."

This time it's Malcolm who has a question: "You believed Karl Schenker posed a real threat?"

"He'd hanged three women in a wood. So yes, I believed Schenker posed a threat."

"What did you expect Cartwright to do?"

"Call Miles home. That would have put an end to it. Otis wouldn't have been able to handle the trap by himself, so he'd have faded into the woodwork, let the legend of the cabinet, the recovered files, die a natural death. And Miles would have been safe in London."

"So you didn't believe what Miles had said, about Cartwright wanting him . . . thoroughly compromised."

"I didn't know whether I believed him or not. It all seemed like . . . boys' games. All that stuff about everyone betraying everyone else—I mean, I could see why he might believe that, but I thought it was just paranoia. Either way, it was less important than whether one or other of them got murdered. But in the end, of course, I was just proving Miles right. By calling Cartwright, I betrayed him."

Malcolm, listening to this, picks up the photograph that is part of the file, and studies it once more, perhaps finding something different in it, now he knows the circumstances in which it was taken.

Griselda says, "Are you all right to continue? We can take a break if you'd prefer."

The witness, answering a different question, says: "But Cartwright couldn't call Miles home, because that would have been an end of it. Cartwright didn't have operational command, so someone else would have to give the order. Explaining that Miles had diverted funds for his own use, or was planning a revenge op, either would have been enough to have Miles recalled, but that would have rendered him useless for Cartwright's purposes. You don't have a hold over someone if everyone already knows what they've done."

Griselda, faltering now, says, "Or we could just . . ."

"I'm fine to go on."

"If you're sure."

The witness, clearly, is sure.

She left work late that evening, having spent hours in an indeterminate state: I am not really here, but nor am I anywhere else. She was in her own head, rather, while her body performed familiar tasks of administrative drudgery, a yellowing ledger open on her desk while she compared long-established spending patterns and payment processes to current more slapdash affairs. This was not how things were supposed to be—things should become more efficient, not less—and she wondered how much of this was due to Miles's influence. When he'd been behind the Wall, procedures were more carefully applied. Now he was among the suits, as he'd put it, the haphazard featured more strongly. But then Miles was an agent of chaos, intentionally or not, and wherever he hung his hat, plaster was likely to fall. How he'd survived the undercover life passed understanding, unless you relied on the spooks' chorus: he'd been a different person then. Unless he was a different person now, of course, and the real Miles, his natural self, remained trapped behind a demolished wall. A notion that caused her to shake her head in disgust: this was what happened when you were trapped in your own head. She was safer among facts and figures; would be better off in a back room at the Park, or one of its underground chambers, guarding its secrets and lies, bound in ledgers like this one. She closed it and rested her head on its cover. Just so long as she didn't have to deal with people.

When Young Alan had gone, after asking—and gracefully accepting rebuff—if she fancied a drink, this or any other night, she used the office phone to call Cartwright. Miles was nowhere about, and she found herself not caring about tradecraft, about traces left on the system. *Boys' games*. Let them all talk. After that she was on her way home, straphanging on the U-Bahn and alighting early, fearful that the press of travellers would make her sick. On the Kurfürstendamm she passed a bar, and was so grateful for the strength of mind that prevented her walking in and ordering a drink that she stopped at the next one to celebrate. A world different to the dives Miles took her to, this one was chrome and

leather, everyone wearing clothes, and a range of wines behind the
bar. She ordered one, and sank gratefully into a booth, where someone had left a newspaper: all heavy print, weighty words, constant
capitals. Cartwright should have sent someone better versed in the
language. But all he had wanted was someone to follow Miles,
collecting evidence of his bad behaviour, like those people you saw
in parks trotting after dogs with little plastic bags in hand. Which
actually was a good idea, and should be compulsory, but not where
Miles was concerned. He should be made to deal with his own shit.
The bar filled. The newspaper was commandeered by someone
else, and soon she was talking to a man in a black leather jacket
over a blue open-necked shirt, his smile a little too wide, his wallet
a little too open. He bought her drinks as if there were a prize
waiting at the bottom of one of them. After a while, it became
apparent that the prize was Alison, but she wasn't so far gone that
this seemed a good idea.

"I need to go home now."

"Sure. I'll take you."

"No. Thank you, but I can manage."

"Of course you can't. It's not safe, pretty young thing like you.
Anything could happen."

"I'll be fine. I'll take a cab."

"That's good. We'll be there in no time."

She slipped away, but not so smoothly he wasn't still there
when she reached the door. Cold air hit her like a flannel in the
face, and then she was on the street and he was still with her, one
hand wrapped round her upper arm. With the other he was
hailing a cab.

"You're hurting me!"

"You'll get used to it."

"Let go!"

"That was a lot of *Wein* I just paid for."

She'd have reached for her purse but her arm was firmly in his grip, until it wasn't: there was a yelp, and a crunch, and someone was on the ground. A taxi stopped, and a gentle hand was guiding her into it. Instructions happened—she recognised her address—and the lights of the Ku'damm cartwheeled as the taxi pulled away.

Her voice was somewhere deep inside her, and came out stained with wine. "You were following me."

"It felt like a good idea. It *was* a good idea."

"What do you want now? The same as him?"

Otis said, "I'll settle for knowing you're home safely."

The driver was Turkish, and keen on establishing his rally driver credentials. Alison was thrown against Otis as a corner was taken, and it was easier not to struggle upright. He smelt of the streets, of air and smoke and loud voices, and his arm across her shoulders felt comforting rather than predatory. *Why does he think I want comforting?* It was, after all, easier to struggle upright.

Otis paid for the taxi, escorted her through the apartment block lobby, and came up with her in the lift.

Her key appeared to have been replaced with a poorly cut imitation, because it took three goes to get through the apartment door. Luckily Carola was a stout sleeper, or she'd have been there with curling tongs, or similar weapon. Inside all was dark, Carola's bedroom door firmly shut, the crockery from her evening meal drying in the rack. If the steamed-up windows were anything to go by, she'd had an evening bath, steaming the windows in the process, and tainting the air with whispers of lavender. When Alison pushed a curtain aside, the city was a foggy blur, and a passing aeroplane's taillights fiery red comets. Otis, meanwhile, was giving the place a swift once-over, even opening Carola's door a crack before Alison could protest. A soft snore drifted out. "Everything's fine," he said. Why wouldn't it have been? But the question swam away. "I'll go now."

"No. Stay."

"You don't need me here. It's all fine. But drink some water."

"I'm not a virgin, for God's sake."

"Me neither." He was still wearing his hat. "Make that quite a lot of water."

But when she pulled him into her bedroom, he didn't protest, and shed both coat and hat before sitting on the bed. Her dress had large buttons, almost saucerlike, which in the cold dark of night were ridiculous really. But at least were decorative, and didn't need undoing. She pulled the dress over her head and stood before him in her underwear.

"Very charming," he said. "Very."

"Are you just going to sit there being a gentleman?"

"No," he said. "I'm going to fetch you that water."

Alison was dizzy when she sat, and still dizzy when he returned, bearing two glasses. He made her drink one, then put the other in her hand, and tucked the duvet round her shoulders after placing the spare glass on her bedside table. She sat contemplating it while she rolled water round her mouth, wondering why her tongue still felt dry. "You can get undressed now," she said. "If you want."

"I don't know that Miles would like that."

"What's Miles got to do with it?"

Otis appeared to give that serious consideration for as long as it took her to finish her water and hand him the glass. He took it from her, placed it next to the first, then sat next to her. His thigh, touching hers through the duvet shrouding her, was warm and solid. When he started to unbutton his shirt, beginning with the cuffs, she didn't know whether to feel happy or disappointed, but this dilemma resolved itself when he kissed her, and before long resolved itself again, and even the very slight worry that she might disturb Carola ceased to be of importance.

She woke in the early hours, heart pounding, but he was still there. He was awake too, calm as a knight on a tomb, his own heart a steady beat beneath the duvet.

"I called London," she whispered.

"You mean the Park?"

The Park meant London. London meant the Park. "Yes."

"What did you tell them?"

"What you're doing."

He patted her shoulder softly. "Okay."

"I had to. I want you to catch this man, of course I do. But if you kill him, if I knew about it beforehand, that makes me as guilty as you."

"It's not necessary to kill him. This isn't a bandit state, Alison. We catch him, he confesses to what he did, he's punished. By law."

"But what if he doesn't confess?"

"He will."

"Miles says it's not the records that are the bait. It's you."

"Of course I am. So is Miles. We both are."

"How sure are you he'll come looking?"

"Pretty sure."

"He can't even know he's named in the records. These non-existent records."

"Miles had a drink with Dickie Bow this evening. You've met Dickie?"

She nodded, which he couldn't see, not with her head buried in his shoulder. But he felt the movement.

"Then you'll know what he does. It was Dickie who first put the word on the streets that we were buying this house."

(She remembered Miles's anger about this. *Last time we got up close and personal, I remember a certain property being mentioned . . .* So Dickie got bollocked for doing what Miles had wanted him to do: so much for the one-two shuffle. Poor Dickie.)

"And now Karl Schenker's name is on the streets too," Otis continued. "And Karl Schenker will want to know who put it there."

"I thought he was pretending to be dead."

"Yes. But me, if I was pretending to be dead, I'd want to know who was digging me up."

She said, "Maybe he'll just lie low."

"Maybe."

"Anyway, if they kill you, if Karl does, how does it help him? The records are still out there, as far as he knows."

"And as far as anybody else knows, it'd be suicide to blackmail him. You kill somebody, it discourages others."

"But it didn't, did it? When he killed Alicia. Your sister. It didn't discourage you from doing something about it."

"It would have done. If not for Miles."

"She was his joe."

He didn't say anything.

She would have liked more water, but it was all gone and she was too comfortable to suggest that either of them move. Or if not comfortable, too welded in place. Any movement now, any shifting of position, might cause time to start again. For as long as it didn't, they were safe.

"Did you really buy the house?"

"A good legend needs a solid foundation."

A good lie, she thought, just needs conviction.

"Go back to sleep, Alison. Everything's going to be all right."

But she didn't go back to sleep, except she must have done, because when she woke in the morning he was gone.

She falls silent, and neither listener wants to break her reverie. The events she is recalling took place years, decades, ago, but there is no statute of limitations on remembered damage, if that is what this is. And how can it be anything else? Happiness takes on a different shade in the light of its consequences.

The rain that has battered London this past half hour is subsiding, though the occasional flurry still wipes the windows. The folders on the desks—Mozart/Q1–94/OTIS/Berlin (BM)—lie closed; thin Manila sandwiches containing the skeleton framework of Alison's story. But of the fresh details being revealed, none will now find their way into an official report, because whatever sins were committed, and whether or not they cry out for redress, Monochrome is no more. Malcolm and Griselda are listening under false pretences. Which makes it more important, not less, that they hear the end of it.

At length Malcolm says, "Was it through Otis that Miles recruited his sister?"

There is a pause while the witness reels herself in from the sea of her past. "I'm sorry, could you repeat that?"

"I was wondering if it was through Otis that Miles met Alicia, and recruited her as his asset? Or was it the other way round?"

The witness stares at Malcolm and then laughs a harsh bark of a laugh, the noise a seal might make with something caught in its throat. "Oh dear. I'm sorry. I'm not making fun of you. I promise I'm not."

But it is another short while before she can continue, and the lump of her upper body shakes with something that could as easily be grief as humour. At last she says:

"Otis's sister wasn't Miles's asset. She was one of the other two who were hanged with her."

This is greeted with silence, as Griselda and Malcolm recalibrate what they thought they knew about the dead woman.

"He let me think otherwise for a while, I'm not sure why. Or at least, I am, but it doesn't speak well . . . He thought I'd be unsympathetic. That I'd care less, because his sister had been a member of the state security police. And I suppose I do. Except I don't, because she was still his sister, he was her brother. He said they 'compartmentalised.' That's something you do so love won't run into duty."

When this happens, her tone suggests, something's got to give.

"So she was a loyal member of the Stasi," Malcolm says.

Alison looks him in the eye. "Well. I suspect she turned the occasional blind eye to her brother's activities. So perhaps her loyalty wasn't all it could be. But she didn't spy for the west, if that's what you mean."

"So Otis wasn't . . ."

The witness waits. So does Griselda.

"I'm sorry, I just meant . . . I don't know what I meant. I suppose I thought his loyalties lay with . . . us."

"I saw the photograph," she says. "Of the three women, I mean. Miles left it on my desk. He wanted me to know what was driving him, why he was prepared to destroy his career. It was . . ." What it was evades description. She shakes her head, looking down at her lap, and then, as if it occurs to her only in the moment of speaking, looks up and says, "I had no idea which was which. Which was Miles's asset, which was Otis's sister. Who the third woman was. But it doesn't matter, they were equally murdered. Loyalty doesn't come into it. It's too small a concept."

Griselda says, "And too easily mistaken for something else."

Malcolm looks her way uneasily, not sure of her meaning.

The witness says, "We're nearly at the end now."

For the next five days, everything was in stasis. Whether Otis had told Miles that she had spoken to London—to the Park—to

David Cartwright—Alison didn't know, and didn't dare ask. Whether Miles knew that she and Otis had spent the night together, she also didn't know. Then again, she didn't get the chance: Miles didn't show up at the Station House. When she raised this with Young Alan, he gave a mournful shrug. The Mileses of this world made their own rules. The Young Alans suffered the impositions of others.

With evenings her own, she indulged in tourist escapades: the Brandenburg Gate at last, and the cathedral. She went up the TV tower on Alexanderplatz to look down on Berlin, words that Otis—inevitably—had said coming back to her: that when the Wall came down, the future came rushing into Berlin from all directions at once, causing a godalmighty pile-up. The way he spoke, it was as if he were viewing one of those places on the outskirts of every city, where dismantled cars were stacked in ziggurats. To Alison, from this perspective, it seemed, rather, as if purpose were establishing itself; as if an intelligence, poking through the rubble, were fashioning a new outcome from old pieces, in the same way, a childhood memory suggested, that Chitty Chitty Bang Bang was built from discarded parts, and ultimately flew. Which in turn reminded her of their attempted outing to Wannsee. Chitty Chitty Bang Bang indeed.

Meanwhile, her job had staled. Her hours were spent trawling through the unholy trinity of outcomes, outlays, deliveries, and in the end, whether these results were about information successfully collected, suspicions weighed in various balances, or simply notions that had roosted in the minds of the watchers and listeners of the Spooks' Zoo hardly seemed to matter. It was a business, that was all; one carried on in an undertone rather than with aggressive marketeering. Its other practitioners had grown surly; Robin in particular standoffish. Some around her assumed a specific cause; that she either had or hadn't succumbed to Robin's advances. Not for the first time, Alison reflected that the Service probably wasn't so different from other enclosed environments: boarding school, or fish tank. Only Ansel remained unaltered, his stick-thin formality brittle as ever. Wishing him *Guten Morgen* she remembered invading his cubby-hole, taking his key to broach Theresa's fastness, and wanted to blush but she'd been doing a job—guilt was simply another outcome, one to bury beneath hours of busywork in an office shared with Young Alan, whose every shuffle and squeak was an irritant. On the ever-absent Cecily's desk lay unopened letters and a discarded lipstick. There are always those who fail to earn their place in a story.

And there are those who turn up without fanfare, leaning on the office door, unlit cigarette in mouth.

"Who crapped in your coffee?"

She didn't know whether to feel relief or its opposite. "Do you mind?" she said. Stalling. "That's a disgusting—"

"Yeah yeah. Come on."

"It's not four o'clock."

"When I need to know the time, you'll be the first I ask," he said, over his shoulder.

She grabbed her coat, sending a rolled-eyed apology Young Alan's way. His petulant grimace in response indicated that here was another example of what he'd been complaining about; the way the world was always tilted in someone else's direction.

Miles was on the pavement before she caught up, adjusting himself to others' speeds never being a big priority with him. The cigarette in his mouth remained unlit. His coat flapped unbuttoned. The bar he chose was not far, and surprisingly ordinary: tiled floor, stools at the counter, a row of tables against the wall; somewhere workers heading home might pause at, but nothing to anchor them there until the early hours. Miles ordered a whisky on his way past the barman, leaving Alison to order her own drink, pay for both, and carry them to the table he'd chosen, against the farthest wall, near the door to the toilets. A lone man at one of the other tables was absorbed in a yellow-jacketed paperback. Miles sat at an angle allowing a clear view of him in the mirrored wall behind the counter.

Red wine. It was early to start drinking, but red wine.

She placed his drink in front of him. "You've been keeping a low profile."

"Not low enough."

"Did you get out the wrong side of—"

"We had a deal." She'd got used to his way of speaking, his drawl, as if—almost—he'd got so used to German that switching to English required putting the brakes on. Now, though, his words came low and fast and angry. "You were supposed to give me a week."

Red wine.

"But you spoke to the Park, didn't you?"

"I gather Schenker didn't take the bait."

"No he fucking didn't."

"And you think that's my fault."

"You're telling me it's not?"

Red wine.

She wasn't going to tell him that, because he already knew. Knew she'd spoken to Cartwright, knew she'd slept with Otis; probably knew she'd been up the tower at Alexanderplatz, and spent an hour walking round the cathedral. Knew she'd lit a candle, and who for. She hunted for a name. "What about . . . Dieter? Dieter Schulz."

"What about him?"

"I thought he was showing interest."

"So did I." Miles picked up his glass, but his eyes didn't shift from her face. "Except if he was, it didn't last. Wonder why that was?"

"How could that have been my fault?"

"Glad you're not bothering to deny it." He revolved the shot glass in his fingers. For a drinker, he liked to fidget; if not for that, he'd put away twice as much. "Schulz might have been who he said he was. A thug for hire, who'd happily break legs for hard currency. But Dickie Bow had the story too, under strict instructions to keep it off the streets, and he leaks like French plumbing. But no one fucking heard. Apparently."

"Maybe," she said, "it just wasn't a very good story."

"Didn't have to be. Even a bad story needs checking out."

Red wine. She'd bought a small glass, and maybe that was a mistake.

She put it down, a little harder than she'd intended. A red wave lapped the rim, leaving droplets like tears on a window. "Okay," she said. "Yes, I told Cartwright. That's what I'm here for, it's my job. And what happened? Nothing. He didn't summon you home, didn't send the Dogs, didn't send a balloon up about the stolen money. So what do you imagine he did do? Spread the word in the Berlin underworld, warning former Stasi officers not to worry about fairy tales? You've kept telling me he's a suit, that he fights his battles from behind a desk, and suddenly he can reach out and warn a man in Berlin he's being hunted, when you and Otis between you can't even discover what he's calling himself now? Make your mind up."

"I never said he wasn't a smart bastard. Just a bastard."

"Then the two of you should get on fine."

"Except he's playing to the wrong rules."

"There are rules now?"

"My joe was murdered. That's against the rules."

She'd never seen him like this.

"And you interfered when you said you wouldn't. That's against the rules too."

"I was trying to make sure you didn't get hurt."

"Well you're too fucking late and you're too fucking useless. You think I need you watching my back? From what I've heard, you're too busy getting on your own."

"You really are a shit, aren't you?"

"When did I pretend otherwise?"

The last thing he expected now, the very last, was for her to hit back. She leaned forward. "How come this one's so important?"

"They're all important."

"And how many of them are dead?"

He didn't answer.

"Come on, that shouldn't be difficult. Or did you stop counting?"

He said, "You never stop counting," and found another cigarette somewhere, and a match somewhere else.

Alison tilted her head, feigning puzzled. "But this one you're sticking your neck out for. And how did they find out about her anyway? They didn't know who she was, that's clear, because two other women had to die too. Unless that was just for the sheer bloody spectacle of it, but I don't think so, do you? No, they didn't know who she was, they just knew she was a woman. How did that happen?"

Miles's match flared. Instead of shaking it out as he always did, he blew on it, his whisky breath offering it a brief hope, swiftly extinguished.

"It was you, wasn't it? What happened, did your tongue slip? You said 'she' instead of 'he' in the wrong company?" She sat back as the truth hit her. "Oh God, that's exactly what happened, isn't it? The wrong company. You told the mole all about your asset. You betrayed her all by yourself. That's how you found out he was the mole. Because she ended up killed."

As soon as the words were out, she'd known she should have kept them to herself. Miles didn't flinch but his eyes deepened in colour. He raised his cigarette to his lips and inhaled deeply, then reached for his glass, and drained it in one swallow. He said, "Top three in your year, right?"

"I'm sorry. I shouldn't have said that."

"Probably needed saying. Bright girl like you."

"It wasn't a betrayal, it was a mistake—"

"Trusting the wrong person," he said, "or trusting anyone at all. That's a mistake. Betrayal's the consequence."

"That's so cynical—"

He put the glass down gently—she'd been expecting damage. "Word of advice. If you're going to cut it in the Service, never apologise for being too clever."

"That's not what I was apologising for."

He might not have heard. "Once you turn your own strength into a weakness, they'll give up on you. They'll put you in a basement, looking after records."

She said, "What Schenker did, it was murder, plain and simple. He and whoever helped him do it. You don't need to concoct plans to lure him out of the shadows. Just make your case. If he's alive, let the civil authorities track him down. Put him on trial, put him in prison. The Park will help."

"The Park's done everything it intends to do." He stood, abruptly. "Turn your keys in to Theresa. She'll book your flight."

"I haven't finished the—"

"You've done what you were sent to do. What do you want, a victory parade?"

Then he was gone, his cigarette still burning in the ashtray.

After a while she mashed it out, making a mess of the process, sending smoke spiralling outwards and burning her finger: she swore, loudly, then once more as Otis appeared from behind her: "Again? You're following me *again*?"

He put his hands up in surrender. "Not following. Not following."

"Just a lucky—"

"Miles told me you'd be here."

"What, he arranged for you to come babysit in case I was in a state?"

Otis thought for a moment, shrugged, and said, "Yeah, I guess. Okay if I sit down?"

"Do what you like."

He lowered himself into the seat Miles had vacated. Down the bar, the man with the paperback was standing, brushing crumbs from his jacket, making his way out.

Otis said, "He was angry."

"He made that clear."

"Was he—"

"And you told him about the other night. Thanks for that. Little bit of bragging to the boys, was it? Screwing the newbie, they call it at the Park. Like we're all still at university, giggling in the bar."

"Alison. Alison? Calm down."

"Don't you *dare* tell me to—"

"I didn't say a word to him. Honest."

"I'm supposed to believe that?"

"It's true. I didn't say a word."

"So, what, he just worked it out for himself?" But even as she was saying the words, she knew that's exactly what he'd done. He'd known about it before it happened. *If I have to listen to you two falling in love, I might just puke all over the table.* Except it hadn't been love. It had simply been Berlin.

She swirled her glass, and watched the drops left inside try to keep up with the motion. "Your plan didn't work," she said at last.

Otis made a small exploding shape with his hands. "*Kaput*!"

"Do you expect me to apologise for that?"

He was quiet for a moment. "I would have liked to see Schenker again. Liked to have spit in his eye."

"Miles planned to kill him."

"We both did. But I'm not sure we would have done. In the end."

Maybe not Otis, she thought. But Miles would.

She said, "I'm going home. Apparently."

"Probably for the best."

"Have you any idea how annoying it gets, men telling you what's for the best?"

"Would another drink help?"

It wouldn't hurt.

He fetched her a glass of wine, and bought a Coke for himself, while she sat thinking about what Miles would do now; whether he'd set another trap for Schenker, and how he'd go about doing so, now Schenker knew he was being hunted. Schenker, who had a track record of obliterating threats.

"I'd offer a penny for your thoughts," Otis said. "But I'm not sure I want to know."

She stirred. "You're drinking Coke?"

"Driving."

"Right." The same penny, or a different one, dropped. "Seriously? The convertible?"

He said, "It's fine. I'm sure it's fine now. I've had it seen to."

"It needs setting fire to, not seeing to," she imagined Miles saying. But she remembered, too, Miles sprawled across the back seats like a Roman, his thinning hair needing only a laurel wreath.

"Who did you get, a miracle worker?"

"This is Berlin," he reminded her. "There is always someone can bring a car back to life."

Just a matter of putting the word on the street, she supposed.

He finished his Coke and slammed the glass on the table as if he'd conquered a flagon of mead. "I'm sorry that we . . ."

She waited, genuinely curious as to how he'd finish this.

"I'm sorry we didn't get to know each other better. Or more slowly, perhaps."

There was still time, she considered saying, but there wasn't, they both knew that. Their time had been while there'd been three of them, and nobody had betrayed anyone yet. *The sad thing is, I could probably get to like you if you were here long enough. And I don't really like anybody.*

She said, "It happened the way it ought to, I suppose. I mean, I'm not staying here. And you're not going anywhere."

He laughed. "No. No, I'm not going anywhere." He looked at her glass, which was almost empty. "I'll give you a lift home."

"I've had a lift from you before. Remember?"

"I'll let you drive this time."

She wouldn't see him again, she knew.

"Come on. How often will you get the chance?"

"I've had two glasses of wine."

"Driving in Berlin, that's the minimum requirement."

"You were drinking Coke," she muttered, leaving the last quarter inch in her glass.

He hailed a cab when they were outside, explaining that they had to pick the car up before they could drive it back. For a moment she wondered what the point was; she should head back to the Station House and collect her things. She was still contemplating that halfway up Karl-Marx-Allee, in the shadow of its monument-like apartment blocks: the evening pulling in now, tidying daylight away. Berlin would always seem dark to her, because this was how she first saw it; when the days were short, and the evenings underground. She glanced at Otis, but he seemed far away. We've already said goodbye, she thought. That happened last week. As for Miles, their goodbye had happened too. The taxi was turning, and Otis offering an extra direction or two: farther along here, right at the end. The city, like most others, changed shape at every junction. No longer on the showcase boulevard, they were among the shadier side streets: low-rise, narrower, lined with cars. The taxi slowed, negotiating a careful passage. Otis was finding his wallet, and scanning the street ahead.

"There it is."

The Camaro: under a streetlight, looking twice as American, somehow. Alison thought of clubs they'd wasted evenings in, the rock and roll décor, the candy-striped walls, and how this effortlessly trumped their childish yearning. The car was childish too, of course; too big, too brash, too look-at-me. As if every journey it undertook became a ride on a tunnel of love.

The cab driver wasn't impressed. "*Amerikaner, sie sollten jetzt nach Hause gehen.*"

Otis paid him off. "Thanks for sharing." While the taxi crawled away they stood on the street, Otis with his hand on his car's flank.

"It looks good," he said.

"Looking good wasn't the problem," said Alison. "Not working, that was the problem."

Otis scanned the house on the opposite pavement: four storeys, three with balconies, most in darkness. "Hansi said he would be here. I still owe him."

"Pay him another time?"

"And he has the keys."

She hoped this wasn't going to turn into a three-act drama. "He lives there?"

"*Jah*. I can't remember which flat."

"Good friend of yours, eh?"

Otis shrugged. "Some friends are better than others. Not all of them fix cars."

There was a row of doorbells by the main entrance. Ring one and ask for Hans, she thought. Or: "Sound the horn?"

"Why not?"

Climbing into a convertible wasn't as easy as it sounded, and she wasn't dressed the part—she needed red lipstick, a white dress, shades—but she managed. She put her hands on the wheel, imagined a freeway. It felt pretty good, actually.

"Alison?"

"I'm doing it." And she did, secretly hoping for an *Arrooga!* but getting an admittedly loud one-note blare instead. Hansi would have to be deaf.

Which he wasn't. A light appeared three storeys overhead, and a figure appeared on a balcony, shouting a greeting. Otis replied in German, and both men laughed, and there was a glinting in the gloom, and the sound of keys hitting the pavement.

Otis scooped them up. "Success."

"Let's see if it starts first."

He laughed and called up to Hansi again. "He's coming down," he told her, and headed over the road to meet him, but tossed her the keys first. When she caught them one-handed, he clapped. "I'm impressed."

"Ain't seen nothing yet," she said in a passable Marilyn Monroe, slotting the starter key into the ignition and turning it.

In the bright moment that followed, her life divided in two.

PART SEVEN

LONDON, NOW

Malcolm made coffee. Somewhere in his papers, up until day 271, was a meticulous record of refreshment breaks, but as with many things—statistics, relationships, novels—the record's being incomplete rendered it worthless. Besides, it did nothing to explain why his hands were shaking.

In the silence that had followed Alison's calm recollection of the bomb that had taken her legs, all in the room had become aware that rain had stopped falling, and two of them that this could not be commented on in the circumstances. Alison herself had fallen quiet not, Malcolm thought, because she had shocked herself, but because this was the natural conclusion to her story. Much of what followed had taken place without her conscious participation. It had been the best part of a year before she was taking an interest in her own life again, let alone demonstrating awareness of those around her. Not that Miles or Otis were any longer in that orbit.

"Otis wasn't hurt, not badly. There may have been . . . bruises."

Alison was talking again. All three now had coffee.

"Or so I was told. I never saw him again."

"What about Miles?" said Griselda.

Alison said, "Him neither. Not for a long time. Fifteen years."

"No hospital visits? No cards or flowers?"

"I doubt he knew where I was. He was recalled to London immediately."

"But he's still working for the Service?"

"The . . . job he did for Cartwright was his guarantee. He

couldn't be kicked out, not after that. He was given his own domain instead. Still there. Still making waves."

The other residents of the Station House, on the other hand, had sunk beneath them.

"Robin killed himself," said Alison. "A few years later. He weathered the fallout from the bombing—he could be quite astute, in his own defence—but there was talk of another love affair ending badly. I think he was one of those people who couldn't help having his heart broken. I don't know about the others. Maybe Young Alan is running the House now. Maybe Theresa is ruling the roost from her cubbyhole, and Ansel still watching the door."

"Not really," said Malcolm.

"No, not really. But there are always parts of the story you never find out. Being blown up feels like an ending, but for everyone else things carry on happening. They'd have talked about it for weeks, for months. Remembered it for years. But sooner or later their own concerns would have taken over. There comes a point when working out whether you've enough milk to see you through the weekend matters more than that somebody you once knew lost her legs to a bomb."

"Was Schenker caught?"

"No."

Griselda said, "Why did he do it, even? What was the point?"

"He didn't do it himself," said Alison. "A man like Schenker doesn't get his hands dirty. He was on the scene when the women were hanged, and I have no doubt he gave the orders. But he wouldn't have tied a knot or climbed a ladder. Same with the bomb. As to why . . . He was a survivor. When he got word there were hunters after him, he did what he always did, and got rid of them. If nothing else, it would give everyone else pause."

"It just seems extreme." Malcolm's train of thought was visible on his face; puzzlement chasing itself in circles. "And how could he have known about Otis and Miles in the first place? That they were laying a trap for him?"

"David Cartwright," said Griselda.

"But how could Cartwright have got word to Karl Schenker? Apart from anything else, Schenker was supposed to be dead."

"Who knows?" said Alison, and sipped her coffee. Then: "Cartwright's dead now. There'll be no answers from him."

Malcolm shook his head. The nearer they got to the end, the more it slipped away. And no one had yet explained the beginning. "Why are we here, anyway? I mean, who leaked the OTIS file?"

Alison said, "I'm sure we all have our own ideas about that."

He wasn't so certain. "There'll be a gap in the report."

"Malcolm," said Griselda, "there'll be no report. Even if we write one, even if we hand it in, it will disappear."

"Why?" said Malcolm. "It'll send a wrecking ball through Regent's Park, which is the whole point of Monochrome in the first place. And a scandal is exactly what the government needs. Something to distract attention from . . . everything."

"Any scandal sends shrapnel flying in unexpected directions," said Griselda. "They'll bury it because it's safer to do so than not."

No, thought Alison. They'll bury it because of who Karl Schenker is now.

But she said nothing.

The richer you are, the better the view—this truth was scrawled across the cityscape, its *T*s crossed by the private jets' contrails vivisecting the sky, its *I*s dotted by the winking lights atop skyscrapers, which made it strange that Ratty's den was a windowless room which might be on any level: dizzy height or doomy depth, it was all the same once you were through the door. The lighting, too, was subdued, not that there was much to see—a large sofa, a drinks cabinet, a widescreen plasma TV fixed to a wall. It could have been the lair of estate agent or banker, or an only mildly successful football player, though in those cases it would likely be put to different use, for this was the room where Fabian de Vries came to think. He had always thought best in the dark.

Now he was holding a glass as he did so, one filled with a seaweedy liquid an expert would recognise as a kale smoothy— doctor's advice, and at his age, doctors were taken seriously. Sipping with neither distaste nor enthusiasm, he cast his mind back to the terse communication he had received earlier. Expressing regret, and a hope that its message would not curtail the friendly relationship between emailer and emailee, it had nevertheless been unbudging in its import: De Vries's tender for the vetting services required by certain government-controlled departments would not be successful, and it was in everyone's interests if he were to quietly withdraw his bid rather than have its failure become a public talking point. De Vries would understand—the sender had been optimistically sure— that nothing personal was inherent in this rejection, nor was there any suggestion that he was considered unfit to provide such services. It was to be hoped that future ventures would have a happier outcome; meanwhile the sender remained his most respectful etcetera, and looked forward to many etcetera etceteras, banalities that De Vries's memory skated around without touching.

Glass empty, he placed it on the floor and forgot about it. It would not be there the next time he entered the room.

Failure, he thought. He should quietly withdraw his bid rather than have its failure become a public talking point.

Had he bothered to reply to the email, he would have thanked the sender for their consideration in offering this advice, etcetera etcetera. And would have done so with a broad smile on his face, etcetera.

Meanwhile, he had a dinner reservation.

Through the wet streets, then, though the rain had subsided; through puddles and along cramped pavements; over cracked kerbs and across treacherous stretches of tarmac, when the lights allowed. She could have taken a cab—Malcolm had been assiduous in reminding her of the expenses allowed; that it would cost her nothing bar some administrative minutes to be collected in a big vehicle with sliding doors and be transported through these same streets in relative comfort, potholes notwithstanding—but Alison North, as she no longer was, preferred to journey home under her own steam. Daylight had slipped away, to hide in corners until needed, and grey evening was on the city like a damp cloth over a cage. Shop lights found reflections on the pavements, and pavements found their mirrors in the sky: the same hard grey surface whichever direction you looked, on only one of which her wheelchair was leaving streaky marks. "Journey home," and that was how she thought of it, but it wasn't home Molly Doran was heading for, but the Park.

After all these years, it was a natural association. Her actual home was a tidy enough apartment, its facilities long since adjusted to her different mobility, but the archive floor at the Park was her queendom, and she belonged to it as much as the other way round. Its shelves bore the tracks of her passage the way wet pavements did; her various obsessions could be traced in the occasional misalignment along the ranks of files, allowed to abide for a while so she could see the paths she'd beaten through their contents. There was a childhood memory buried in this habit, a memory of trudging up a Berkshire hillside, its dips and mounds freshly covered in snow, and looking back to see her visible journey, an untidy scrawl across a clean white page. Not yet a spy, she'd rejoiced in leaving her signature. Not yet an amputee, she'd taken her footprints for granted.

Footprints that had once been hers alone, but for some while now her solitary court had been shared with a newcomer.

"I don't need an assistant," she'd said, when this news had dropped.

"That's too bad. Because I want her somewhere I won't encounter her again."

Offered as a trade: take the cast-off in, and Molly would be guaranteed First Desk's absence.

"She'll quit within the week, you realise that?" she'd said.

But that's not how it had worked out.

On their first encounter, Erin Grey—a young woman with abundant red hair, wearing jeans and a cream-colored sweater—had been, if not exactly truculent, not exactly the opposite either. She clearly regarded her new role as both a punishment posting and a mistake, and seemed prepared to make the best of the first on the assumption that the second would be rectified soon. Which meant that, however long she'd been at the Park, she hadn't yet come to grips with its prevailing ethos: that nothing that happened, however erroneous, was a mistake, rendering any need for correction obsolete.

"I'm here as your support," was how she introduced herself, the word *apparently* hovering unseen over the assertion.

"That's nice," said Molly. "But as you can see, I'm completely without the need for assistance of any kind."

There were those—she was thinking of one in particular—whose answer to this would have included the phrase "high shelves." But Erin, to give her credit, looked like nothing of the sort crossed her mind.

"Well, that's awkward," she said. "Because that's what I'm here for."

"It seems we've reached a pretty swift impasse. What do you propose we do about it?"

"I generally wait for instructions."

"They'll be a long time coming. Better all round if you keep yourself busy, and ideally out of my sight. It's not that I dislike company, it's more that I can't stand it. And if you're inclined to make a joke now," she added, slapping her palms on the wheels of her chair, "do go right ahead."

But whatever humour Erin was finding in the situation, she kept wrapped up.

Which she also did with herself for the next weeks. That she was there was indisputable—the archive floor was large enough that you could remain unseen if you so desired, but Molly was attuned to its moods and graces, and to go entirely unsensed wasn't possible—but she made no demands and caused no inconvenience. Given Molly's previous form in establishing the extent of her dominion, which had included imposing the iron law that no Dogs were allowed, it wouldn't have overtaxed her to purge her borders and see Erin off, but something stayed her hand. That every sorcerer needs an apprentice, perhaps. This young woman would not be here permanently, but she might serve a purpose in the meantime. It was just a matter of waiting for her to discover what that purpose might be.

A process that needed, by Molly's calculation, fourteen days to complete.

Erin found her one afternoon in the 1930s, an area Molly took herself to when she needed reminding that no matter how badly governed a nation might be there was always room for deterioration, and announced her new-found objective. "This Green Shoots business," she said.

"Ah, yes," said Molly. This had been on her own mind lately; the initiative whereby so-called ancillary departments of the Service were put out to tender. "Funny they gave it a name suggesting new life. Though I suppose calling it The Knackers' Yard might have been a little on the nose."

"First Desk is anti—"

"Of course she is. And you think helping her fight her battles would put you in her good books? An interesting position." She allowed the word "interesting" to do all the work, not bothering to lay stress on it. "I'd have thought five minutes of being her PA would have told you the last thing she does is favour those who observe her in moments of weakness."

"It's not her benefit I'm thinking of. And I'm not eager for her patronage either."

"Patronage. Hmm. Your degree was in history, wasn't it?"

"Yes."

"Well, there's plenty of that round here to keep you busy if you've still a hankering. But you'd rather occupy yourself with the present. Why?"

"Because it's only the present for a moment. In the long run, it's all history." Erin looked around the archive, its collected stocks and balances. "This place more than most. It won't be long before someone notices that a basic digitisation process would free up all this real estate. A couple of scanning machines and a crew of bright school-leavers on work experience, and your entire *raison d'être* disappears."

"Nice of you to sum me up so succinctly," said Molly. "But I've been under threat of eviction before. And as you can see, I'm still here."

"Oh, I'm sure you run rings round First Desk," said Erin. "But what about afterwards? Forgive the bluntness. But five minutes after they've draped you in a shroud, there'll be men with tape measures here, working out how many water coolers they'll need when they refit the floor as a break-out area. Possibly not the legacy you're hoping for. Why are you laughing?"

"That's not important. All right, then, Green Shoots. What precisely are you intending to do?"

"What an archivist does. Even a reluctant one. I'm going to do some research."

"Are you expecting my blessing?"

"No," said Erin. "I just thought you'd like to know what I'm up to."

This had been the previous autumn. It was early December when the young woman brought the first fruits of her endeavours to Molly's desk; less, Molly was pleased to note, in the expectation of praise than with the air of one paying a tithe.

A tribute that had turned Molly's universe upside down.

This evening, Erin was at her desk when Molly arrived, a book in her hands and an opened envelope in front of her. The envelope looked official, and Erin, if not precisely beaming, seemed reasonably content, all of which prompted Molly to ask, "Success?"

"I think so. They want me for interview, anyway."

Erin had applied to do postgrad research, at the obvious place; the one they called the Spies' College, on the Woodstock Road in Oxford.

"You'll do well there." And it was high time she moved on, Molly thought. Spend too long among other people's secrets, you fold in on yourself, and become unable to move except sideways, unable to think except in paranoid loops. It was way too late to help herself, but Erin had a future.

"How did today go?" Erin asked her.

"It went."

"So what happens now?"

What happens now would already have happened, thought

Molly. What happens now was that Karl Schenker, as he once was, would have made a move against Otis, because that was how Schenker operated. *When he got word there were hunters after him, he did what he always did, and got rid of them.*

"You're sure he'll have found out?" Erin continued, reading her thoughts.

"Of course he will. This is Spook Street, remember. Information leaks like light from a bulb."

"You never get tired of it, do you?" Erin said. "Your generation and its self-mythologising. Spook Street. London Rules. Just listening to you answer a simple question is like being offered a Masonic handshake."

"Fair point. But the fact remains, Monochrome will have leaked. It will have leaked yesterday, when there was a whole panel sitting. And it'll have leaked today, when there were just the three of us. Or four, if you count Clive."

"Oh, let's not forget Clive. And your friend Otis—if we can call him your friend, when you've not laid eyes on him for thirty years—your friend Otis will find himself with crosshairs on his back. If he's even still alive, and somewhere accessible."

"He was fed into the system by David Cartwright." Who had been protecting his own back more than safeguarding others, thought Molly. It had been Cartwright's hand that had primed the bomb that robbed her of her legs, once you'd stripped the layers away. He schemed and plotted here in London, and the price was paid by others. Best to hide those others away, in case the auditors took too close a look. "There's no reason he'd not be still alive. Beyond life's usual vagaries, I mean."

"And you've never tried to contact him?"

"Like I said—"

"Like you said, he's in the system. But you're not telling me you couldn't have tracked him down if you wanted."

If she'd wanted. Certainly, there'd been times when she had, and even at the best of them, she'd not known whether she'd have embraced him or opened his throat. But the years had a way of smoothing the edges—among other things, they did that—and Molly hadn't thought of Otis in a long time, not until Erin had placed the Green Shoots folder in her hands, igniting a memory she'd not been aware was still ticking in the back of her mind.

A man in a black leather jacket over a blue open-necked shirt, his smile a little too wide, his wallet a little too open.

"If I could do that," Molly said, deliberately ignoring Erin's point, "then so can Schenker. He's not without contacts."

"He's also not without brains. Why risk his new life just to plug a gap that might not even be there? Otis wouldn't recognise him. Wouldn't have a clue who he is now."

"That's a ninety-nine per cent certainty," Molly agreed. "But Schenker's a one per cent player. If he gets wind Otis is out there, he'll make a move. And even if he's just pushing buttons, he'll have to show his hand."

"So Otis gets to be bait once more. I hope I'm not going to regret helping make that happen," said Erin. She meant the moment in the supermarket, when she'd crashed trolleys with Malcolm Kyle, and slipped the OTIS folder into his shopping. "And you're okay with all of it? Putting Otis in danger, I mean," she said. "Because Schenker's not going to be throwing a reunion party."

Molly barely glanced at the stumps of her legs. "Yes," she said. "I'm okay with that."

Anna Livia's—no one used the "Plurabelle"—was on Park Lane, and if Max had been unaware of the pissy stricture about not calling it what it called itself on its awning he couldn't fail to notice that this wasn't a gaff where the house wine came in jugs.

When Carl Singer entered, he was recognised by the woman playing front of house, a woman with a headset, a lectern and a smile so professionally polished Max could see it from across the road. This was where Shelley had dropped him before cruising off into the traffic, one element of which was the taxi they'd been following since it collected Singer from his apartment on the South Bank. Singer was alone. So was Max, now; however this played out, Shelley's role was done.

"Do you plan to use violence?"

True, Max still had the baton he'd acquired earlier, but he couldn't see himself using it to beat a story out of a well-known business figure. Not in a high-class restaurant, anyway.

"Because either way, I'm out of this now."

"Yeah, you have to be careful," he said. "What with your bad leg and everything."

"Max—"

"Kidding." Which he had been. Everyone needs an escape route; everyone needs an exit strategy. He'd lived for years with a flight kit under his floorboards. If Shelley needed a payoff to fund her own departure, Max didn't care how she secured it. And if the Park ended up holding the bill, that was fine too. "Take care of yourself," he'd said, and then she was gone, her anonymous car one more pixel in the wide-screen streets of West London, and their shared history no more substantial than the exhaust fumes painting its wake.

There was a bench in an alcove on the pavement facing the restaurant—*dedicated to the memory of*, Max didn't read the rest—and there he sat, resigning himself to a wait. Who Carl Singer was, he had no clue. The face rang no bells, and while history's cupboards were full of skeletons, Singer was too young to have been a player when Max was active. The likelihood was that he was a cutout; that his security firm had been hired to do a job in which he had no personal stake. But that worked for Max. Just so long as Singer could let him know who lit the fuse, he'd wait as long as it took.

There was a camera on a lamppost twenty yards away, tilted towards the traffic, but all the same he positioned himself so that it had as narrow a view of his profile as possible. The street was busy, but a man on a bench was as good as invisible. Max ran a hand through his recently tinted hair, and hoped it wouldn't rain.

"Let's get eyes inside, shall we?" First Desk said.

She'd had a watch put on Singer once the penny dropped: that the new front-runner in the tendering process for Landscaping had also sat on the Monochrome inquiry. First Desk enjoyed coincidences the way she liked happy endings: outside of fiction, they were as trustworthy as a Tinder profile. So the boys and girls had added Singer's name to the roster of suspected terrorists, former PMs and other bad actors, which meant their face-recognition programs—face-huggers, in the jargon—had another target to play with, one that didn't tax them long. Singer had been picked up getting into a taxi outside his apartment block, and First Desk had joined the team as he was alighting at Anna Livia Plurabelle's, once Mayfair's hottest meal ticket, until it had a body dumped outside its windows a few years back. The resulting rush for tables had led to a decline from A-list to C-list for a season, and even now regularly featured on Instagram. Singer's presence didn't necessarily mean it had turned a corner, but at least there was money tucking in. Precisely how much money, First Desk was busy establishing. She took billionaires on trust the same way she accepted coincidence.

"Haven't got all day."

Anna Livia's door-cam was already being piggybacked, and

a panoramic shot of the dining room coming into view: a number of couples, a few larger parties, and some fuzzy corners where over-ambitious pot plants allowed shyer diners privacy.

"I want to see nooks and crannies. And if there are private rooms, I want those too."

Someone was already working on it, swivelling a camera mounted above the fire exit at the back of the dining room.

"That's not helping."

But it came to rest aiming at a mirror, in which a table previously hidden by internal foliage could now be seen.

"All right, smart arse." First Desk's occasional crudities were cherished by those at whom they were aimed. The smart arse thus honoured couldn't help the smirk reaching her lips, but she converted it into a frown of concentration as First Desk went on: "That's Singer, then. But who's he with?"

Because while the new angle clearly showed Singer, his companion remained a rear-view only: the back of a bald and cratered head.

"Working on it," someone whispered. It wasn't a church, the hub, but you wouldn't necessarily have known that by the comportment of some of its familiars.

A face-hugger had already locked onto the available image, milking what it could from the shape of the ears. It stuttered once, twice, and for a moment seemed to suggest that Singer was dining with a former captain of the Starship Enterprise.

"Please don't make it so," muttered First Desk, a prayer granted almost immediately as the program shuffled through more choices before picking another face from its library.

The team released a collective breath, and First Desk leaned in closer.

"Well, there's interesting," she said. "What's Carl Singer doing breaking bread with Fabian de Vries?"

Or, in the first instance, breadsticks. Which snapped with the same sound fingers would, an image Singer brushed away as soon as it occurred. "Anything on the wine list grab your attention?"

De Vries said, "I have three important calls to make after this. But you order whatever you like."

The tone of his voice made his meaning clear.

He was in his seventies, Singer thought, though this was speculation. But if so, it was a fit and healthy seventies, his cratered head a stronghold of secrets that his broad shoulders were clearly equal to carrying. His eyes were brown, he never seemed to blink, and his hands were large and strong. Somewhere in his past, Singer imagined, lumber had been stacked and coal sacks shifted. Scarring at the jowl line was perhaps a souvenir of youthful misadventure, though if he'd seen the same evidence on a woman he'd have assumed cosmetic surgery. His suit, meanwhile, was a thing of sombre beauty, to which his tie added the only flamboyant note; from a distance a rich dark blue, that only up close betrayed swirling dragons.

They had taken different roads to riches, Singer knew that much. He himself had become wealthy the traditional British way, by having landowning parents who died. De Vries, meanwhile, had arrived from his native Holland having made his money in property, the details of which remained obscure, as did his background. Given his apparent age, this couldn't be down to a shyness about his war record—though it wouldn't have surprised Singer to learn that those hands had wrought violence—but whatever the reason, a thick curtain had been drawn that no journalist or business partner had ever pulled back. Which was not, in the long run, a reason to shun him. Clearly De Vries had a past he wanted kept hidden, but equally clearly he was good at hiding it, which in today's world amounted to squeaky clean.

Since settling in the UK, however, he'd availed himself of the moral latitude London allowed, and increased his fortune by means of, in turn, a payday loan company, online gambling, a national chain of escape rooms, and virtual reality porn, this last being dressed up as "a breakthrough in distance caring," possibly with medical applications. It had certainly involved nurse's uniforms. But any way you looked at it De Vries wasn't the first businessman, and wouldn't be the last, to grow rich exploiting his fellow man's weaknesses. And given that Singer's own weaknesses currently included a hole in his finances big enough to pass a camel through, Singer wasn't about to risk his displeasure by ordering a bottle of wine.

One of the waitstaff, a pretty young man with a white smile, was approaching, the blue light on his headset winking three times in quick succession just as First Desk, back at the Park, was asking, "And what about ears?"

"Piggybacking now," the young woman said.

First Desk leaned forward.

I see [. . . crackle . . .] *the best table.*

If you want to be seen, you should choose other [. . . crackle . . .]. *I value discretion above* [. . . crackle . . .].

"There's a little interference," someone apologised.

"Do you think?"

"It'll tidy up when we—"

"Quiet!"

And then a booming delivery; a whisper writ large, as if the speaker were delivering an aside to the gods.

Gentlemen, would you like to see the cocktail list?

They waved him away.

De Vries said, "Dare I ask how your supposedly crack team's mission went this afternoon? A simple case of collecting a disgruntled party, that shouldn't have been too much of a challenge. Even given the pig's arse they made of the initial attempt."

Singer said, "I'm awaiting word. I'm sure it went smoothly." If it had gone smoothly, he'd have heard about it by now. "I don't suppose there's any point in asking what your interest in this Max Janáček is?"

"None at all, no."

But whatever the reason was, thought Singer, he—Singer— was thoroughly implicated in it now. But then, this was what happened when you sought alliance with the powerful: the price they exacted was measured in coils. If he'd had any choice in the matter he'd have steered clear, but given the state of his finances, a refusal to submit to De Vries's suffocating embrace was to accept fiscal catastrophe.

It was to bolster his own esteem as much as to defend the team in question that he said, "They're ex-military."

"Really. And did you inquire as to why they're ex? Because my guess is, they were let go because they're useless."

There was no point prolonging this. "I'll let you know as soon as I have word."

"And meanwhile, Monochrome is over."

"Inasmuch as it ever got off the ground," Singer said. "Regent's Park—well, First Desk—made sure of that."

De Vries waved a hand. "It doesn't matter. Monochrome was intended to expose the Park's weaknesses, and show it ripe for overhaul. First Desk's manoeuvres might have prevented that, but the overhaul is happening anyway. Green Shoots work both ways, you realise. New buds opening in the air, and fresh roots taking grip in the earth." Singer had grown used to this: the way De Vries would occupy a lectern during conversation. He might shrink from public attention, but demanded the spotlight in private. "The Park is fighting a losing battle, not least because the ideologies that will dismantle it are precisely those it was established to protect. Capitalism always eats its young in the end. Any history book will teach you that."

"You sound like an old-school red."

De Vries laughed, something Singer hadn't seen before. "Maybe in my youth. Never trust anyone who wasn't a socialist when young, isn't that the saying? But only a fool hangs on to such ideals in age, when the winds start to blow."

Their starters were delivered. Singer had liked the look of the teriyaki beef, but De Vries had ordered that, so he had opted for the crab cakes. These, it turned out, were very small.

"Meanwhile, congratulations are in order." De Vries picked up his fork. "My bid for the government's vetting services has been, for reasons nobody is prepared to discuss, unsuccessful. Making you the front-runner and almost certain victor. In fact, just between the two of us, there's no 'almost' about it."

"I hadn't heard that."

"Officially, neither have I. But it's a foregone conclusion."

"Meaning you've effectively won after all."

"Nobody needs to be told you're my proxy. We'll allow appearances to prevail."

"And if we're seen dining together?"

"A good loser's tribute to the better man. I'll be picking up the bill, naturally."

"I'm not entirely without resources."

"Not entirely, no," said De Vries, spearing a pound-coin-sized piece of beef. "Not entirely."

We have an Instagrammer."

A photograph of one of Anna Livia's signature dishes had just uploaded to the platform, and before its colours were dry its originating mobile phone had been swooped on and recruited for the cause, and was now, despite its apparently innocent idleness, acting as a microphone one empty table's distance from where De Vries and Singer sat.

"Shall we give it a like?" someone suggested, and all round the workstation were momentarily gobstruck when First Desk said, "Yes, why not? Always nice to show a little appreciation."

The conversation coming through was patchy at best, as if it were held at the other end of a subway, but would clear up in the edit as nobody quite dared suggest a second time.

"And while we're at it, let's do a trawl of the surrounding area. Be good to know whether our friends have a travelling band."

Someone got to work on it before the sentence was done.

Anna Livia's windows were tinted, and Max might as well be staring at an unlit aquarium. The thought that he could simply cross the road and gatecrash Singer's dinner hadn't tarried long. Singer had arrived alone, as far as Max could tell—and Singer's stormtroopers weren't good enough to blindside him—but an alarm call from this postcode would have a police response measured in minutes. Better to wait and choose a private moment.

A life lived between green lanes had taught him patience.

Anyway, there were other thoughts to occupy him while waiting. Images of Berlin emerged unbidden, particularly of those last weeks, when Alison North had arrived in the city, wide-eyed and fresh as a dandelion. After the bomb, he'd never seen her again. Why had he allowed that to happen? Guilt, obviously. And because he'd been spirited off by the Park. "For your own good," Miles had said, in the last conversation they'd had. "It's not like Schenker's going to shrug and walk away. He wanted you dead, you're still alive. Do the fucking maths."

"What about you?"

He hadn't answered, but hadn't needed to: what about Miles was, Miles was sent home.

Among the things left unsaid was that Max's long-term good was to the Park's benefit too. Someone high up the food chain had sent Alison to Berlin, and look how that had turned out. So, as was the way with the Park, a cover-up had been launched, or at any rate, a scattering of those involved, so the stories they left behind would remain a collage of obscure origins. Alison, he guessed, would have been tidied away, a disability pension breaking her fall. Miles, he didn't want to think about. When he did, he imagined suicide, though could never determine whether Miles would opt for the swift exit or the slow-drawn kind. As for himself, never an employee of the Park—merely a cash-in-hand contact of one of its agents—he'd ended up with the full passport package: a life, a home and a salary, and all he had to do was let himself be uprooted.

It had helped that someone else had already attempted to hack those roots away.

Miles is hunting a tiger, Max had told Alison, and that same tiger had turned its attention to Max. It was his friend's legs that were bitten off, not his own, but was it any surprise he'd gone through the door the Park held open? The only wonder was he'd sunk so comfortably into his new life, and wouldn't have left it if that same door hadn't swung open again, letting the old light through . . . And that was it, that was why his mind kept pushing him towards Berlin. Because danger had opened its mouth again, and how many tigers did you encounter in the average life? No, it was the same old tiger back again, using Carl Singer to find him.

Max cracked his knuckles, and looked towards the restaurant. He—Max Janáček—might not be up to bracing Singer in a public space, but his younger self would have known how to handle him. And he felt an old grin creep across his features, one picked up by the team at the Park studying him through incoming CCTV, the face-hugger having identified him in moments. "Well, look at that," First Desk said. "Losing an old spook, that could happen to anybody. But having him turn up in the middle of something else, well. Makes me wonder who's playing games. And who's the football."

She paused, giving it thought. All this time she'd been standing bolt upright, while the youngsters around her sprawled in chairs or leaned on desks. Thus assembled, they waited for her ruling.

"Let's bring him home, shall we?"

At the dining table, De Vries was in full flight. "It's not about the money. It's about control, and control means data. If you own the platforms on which people conduct their business, you effectively own that business. And if you own the platforms on which those same people pursue their leisure interests, you effectively own their lives. Any fool with a Twitter feed, a Facebook page or an Instagram account has to all intents and purposes ceded autonomy. But don't look so worried. It's just a point of view."

Singer was wishing he had wine. "If you really believe that, how come you don't own a chunk of social network?"

"Because I came along too late. But we are where we are, as our politicians are so keen on emphasising, perhaps to distract attention from the reasons why that might be so. And we seek opportunities where we can. The online world is a marketplace, and data is its leading commodity. A man who has control of the government's background-checking services would have to be very short of imagination not to recognise the potential for personal growth."

"That's obviously a . . . I mean, there'll be controls. Oversight. It's not as if I—we—it's not as if we'll have *carte blanche* to use information gathered during vetting processes for other purposes. There's data protection in place, apart from anything else."

"There are always protections, always controls. There'll always be legislation. And yet people always get rich. I'm not talking about illegality. I'm talking about the areas no one's fenced in yet, because they haven't thought about it. And it's those unfenced areas we'll be laying claim to. Nothing criminal about it. Not until the lawmakers get around to paying attention."

"And what happens then?"

"Who cares? The sheep'll be sheared and we'll have moved on." De Vries reached for his water glass, studied it a moment, then apparently decided against offering a toast. "Always move on. If it's lessons you're looking for, write that one down. Never be there when the bill comes due." He gave a hard smile, which might easily be mistaken for contempt. "Present circumstances excepted, of course. I don't think we'll be needing the dessert menu, do you?"

There was movement at the restaurant; taxis arriving, people leaving. Max stood and shuffled blood back into his legs. This was one of those London streets where darkness was a visitor, only ever hovering on the edges; these restaurant lights, these hotel lobbies, would shine all night, in case it looked like they'd grown poor. He stretched, grimaced, flexed fingers. No Singer yet, but if the first sitting was done, he might emerge at any moment. What Max would do if he was in company, he didn't know. But if there was a chance of a private word, Max would be taking it. Which meant ushering Singer from the main drag before he hopped into a cab: a two-man job he'd have to undertake on his own.

There was a gap in the traffic and he started across the road, just as two men emerged onto the pavement.

The woman with the headset who'd shown him to the table helped Singer with his coat, and he might have imagined it—no, he definitely didn't—but her hand squeezed his elbow. He'd already folded a twenty for her, and made sure it was wrapped around his card before slipping it into her palm: just his name and mobile number. His arm tingled. He smiled when she thanked him, but did not speak.

De Vries said, as they stepped onto the pavement, "Neatly done."

Singer gave the merest suggestion of a nod. For a moment, the evening's run of play had been reversed: at the table De Vries had been in control, and not shy about showing that he knew it. But all of his fables about money and power, what were they worth if women didn't come to you of their own accord? He wondered about saying this aloud, but if it came out wrong De Vries would step on him, right here on the pavement—few people would dare do that, but De Vries would; De Vries knew what he was worth, underneath the smart suits and the headlines. De Vries would smile while he was doing it. Though De Vries, right now, looked more puzzled than anything else.

"Friend of yours?" he asked, and with a nod indicated the man crossing the road in a hurry, heading directly towards them.

Max was letting the moment carry him, which was bad tradecraft, but thirty years out of practice, what could you do? Singer had appeared on the pavement, beside an older man; they were hovering, exchanging words, but a car would arrive any moment—a simpleton's prediction: Singer was a rich man; rich men don't walk . . . Max paused while a cab rushed past, giving him the full benefit of its horn. Singer was familiar, Max having studied online images earlier, but his companion was a stranger, except . . . Another car, and here he was, stranded in the middle of the road. The second man was older, wearing an expensive coat; he was bald, and something about the shape of his head . . . Ridiculous. Now an SUV was coming, tint-windowed, black. It cruised past Max like a shark ignoring fry, its driver all stony concentration on the road ahead.

He thought: something about the way this man is standing. Add thirty years, more . . .

But it was too big a leap, and he'd only met Schenker once.

Another gap, and he ran the rest of the way across, barely aware that his fists were clenching. An old photograph was stirring: a man in a wood, three bodies hanging from the branches behind him. One of them Max's sister. His back was to the camera, his head half turned, allowing a quarter profile at best . . . Max had met the same man at a party; had noted his habit of standing with his hands behind his back, and the way his apparently lazy gaze took in everything around. This man he was approaching held his hands ramrod straight by his sides— but then, the first things you lose on becoming someone new are the habits that held you together. Max knew about that. So would Schenker, whoever he was now. But Max doubted he'd be able to lose that gaze, that predatory gaze.

Reaching the pavement he tugged at his collar, for that too was habit. Singer and his friend were yards away; he was entering their space, and any moment they'd be turning, offering puzzlement or alarm or fear—or understanding, which would answer Max's question. But first something black dropped over his head and his arms were pinned behind him; before he could make a sound his legs were whipped away and he was airborne, then flat on his back—not the pavement, but a gap between seats. A door slammed and someone knocked twice. *Go.* The SUV moved off. On Anna Livia's pavement, two men stared after it.

"What was all that about?"

De Vries, watching the vehicle turn the corner, said, "Just a little local difficulty, I'm sure. Aren't our security services wonderful?"

An hour passed, or it might have been two—after dark, hours were hard to count; they flocked together like birds in flight. But however many there were First Desk spent them in her office, listening to the cleaned-up tape of Singer and De Vries in conversation, and poring through a hastily assembled financial portrait of the former—"Warts and all," she'd demanded, and there were warts, there were warts—alongside the sparse account of the latter's pre-history. It was still possible, just, to appear on the modern landscape as an innocent, having recently wandered out of the woods. But it wasn't possible to do so and actually be innocent. Nobody wandered from the woods with clean hands. The corpse of Little Red Riding Hood was always buried somewhere.

Unless it was hanging from a tree in plain sight, its sisters swinging beside it.

Meanwhile, there were questions to be answered, and people to answer them. Leaving her office, she took the lift to −2, IR3. The archivist, she knew, would appreciate the nod to her own history.

The archivist was in the room, thoroughly absorbed in her own present. She had been there, unoccupied, since First Desk had had her collected from her domain.

"You've been a busy woman."

"Well, you know how it is. Idle hands, devil's work and all that."

First Desk pulled a chair from under the desk, smoothed her skirt and settled into it. "There's only one way I can see that the OTIS file got to Monochrome. You had Erin Grey deliver it."

"You're the one assigned her to me. You can't punish her for following my instructions."

"You have interesting ideas about management structures. You must tell me about them one day. Meanwhile, the OTIS file. Monochrome. Why?"

Molly said, "I had Erin plant the file on Monochrome—have you met him, by the way? Malcolm Kyle?"

First Desk stared.

"Nice boy. A little unsure of himself, but he'll find his legs." She paused. "See what I did there? Never mind. I had Erin plant the file on Malcolm to flush De Vries out. Spoiler alert, but he used to work for the Stasi."

"And you thought using Monochrome—a pointless paper-shuffling exercise with zero authority—was a wiser course of action than, say, coming to me?"

"Well, it seemed less likely to end in a cover-up. De Vries is a well-connected man. Rich, party donor, friend of prime ministers. Meaning virtually untouchable, unless he did something stupid like disrespecting Trans people on Twitter."

"He hanged three women in a wood," said First Desk. "One of them worked with the Park. Do you really imagine I'd have allowed a cover-up?"

"Karl Schenker hanged three women in a wood," said Molly. "Fabian de Vries wasn't there at the time. In fact, Fabian de Vries wasn't anywhere then, because he didn't exist. As for what the Park will and will not cover up, I work in the archive, remember? So let's not act like we have a moral high ground. We wouldn't recognise one of those if it came with a gradient warning sign."

"If it pains you to work for such a grubby organisation, I'll happily accept your resignation. Meanwhile, why Monochrome?

You might as well have reported him to the post office. It would have made as much sense."

"But there'd have been a longer queue," said Molly.

The room they were in had no two-way mirror, because there didn't need to be; the suite was wired for sound and vision, available live to anyone in the monitoring room down the corridor, a room First Desk had had cleared before this interview began. If what Molly was going to tell her contained bear traps, she wanted to hear about them before anyone else.

Molly said, "I knew nothing about De Vries until Erin did her Green Shoots research. Which was . . . interesting. You already knew De Vries was tendering for the Landscaping contract, because he wanted control of the vetting service. But did you know the hold he had over the old PM, before Erin revealed it for you?"

First Desk said, "The PM's well-known liquidity problems always threatened to throw him into bad company."

"I'll take that as a no. Erin found out about the superinjunction the old-fashioned way, by having a friend from college who worked for the judge involved. She—the friend—was somewhat hostile to the PM in question, and thought, in Erin's words, that 'someone ought to know.' Going to the press, obviously, was out of the question."

"Erin's handier than I realised."

"I think you've missed that boat. Anyway, Monochrome. Given De Vries's ambitions, it seemed likely he'd have an ear to the ground for any mention of his former existence. Monochrome, in its trawl for naughty Service doings, had the freedom to call any file it wanted from our archive, and since De Vries had been the target of an illegal op run by Berlin Station, it wasn't out of the question his name would arise. The fact that you'd pulled the rug from under the inquiry on Day One didn't change that. One disgruntled agent with the right memories, and any manner of old secrets might have come tumbling out."

"And you made sure that happened."

"And he got to hear about it."

"Via Carl Singer, I assume," First Desk said. "We know they're in cahoots. It was Singer's company De Vries used to establish Otis's new identity. And then attempt to abduct him. Which is down to you, incidentally. Putting Otis, Max Janáček, in the firing line."

"True. But as far as Singer's concerned, I rather think it was the other way round. De Vries established . . . cahoots with Singer precisely because Singer was on Monochrome. That was their point of connection. No, if De Vries already had a spy on the panel, it must have been someone else."

"Who?"

"Isn't finding that out your job? I'm just the archivist, remember?"

"Did you know De Vries would go after Otis?"

"It's what I'd have done, in his shoes. If I wore shoes. De Vries is really Karl Schenker, who had three women murdered, remember? One of the others involved that day, who was arrested a few years later, named Schenker in court. Schenker was thought to be dead at the time, so it was safe enough to do so. But Otis was one of the few who knew he was still alive. And De Vries is a hunter. Anyone who presents a threat to him, he'll come after them."

"He might have come after you instead."

"I'm aware of that."

First Desk waited, but Molly had nothing more to offer on that subject.

"De Vries doesn't like having his picture taken," First Desk said at length. "But there was a photo of him in the file Erin prepared. An old one, from some charity event, more than a decade ago. Is that how you recognised him as Schenker?"

"Yes," said Molly.

"How? How, exactly, did you do that? For a start, he'd have changed his appearance after faking his death. And for another thing . . ." She leaned forward. "For another thing, you never laid eyes on Karl Schenker. He was long gone when you arrived in Berlin."

"Was he?"

"Oh, wonderful. Now you're being mysterious."

"I'm in a wheelchair. I can be as mysterious as I like. It's in our charter."

"I need to know this, Molly."

"But I'm not about to tell you. I will tell Otis, though. Or Max, as I suppose I should call him now. It's our story, not yours."

"When was the last time you saw him?"

"Last time I stood up straight."

"And you think I'm going to allow the pair of you to have a little catch-up?"

"I'm pretty sure you're going to, yes. It's not as if you won't be listening in."

"Oh, I'm First Desk. I can eavesdrop all I like. It's in my charter."

The two women glared at each other. On First Desk's wrist, the second hand glided round a full circuit, then most of another.

"I can sit here all day," said Molly at last. "If memory serves, my chair's more comfortable than yours."

"I'll give you ten minutes. And if I don't start hearing answers, any comfortable sensations you have will be a distant memory." First Desk stood, not waiting for a response, but before opening the door, she paused. "Brinsley Miles . . . He's who I think he is, right?"

"Of course he bloody is," said Molly.

By the time they unlocked the room and walked him down the corridor, Max was past asking questions. He was in the Park, he assumed. He'd never been there before—strange; it occupied a weighty presence in his history, but he'd been Miles's recruit, not the Park's, and had never laid eyes on the place, tonight included, because in the SUV he'd had a bag over his head. This was how spooks were: Regent's Park was on Google Maps, and had its own website, but if you worked there you pretended it was invisible.

Here on the inside it was visible enough but unappealing; just a well-lit corridor, with closed doors at regular intervals, some numbered, others not. It might be a code, but was more likely a bureaucratic muddle. Other muddles included that, while he hadn't been cuffed, he hadn't been listened to either. He was three-quarters certain he'd just seen Karl Schenker in the middle of busy London, but nobody seemed bothered. They were probably too busy planning a new numbering system for their offices, here on this subterranean floor of Regent's Park.

Whose recruit he'd never been.

In truth, though, Miles had been Max's recruit as much as the other way around. They'd made each other who they were, back when they'd been different. Berlin was a zoo but also a playground, and it had been theirs for a while. All those nightclubs, all that noise. A lot of drink spilled on a lot of sticky surfaces. Looking back on it was like gazing down a green lane; all twists and overgrowth, the very thing you were looking at obscuring your view. And then a door was opened and he was being ushered through, and the first thing he saw was Alison North.

"Jesus," he said. "Alison?"

"I know, I know. I used to be taller."

But when she brushed at her eyes as Otis bent to embrace her, it was an attempt to hide her tears.

"**What's there** to say? I lived a life, and it went by faster than you can imagine. Don't they all? I taught. Distance learning, Open University, some other courses. I wrote a book and read a lot, mostly Dickens. I was even married for a while, though that feels like something I saw on TV." He paused. "Sitting here, it feels like it all happened to someone else. That everything that's happened since Berlin has been a fantasy. Do you ever get that?"

"No. Were you always in Devon?"

"No. I was shunted around at first—I spent the best part of a decade up north, on the east coast. They want you to be a moving target, you know? Then they get sick of playing games, and just want you to be forgotten. Devon's a good place for that, it turns out."

"I never quite forgot you, Max." She paused. "Max. No, that's not working for me. I never quite forgot you, Otis."

He blinked. "Now I'm Otis?"

"Your codename."

He laughed. "What happened to . . . Miles? That's not his name either, is it?"

"Not Miles, no. But he's fine." She amended this. "Well, that overstates the case. But he's alive. Still in the Service."

"Jesus. Can't imagine him doing a desk job."

"Again, overstating the case."

"Miles, though . . . Christ. He struck some matches in his day. Started a few fires."

More than a few. There'd long been whispers about Miles's exploits behind the Wall, whispers she'd tried to track down to their sources, never with any success. That this left her convinced of their truth revealed more about her than about him.

Max was speaking. "I wanted to see you, you know. After-wards."

She nodded.

"But they hustled me out of the city pretty quickly."

"The Park doesn't like it when its agents are targeted."

"I wasn't Park. And you—that bomb was meant for me, Alison. We both know that."

"Yes."

"I'm sorry."

She said, "I was doing my job. Betraying you, betraying Miles, that was my job. So what happened to me was never your fault, or his. If you want to blame anything, blame this place. The Park."

"And you work here still."

"Where else was I supposed to go?"

A question she hoped he wouldn't answer, because he could have done so with a single word: anywhere. It had once seemed to Molly that, rather than grieving a lost future, she was building a different one in the only place it would be allowed to flourish, but these days she knew she'd been wrong about that; that she was strong, and always had been, and could have conquered worlds, chairbound or not. She'd settled for the tiny queendom of her archive instead. Well, we are all diminished by our wrong choices, she thought, and wondered whether Miles had discovered this too, in the years since.

Of course he had. Of course he had.

Max said, "They're listening to us?"

"Of course."

"Well, there's no point keeping secrets now. I saw him tonight. Karl Schenker. He's still out there."

"Yes."

"This isn't news to you."

"If Schenker came looking, that's because of me. I set a trap for him, like you did."

"A trap?"

Molly reconsidered. "I laid bait. It's nearly the same thing."

She told him about Monochrome, about the file, about how he—Max—had been the bait. There was no suggestion of apology, nor did Max expect any. When she'd finished he remained silent, sifting through the new information, slotting it alongside his own recent experience. It seemed to fit. At any rate, he nodded to himself. Then said:

"How did you recognise him? And how did you know he'd keep tabs on Monochrome, and bother to search me out?"

"Because he's getting more rich and powerful, not less," Molly said, answering the last question first. "And the richer and more powerful he gets, the more he wants to stay that way. You're a threat."

"So was Miles."

"Miles never laid eyes on him."

"I only did once, and he looked different then. He'd have changed his appearance after faking his death."

"Oh, you saw him a second time."

"When did that happen?"

She said, "He wore a black leather jacket over a blue open-necked shirt, and his smile was a little too wide and his wallet a little too open. I thought at the time he was simply after a pick-up, but it wasn't random. He knew who I was."

"I don't follow."

"But you did. Remember? When he tried to get me into a cab, you stepped in. Dropped him on the pavement."

Light was dawning. "That night on the Ku'damm . . ."

"That night. Yes. He said something about wanting to hurt me, I thought it was just standard male behaviour. It was probably something more. Anyway, that's the man in the photo. The one my assistant put in her research folder."

"I laid him out."

"You did. I wonder how much that had to do with his determination to hunt you down."

"Seriously? Wounded male pride, after thirty years?"

"You've read your Dickens," said Molly. "You tell me. On the other hand, if things work out his way he'll be running a chunk of what used to be the Park's business. I suppose safeguarding that, along with protecting himself from a triple murder charge, might take precedence over avenging himself for a sucker punch back in the dark ages."

"It wasn't a sucker punch," said Max. "Well, okay, maybe it was. But I still put him down."

"And that's the main thing."

They shared a smile, and for a moment they were back in their old lives, the ones that had turned out to belong to other people, or at any rate, to no longer belong to them.

"So what happens now?"

"Oh, I expect we'll find out," Molly said, even as the door was opening, and First Desk coming in.

"I want a timeline from all involved. Since the moment Erin planted that file on Kyle."

"Yes."

"And hourly reports on Singer and De Vries. Phones, laptops, the works."

"Yes."

"And a damn sandwich. Anything but cheese."

"On its way," said Hari.

It arrived with coffee, which was equally welcome. First Desk ate, drank, read the timelines, studied the walls. She re-read the dossier Erin Grey had compiled on Green Shoots, with its rare photograph of Fabian de Vries. Schenker's file, she'd called up from the archive too. He had been listed as dead shortly after the Wall fell, a development prompting a scrawled *Good career move* in the file's margin. Subsequent activities, including the car bomb which had taken Molly's legs, were listed as "Unsubstantiated." Small wonder Molly, having learned of his new identity, had taken an unorthodox approach to forcing his hand.

And this was the man who, via his glove puppet, would be taking over the Service's Landscaping functions, vetting those appointed to sensitive positions in government-controlled institutions. Not to mention applicants for employment in the Service itself. She could prevent all this with a phone call now. With a second, she could have him arrested. It would be a good day's work, and go some distance to pulling the rug out from under Green Shoots. Except it would be a temporary respite; an interlude before the next bankrupt government began checking down back of its sofa for coins.

She frosted the wall. Out on the hub the boys and girls steered the Park through the secret hours, and she didn't need to see them to know they were doing their job. As for her own job, there were days she could be standing right in front of it and not recognise it for what it was. *Protecting the nation.* Which meant the workers, the concertgoers, the shoppers; those on the front line when hate crimes were planned in curtained back rooms. Which to her mind justified intrusions into the lives of those same workers, but not everyone took that line. To some, she was the enemy. *Protecting the Establishment.* A familiar jibe, and not without foundation, but it ignored the fact that the Establishment had been dismantled these past decades, its old-school champions of industry and the Civil Service supplanted by the new breed: on one flank the media, on the other the rich, and in the middle, that huge overlap between the two. Their battle cry might make a pretence of anti-elitism, but underneath the covers they'd been to the same schools, joined the same clubs, and flew the same flags over the same country estates ... No: the Establishment didn't need protecting, because the

Establishment always won. It just wasn't always the same Establishment, or not at first.

Protecting the Service. That got to the heart of it. Protecting the Service, because if the Service fell, everything else would tumble. Or that was how she had spent her adult career viewing the world, and it was too late to change her outlook now.

Down in the interview suite—First Desk accessed the audio link—Molly Doran and Max Janáček had fallen silent. Perhaps their earlier selves, Alison and Otis, were still wrapped in conversation. It was hard to know what our earlier selves were capable of, she decided. We can't always know what our current selves will do.

It was after three, but that didn't stop her: she made a call, but not the one she'd been contemplating earlier. Then stared at her frosted wall a while longer before summoning Hari. "I've someone to see, something to borrow. I won't be long."

"Change of outfit?"

"You could say that," said First Desk. "The new PS. Is she still on shift?"

First Desk's Personal Security, who'd be with the Service chief every step she took out of doors.

"She is, yes. Did you want to meet her?"

"No. Just so long as she's on the ball." First Desk hesitated. Then: "No soft landings. Make sure she knows."

"Ma'am."

Hari tidied away her coffee cup, her sandwich plate, and left her desk lamp lit for her return.

The phone woke De Vries, though long habit ensured he gave no hint of this, and his voice was steady when he answered. It was 4:27 A.M. There was no light and little noise outside. London had been dimmed and dumbed, its settings adjusted for the wary.

"It's me."

He knew who it was: the only person who called this number. Toad. "It's very early."

"We need to talk."

"And why do we need to do that?"

"Because the Park want to talk to me. First Desk has just rung. *First Desk.*"

"Yes, all right." First Desk, at four-something in the morning. It sounded like an emergency. Whether it was his emergency had yet to be determined, but he hadn't lived his second life this long without taking all precautions.

"She woke me up. I'm frightened."

"I'm sure you have nothing to be worried about."

"But maybe you do."

He was used to listening for more than one thing at a time: a voice on the phone, a noise on the street. A car door slamming, or an engine starting up. The small things that suggest bigger things happening. If they came for him they'd come politely, because he was a friend of prime ministers, even notoriously poor ones. He was a party donor. He was not immune to bad headlines, arrest, even punishment, but such things would accumulate slowly, not drop from the sky like an unexpected tortoise.

If First Desk was gathering evidence—if Max Janáček had sought sanctuary at the Park—then it would be as well to know about it. Forewarned, as the saying went, was get-the-fuck-out-of-here-now.

"Are you going to tell me what she said?"

"I want to see you face to face."

"There's no need—"

"Bring cash."

"I see." The clock on his bedside table silently threw another minute to the floor. "Well, you can't come here."

"There's a flat I can use. On Calthorpe Street?" He noted the number that was read out. "Now. You have to come now."

He wondered how a flat on Calthorpe Street came within Toad's ambit, but not out loud. The call had ended. No sum of money had been specified, which De Vries found quietly admirable. When dealing with the rich, it was tactful to allow them to set their own parameters. Many—most—were irredeemably parsimonious but didn't enjoy being reminded of the fact. The clock let slip another minute. De Vries dressed, and summoned his driver.

The flat was on the third floor, and its big windows fully lit, uncurtained. Looking up as he stepped out of the car, De Vries wondered if this were a protective measure; if Toad were worried he might, instead of buying information, seal it up instead. But his days of inflicting violence were over, the occasional prostitute notwithstanding. Otherwise those uncurtained windows would be an issue.

He pressed the doorbell and was buzzed in.

The stairs were narrow for such a grand house. On the landings were small watercolours, talentless but old and pleasingly framed. When he reached the flat he rapped twice on the door. It had just gone five. Toad—or someone—invited him to enter; when he tried the handle, the door was unlocked. He stepped into the same lit room he'd gazed up at from the street. It was sparsely furnished—a sofa, two armchairs, a cabinet, a coffee table—with three other doorways, two of which were ajar, and led to, he suspected, a kitchen and a bathroom. The closed door would be a bedroom. It was all quite pristine and unfussy, a flat for brief occupancy: overnight stays or weekend interrogations. De Vries recognised a safe house when he saw one. On the coffee table were a half-full cafetière and two mugs, one of them gently steaming. The armchairs were unoccupied. On the sofa sat First Desk.

He closed the door behind him. "Well, isn't this a surprise?"

"Not who you were expecting, I know. But Toad—Toad?"

"Toad," he agreed.

"Sends apologies. Coffee?"

"Please."

She poured. "Do sit down. You know who I am, of course."

"Of course. We once dined together, in fact. In a manner of speaking."

"Really? I'd have thought I'd recall the occasion."

De Vries sat on an armchair, having first removed his coat, folded it carefully, and placed it on the other. "There were quite a few of us there. A dinner to celebrate one of your triumphs. Peter Judd was hosting."

"Oh, yes. Yes, I remember. Though there were, as you say, a number of people present."

"And I hesitated to put myself forward."

"I can't imagine why."

He shrugged, an expansively European gesture. "I consider myself a background man. Not one to shuffle into the limelight."

"How very wise." First Desk's own coat was hanging somewhere unseen. She wore a dark green long-sleeved dress, and in her ear was a white nodule: wired for sound, De Vries assumed. Her gaze was steady, and fixed on him. It could easily grow uncomfortable.

He sipped coffee, which wasn't as hot as it might have been. Perhaps she'd been waiting a while, planning a posture—a relaxed attitude—with which to disconcert him when he arrived. As if she'd dug a pit, and was peering down at him. She'd find he wasn't as easily penned as that.

First Desk said, "Ms. Fleet—I'm sorry, I can't take the whole

Toad nonsense seriously—Ms. Fleet says you approached her to report on the activities of Monochrome within a week of its being established. Why did you do that?"

De Vries took another sip of coffee. It was somewhat bitter. "I take it we're being recorded."

An earpiece was unhooked and placed on the coffee table. "Not any more."

"How very civilised. This Ms. Fleet—she came to you with this story?"

"Do you know, in time, I think she would have done. I suspect her decision to become your ears on the panel had more to do with the nature of her recruitment to Monochrome than with any desire to profit from it. But as it happens, no. I realised she'd been reporting to you before she had the chance to confess. A matter of timelines."

"This smacks rather wonderfully of tradecraft. I've a weakness for spy stories. Please go on."

"You orchestrated the raid on Cornwell House—to trace Max Janáček's handler—the night before the Monochrome panel received copies of the OTIS file. So it could only have been Fleet or Kyle who alerted you to its contents. And it wasn't Kyle, or he'd not have delivered the file in the first place. He'd have told you about it, and you'd have told him to destroy it."

"Max Janáček?"

"Referred to in the file as Otis. You know, this is going to go more quickly if you drop the innocent act. I should probably let you know that I have tapes of your meeting with Carl Singer earlier this evening."

"Is that quite legal?"

"If you were at the meeting Peter Judd hosted, you'll be aware that legality isn't always my strong point."

"Quite so." He placed his coffee mug on the table. "Very well.

I've always taken a keen interest in the security services. You know this. Until recently, I was in the running for one of the Service contracts being put out to tender. We could easily have been colleagues."

"I'm not sure that's how I'd put it."

"Semantics. As for Ms. Fleet, she needed money badly. There's a regrettable ex-husband in the picture. When I approached her for advance information on the panel of inquiry's findings, I assured her—and she accepted—that this was purely a form of due diligence on my behalf. Nobody buys a used car without checking under the bonnet. In that same spirit, I was eager to know that no major misbehaviour was about to come to light just as I was preparing to become, what shall we call it? A shareholder in the business. It amounted to no more than that. I hope you won't judge her too harshly."

"Oh, she's judging herself harshly enough for both of us. But she was amenable to the idea of arranging to meet you here. Leaped at the chance, in fact. Some small form of redemption, I suppose." She placed her mug on the table. "Not that she ever believed it was due diligence you were after. On the contrary, she suspects you had personal reasons for wanting to be abreast of the inquiry."

"Personal?"

"Yes. Which was bright of her. I mean, you had good cause for wanting to know if the name Karl Schenker came up. That would have given you a scare. More so once you knew there were those who remembered Schenker, and what he did. Who would have been prepared to offer testimony in court."

"You're going to have to explain who this Karl Schenker is, I'm afraid."

"No I'm not."

Still the steady gaze.

De Vries looked at the discarded earpiece. Always treat a microphone as live, that was the broadcaster's mantra. It would be foolish to take this woman at her word. On the other hand, something about her gaze suggested she could be trusted, in this much at least. She would destroy him if she could, they both knew that. But he didn't think she'd lie to him, or not so transparently.

Best to be cautious, though.

He said, "We may have reached an impasse. I came with a farewell gift for Ms. Fleet. As she's not here, there's little purpose in my staying."

"Fair enough. I simply wanted to put you on notice. Your life as you currently know it is over. Soon, very soon, you'll be paying for your past."

"That's confident of you. But forgive me, because it's not my place to offer you lessons in realpolitik, but I habitually dine with cabinet members. The former PM, as you know, is a close friend. Do you really need to be told that any attempt to smear my name will meet with official resistance? Sour grapes, they'll say. You'll do anything to undermine Green Shoots, and that includes blackening the names of those involved."

"Which doesn't include you any more. Remember?"

"You already know I have a significant amount of influence over Carl Singer."

"You're pulling his strings."

"It's a financial relationship, of the sort the current government understands all too well." He paused. "It's how business is done. Here, and everywhere else."

"Business interests only stretch so far. We both know you plan to use the vetting service to make money."

"Well, obviously. Nobody's going to take it over on the promise of *losing* money." A sudden twinge from his bladder disconcerted him, but he spoke on. "Let's not be naïve. Green

Shoots isn't simply about cutting public funding. Those who initiated the scheme, who've backed it from the beginning, their support won't leave them poorer. Whether it's my company that take up the reins, or Carl Singer's, or any one of a dozen others, we'll all have positions that need filling in the future, when current members of parliament find themselves in need of employment. This shouldn't be news to you. It's how the world works."

"There are limits to self-interest too."

"You think so? And is your own position secure enough to gamble on that? Monochrome was set up for a reason. You're part of that reason. You'd be wise to consider your hand carefully before you play a card."

"Any resistance I meet will disappear once it's clear who you are."

"I'm Fabian de Vries. No amount of scandalmongering will change that. Do you think I'd be so slapdash as to assume an identity that wasn't made to measure?" He pursed his lips. "You could investigate. You might, possibly, find some tentative connection between me and this Karl Schenker. But in truth, you'd hit wall after wall. It's a cold piece of history, and you won't get a lot of cooperation. Bad times are best forgotten, and besides, who wants to cooperate with the British? You're the outcasts of Europe, through your own choice."

"This isn't about hunting down some tax-evader. Karl Schenker is known to be involved in the murder of three women."

"And is also known to be dead. And nothing you've said, or can prove, will change that."

"DNA analysis would put the matter to rest."

"You're confident that Schenker's records remain extant. And include DNA evidence. And that mine would match. Even supposing you had grounds for collecting it." He shook his head. "You're clutching at straws."

"Regardless of which identity you're hiding behind, you tried to abduct Max Janáček."

"I have no idea what you're talking about. Or, indeed, who."

"You set Carl Singer's security people onto him. They thought they were apprehending a paedophile."

"That sounds like vigilante behaviour to me. Which isn't best legal, is it? So I doubt you'll get much cooperation from Mr. Singer, either."

She was silent for a few moments and then, to his surprise, gave a rueful smile. "It sounds as if you've thought all this through."

"It's not a matter of thinking it through. More about seeing things as they actually are."

"I bow to your broad perspective. But perhaps you'd agree that I could, if I wanted, make things difficult for you. To no small degree."

"You could be a nuisance, no more." But he conceded a nod. "But yes, a nuisance."

"Then perhaps we could seek a middle way."

"I'm listening."

"More coffee?"

"Thank you, no." He reached for his mug, though, and took another draught. "Go on."

"Carl Singer, as you established earlier this evening, is to be your—you said proxy?"

He nodded again.

"So much more seemly than 'sock-puppet.' Well. Whatever he is, he'll no doubt be in a position to do you the occasional favour, even aside from the, ah, financial leverage that control of vetting will allow."

Light dawned. "And you're hoping for a share in this?"

"Not for myself." First Desk picked up the cafetière and

poured. "But for the Service. There will always be times when a thumb on the scales would be welcome. When, regardless of any evidence to the contrary, the subject of a vetting procedure might be found acceptable, say, or unacceptable. Depending on the circumstances."

"You're not capable of arranging this for yourself?"

"We've never had difficulty doing so. But then, we've always had our hands on the reins before now."

"Of course. So you're seeking, what? A partnership?"

"Let's call it a non-aggression treaty. I'll back off from further investigation into Karl Schenker. You'll agree not to use your control of Landscaping to impede the work of the Service, and indeed to offer aid when required."

"That seems . . . workable." Their conversation had amused him, as negotiation usually did, when he was on the winning side. He couldn't remember the last time it had been otherwise. "But tell me, was this what you were after in the first place? An arrangement of this sort?"

"It occurred to me," she said carefully, "that it was a likely outcome."

"Then congratulations."

"Oh, it's a win for both of us. I mean, I'm sure you can use your newfound role to bury your own past even deeper."

De Vries wagged a jocular finger. "Now now. As I think we've just agreed, I have no past to bury."

First Desk gave a slight bow.

He rose. "And if you'll excuse me, might I use the bathroom?"

"Of course." She indicated the door he needed. "Through there."

He went into the bathroom, keenly aware of the demands his bladder was making, but not so keenly that his attention wasn't grabbed by what was sitting on the toilet lid. "What the hell?"

"What's the matter?"

"There's a *gun* in here." He picked it up. It felt real. A Russian make, a Makarov. He'd used one in the past.

"I don't—what do you mean, a gun?"

"I mean a bloody gun—what the hell is this doing?"

Her reply was drenched in panic. "It must be a mistake. I mean—good God!" He could hear her getting to her feet. "It's a safe house, not an armoury. Some idiot must have—I'm so sorry. Bring it out. Are you sure it's real?"

De Vries was sure. But grounded enough to say, "How would I know? I'm not a gangster."

He pushed through the door, gun in hand. As he did so, First Desk threw her own hands in the air and screamed. A chip of glass burst from the window, but De Vries stopped noticing anything long before it bounced off the coffee table and came to rest on the carpet, the bullet that had dislodged it having entered his right eye moments earlier. His body hit the floor as his bladder relaxed for the final time.

First Desk reached for her comms device and switched it on. "Good job," she said. "Damn good job." She glanced at Schenker's body, lying in a spreading pool of urine. "Bastard was going to kill me."

Her PS, stationed over the road, responded, but First Desk didn't take in the words. She was, rather, addressing the body, if not out loud.

Now *that*, she told him. *That* was what I was after.

Already there were people running up the stairs.

The morning, when it landed, was cold and grey, and First Desk had had more than enough of it by the time she left the Park, having suffered the sympathy of her staff and an almost, but not entirely, suspicion-free interview with Oliver Nash.

"He came at you with a gun?"

"He was a desperate man. He knew the game was up, that his past was uncovered. If it wasn't for my security woman—"

"She does have a name."

"—I'd be on the carpet, he'd be in the wind, and you'd be writing a eulogy. Forgive the self-interest, but I'm happier this way round even if you're not."

"Of course I'm glad you're not dead."

"Thank you, Oliver. Perhaps we could work that into a sampler. I could hang it on the hub."

"But there's bound to be . . . discussion."

"Oh yes. The times when we could just shoot someone and agree not to mention it are long gone. Which I'm fine with, in case you were wondering."

"You're very skittish."

"Having my life flash before my eyes does that. It kills the appetite too, by the way. If you're after a new plan."

"I'm on the eight-to-eight." He patted his stomach. "And it's working."

"Glad to hear it."

"I gather you put your PS on an emergency setting."

"How did you come to gather that?"

"Your boy Hari. You passed on an instruction. No soft landings, you said."

"It was her first solo shift. We always specify, when they're new to the duty, that there are no practice drills. Which was just as well in this case."

"As you say."

"If she'd thought it was a trial run—"

"You'd be on the carpet, yes. You said." An attentive Hari—with whom she'd be having words later—had delivered a tray of pastries: Nash's eyes kept wandering there, though he had so far proved strong enough to resist. "None of this will stop Green Shoots, you know."

First Desk raised both eyebrows. "You think I engineered this to derail the initiative?"

"No, of course not. All I meant was that De Vries was already out of the running. Whatever ructions his passing causes, it won't affect the handover."

"Well, I'm sure Carl Singer can be trusted to do a good job."

It was Nash's turn to affect surprise. "That's a very fair attitude."

"Yes, isn't it? Though I can't help thinking he could do with a trustworthy project manager. Someone who'll know their way round the regulations."

"Why do I get the feeling you're up to something?"

"Because you're a hopeless cynic. Now, do have a pastry. You know you want one."

In the car, being driven home, she ran the numbers. Schenker was dead, which closed the book on a number of crimes, a dead joe and a maimed Park officer among them. As for Carl Singer: the acceptable face of capitalism was on the brink of collapse. On top of which, she had him on tape with De Vries, discussing ways of milking the vetting protocols, so a conspiracy charge was a slam dunk . . . Or . . . Or she could let him take over the contract, on the understanding that, no longer De Vries's proxy, he was now the Park's creature. It would be useful to maintain control over such an essential part of the business. Of course, she'd need Singer to appoint a manager, which was where Malcolm Kyle came to mind. *Nice boy. A little unsure of himself, but he'll find his legs.* She didn't have time for nice boys, and Kyle would be a weak link in any chain, but an independent-minded project manager would defeat the purpose. Besides, it wouldn't be a long-term proposition.

Singer Enterprises would crash and burn within the year, and that would bury Green Shoots for good.

As for Griselda Fleet, it wouldn't do for there to be close examination of her role in arranging De Vries's appointment at the safe house.

Her call to Fleet in the early hours had been brief, with Fleet more than ready to admit her association with De Vries, a burden she'd been carrying too long. Her only show of reluctance had been an irrelevance. "Please don't tell Malcolm," she'd said.

First Desk, who had no intention of doing so, since it would be of no benefit, had made no response.

"I told him I was taking money from my in-laws," she'd said, giving First Desk a glimpse of a conscience at work, as if she'd momentarily become a character in a Christmas fable. Thank fuck that didn't happen often.

The car arrived. She got out, dismissed the driver, took some lungfuls of breath and entered her house.

Winter's trees were stark and spare. Her back garden was an unloved space, tended by professionals; its lawn mown, its paving swept, its furniture bleached of bird shit. Out there now—through the glass doors in the sitting room—she could see an untidy shape slumped over the wooden table, cigarette fizzing in its paw. She sighed, and went to join him via the kitchen, collecting a bottle of wine from the fridge and a glass from the rack on the way.

"You read about families in Canada coming home to find a grizzly bear squatting in their garden," she said, pulling out a chair. "I know how they feel."

"Yeah, I hear you're a magnet for endangered species today. You mounted his head for your wall yet?"

"No, but I've been promised his thumbs for my collection." She poured wine into her glass, while her companion produced a bottle of Talisker from the pocket of his grubby overcoat. It was already uncapped. He held it out, and they clinked glass.

"What impresses me," he said, "is that you didn't get your hands dirty. Do you even know the name of whoever took the shot?"

"She's called Personal Security, Night Detail," said First Desk. "Sometimes the job title's more important than the individual. Anyway, it was a fitting end for an arch manipulator. He wasn't the type to do dirty work either. I bet he hadn't wiped his own arse in twenty years."

"Well, that'd make his thumbs more collectible," her companion agreed. "But as far as manipulation goes, are we pretending you did this for a dead joe?"

"In part, yes."

"But mostly to prevent him getting those nice clean hands on your precious Service." His own hands were wrapped around his bottle. "Because letting an amoral, self-serving, ruthless bastard through the door would harsh the Park's mellow."

"Someone once said you'd either end up running the place or buried underneath it."

"It's early yet."

"It really isn't." She held out a hand. "Cigarette." He stared at her palm for a moment, then fished in his overcoat. Instead of offering a packet, he produced a single cigarette. She took it, and accepted his light. "I'm in charge of the Park, like it or not. And that doesn't involve sentiment or score settling, even if it does sometimes require extreme action. You can chalk this morning up as just another day's work."

"I'm not arguing with that. I'd just sooner pull my own triggers."

"Don't undersell yourself. You pull a lot of people's triggers."

"What if Schenker hadn't needed a piss?"

She squinted through the smoke. "Was that intended to impress?"

"Well it was either that or you'd put the gun in the bedroom. And if you'd sent him into the bedroom, I wouldn't need to ask how."

"Someone, somewhere, probably regards you as a breath of fresh air." She exhaled. "I doctored the coffee."

" 'Course you did."

"A precaution, that's all. Old man, cold morning. You don't need me to tell you about that."

"I've already pissed on your rhododendron twice."

"Which one's that? No, I don't want to know." First Desk examined the lit end of her cigarette, then took another sip of wine. He mirrored her movements with his bottle. She said, "Something I'm not clear about. Apparently it was David Cartwright warned Schenker you'd laid a trap for him. If you can call it a trap. It sounded like a half-arsed rag week prank to me. But that aside, how did Cartwright get word to Schenker? Classified ad?"

"I'm supposed to know?"

"You've been thinking about it longer than I have."

He put the bottle to his lips again. After a moment, he belched. "I've said it before and I'll say it again. David Cartwright was an old bastard, soaked in blood up to his cardiganed elbows. He never did anything that didn't pay off both ways. His grandson thinks the sun shone out of the old man's arse, but that wasn't the sun. It was a death star."

"Well, that clears that up. So Cartwright what, sent out a solar flare? And Schenker saw it?"

"No, Cartwright told Charles Partner what Otis and I were up to. He knew Partner would send word to Moscow. The KGB were on friendlies with the Stasi, when it didn't pay them not to be, and they'd have known how to reach him."

Understanding dawned. "Cartwright used our own traitor to blow your op."

"And in doing so, made sure I'd end up under his thumb. After what happened in Berlin, I'd have been put out with the empties unless I did what Cartwright wanted."

"Which was to kill Partner." First Desk was nodding. It might have been admiration. "You're right. He was a twisty bastard."

"Welcome to our world." He raised the bottle again, but this time capped it and tucked it into a pocket. Looking her in the eye, he said, "I'll not get my gun back, will I?"

"I'll have to owe you."

"Everyone does," he grumbled, and stood suddenly only to freeze in place, staring down the garden as if something had caught his attention. Whatever it was didn't stay, or perhaps had never been there at all. But in that moment he looked, she thought, not younger exactly, and certainly no tidier or happier, but different, as though caught in the act of remembering another life, one which had never found fulfilment, but might still be seeking it somewhere. This didn't last more than a second or so. Still, she wondered who she'd glimpsed, and thought about it on and off for the rest of the afternoon, long after he'd left.

ACKNOWLEDGEMENTS

My thanks to all at Soho Press over here and Baskerville and John Murray over there, especially Juliet Grames and Yassine Belkacemi; to Juliet Burton, who's been with me all this way, and to Lizzy Kremer and her colleagues for picking up the reins; to Micheline Steinberg; to all who've graced the writers' room with their talents; to the brilliant cast and crew of *Slow Horses*; to Lucy Atkins, and every other novelist I've ever drunk coffee, broken bread, clinked glasses and talked books with; and to booksellers and librarians everywhere.

Janet Beckett's name appears in this book in return for the generous donation she made to Croak & Dagger's Great (Little) Library Adventure, a community-outreach programme benefiting small public and community libraries in New Mexico. Big or small, wherever they are, libraries make things better. May they always survive.

Love and thanks as always to my mum and my siblings and in-laws—especially David and Tig, who walked me down some green lanes, and allowed me to make use of a modified version of their home—and to their offspring and attachments. And to Tommy and Scout, for being the extra heartbeats in the house.

But most of all to Jo, for everything.

Continue reading for a preview of
the first book of the Oxford Series

DOWN CEMETERY ROAD

When he opened his eyes he expected to find all the light squeezed from the world, but no: he was alive still, strapped to a bed in a sterile room, angry red claws of pain scratching channels in his flesh. *They have tied me down to keep me from shredding myself,* he managed, in a moment of clarity. *To prevent me ripping the skin from my bones, and not stopping until I'm dead.* This was a good thought: it pretended they had his welfare in mind. But the pain remained, like being chewed by fire-ants, and even when he slept he felt it working in his dreams. In his dreams, he was back in the desert. His companions were dead soldiers, their meat dropping off their bones.

The loudest thing in life was a helicopter. All around, the boy soldiers disintegrated; made puddles in the sand.

Here, when he was awake, there were other noises to occupy him. Outside his room, he imagined a long corridor of swept tiles and white light; an echoey tunnel that carried sounds past his door, some of which lingered to mock his boredom. A dropped fork rattled in his mind for hours. He heard voices, too, a low mumble that never separated into language, and once he thought he heard Tommy; thought he recognized a man he knew in a noise mostly animal: a rising scream, cut off by a slammed door. Footsteps clattered into distance. Something on wheels might have been a trolley. He tried to shout a response, but his voice got lost in the deep red caverns of his pain, and all he could do was weep silent tears that scorched his cheeks.

A doctor came once a day. He had to be a doctor: he wore a white coat. The nurse with him carried a tray; on it, a precise array of tools—different-sized needles, small bottles of coloured liquids. Both nurse and doctor wore gloves and surgical masks, and both had olive skin and hazel eyes. Only the doctor spoke. His sentences were short and to the point: Breathe in. Breathe out. I take blood now. Even without the mask, he'd hardly have been fluent. It was another clue to his whereabouts . . . Not all the needles were for him, so he knew he wasn't alone here; there were other rooms, other patients, though *patients* wasn't the word he meant. *Prisoners*, his mind supplied. He was a prisoner here, though where *here* was, he couldn't be sure.

The doctor said, "Sleep now." As if it were a magic instruction, and he was a rabbit being put back into a hat.

The nurse, though, was beautiful, as nurses have to be. The nurse came more often and fed him, wiped him, saw to his bowel movements. Nothing he did made her speak. Even an erection, to him little short of a miracle, left her unmoved. For the rest, all he had were a few schoolboy phrases—*Parley voo? Spreckledy Doitch?*—which it wouldn't have helped him if she'd answered. And anyway he knew, was certain, that if she spoke it would be in a sand language, whose vast syllables would leave him adrift and uncomprehending, like a traveller caught between settlements. Soon, he forgot she was human. When he didn't want to see her, he turned his face to the wall.

Days passed. There was no way of knowing how many.

His body was healing, but slowly: red weals marred all his flesh he could see, and a small detached part of his mind—his black box—told him he'd always be like this now; that his body was scarred and monstrous for ever, but at least the pain was dimming. He was no longer kept strapped down. An ankle-chain secured him to the bed. In time, he might do something about that.

Once, he stole a spoon during a careless moment; filched it from the tray when the nurse looked round at a noise from the corridor. He hid it under the mattress, but within the hour they'd come to fetch it—three of them: male, silent, dark-featured. Two held him against the wall while the third retrieved his prize, though not roughly. He didn't struggle. But the effort exhausted him anyway, and he crashed as soon as they'd left. His dream took him back to the desert and the boy soldiers. Sand crunched as he fell from the truck, and the chopper's whine was the loudest noise in the world. And the boys were melting again, their faces turning runny while his black box recorded it calmly, noting that *it's like watching a very wet painting hung in the wind*—but he was sweating when he woke, and sure he'd been screaming. There was nobody to tell him if that were true. Just as there was nobody to tell him if it were night or day.

He'd have sold his soul for a window. For natural light.

And then one day—he had an idea it might be the winter; there was a cold bite to the air—they took him out of the room. The same three men came to secure him to the bed. He was blindfolded and taken through the door, down the corridor he'd only imagined; wheeled past—he was sure of this—windows, from which light fell on to his face in a gentle strobe. He racked his body against the bed, but remained locked in place. When they removed the blindfold, he was in what looked like an operating theatre. The doctor was there, masked, suited up, and had the three interns—guards—untie him and fasten him in what resembled an open coffin. Because he thought they were going to kill him at last, he didn't struggle. But instead he was loaded into a large mechanical device, of a kind he might have seen in hospital films. Some kind of scanning machine. He was kept there for twenty minutes or so. The noise was constant but not too loud, like knowing there were bees nearby. He almost fell asleep.

Afterwards the doctor said, "Good." He was strapped down again, eyes covered, and wheeled back to his room. Again he felt the windows pass, and his one wish in the world was not even escape, but just to be able to stand in the light, and imagine the wind pulsing against his damaged skin.

After that, it became regular. Once every three days, as far as his body could tell . . . There were no other clocks available. That was one of the discoveries he'd made: that the body was a kind of clock. It couldn't be rewound, and couldn't be replaced. When it finished telling the time, its job was done . . . Once every three days they took him to the theatre, and scanned him with their device. He never asked a question. This was his plan: for them to forget he was there, and turn their backs for one moment. Even without a spoon, he thought he might win an eye or a tongue.

. . . He never knew this, but it was on a Wednesday that it all changed; that he caught his glimpse of the outside world, and found it upside down.

He was asleep when the nurse came. Genuinely asleep. The pills did this, along with the blood they took: he never did anything, but often felt weak and sleepy. By the ankle-chain, he was tethered to the bed. She must have thought this enough. Perhaps the others, the men, were having a day off. He never knew. It didn't matter. She wheeled him from the room like that, just the ankle-chain holding him down.

It was the movement woke him. He'd been dreaming again—the dream never left him, or perhaps he never left the dream—his head full of boiling faces when he forced his eyes open, the way he always woke. For a moment he thought it hadn't started yet, that he was back in the truck, and instinct tipped him over the side where he hit the floor with a crash of spilled metal. The bed jerked to a halt. And with his gown flapping open, bare-arsed to the world, he lay with a window just two feet above him, its blinds pulled tight against the light, and both his hands untethered.

Even then, the nurse didn't speak. She pressed something on her belt instead, though he heard no alarm, and as he reached a hand for the blind, came round to arrest him. He thought she'd be soft. She punched the back of his head. It had been a while since he'd been hurt quite like that, and he collapsed back to the floor, taking the blind with him. It sounded loud as a helicopter. And then there were feet coming, and a pricking in his arm to send him back into the desert, where he really didn't want to go, not now he'd seen the light—not now he'd seen the sky, and the treetops, and the arch of the building opposite, with its grey stone scrolls and pigeon shit and everything about it screaming *England*—but then the needle opened the window in his head, and he flew back to the desert. The light was just the morning sun, building its killing heat. The boy soldiers were dying again, but nobody heard their screams.

CHAPTER ONE

BHS

I

On discovering a fire, the instructions began, shout Fire and try to put it out. It was useful, heart-of-the-matter advice, and could be extended almost indefinitely in any direction. On discovering your husband's guests are arseholes, shout Arseholes and try to put them out. This was a good starting point. Sarah was one glass of wine away from putting it in motion.

But the instructions had been pinned to the wall in her office when she'd had a job, and did not apply in the kitchen. Here, Mark would expect that all emergencies be met with predetermined orderliness—crisis management was his Latest Big Thing—and graded instantly by size, type and career-damaging potential: earthquake, conflagration, shortage of pasta. His guests would not figure on the chart, since they came under Acts of God, and were to be borne as such. Of course they're arseholes, Sare, he'd say, when they were gone and he could afford to be ironic. He's rich and she's dumb: what did you expect, they'd be *nice*? But if Sarah asked when rich got important, he'd lose a little of the irony. Since rich got on my client list, he'd say. Since rich started buying lunch. Self-promotion was his other Latest Big Thing. He had these in pairs now, so as to be sure of not missing anything.

And now he came into the kitchen, to make sure she missed nothing either. "Coffee done?"

"Just about."

"Anything I can do?"

"You could try asking that first in future."

"In *future*? You think I want to go through this again?"

She banged a cupboard, just quietly enough to sound accidental next door, but loudly enough to leave Mark in no doubt.

"I mean," he went on—hissing—"Wigwam? *Rufus*?"

"You said," she said, through gritted teeth, "another couple. You wanted company."

"I *wanted* Stephen and Rebecca."

"Busy."

"Or Tom and Annie. Or—"

"*Busy*." She took a breath. From the living room came that awful dead sound you probably got on battlefields before the buzzards swooped. "And you said, when I said it was awful short notice, you said *just get anybody*. Anybody who could make it."

"I didn't mean—"

"Well, you should have said so at the time. Because it's a bit late now, isn't it?"

Mark gave a short laugh, which might easily have been aimed at himself. It was one of his characteristic declarations of surrender, though she had no doubt this would be temporary. And his next words, anyway, were "You did get some of those mints, didn't you?"

"Yes. Mark."

So he changed tack, put his arms round her: "Come on. It's not been that bad, has it?"

He really didn't get it. Two hours he'd sat watching war being declared in slow motion, and he still thought it hadn't been *that* bad. "Did you just arrive?"

"He has firm opinions, that's all. Gerard does."

"Well, I didn't think you meant Rufus."

"He's used to playing rough. Cut and thrust sort of—"

"He's a vampire." She pulled free and checked the kettle-flex, for something to do. It was plugged in okay. It just hadn't boiled yet. "Get back in there and stop him biting my friends."

"It won't hurt them to have their Greenpeace sensibilities challenged once in a while."

"Challenged is fine. But he wants a pissing contest, and that's not."

"Sarah—"

"Just go away. Go and smooth his ego. Use the bloody iron if you think it'll help."

"He's nearly a *client*," Mark hissed on his way out. "I'm *that* close."

And you were staring at her legs, she added. *The Trophy Wife's. You shit.* But Mark had gone.

She poured the water, found a tray, emptied the mints into a bowl. They were foil-wrapped, chocolate-covered mints, and she ate one while waiting for the coffee to draw and another while hunting spoons. The cups did not match. One comment from Mark and it was a separation issue. Then she counted the mints: two each and one over. She ate it, and carried the tray through.

"Guns," Gerard was saying, with the air of a conjuror producing a toad when the kiddies had been expecting a bunny.

"You collect *guns*?" Wigwam asked. You molest *babies*? Wigwam apologized when people trod on her foot. Gun collectors were out of her range.

"What did you imagine, stamps?"

"Well, I don't . . ."

"Gerard has some *awfully* expensive guns."

"Cheap guns," Gerard said, "being better avoided."

"I thought," said Rufus bravely, "that sort of interest was, you know, compensating . . ."

"That's easy for you to say. I don't suffer penis envy myself."

Sarah put the tray on the low table around which they sat: Gerard in an armchair; Wigwam on the floor; the others sharing the sofa. Gerard *needed* a whole armchair, but did not act like he did, and this Sarah found irritating. The overweight should own up, and be made to suffer. But Gerard moved like a man half his size. She had read of the peculiar grace to be found in heavy men and had assumed it propaganda, but his gestures were small and controlled, as if part of his overactive mind were engaged in choreography. He made dainty movements now with his unlit cigar, punctuating sentences with careful darts and jabs. He had asked permission to smoke and seemed hardly put out at all by her refusal. Now it wagged like a totem in his long but chubby fingers, as if he were warding off evil. She'd have felt happier with a crucifix herself. Gerard Inchon was a total bastard.

"What *do* you suffer, then?" she asked.

"I beg your pardon?"

Mark sprang forward and began rattling cups. "Who's for sugar?"

"I said, what do you suffer? We've heard a lot about your perfect life, there must be something goes wrong occasionally. The Porsche's ashtrays fill up? Your tailor sleeps in?"

"Gerard gets all his suits—"

"Sarah's making a joke, dear."

"Or is this as good as it gets? Flaunting your wealth in front of the help?"

"I'm hardly the help," said Mark. "I wasn't talking to you."

Gerard Inchon smiled. "I suppose you get a lot of this," he said.

He was talking to Sarah. "Dinner guests at short notice. Strangers you're supposed to be polite to."

"Not a lot, no. Mark's not that important yet."

"Sarah—"

"Well, he will be. So you'll have to get used to it. Because a lot of them'll be worse than me."

She found that hard to believe.

"And they'll find your perfunctory small talk and poorly hidden contempt rather more unpleasant than I do. And then your husband's career will suffer. And then what will you do?"

"Hire a band," she told him. "Throw a real party."

Wigwam said, "Gosh, I'm *dying* for a coffee. Are those mints?"

"So it's not me you're objecting to, it's your husband's job?"

Mark said, "Look, I'm really sorry about this—"

"Don't you *dare* apologize for me!"

"No apology is called for. But I am interested to know what Sarah proposes to adopt. As a matter of policy, I mean." Gerard Inchon surveyed the company as if awaiting suggestions, then turned back to her. "You don't work, do you?"

The switch threw her. "I—no. Not at the moment."

"Publishing, was it?"

She gave Mark a hostile look. "If you know, why ask?"

"I didn't. I was guessing. Let's see, not one of the big ones. Something worthy. Third World? The Environment?"

"Is this meant to be funny?"

"Alternative Medicine? All of the above?"

"Green Dolphin Press," said Sarah. "If it makes you happy."

"With print runs of three hundred, and selling less than half."

It sounded like he'd seen the books. "Lots of businesses fail."

"And lots don't. So what happened then, charity work?"

"Christ, what a phrase. But then, you'd like that, wouldn't you? Soup kitchens. Workhouses."

"Don't get me started. What was it, one of these homeless shelter places? That's the guilt-trip of choice, isn't it?"

Wigwam said, "Oh, there are so *many*—"

"Let me guess," said Gerard. "They couldn't use you."

Sarah was shaking her head in disbelief. "What is this?"

"Oh, I see a lot of it. Hubby brings home the bacon, and the little woman has nothing to do. The ones that don't have affairs, shop. The ones that don't shop get charity jobs."

"You really are disgusting, aren't you?"

"So these jobs are oversubscribed. The interesting ones, anyway. What was it, you didn't have the experience?"

She'd failed the screening.

"Which leaves the dull end of the market. The retail bit. I can't see you sticking that, though."

The Oxfam shop had let her go.

Gerard Inchon leaned back into the armchair. "What I like to call it, I call it BHS."

Nobody ask him, Sarah prayed.

"Bored Housewife Syndrome. Most women enjoy being bored, of course, but you still get some who—"

"You insufferable bastard."

"—end up throwing wobblies at dinner parties. You're enjoying it now though, aren't you?"

"*What?*"

"Little bit of aggro, little bit of rough." He made his cigar pass from one hand to the other, like an amateur conjuror. "I bet you haven't had a scrap in ages. What you need is more excitement."

That was when the house blew up.

Other Titles in the Soho Crime Series

PETER LOVESEY
(England)
The Circle
The Headhunters
False Inspector Dew
Rough Cider
On the Edge
The Reaper

(Bath, England)
The Last Detective
Diamond Solitaire
The Summons
Bloodhounds
Upon a Dark Night
The Vault
Diamond Dust
The House Sitter
The Secret Hangman
Skeleton Hill
Stagestruck
Cop to Corpse
The Tooth Tattoo
The Stone Wife
Down Among the Dead Men
Another One Goes Tonight
Beau Death
Killing with Confetti
The Finisher
Diamond and the Eye
Showstopper

(London, England)
Wobble to Death
The Detective Wore
  Silk Drawers
Abracadaver
Mad Hatter's Holiday
The Tick of Death
A Case of Spirits
Swing, Swing Together
Waxwork

Bertie and the Tinman
Bertie and the Seven Bodies
Bertie and the Crime of Passion

SUJATA MASSEY
(1920s Bombay)
The Widows of Malabar Hill
The Satapur Moonstone
The Bombay Prince
The Mistress of Bhatia House

FRANCINE MATHEWS
(Nantucket)
Death in the Off-Season
Death in Rough Water
Death in a Mood Indigo
Death in a Cold Hard Light
Death on Nantucket
Death on Tuckernuck
Death on a Winter Stroll

SEICHŌ MATSUMOTO
(Japan)
Inspector Imanishi
  Investigates

CHRIS McKINNEY
(Post Apocalyptic Future)
Midnight, Water City
Eventide, Water City
Sunset, Water City

PHILIP MILLER
(North Britain)
The Goldenacre
The Hollow Tree

FUMINORI NAKAMURA
(Japan)
The Thief
Evil and the Mask
Last Winter, We Parted
The Kingdom
The Boy in the Earth
Cult X
My Annihilation
The Rope Artist

STUART NEVILLE
(Northern Ireland)
The Ghosts of Belfast
Collusion

STUART NEVILLE CONT.
Stolen Souls
The Final Silence
Those We Left Behind

So Say the Fallen

The Traveller & Other Stories
House of Ashes

(Dublin)
Ratlines

GARY PHILLIPS
(Los Angeles)
One-Shot Harry
Ash Dark as Night

Violent Spring
Perdition, U.S.A.
Bad Night Is Falling
Only the Wicked

SCOTT PHILLIPS
(Western US)
Cottonwood
The Devil Raises His Own

That Left Turn at Albuquerque

KWEI QUARTEY
(Ghana)
Murder at Cape Three Points
Gold of Our Fathers
Death by His Grace

The Missing American
Sleep Well, My Lady
Last Seen in Lapaz
The Whitewashed Tombs

QIU XIAOLONG
(China)
Death of a Red Heroine
A Loyal Character Dancer
When Red Is Black

NILIMA RAO
(1910s Fiji)
A Disappearance in Fiji